THE ASSAULT

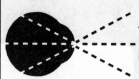

CYCLE TWO OF
THE HARBINGERS SERIES

THE ASSAULT

THE REVEALING BY BILL MYERS
INFESTATION BY FRANK PERETTI
INFILTRATION BY ANGELA HUNT
THE FOG BY ALTON GANSKY

THORNDIKE PRESS
A part of Gale, a Cengage Company

GALE
A Cengage Company

Farmington Hills, Mich • San Francisco • New York • Waterville, Maine
Meriden, Conn • Mason, Ohio • Chicago

LIBRARY OF CONGRESS CATALOGING-IN-PUBLICATION DATA

Names: Myers, Bill, 1953- Revealing. | Peretti, Frank E. Infestation. | Hunt, Angela Elwell, 1957- Infiltration. | Gansky, Alton. Fog.
Title: The assault.
Description: Large print edition. | Waterville, Maine : Thorndike Press, a part of Gale, a Cengage Company, 2017. | Series: Thorndike Press large print Christian mystery | Series: The Harbingers series ; Cycle 2.
Identifiers: LCCN 2017026578 | ISBN 9781432841300 (hardcover) | ISBN 1432841300 (hardcover)
Subjects: LCSH: Christian fiction, American. | Large type books.
Classification: LCC PS648.C43 A88 2017b | DDC 813/.01083823—dc23
LC record available at https://lccn.loc.gov/2017026578

Published in 2017 by arrangement with Bethany House Publishers, a division of Baker Publishing Group

Printed in the United States of America
1 2 3 4 5 6 7 21 20 19 18 17

CONTENTS

THE REVEALING
   BY BILL MYERS. 11

INFESTATION
   BY FRANK PERETTI 115

INFILTRATION
   BY ANGELA HUNT 229

THE FOG
   BY ALTON GANSKY. 367

In this fast-paced world with all its demands, the four of us wanted to try something new. Instead of the longer novel format, we wanted to write something equally as engaging but that could be read in one or two sittings — on the plane, waiting to pick up the kids from soccer, or as an evening's read.

We also wanted to play. As friends and seasoned novelists, we thought it would be fun to create a game we could participate in together. The rules were simple:

RULE #1
Each of us would write as if we were one of the characters in the series:

Bill Myers would write as Brenda, the street-hustling tattoo artist who sees images of the future.

Frank Peretti would write as the professor,

the atheist ex-priest ruled by logic.

Angela Hunt would write as Andi, the professor's brilliant but geeky assistant who sees inexplicable patterns.

Alton Gansky would write as Tank, the naïve, big-hearted jock with a surprising connection to a healing power.

RULE #2

Instead of the four of us writing one novella together (we're friends but not crazy), we would write it like a TV series. There would be an overarching storyline into which we'd plug our individual novellas, with each story written from our character's point of view. If you're keeping track, this is the order:

Harbingers #1 — *The Call* — Bill Myers

Harbingers #2 — *The Haunted* — Frank Peretti

Harbingers #3 — *The Sentinels* — Angela Hunt

Harbingers #4 — *The Girl* — Alton Gansky

Volumes #1–4 omnibus: *Cycle One: Invitation*

Bill's first novella, *The Revealing,* sets the stage for the second cycle, *The Assault.* It will be followed by Frank's *Infestation,* Angela's *Infiltration,* and Alton's *The Fog.* And if we keep having fun, we'll begin a third round and so on until other demands pull us away or, as in TV, we get cancelled.

There you have it. We hope you'll find these as entertaining in the reading as we did in the writing.

Bill, Frank, Angie, and Al

■ ■ ■ ■

THE REVEALING

BILL MYERS

■ ■ ■ ■

CHAPTER 1

"What're you sketchin' now?" Cowboy asked.

I flipped my notebook shut like a kid caught with porn.

The big guy smirked. "You know, Miss Brenda, you don't have to keep hidin' your gift under a bushel."

I gave him a look. He gave me one of his good-ol'-boy shrugs. Daniel, who's sittin' on my other side, stifles a giggle.

I shoot him a look. "You think that's funny?"

He grins and imitates Cowboy's shrug.

I scowl. But the truth is I like that grin. It don't happen much, but whenever it does, it warms somethin' up inside me.

The sketch is a blue velvet armchair. It's got peeling gold paint on its arms. I've been seeing it ever since we got on the plane to Rome. Never left my head. Not during the twelve-hour flight with its crap food and rerun movies, not during Mr. Toad's wild taxi ride from Da Vinci airport to the Vatican, and not as we sat on this butt-numbing wooden bench listening to the professor lay into some pimply-faced man-boy receptionist.

"Well, look again." The old man waved at the computer screen. "Cardinal Hartmann. You do know what a Cardinal is, do you not? *Cardinal* Hartmann invited us to this location at this particular date and this particular time to —"

"*Mi scusi,* signor, but you cannot have an appointment with —"

"Blast it all, don't tell me what I can and cannot have."

"But, such a thing, it is not —"

"I'm sorry, are you part of some special-needs program?"

"Professor . . ." As usual, Andi, his ever-cheerful assistant, stepped in to try to prove her boss was a human being. As usual, the odds were not in her favor.

Meanwhile, Daniel scooted off the bench to get another drink of water. At least that's what I figured. But the way he cocked his head upward like he was listening told me one of his "friends" was around.

Miss Congeniality continued smoothing things over. "What the professor means is,

14

we've just come from the airport. In fact, we haven't even gone to our hotel because Cardinal Hartmann sent a very urgent and very personal request for us to visit him today."

All true. It hadn't even been a month since the professor sent the Cardinal that scroll with the fancy writing on it. The one some kid, supposedly from another universe, gave us. I know, I know, long story, and I'm not in the mood. The point is, this Cardinal guy, who used to be the professor's mentor back when the professor believed in God, begged us to come. He sweetened the deal by e-mailing each of us plane tickets. And since I couldn't cash them in, and since neither me nor Daniel have ever been out of the country, and since the professor pulled some strings to get us some fast passports . . . well, here we were with our ol' pals, stuck in some backroom reception area that smelled like old men and floor wax.

I glanced over to Daniel. He'd passed the water fountain and stood at a wooden door built into the wall. Hardly visible. He looked back at me like he wanted something.

What? I mouthed.

He just stood there.

What?

Meanwhile, the professor cranked up his personality to super-jerk. "Okay, you do that."

The receptionist had gotten up and was heading out of the room.

"Only make sure you bring back someone with rudimentary communication skills."

Daniel cleared his throat, real loud to get everyone's attention. We turned to him as he reached for the door. He pushed it open and motioned for us to join him.

"What is it now?" the professor said. "Do you wish for us to follow? Do you believe there is something inside there?"

Daniel sighed like it was obvious. And for him it probably was. 'Cause like it or not, the kid heard things we never heard. Saw things we never saw. And whether the professor believed in any type of "higher power" or not made no difference. Our last couple of road trips made it clear Daniel was connected to something.

So, without another word, Dr. Stuffy Butt headed over to join the boy. Something was up, and he knew it.

So did Cowboy. "What's goin' on, little fella?" the big jock asked as he rose to his feet.

Daniel pointed to the open doorway. It was dark, but you could just make out some narrow steps. Me and Andi glanced at each other then got up and followed. None of us knew what was going on in that little head of his, but whatever it was, it wouldn't hurt to pay attention.

CHAPTER 2

"Surely you're not serious?"

"Have I ever lied to you before?"

"Other than matters pertaining to God?"

Cardinal Hartmann waved the professor off with a bony, arthritic hand. "Please, James, do spare us your sophomoric wit. If I've taught you anything, was it not to put aside your prejudices? Weigh all the facts and only then reach a reasonable conclusion."

The professor wasn't thrilled about being lectured in front of us, but I didn't mind. It was good to see someone other than me putting him in his place.

We'd found the frail old priest stashed away in some musty little apartment on the third floor. If it wasn't for Daniel's inside info we'd never have gotten to him . . . or dodged the locals who would have busted us for skulking around. Even then, it took twenty, maybe thirty minutes to wind through all the halls and stairs before we found him.

The assistant who'd opened the door for us was even skinnier than Hartmann. He wore thick Coke-bottle glasses that hadn't been cleaned in years. He didn't say anything, just greeted us with a polite nod and ushered us inside.

Hartmann sat in the center of the room. He was hunched over in the exact chair I'd been sketching all these hours. He was too old to stand and greet us. And when the professor tried to shake his hand, he refused, laughing it off about being a closet germophobe. There was something more, but I couldn't put my finger on it.

Over on the desk was the scroll the professor had sent the Cardinal. But so far no one had brought it up. Instead, we were sitting in some broken-down apartment listening to some broken-down priest tell us an unbelievable story. Most of it had to do with the small display case the assistant had wheeled in and the rusty spearhead inside.

The professor tried to be cool, but you could tell he wasn't happy. "Can you honestly tell me with a straight face that the artifact before us is the reason Hitler started World War II?"

"No." Hartmann shook his head. "Though

my brothers here insist upon this one's authenticity, there was another lance with greater credentials in the Imperial Treasury in Vienna. That was the one Hitler insisted upon owning — the one both he and Himmler believed had great supernatural powers. A fact underlined by Hitler's immediate visit to the museum to take possession of it when his troops marched into Vienna."

The professor said nothing — a first, as far as I could tell. He just sat there, eyeing his old mentor, wondering if the priest had lost his mind. And the more he talked, the more I figured he might be right.

"Because of Hitler's deep involvement with the occult, he believed whoever controlled the Spear of Destiny would control the world."

Andi motioned to the display case. "The Spear of Destiny. The one that supposedly pierced Christ's side at His crucifixion?"

"That is correct. Because it was used to kill God's Son and because some of His blood remained on it, Hitler believed whoever owned the spear would be invincible."

We sat in silence a long moment until the professor answered. "Poppycock."

"Perhaps. But do keep in mind that it is the exact spear Emperor Constantine claimed gave him his power. Then there is the overwhelming evidence that Charle-magne actually slept with it. Finally, we have the minor fact that over forty-five emperors for over a thousand years possessed it and claimed it facilitated their ability to rule."

"Proving absolutely nothing."

"And the very day the Nazis lost the spear to General Patton, who later returned it to Vienna, was the very day Hitler committed suicide."

"That may be true," Andi said. "But as you said, that's not this spear here. That's the one in Vienna."

"Yes and no. Granted, it is not this spear. However, I do not believe the spear Patton returned to Vienna is the same spear Hitler stole."

"But you just said —"

"The Nazis were notorious for creating replicas of the treasures they stole. Paint-ings, statues, religious artifacts —"

"And spears," Cowboy said.

"That is correct."

Cowboy stole a glance at Andi, no doubt hoping she noticed his powers of deduc-tion.

She didn't.

"So if this isn't the real spear," she said, "and the one in Vienna isn't the real one, then —"

There was a knock on the door. Andi stopped as Hartmann raised his hand for us to be quiet. There was another knock. Again he motioned for us to be silent. After what seemed forever, the footsteps faded down the hall.

When they were gone, Hartmann answered Andi's question. "That is the very reason we have summoned your team here."

"Team?" I couldn't help but smirk. "I wouldn't go calling us a team."

The priest looked at me. I held his gaze, but he didn't blink.

He answered. "We have decided you are the ones called to find and retrieve the real Spear of Destiny."

"We?" I said. "Who's *we*?"

He started to answer, then stopped and shook his head.

"And what's all this got to do with the scroll?" I nodded to the scroll sitting on the desk.

"Everything. And more."

"Yeah? Like what?"

"You shall find out soon enough."

I kept staring. There was something about him. He seemed honest enough, I'll give him that, but there was something.

The professor gave a heavy sigh. "So you brought us halfway around the world to find some mythical artifact with a questionable history that may or may not even exist."

"Oh, it exists, James."

The professor continued. "And to what purpose are we retrieving it? To add yet another item to your obscenely bloated Vatican collection?"

"No. To prevent the others from adding it to theirs."

"Others?" Andi said.

The priest nodded. "Hitler is dead, this is true."

"At last, a verified fact," the professor said.

"But there is another force far more powerful." He turned to the professor. "The very one your overinflated sense of logic keeps denying. One whose power grows stronger every day."

"I kinda got lost," Cowboy said. "What force are we talkin' about?"

"You've already encountered it. More than once." He turned to Andi. "On your beaches."

Andi frowned. "All those dying fish and birds?"

"And earlier. As far back as your first meeting at the Institute."

"The Psychic Institute?" I asked.

"It was one of their training grounds."

"Sridhar," I said. "The kid mentioned

something about an organization. What did he call it?"

A moment then Cowboy beamed. "The Gate."

"That's right," Andi said. "The Gate."

Cowboy beamed brighter. She didn't notice.

The priest continued, "Should the spear fall into their hands they shall —"

"— rule the world and make us all their slaves." The professor's voice dripped with sarcasm. "No doubt ushering in the post-apocalyptic nightmare that will destroy all mankind."

Hartmann looked at him then answered. "No, not yet. They still need to secure the appropriate items and people. But possessing the spear will greatly expedite their plans."

Daniel gave a start and spun to the door.

"What's the matter, little guy?" Cowboy said.

The priest lowered his voice and spoke quickly. "We haven't much time. It is imperative you find the spear and bring it here as quickly as possible."

"But . . ." Andi frowned. "How? Where do we start? Where do we —"

There was another knock on the door. Hartmann traded looks with his assistant, who nodded and shuffled over to answer it.

Hartmann turned back to Andi and whispered. "The Appian Way. The catacombs."

"The catacombs," the professor scoffed. "Aren't we being just a bit melo—"

More knocking, louder.

The assistant reached for the handle but was a fraction too late. The door flew open and five wannabe linebackers stormed in. We jumped to our feet ready to defend ourselves.

"No," Hartmann cried. "Do not resist them. Our meeting is over."

The first fellow grabbed me. I swore and tried to land a good kick, but he saw it coming. The second guy reached for Andi. Big mistake. Cowboy saw it and threw all 275 pounds at him. They crashed to the floor and traded punches.

"Don't resist," the priest kept shouting. "We have finished. Do not resist."

I searched for Daniel who was off to the side, safe.

"Unhand me, you Neanderthal!" the professor was yelling at the third man.

The other two had joined the one fighting Cowboy. Even at that the odds weren't exactly in their favor.

"Don't resist! Bjorn Christensen, there is no need to resist."

The sound of his name brought Cowboy up short. He turned to the priest.

"We have concluded our business. There is no need to resist."

They got Cowboy to his feet. "Okay, fellas," he said. "Take it easy. I heard the man, take it easy."

They guided us to the open door. I looked over my shoulder to see Daniel trailing close behind. We'd barely made it into the hallway before Hartmann called after us. "The feast is in the kitchen."

I turned to him.

He nodded and repeated, "The feast is in the kitchen."

His assistant also nodded, then smiled, then shut the door as the big boys escorted us down the hall.

CHAPTER 3

I wanted Daniel to see some of Rome, especially the Colosseum. We caught a glimpse of it as our taxi shot past. I even got a couple of blurred selfies. But it wasn't quite the same. Still, it would be somethin' to show Social Services next time they come snoopin' around seein' if I'm a fit guardian.

It took us half an hour to get from the Vatican to the creepy church basement full of human skeletons. Which, to be honest, was probably more exciting to a ten-year-old kid than a bunch of old ruins. And we're not talkin' one or two skeletons. According to Andi, our self-appointed tour guide, and with a little help from Wikipedia on her cell phone:

"The crypt consists of 3754 bodies, all Capuchin Monks who fled the French Revolution and took refuge in the church immediately above us. The Capuchin order separated from the Franciscan monks in

1525 in the belief that they needed to be more austere. Oh, and here's something you'll find incredibly fascinating . . ."

"I'm sure we will," the professor muttered.

"Cappuccino coffee actually received its name from the color of the monks' robes."

On and on she went. And just when it couldn't get any more boring, she went on some more. 'Course Cowboy hung on her every word, but me and Daniel couldn't care less. Who cares about the history of a bunch of dead monks when their actual skeletons were all around? And not whole skeletons. They were separated into lots of feet, legs, ribs, and skulls. Piles and piles of skulls.

Some were used to build altars. Others made up a giant clock with toes and fingers. There were chandeliers made from hundreds of vertebrae and hipbones. Nearly every wall was covered with complex patterns of bones.

And not just one room. I counted six. Each one labeled. Things like: *The Crypt of Skulls. The Crypt of Pelvises. The Crypt of Leg Bones.*

Yeah, it creeped me out a little. But Daniel's wide-eyed wonder said he was in kid heaven.

"Anybody see anything?" the professor

asked. "Clues? Diagrams? Something to tell me this isn't a complete waste of my time?"

Nobody saw nothing.

Except Andi. "Guys, check this out." She was looking at a wall up ahead. It was covered with arm bones that made up different squares and boxes.

"Lovely," the professor said.

"No, don't you see it?" Andi asked.

He didn't. No one did.

Except Cowboy. "It's a window box," he said. "Like my mom use to have to show off her knick-knacks."

"Well, that's one possibility," Andi said. "Or . . . ?"

She waited, but there were no takers.

"It's a floor plan. Don't you see it? There's the front door down here at the bottom. It's even open. Here's the entry hall with one set of stairs. The living room, hallway with another set of stairs, dining room, kitchen. And over here is . . ." she slowed to a stop.

"Over here is what?" Cowboy asked.

She got real quiet. "I've seen this before."

"Where?" Cowboy said.

We waited. Daniel reached up and took my hand.

When Andi continued, her voice was a little unsteady. "When we were up in Washington State. . . . It's the House. The one

29

that kept haunting Van Epps, the professor's friend. It's the floor plan to the House."

CHAPTER 4

I grabbed shots of the floor plan with my cell phone . . . which pissed off some caretaker . . . which I ignored . . . which got him in my face . . . which got my elbow in his gut . . . which got us thrown out . . .

Which was getting to be a habit.

I squinted as we stepped out into the late afternoon sun. "Now what?"

"Cardinal Hartmann said catacombs," Andi said. "Not catacomb, singular, but catacombs, plural."

"There's more?"

"Actually, 186 miles of them."

"One-hundred-eighty-six miles of —"

"I suggest we continue next by exploring the Domitilla Catacombs," she said. "They're quite close and one of the oldest and best cared for."

"How many rooms?" I asked.

"Tunnels," she said.

"How many tunnels?"

"Nine miles."

I swore. The professor joined me. But it didn't stop our personal cheerleader from leading us forward.

When we got to the entrance, the ticket guy at the door shook his head. *"Chiuso,"* he said. "Too late. Come back tomorrow."

Andi pleaded, said we were on an urgent mission. The professor even played his priest card (which had expired a few decades earlier). Nothing worked. The guard shook his head, pretending he didn't understand . . . till I slipped a handful of euros into his palm. He understood that perfectly.

Andi had reconnected to Wikipedia. So as we headed down the narrow steps into the cooler air, she resumed the tour. "There are roughly forty catacombs built under the city. Despite legends that Christians hid in them during the time of persecution, it is more probable that due to restricted land use, as well as their insistence upon being buried instead of cremated, these underground chambers were dug to serve primarily as cemeteries."

"More dead bodies," the professor sighed.

"Actually, in these particular catacombs there are indeed a few remaining. However, in the others, the bones have long since been removed."

"No doubt sold as picture frames," he said.

Daniel giggled.

"Named after St. Domitilla, their history is as lengthy as their tunnels and tributaries, which, by the way, are stacked on top of one another up to four levels high. Now, coming up to our right you'll note a delightful fresco painted by . . . by . . ." She lost reception. She waved her phone around to find the signal. The professor gave another sigh — this time out of gratitude.

"Hey, check out these symbols," Cowboy said. I crossed over to look at his wall. "Here's a guy with a lamb on his shoulders. I bet that's Jesus. And here, look, it's a dove with some sort of branch."

"That would be an olive branch," Andi said. "Together, the dove and olive branch would represent divine peace with God. In fact, in Greek, the very word *cemetery* means 'place of rest,' and in the Hebrew —"

"They're here," Daniel said.

It was the first words he'd spoken all afternoon.

"Who?" I said.

He pointed down the tunnel behind us.

"Someone's coming? Who?" I asked.

"For us."

The bare bulbs hanging along the ceiling gave off plenty of light, but I didn't see anything.

"Listen," the professor said.

I strained to hear. There were footsteps. Running. And getting closer. And hushed voices speaking a language I couldn't make out.

I traded looks with the others.

Daniel didn't wait for a discussion. He grabbed my hand and yanked me forward. We started down the tunnel. The others followed.

"Faster," he whispered. "Faster."

We broke into a run for, I don't know, forty, fifty yards, when he darted to the right. It was a little niche off to the side. Unlit, almost invisible. Stairs were cut into the wall. Steep and narrow. Almost a ladder. He started up them. I hesitated, then followed. Then the others, and finally the professor.

As we climbed, pieces of rocks crumbled and fell.

"Be careful up there," he hissed.

The steps got steeper. The sides of the wall came so close they touched me. After a few minutes or so I saw some blue-green lights above us. Parking lot lights. The sun had already set and the parking lot lights had come on.

Down below a man's voice shouted, "Up there!" It sounded Swedish or something. "You there. Halt!"

We kept going, not bothering to answer.

The light above got brighter. Pretty soon you could see it was coming through a round opening. In another minute we arrived at an iron grate.

The good news was there was a way out. The bad news was the grate wouldn't budge.

"Keep going," the professor whispered. "Why have we stopped?"

The voices below got closer.

Me and Daniel both tried pushing against the grate with all we had. "It's no good," I said. "They got it locked."

Cowboy tried squeezing past. "Maybe, if I could just —" But things were too cramped. No way could he get past us.

"Doesn't matter," I said. "It won't budge." I gave it one last push. "It's welded shut or something."

"We're trapped?" Andi asked.

I swore and nodded . . . until I spotted the girl. Her face so close to mine I gasped. It was the kid from that other world, Cowboy's and Daniel's friend. She was on her hands and knees, hunched inside a small tunnel connected to ours. A tunnel I was sure hadn't been there till now.

Cowboy saw her, too. "Helsa?" He moved up closer. "Littlefoot, is that you?"

She smiled. Even in the dim light I could see the silver in her eyes sparkle. A sure sign she was happy.

"What's going on up there?" the professor whispered.

"We missed you," Cowboy said. You could hear the softness in his voice. "You come back to visit?"

She nodded, then reached out for Daniel's hand. He let her take it and she pulled him into the tunnel. Once inside, he turned to help me. I took his hand and he pulled me in. I did the same for Cowboy, who did the same for Andi, who did the same for the professor.

Now we were all in the side tunnel crawling as fast as we could. No talking. No sound. Just lots of hands and knees scraping along the rocks. I felt something long and smooth in the wall beside me. Then it got bumpy, then ridges. Ribs. I yanked back my hand, not wanting to feel more.

Finally, the girl came to a stop.

The professor whispered, "What's going —"

"Shh," Daniel said.

36

For once in his life the professor obeyed. A good thing, too, because the men behind us had reached the top.

One of them was speaking Swedish again. Another answered.

We held our breaths.

You could hear them strain and push against the grate as they kept talking and getting madder.

Finally the first one shouted in his heavy accent, "Hello? Is anyone there? Is there anyone who can hear us?"

We kept silent.

They talked some more. They pushed and grunted some more. Finally they gave up and started back down.

The girl motioned for us to wait till the sound of their climbing had nearly faded. Then she started forward again and we followed. After another minute or so the tunnel angled up. A moment later we were out in the open surrounded by bushes and shrubs.

It was good to finally stand up and breathe. And despite my promise never to light up around Daniel, I pulled a cigarette from my pocket. Things were eerily quiet. We were pretty far from the parking lot, but could still see each other's faces in the

shadows. Except for the girl's.
She was gone.

CHAPTER 5

"Hello?"

"Signora, the taxi, it is here."

"We'll be there in a sec," I said.

"For your bags, shall I send him up?"

"No, we're good." I hung up the phone and faced the others. They'd been in Daniel's and my room the last forty-five minutes begging us to stay.

"But you just can't leave," Cowboy whined.

"Watch us." I crossed to the bathroom and dumped the free soap and shampoo into my bag.

"But what about the spear and the diagram and the Cardinal?"

"And saving the world?" Andi added.

The professor answered, "She's more concerned in saving her inconsequential derrière."

"You're one to talk," I said as I reentered the room. "I'm surprised you even bothered to come."

"Call it scientific curiosity."

"And the scroll," Cowboy said. "Remember, he was going to tell us what it meant."

"Which he didn't." I opened the mini-fridge, grabbed the two Cokes but left the booze — too many bad memories.

"We really need you, Miss Brenda."

I slammed the fridge. "I got Daniel to look out for now."

"And some enormous guilt to work off."

I turned back to the professor. "Meaning?"

"We all saw what you went through at the Institute. All those fears . . . all that guilt."

"Professor," Andi warned.

"Not that I fault you. It must be a tremendous burden — giving up your spawn, knowing you were an unfit mother to raise it."

The muscles in my jaw tightened.

He motioned to Daniel. "It doesn't take a genius to see the boy is simply serving as a surrogate, a vain attempt on your part to work off all that —"

I didn't hear much after that — saw nothing but his smug face as I sprang at it. I landed a couple good blows before Cowboy pulled me off. "Hey, hey, Miss Brenda! Miss Brenda, come on now!"

When things settled down, I turned to my backpack and finished shoving clothes into it. Daniel was already at the door, sitting peacefully on his own pack.

"She's not going anywhere," the professor muttered. He was nursing what would likely be a shiner. "The tickets are nonrefundable. She can't leave until the date of departure, just like the rest of us."

"Is that true?" Cowboy asked.

"Not without buying another ticket," Andi said.

"Which means cash," the professor said. "Something of which I'm sure she's a bit lacking."

I reached into my pocket and tossed his American Express back to him.

Now he leaped at me.

"Professor!" Andi and Cowboy shouted. It took both of them to stop him.

I zipped up my backpack and headed for the door. "Let's go, Daniel." But before I reached it, there was a knock. I glanced to the others, then opened it.

Two men in silver sunglasses stood there. "Taxi?" the biggest said. There was no missing his Swedish accent. I tried slamming the door but his size-14s blocked it. I yelled and swore as they threw it open and stormed in.

Cowboy was on his feet, doing what he did best. He flew across the room, decking the first guy, knocking off his glasses. We all stood and stared. And for good reason. The big Swede lay on the floor with no eyes. That's right, his sockets were completely empty.

The second guy took advantage of our shock and landed a good punch into Cowboy's gut and then his face. Not enough to ruin him, but enough to make his point.

"Run!" Cowboy shouted to us. "All of you, run!"

I didn't need a second invitation. I grabbed Daniel and we headed for the stairs, the professor right behind. Andi needed more convincing. "Tank!"

"Go, Andi! Go!"

We got to the bottom of the steps, raced through the lobby and out onto the street. Wheels screeched and I spun around just in time to see a taxi mini-van. It barely missed us. The driver shouted through the passenger window, "Taxi?" He had a black beard and a Middle Eastern accent so thick I could barely understand.

"What?" I said.

"Taxi? Taxi?"

I saw Cowboy stagger from the lobby, a little worse for wear.

"Taxi?"

"No." I turned from Cowboy back to the driver. "I mean, yes. Maybe. You'll go to the airport?"

"Defeats," he said.

"What?"

"I take you to defeats."

"Defeats? What are you —"

"No. Defeats! Defeats!"

"The feets?" Cowboy asked. "You want to take us to the feets?"

"Yes, yes. Get in. All of you. Hurry."

"Whose feet?" Andi said.

"Are you speaking of more skeletons?" the professor asked. "The catacombs?"

"No! No! Defeats!"

The hotel doors flew open and the two Swedes stormed out. During the brawl the second one had also lost his glasses. His eye sockets were as empty as his partner's. And yet they raced toward us like they could see perfectly.

"Some folks." Cowboy sighed. "I try to be polite, but they just won't take a hint." He positioned himself at the back of the taxi between us and them for another round.

"Hurry!" the driver shouted. "All of you, get in!"

The men kept coming. "Stay calm," the first said. "No one need be hurt."

"Get in!" the driver kept yelling. "Every-one, get in!"

I threw open the back door and shoved Daniel inside. Andi raced to the other door as the professor squeezed in beside me and Daniel crawled into the rear seat.

"Stay calm. No one need be —"

"Cowboy!" I shouted.

The first guy came at him. But the second headed around front for the driver, who panicked and dropped the van into reverse. A good idea, except for the first guy. The taxi slammed into him and knocked him to the ground. The wheels bumped over some-thing that was not a curb. And when I looked out the back window, there was no bad guy.

Cowboy dropped to his knees, looking under the car. "Mister? Mister, are you okay?"

Off in the distance, I heard a police siren. "Cowboy," I shouted. "Get in!"

"But, he's —"

Meanwhile, Bad Guy #2 had reached the driver's window and was banging on it. "Stay calm. No one need be hurt. Stay calm. No one need be hurt."

"Now!" I shouted at Cowboy. "Get in, now!"

Reluctantly, he rose, headed to the front

door, and climbed in.

"Stay calm. No one need be hurt. Stay calm. No one —"

The driver stomped on the gas, throwing the attacker to the side while again bouncing the rear wheel over his partner.

"I take you to defeats," the driver shouted as he picked up speed. "Defeats in the kitchen!"

"What are you saying?" the professor demanded. "What defeats?"

"No," Andi said. "Not defeats." She turned to the driver. "Are you saying *'the feast'*?"

"Yes, yes! De feasts, it is in the kitchen! That is what I am saying!"

She looked to the professor. " 'The feast is in the kitchen.' Cardinal Hartmann's parting words."

"Yes, yes! Defeats in the kitchen. Hurry! We must hurry!"

I looked out the back window. The bad guys were nearly a block away. And the one we'd run over twice? He was getting back to his feet.

CHAPTER 6

For half an hour we'd been playing Q and A with the taxi driver. The problem was, he did most of the questioning.

"Why do you persist in asking us?" the professor called from the back seat. "You seem to be the one with all the answers."

" 'The feet are in the kitchen.' " Cowboy chuckled. "That's a good one."

"I do not know, that is why I am asking. You said the airport, but there is no airport on the beach."

"Beach?" I said. "Why are we going to the beach?"

The professor interrupted. "Cardinal Hartmann instructed you to pick us up, did he not?"

"I know no Hartmann. I know very little of nothing."

"But you knew where we'd be," Andi said.

"I know only what I hear."

"From whom?" the professor asked.

"From my head. Words. I hear words. And sometimes, as you may tell, I do not always hear so well."

Cowboy chuckled. "The feet are in the kitchen."

There was a loud thud on the roof and we gave a start. I looked out the windows. Nothing to see but the thick blanket of fog we'd been driving through for the past few minutes.

"We're at a beach?" I said.

"Yes, yes. But as I have told you, there is no airport at the beach."

"Then why are you —"

There was another thump, and then another. I saw something bounce off the hood.

"What was that?" the professor demanded.

More thumping.

"What is going on?"

"That is what I keep asking you."

I looked out the side window. There were dozens of birds, mostly seagulls, flapping around on the road.

"Well, will you look at that," Cowboy said.

One hit the windshield. Blood and feathers everywhere.

Andi shuddered. "That's gross."

The driver turned on his wipers. It pushed off most of the feathers but left a smear of blood that took several more swipes to get rid of. Another one hit the roof. And then another. They came faster, like a hail storm — hitting the roof, hood, windshield, the rear window.

The professor turned to look out back. "Remarkable" was all he said.

Another hit the windshield, so hard it left a spiderweb crack. Another one followed. Faster and faster. With the smearing blood and feathers, the wipers couldn't keep up. Unable to see, the driver hit the brakes and we slid.

"Careful, man!" the professor shouted.

But the birds were slippery. We veered into the other lane. No problem except for the one and only vehicle we'd seen on the road — a produce truck. It appeared out of nowhere through the fog. The driver blasted his horn. When I looked out the side window I was looking straight at him, straight into his terrified face.

It was close. We missed each other by only inches. Our car shot up and over a small embankment. We landed hard on the sand, bouncing several times before coming to a stop.

We sat a moment, catching our breath.

The birds continued to fall. Nonstop pounding.

"Everybody is okay?" the driver shouted

over the noise.

We were — if "okay" meant being in the middle of a storm of falling birds. Everywhere we looked, they were falling and flapping.

"My grandparents' beach," Andi said. "It's like what happened on their beach."

The driver dropped the car in reverse and hit the gas. The wheels spun. The windshield cracked into another spider web. More blood and feathers.

"We can't stay in here!" the professor shouted.

"Where do we —"

"There!" the driver pointed to a bus stop or taxi stand or something. Whatever it was, it had a roof and it was close.

The back window shattered. I grabbed Daniel and yanked him toward me, away from the raining glass.

"Hurry!" the driver shouted. "Go!"

We didn't need a second invitation. As soon as the professor threw open his door, I pushed him out and spun around for Daniel. "Come on!" I did my best to protect him as the two of us ran for cover. I got hit two, maybe three times, but nothing bad. Daniel, too, but he looked fine. Actually more than fine. Not that he was enjoying himself. But almost.

We got under the corrugated roof, which made the falling birds even louder. Cowboy followed with Andi tucked under one arm, the professor under the other. The driver stayed behind. Revving his engine, spinning his wheels.

Cowboy shouted to him over the noise. "Best you get out of there!"

The driver ignored him. It looked like he was going to go down with the ship.

Or not.

Suddenly, the wheels found traction and the taxi took off.

Cowboy cheered. Andi clapped. Of course they'd be happier if the driver had circled around to join us. But he didn't.

"Hey!" Cowboy shouted as the car bounced back onto the road. "Hey!"

"Return here at once!" the professor yelled. "You are not leaving us stranded!"

But the driver had other ideas. He swerved hard, sliding into a U-turn. He stomped on the gas, wheels spinning, until they caught and sent him racing back down the road toward the city.

The others shouted. I didn't bother.

In a minute or two the bird storm slowed to a stop. Now they just lay there, flapping and gasping for breath. I knelt down to take a better look.

Cowboy stooped to join me. "Wow."

I nodded.

"Look, they got no eyes."

I nodded. "Just like the fellows back at the hotel."

"And the birds and fish back at Andi's grandparents. Poor things."

I grabbed a twig and poked at one. It kept opening and closing its beak like it was trying to talk, but no sounds came.

"Great," Andi sighed. I glanced up to see her peering out into the fog. "Now what do we do?"

Not a bad question, considering the produce truck had been the only car we'd seen on the road. And houses? Forget it. At least none we could see in the fog.

Andi pulled out her phone and tried to get a signal. I stepped away from the group and lit a cigarette.

"What's that over there?" Cowboy said.

I followed his gaze up the beach. Through the grayness and off to the right you could just make out some pillars of rock rising from the water. And to the left above the beach, a cliff thirty or forty feet high. But it wasn't the cliff that got my attention. It was the tiny squares of light coming from it.

"Are those . . . windows?" I squinted. "Is somebody living there?"

"Sure looks like it," Cowboy said. "Like them cliff homes the desert Indians built."

"Are you getting any reception?" the professor asked Andi.

She shook her head. "Nothing."

"Looks like someone's got some real nice beachfront property," Cowboy said.

The professor muttered something, then stepped out from under the covering. Without a word, he headed up the beach.

"Professor," Andi called, "where are you going?"

He shouted over his shoulder. "I have seen enough." He cursed as he tripped over a seagull and nearly fell. He motioned to the cliff. "If that's light coming from those windows, it has electricity and most likely a telephone. And if it has a telephone, I am calling a real taxi to take us to a real airport."

We traded looks. The feeling was unanimous. I butted out my cig, grabbed Daniel's hand, and followed.

CHAPTER 7

A hundred yards up the beach and we were out of dead birds. The walk was short. But not short enough to stop Andi from chattering away with more fun-filled Spear of Destiny facts. Not that it wasn't interesting. But it had been a busy morning. A little quiet wouldn't hurt.

But, since quiet wasn't one of her high cards . . .

"There's one theory, quite popular, that says that after Hitler made the duplicate of the spear, he shipped the original off, along with other priceless art treasures, to a special bunker in Antarctica."

"No kidding," Cowboy said.

"Yes. His idea was that should the Third Reich fail, the Spear would be there to empower the Fourth Reich when it resurfaced."

"Wow," Cowboy said.

"And after the war, a secret German

53

convoy returned the spear to a secret organization called The Knights of the Holy Lance, whose sole purpose was to keep it hidden until the proper time."

"That's really impressive," Cowboy said.

Truth is, Andi could be reading the phone book and he'd be really impressed. Too bad. 'Cause the big guy was setting himself up for a massive heartbreak. And you didn't need someone like me to see that in his future.

By the time we got to the cliff, the cold dampness had worked its way through my thin SoCal clothes. Not Daniel. He wore the UW sweatshirt Cowboy's uncle had given him. A little salt in Cowboy's wounds, since earlier he'd been bounced from the football team for helping us.

"You okay?" I asked Daniel.

He nodded, but I'm not sure he heard. He was too awed by the cliff and whatever was carved into it. Those little squares of light really had turned out to be windows. Two stories' worth. Well, three if you count the dormer that stuck out above the center. It had the vague outline of one of those old Victorian houses. Strange. Stranger still, there was something familiar about it.

Once we got there the professor headed up the stone steps and knocked on a front door of thick, wooden planks.

There was no answer. We joined him as he knocked again.

Nothing.

He was about to try a third time when the door suddenly opened. And there in front of us stood some old, jolly-faced nun. The moment she saw us she broke into a grin. The professor started to introduce himself, but it didn't matter. She opened the door wider and motioned us inside like we were old friends.

It was like stepping into a giant, elaborate cave. Even though it was carved into rock, the entry hall was like a real house. There was an antique bureau with a mirror, a hall tree, and a grandfather clock. To the right was a fancy staircase with polished wood. I couldn't put my finger on it, and maybe it was just my "gift," but I definitely felt I'd been there before.

"So," the professor was saying, "if you would be so kind as to allow us to make a phone call, we shall be out of your hair in no time."

The nun's smile grew bigger. She still didn't speak but motioned us toward some double doors. I glanced to Daniel. The kid was a pretty good barometer when it came to danger, and he looked more intrigued than nervous.

We stepped through the doors and into what could only be a living room. Sofa, end tables, lamps. No feeling of being in a cave. Instead, it was all very Victorian . . . and very familiar.

"The House," Andi whispered.

We all looked to her.

"It's like the House in Washington."

The double doors behind us shut. I turned, and the nun was gone. There was a quiet click of a lock. We traded looks.

Andi crossed back to the doors. "Hello?" She tapped on them. "Hello? If you could just tell us where the telephone is? Hello, are you there?"

The professor brushed past her and tried the handles. They didn't move. He shook them. "Come on." He pulled. He pushed. Then he stopped and took a step back. So did Andi. And for good reason.

The doors were . . . melting. And not just the doors. The wall around them. And the pictures on the wall and the shelves.

And the floor.

Starting at the doors, the floor was turning to liquid . . . which flowed toward us.

"Step away!" The professor motioned. "Everybody step away."

It seemed a pretty good idea, so we all

took several steps back.

It kept coming. Daniel gripped my hand. Not a good sign.

It flowed under a chair against the wall in front of us. The legs dissolved and the chair slumped into itself. Then it sank into the floor. Gone. Completely melted. The same with the nearby sofa.

"What's goin' on?" Cowboy said. "What's happening?"

If anyone had an answer, they weren't telling.

"To the other side of the room!" the professor ordered. "Quickly." We crossed the room and reached a single door at the opposite end. It was closed and locked. No problem. Cowboy leaned down and slammed into it with his shoulder. It budged, but not much. He tried again.

The tide of melting floor kept coming. By now half the place had dissolved — the sofa, end tables, lamps. But only for a second. Because a few yards behind all that melting, the room was getting solid again. Reshaping itself. It was the same room, but instead of rock, the far wall had changed into light-colored oak paneling. Where the furniture had been, desks were appearing. Lots of them.

"Remarkable," the professor said.

"Everything's morphing," Andi said.

I turned to her. "It's what?"

"Everything is morphing into another reality."

Whatever she called it, it didn't help. The melting was closing in fast.

Cowboy finally broke down the door. He stared at the pieces, not happy with the damage he'd caused. The rest of us were just happy to get out of there.

We stepped into a short hallway — a dining room was just ahead with eight high-back chairs, dishes already set, and a fancy chandelier. Beyond that you could see a little kitchen with an eating area. To our right was a back set of steps.

"Which way?" Andi said.

After a quick look, the professor ordered, "The stairs."

We started up them. Everyone but Cowboy. He stayed at the broken door figuring how he could fix it.

"Tank!" Andi called.

He looked back to the living room. The melting tide had just about reached him. Figuring now was as good a time as any, he decided to join us.

Safe and out of the way, the professor stopped in the middle of the stairs to watch. We all did. The melting swept through the doorway, dissolving the broken door as it went. Not far behind the melting, the floor kept turning solid as more and more desks appeared. And what looked like, and I know this is crazy, but computer monitors with people beginning to appear in front of them.

The melting washed in and swirled around the base of the steps. They lurched, then dropped. They were also melting.

"Up here!" the professor shouted.

We scrambled up after him as the steps continued to slip and shift.

"Miss Brenda!"

I spun around. The step below Cowboy had given way. I threw out my hand to him. An idiot move. He could have dragged me down with him. But he hung on just long enough to steady himself before letting go and continuing.

We reached the top of the steps and another hallway.

The professor tried the first door. It opened easily. But . . . well, things were getting even weirder.

On the other side of the door, directly in front of us, was the outside of the same cliff house we'd just entered. We were back at beach level looking up at the same cliff house with the same stone steps leading to the same front door.

Behind us, the last of the stairway gave way and splashed into the liquid. The hallway was next.

"Come!" the professor shouted. He stepped outside onto the sand.

More crashing and splashing. The hallway was falling.

"Quickly!"

It seemed a pretty good idea.

CHAPTER 8

We stepped through the bedroom door and back onto the beach, leaving the melting hallway behind us.

It was a useless idea, but I figured I'd slow it down by reaching back and shutting the door. Only problem was there *was* no door. When I turned, there was nothing but the beach and sea behind me.

"What the heck's goin' on?" Cowboy said. "Am I dreamin'?"

"If you are, we all are," I said.

Andi turned to the professor. "Do you suppose . . . is it possible we are experiencing some sort of multiverse?"

"A whatee verse?" Cowboy said. Then his face brightened. "Oh, like where you said Littlefoot is from. One of those higher dimensions all around us."

Andi shook her head. "Higher dimensions are something entirely different."

"Like angels and stuff," I said.

The professor scoffed.

Andi ignored him. "Perhaps. Whereas the theory of the multiverse believes in an infinite number of realities, each branching off and forming another reality whenever a decision is made."

"Another reality." I motioned over my shoulder to the door, or where the door should be. "Is that what we saw in there? One reality changing to another?"

Andi frowned, then turned from the sea back to the cliff house. "If that's the case, then that would make this structure some sort of transporting device."

"A depot," Daniel said.

We turned to him.

"Like a train depot."

Andi slowly nodded. "Like a train depot. A place that connects universes."

"Well, whatever it was," Cowboy said, "I'm sure glad we're out of it."

"We're not." The professor motioned back to the beach and sea beyond . . . or what had been the beach and sea. Like the hallway we had just left, it was melting. And behind the melting something else was forming. Tall, huge, and spreading toward us. With people, thousands of them. They sat in bleachers that kept multiplying, growing taller and taller. And with the people came the sound of cheering.

"Is that . . ." I blinked, trying to understand the impossible.

Cowboy helped out. ". . . a stadium."

The professor turned and started up the steps to the front door.

"What are you doing?" I called.

He nodded back to the melting sand and the growing stadium behind it. "I have no intention of waiting here."

He knocked on the wooden door. There was no answer. He knocked harder. The melting sand was getting closer. So was the stadium behind it. And the roar of the crowd. He was about to bang again when the door suddenly opened. And there stood the old nun, as bright and cheery as ever.

She opened the door wider, and the professor barged in without a word. Unfazed, she stood there smiling, waiting for the rest of us. Daniel grabbed my hand and pulled me up the steps. We hurried through the door, followed by Andi and Cowboy.

Inside, the entry hall was exactly the same. Same bureau and mirror, same coat tree, grandfather clock, fancy stairs with polished wood. The nun stepped to the same double doors, opened them, and motioned us into the same living room.

"She gonna lock us inside again?" Cowboy asked.

"Most likely," the professor said.

I glanced over my shoulder. The stadium had just finished building and towered over our heads. But the melting sand kept coming. It had reached the bottom of the steps and was beginning to dissolve them.

"Considering the alternatives," Andi said, "it's probably best we enter."

The professor grunted and stepped into the living room along with the rest of us. Everything was back to normal, if that's the right word. Same stone walls, same pictures, same Victorian furniture.

The nun reached for the double doors and started to close them when the professor blocked her. "Must you?" he asked.

She smiled and motioned back to the entry hall. The melting had reached the front door. The professor sighed and let her close the doors. A quiet click followed.

"Now what?" I said.

"I reckon we should get as far away from this side of the room as possible," Cowboy said.

We hurried across the living room to the opposite door — the one Cowboy had destroyed, but was now in perfect condition.

"We can't just keep doing this," I said.

The professor was catching his breath. "You have an annoying habit of stating the obvious."

Across the room, the double doors had started to melt. So had the walls and furniture closest to them. And growing up just a few feet behind them? Not the bright oak paneling. Not all those desks and computer monitors. Instead, some sort of training room was sprouting. It had lots of tables and giant monster-looking men lying on them. Only one guy looked normal. He was standing, working over the others like some kind of doctor or trainer or something. And he looked exactly like —

"Tank?" Andi gasped. She took a half step closer to see, then turned back to Cowboy. "Is that you?"

Cowboy could only stare. We all did.

"This is much too unusual," the professor said.

I shot him a look. "Now who's stating the obvious?"

The melting floor kept coming. The professor opened the door. There was the hall with the back stairway, the dining room, and kitchen just like before. And just like the House in Washington.

"What do we do now?" Andi asked.

"The catacomb," the professor said. "In the Capuchin Crypt." He turned to me. "You took photographs of the floor plan with your cell phone."

I pulled the phone from my pocket and flipped through the photos.

"Andrea, you said the bone pattern on the wall was identical to the floor plan of the house in Washington."

"Precisely. Other than the double doors sealing off the entry hall, they are identical."

I found the photos and enlarged one.

She pointed to it. "See. There's the entry hall with the formal stairway. Here's the living room we just crossed through. The hallway we're currently standing in, the back stairs, the dining room, and . . . what's this?" She pointed to a knuckle bone or something in the middle of the kitchen. It was slightly darker than the others, almost red.

The professor looked a moment then quietly answered. "The feast is in the kitchen."

We turned to him.

"That is what Hartmann said about the spear."

"The taxi driver, too," Cowboy said.

I glanced over to the door. It had started

66

melting.

"Do you suppose . . ." Andi looked down the hallway toward the kitchen.

The professor repeated, "The feast is in the kitchen." He turned and started down the hall. We traded looks as he said it again, louder. "The feast is in the kitchen."

Without a word, we followed.

CHAPTER 9

"I don't see nothin'," Cowboy said. "It's just a kitchen."

And he was right. Fancier than mine (its cupboards actually had food), but nothing special. Sink, stove, fridge. A little eating area to the side. There was an island in the center, but nothing to write home about.

"What did you expect," the professor said as he opened the fridge, "a sign reading, 'Look here for the spear that pierced Christ's side'?" He began riffling through the usual suspects and tossing them on the ground — milk, bread, eggs. "Don't just stand there, people. Search!"

We moved to action. Andi and Cowboy took one side of the kitchen with its cupboards and drawers, me and Daniel took the other. I looked behind the plates and glasses. Taking the professor's cue, I swept them off their shelves, letting them crash to the floor. No one bothered looking down the hallway. We knew what was coming.

"Alrightee!" Cowboy shouted. "Hold up. Hold up, I said! Ain't no need lookin' further. I found it."

We turned to see him holding an old piece of metal — five, six inches long, with some wood attached. I'm guessing it was the head of the spear. Well, half of it anyway. The thing had been cut long ways, right down the middle.

I stepped closer to look.

"That's far enough," he said. "No need for you to come closer."

"I'm just taking a look at —"

"Stop, I said! Stop right there!"

I slowed to a stop and frowned.

"This is mine! I found it fair and square. And no matter how you try, there's no one gonna take it from me. You got that?"

I traded looks with the others. The good-ol'-boy accent was the same, but the charm was gone. "What's goin' on, Cowboy?"

"My name's not Cowboy." He turned to Andi and the professor. "And it ain't Tank, either. It's Bjorn Hutton Christensen . . . the third."

"Yeah," I said, "very impressive." I started toward him again. "So why you gettin' all hot and —"

"Aha!" Andi cried.

69

I turned to see her pull what looked like the other half of the spear from the back of a utensil drawer. You couldn't miss the look of triumph on her face.

Or the anger on Cowboy's. "That's mine," he shouted. "It belongs with this one here."

Andi shook her head. "Wrong. Your piece belongs with mine."

The professor and I glanced at each other.

Cowboy broke into his smile and took a step toward her. "No big deal. I'm sure we can work it out. For starters, why don't you be a good little girl and just hand that over —"

"It's mine!" She yanked her piece to her chest. "It's in my possession and you can't have it."

"Yeah?" he said. "Just watch me."

He started at her until the professor stepped between them. "This is hardly the time to quibble over —"

"It's mine!" Andi pulled away. "I found it, and by all rights, his piece should also —"

"I found mine first! That half belongs to me!"

"And that?" The professor pointed to the melting floor just coming into the kitchen. "Who would like possession of that?"

"I can stop it," Andi said. "If he gives me my other half, I'll have more than enough power to stop it."

"*Your* half?" Cowboy shoved the professor aside and started for her. "You give me *my* half!"

"Stop it!" I shouted. "Cowboy!"

But Andi didn't need my help. She squared off to face the big guy, holding up her piece like a weapon. "My intelligence is greater than yours. I can manage this power far more wisely than some ignorant farm boy."

Cowboy slowed and sneered. "You think you're so smart with your brains and all. Well, brains got nothin' over real strength. Not when it comes to —"

"Look!" I pointed at the melting floor closing in.

Cowboy started at her again. "It needs strength. Not some brainiac with —"

"Stay back!" Andi crouched, ready to spring. "You've been warned!"

He laughed, then lunged at her. She screamed as he grabbed her arm. But he was too focused on getting the weapon to see her knee come up sharp and hard.

It found its mark. He was more startled than hurt. She used that split second of surprise to pull his hand into her chest, bringing his piece next to hers.

There was no flash, no sound. Just a look

71

that came into her eyes. Wild, full of wonder.

Cowboy saw it, too. He blinked. Surprised at his actions. Surprised at hers. "Andi?"

She yanked the metal out of his hand and pulled away. Now she had both pieces, clutching them, hunching over them like some crazed animal.

"Andi?" Cowboy reached for her. Not the spear. Her.

She looked up at him. She smiled. Then she threw herself at him — shoving him backward. Not much, but enough. His left heel caught the edge of the melting floor. He tried pulling it away, but it had him. It quickly ran up his foot and turned it into liquid. Then his ankle. Then his leg.

He looked down at it, puzzled. Then to us. There was no pain on his face. Just confusion. The melting spread up to his knee, his thigh. And, as it melted, he sank.

By the time I got to him the liquid had reached his other foot and started melting his other leg, sinking him into the floor. I reached down to him — the liquid just inches from my own feet. "My hand!" I shouted. "Take my hand!"

He saw the floor coming at me, knew the danger.

"Take my hand!"

72

He looked back up. Now he was up to his waist.

"Take my hand!"

But he wouldn't.

I took half a step back, the floor nearly touching the toe of my shoes. But I kept reaching, arching my back, trying to stay clear. "Take my hand!"

He'd melted up to his chest.

"No, Miss Brenda."

"Cowboy!"

He kept sinking until he was up to his neck. Only his head was above the floor, more than a little creepy.

I stretched with all I had. That's when I lost my balance. I swore and fell . . . until the professor swooped in and grabbed my waist. He yanked me back so hard we tumbled onto the solid floor.

By the time I scrambled to my hands and knees, Cowboy was gone.

Chapter 10

I leapt to my feet and spun around to Andi shouting, "What have you done?"

She stared, as surprised as the rest of us. But there was no missing the awe on her face and in her voice. "The power . . . don't you see it?" She motioned to the floor. It melted at the regular speed, but the area closest to her had slowed. It was circling, going around her. "I can feel it. Energy is flowing through me."

We watched as she put the two pieces of metal into one hand and raised it high over her head. "I order you to stop!" she shouted.

It didn't. Not completely. But the melting had definitely slowed. She was standing close to the island, and all three of us edged next to her.

"That's right," she said. "Good. There's no need to be afraid. Come closer. I'll protect you."

Nobody was crazy about the idea. But

nobody liked what happened to Cowboy, either.

She turned back to the floor and shouted, "By the authority granted to me, I order you to stop!"

It may have slowed some more, but it kept inching forward. We backed up until we were pressed against the island.

"I command you to stop!"

"It won't," Daniel said quietly. I looked at him. "It's purer than her."

"Purer?" the professor said.

Daniel nodded, then hopped up on the kitchen island.

"What are you doing?" Andi said. "I have the spear, the one that killed Christ."

Daniel motioned for me to join him. With the melting floor just feet away, it seemed a good idea.

Andi tried again. "I order you to halt!"

Still no luck.

The professor decided to join us. It took a little effort with his old bones, but we got him up on the counter, too.

By now the whole kitchen was pretty melted — cupboards, sink, fridge — everything but the shrinking circle around Andi and our island.

"Andrea, come up here," the professor ordered. "Join us."

"But . . ." She looked back at the floor. It was inches from her feet.

"Get up here. Now!"

She had no choice and finally hopped up on the island.

The last of the floor quickly melted. Now all four of us sat there. A little boat in an ocean of a melting kitchen.

But the boat was also melting. It shifted, then dropped half a foot. We pulled in our feet, scrambled up until we were standing. It slumped again, hard. So hard we could barely keep our balance. Like an ice cube on a griddle, the whole thing kept getting smaller and smaller.

It lunged to the left, throwing all of us off balance. The professor the worst.

"No!" he cried.

His feet slipped until they touched the liquid. Me and Daniel grabbed his hands, but we were too late. It washed over his feet, dissolving them as fast as they had Cowboy.

"Let go!" he shouted.

We wouldn't.

It rose to his ankles, his calves.

"I order you to release me!"

"Shut up!" I yelled.

He fought us, trying to break free as he kept sinking . . . up to his thighs, his hips.

"Release me or you'll also perish!"

"I said shut up!"

He was up to his chest.

We wouldn't let go.

But the professor had other ideas. He twisted until he wrenched both hands free.

"NO!" I yelled.

He threw himself backward.

"Professor!"

He didn't scream. He didn't shout. There was a brief second as the back of his head lay on the surface then sank, followed by his face. Now there were only his flailing arms and hands until they also disappeared.

"Professor!"

The island was three feet off the floor. It pitched so hard, me and Daniel could barely stay on top.

Andi wasn't so lucky. "Help me!" she screamed as she fell.

She sank like a stone, throwing out her arms, holding the spear high over her head as the floor swallowed her . . . but not before Daniel lunged forward and grabbed it.

Even that didn't help. The last of our little island was quickly melting. I grabbed Daniel and hoisted him onto my hip . . . just as the floor swept over my feet. There was no pain. Just a warmth. It kept rising, absorbing my legs, my thighs.

Daniel scampered higher — clinging to

my neck with one hand, holding the spear with the other. I felt the warmth wash around my belly, rising to my chest. I helped him up onto my shoulders.

A moment later I saw it touch his feet. He didn't cry out, just lifted the spear high over his head. The floor surrounded my neck now. I lifted my head to breathe. One gulp of air, two — before it rose over my mouth and nose. And then I was gone.

CHAPTER 11

It was like a dream.

But it wasn't.

The art studio. The dozen or so kids at their easels. I'd never been here, but I'd also spent years teaching in this very classroom . . . and loving every minute of it.

They were special-needs children — Garret, the Asian kid with MS, Lucy sitting in her wheelchair in the final stages of leukemia, sweet Melissa with her severe learning disabilities. I knew them all . . . yet I'd never met them.

"That's good," I said to Rupert, his genetic disorder so severe he could only paint with a brush between his clenched teeth. The canvas was smeared in blacks and browns. "What would happen if you put a splash of red in there? Maybe even yellow?"

He looked up at me, his eyes beaming. And my heart melted.

That's why I do what I do. Art therapy.

Letting these kids express themselves when nobody else will listen. This month it's paint. Next month it'll be clay. Anything to give them an outlet . . . and to take their minds off the ugliness of the world destruction.

World destruction? The phrase surprised me. I looked around the room for a window. It was the same dimension as the living room in the cliff house, the one I'd spent so much time dreaming about.

Or was this the dream?

But it wasn't a living room. It was a classroom. Bright lights, cheery colors, rainbows and animals painted on the walls.

I found a window and crossed to it. The shutters were closed.

"Miss Brenda, Miss Brenda, come see what I've done." It was Lindsey, an eight-year-old who had been abandoned at the church by her parents. There was a lot of that now. With the plague, the famine, and the war, parents were unable to care for their children, particularly those with special needs.

I stopped. Were such things true? They hadn't been before.

"Miss Brenda?"

"I'll be right there, kiddo." I pushed open the shutters. We were in a big city, crowded, buildings packed super tight. Three stories below on the sidewalk people wore face masks. Like in a hospital. Some even had gas masks. And for good reason. The air was a thick puke-green.

I stared, trying to understand . . . until someone touched my sleeve.

I turned. It was Daniel. Littlefoot was beside him. I knelt in front of them, remembering the other dream, the one in the melting kitchen. "What are you doing here? You all right? Where are the others?"

He shook his head.

"What?" I said.

"Gone."

I searched his face. "Andi? Cowboy? The professor?" I knew the names, but not from here.

"All dead."

"When? How?"

He pointed out the window.

"I don't understand."

"Everyone dies."

"But —"

"In this world everyone dies."

"In this . . ." my mind spun, trying to fit the pieces, remembering what Andi had said about a multiverse. "In this world, in this . . . *universe?*"

He nodded.

81

"Everyone will die in *this* universe?"

"Yes," he said.

"But in the other — Cowboy and the others, they won't die? This" — I turned to the window — "this won't happen?"

"If you come back and help."

I rose and looked around the classroom. "But this . . . this is my life. This has always been my life."

"No."

He was right, of course. The other world had been too real.

"This is what makes me happy."

He shook his head and pointed out the window.

"What?"

His voice filled with emotion. "We can stop this."

"If we go back?" I said. "If we go back to our other world?"

"Yes."

I looked to Littlefoot. Her eyes had shifted colors. Now they were a deep cobalt blue. She reached out her hand to me. I stared at it, then turned back to Daniel. He looked more serious than I'd ever seen him.

I turned back to the girl. She nodded, did her best to smile. Daniel gently reached for my hand, took it, and placed it in hers.

I didn't pull it away.

Without a word she turned and we threaded our way through the classroom. Daniel followed. One by one the children stopped painting. They turned and stared. More like glared. But not at me. At Daniel and the girl.

"Miss Brenda . . . ?" It was Lindsey. "Are you okay? Are they hurting you?"

"What?" I smiled. "No, of course not, we're just old friends."

She didn't look convinced. Neither did the others.

I leaned down to Daniel and whispered, "What's going on?"

He motioned to Littlefoot and himself. "We don't belong."

"What?"

"It's not our universe."

"But it's mine?"

"Only if you want."

We continued around the artwork and the kids that I loved so dearly. When we arrived at the double doors, they opened as if by magic and there stood the roly-poly nun with the perma-smile.

I stepped into the entry hall.

"Miss Brenda?" It was Lindsey again.

I turned and called, "Don't worry, sweetheart. I'll be fine."

Littlefoot reached for the front door.

"Wait." I turned to Daniel. "If I leave, can I return?"

He held my gaze and slowly shook his head.

I turned back to the classroom. There was such joy here. Such . . . purpose. "I love this place," I said. "And these kids. They're my life."

The moisture welling up in Daniel's eyes said he understood. "It will be better," he said. "If you come with us, *they* will be better."

I stared into those deep brown eyes. There was no missing their sincerity. He'd never lied to me before. I glanced up to the nun who stood beside him. She gave a nod of silent assurance. I looked back into the room, the children, my life's work . . . and slowly returned the nod.

The nun gently closed the double doors. I turned to face the girl. She reached for the front door, opened it, and we stepped outside.

CHAPTER 12

Our feet had barely touched the stone steps before Littlefoot turned around and knocked on the door again.

The nun answered, beamed like she hadn't seen us in forever, and ushered us inside. But when Sister of the Perpetual Smiles opened the double doors to my classroom, things were completely different.

Instead of kids with easels, there were all those desks that I'd seen before — back when we were running from the melting floor the first time. Same light oak paneling, same computer monitors manned by the same computer geeks. Everything the same, except . . .

Near the end of the room, on a raised platform, behind an expensive desk sat . . .

"Andi?" I shouted.

She looked up, along with the rest of the room. I raced to her — not running, but not exactly walking, either. The two kids followed.

When we got there she was already standing, taking off her glasses. "Do I know —"

"It's Brenda."

She frowned. "I . . . I dreamt about you. Just last night. And the night before." Her frown deepened. "But . . . we've never met. Have we?"

"Of course we've met. We've been together all day. And a few months on top of that."

"I'm sorry, I —"

"In the other universe. *Our* universe."

"I beg your pardon?"

"The multiverse thing."

"Multiverse? But that's . . . just a theory."

"You tell that to the melting floor and everything else happening to us."

Her eyes widened. "It wasn't a dream? It *was* you." She looked at Daniel and Littlefoot. "And you. I saw you, too."

"The professor," I said, "is he here?"

"The professor. He was with us, too, wasn't he?"

"Yeah, yeah. Is he with you?"

She hesitated. I looked out over the room. By now every computer jockey was staring at us. And they weren't exactly smiling. "Who are these guys?" I said.

"What? Oh, they're my employees. This is an information and research facility."

"Not very friendly."

"Yes." She put on her glasses for a better look. "I don't understand. They're normally quite congenial."

"They don't want us here," I said.

She looked at me.

"And trust me, the feeling's mutual. Get the professor and let's go."

She scowled and looked over to the far wall.

"So is he here or not?"

She stepped off the platform and started across the room. I traded looks with the kids and followed — the geeks watching our every move. When I caught up to her I said, "Daniel and his girlfriend here say we got to get back to our own universe. So let's find the professor and get our butts outta —"

We'd reached the opposite wall and she pointed to it. "What?" I said.

She motioned to a small drawer built into the wall. A brass plaque was on it.

I leaned in and squinted to read:

Dr. James McKinney 1955–2013.

I turned to her. "The professor, he's —"

She nodded. "Several years ago.

"And that's him? In there?"

"His ashes, yes. He asked to be interred here. It may interest you to know that this entire center is named in his honor."

"But he's not dead. Not in the other universe. Not in ours."

"This *is* my universe. This is what we lived for. What he . . . died for."

I looked out over the angry faces and gave a snort.

"You have no idea what joy I have here," she said. "The thrill of all of this information right at my fingertips. Anything and everything. It's a dream come true."

"And the rest of the world?"

"You mean the riots? The radiation poisoning?"

"Riots? There aren't any riots."

She frowned.

"Yeah, well, maybe in this universe," I said. "Whatever they got going here, I'm betting it's pretty ugly. But the thing is, you and me, all of us, there's a chance we can change it. If we go back we can fix things so they —"

"That's extremely doubtful."

It was my turn to frown.

She lowered her voice to a whisper. "The odds of us, of anybody, overthrowing The Gate are extremely —"

"I'm sorry, did you say 'The Gate'?"

She motioned me to lower my voice.

I continued, "They're the ones we're supposed to keep the spear from. Remember the Cardinal? That was our whole purpose. To get the spear before The Gate did."

She glanced around, afraid someone would hear.

"Look, we're in the middle of something here. I don't know what, but it looks like we're a team or something. All of us." I motioned to the drawer. "And the professor, if we go back, he'll still be alive."

She stood a moment looking at the plaque.

"Trust me, the jerk is still alive. You saw him an hour ago. You dreamed 'bout him. About us."

She shook her head. "No."

"Of course you did. You —"

"No. It was not a dream." She grew more confident. "It was an alternate reality. The multiverse." She turned toward the double doors across the room. "And if this structure is indeed a portal —" She looked to Daniel. "Or as you've stated, 'a depot,' it should be fairly simple to return." She started forward.

The kids and I traded looks. She was in.

We followed her across the room. The geeks were getting out of their seats. One or two tried intimidating us by flexing their geek bodies. Good luck with that.

We were practically there when Andi slowed. "But Tank? Where is Tank?"

"He's not here with you?"

"No."

I swore.

Then her face brightened. "The training room!"

"What?"

"The room we saw next to the stadium, do you remember it?"

"Yeah, but —"

She crossed to the double doors and opened them. There, waiting in the entry hall was who else but Sister Smiles. The old lady motioned us forward and we stepped in. Littlefoot reached behind us to shut the double doors. Andi touched her shoulder, and she stopped just long enough for Andi to look out over the room one last time.

Then, taking a breath for courage, she turned and nodded to the nun. The woman opened the front door and we stepped outside.

Actually, inside.

The door opened to the entrance of the giant stadium we'd seen before. They were playing football. Well, a type of football.

CHAPTER 13

For starters, every lineman had some sort of club, or battle axe, or something. Like those old gladiator movies. Only these guys were monsters. Literally. Five, six hundred pounds apiece. Real knuckle-draggers.

I turned to Andi and shouted the obvious, "Steroids?"

"Perhaps. More likely genetic manipulation. In fact, if you notice the ratio of height to weight you can see a reoccurring pattern of —"

A play began, and she was drowned out by the roar of the crowd. Each team went at the other — grunting, shouting, clubbing, hacking. And blood. Lots of it. The quarterback got sacked. And for good measure they started bludgeoning him to death.

The crowd cheered.

Andi leaned over and puked.

"See any sign of Tank?" I shouted.

She shook her head. So did Daniel and the girl.

Andi looked back up and groaned, "Oh no."

I followed her gaze to the field. The monster boys on the sidelines were turning toward us.

"What's the deal?" I shouted. "What are they looking at?" But I already knew. So did Andi. And it wasn't just the players. The fans were also turning toward us.

"They know we don't belong," Andi said. "They sense it."

"We got as much right bein' here as them."

She looked around. "You may think so and I may think so . . ." She nodded toward the dozen Neanderthals leaving their bench and lumbering up the steps toward us. "But they don't."

"Any suggestions?"

"Just one."

She looked at me. I looked at her. We spun around to the cliff behind us and began banging on the wooden door.

Sister Happy Face took her sweet time to answer, so I threw in a little R-rated language to speed up the process. By the time she opened the door the goon squad was a dozen yards behind us. We ran into the entry hall and she slammed the door a second before they arrived with their own version of banging and cussing.

Daniel pushed open the double doors to the living room. Only now it was the training room. A handful of the big bruisers were stretched out on the tables groaning and moaning. Some were bleeding. All were waited on by the one and only —

"Tank!" Andi rushed to him.

The big fella barely had time to look up before she threw her arms around him. He returned the hug, more than a little awkward. When she stepped back, she pulled herself together, even more awkward.

He broke into that bighearted grin of his. "Andi."

"You remember."

"Remember? Shucks, I dream about you all the time! I mean, that is to say, well, not all the time, but what I mean is . . . It's you! You're real!" He spotted me and the kids and broke into an even bigger grin. "You're *all* real!" He reached out his arms to Little-foot, and she ran into them for a hug. "It's sure swell to see you again!"

She looked up to him and grinned back, those blue eyes now liquid brown.

The goon lying on the table in front of him groaned. Probably because of the bone sticking out of his arm.

"Oh, sorry, partner." Cowboy reached down and wrapped both of his hands around the arm. He closed his eyes and began silently moving his lips. Just like old times.

Meanwhile the bruisers kept banging on the front door until you could actually hear the wood planks starting to crack.

When Cowboy pulled away his hands, the arm was as good as new. Not even scar tissue.

"That's what you do here?" I said.

"Yeah." He shot me his good-ol'-boy grin. "It's pretty fun. And I get to make lots of new friends." He turned to the guy on the table. "Ain't that right, Gus?"

Gus moved his arm, grunted, and showed his appreciation by lunging for Andi.

She screamed and jumped back.

Cowboy slammed him back down on the table. "Come on, now. That's no way to treat our guests."

Gus groaned. Too weak to try again. But he wasn't the only one with an attitude. The whole room was turning and staring. Several even managed to growl.

"What's wrong, fellas?" Cowboy called. "These here, they're my pals."

"We don't belong," I explained. "We're in

the wrong dimension."

"Universe," Andi corrected. "We're in the wrong multiverse and they sense it."

The front door was beginning to splinter.

"We gotta get outta here," I said.

"Brenda's right." Andi grabbed Cowboy's hand and tried pulling him toward the hallway. But he wouldn't budge.

"These . . . are my friends."

"Maybe your friends," I said, "but not ours. Look how much they hate us."

Gus made my point by sitting up and lunging for me. He was stronger than before, and it took more effort for Cowboy to shove him back down. "But I help these guys," he said. "Me and the Lord, we fix 'em up. And I really like it. I like it a whole bunch."

Some of the goons from the other tables were struggling to their feet.

"We know you do," Andi said. "And that's very commendable. But there's something even greater."

"Greater than this?"

"You can make things better," I said. "*We* can make things better. But you gotta come back with us."

The bruisers who'd made it to their feet began hobbling toward us. It was like a scene from *The Walking Dead.*

Andi quickly explained. "In this reality, you're only a Band-Aid, you're only fixing something that's already broken. If we go back, there's a chance we can prevent the multiverse from splitting like this; there's a chance we can stop all this from happening before it begins."

"She's right," I said. "We can do it. If we roll up our sleeves and all work together, we can do it!" I winced at my cheesiness, not really sure I believed it.

But Cowboy did. He looked from me to Andi. Then he looked to Littlefoot, who was nodding. He turned back to Andi and she reached for his hand again. This time he took it . . . just as the front door exploded open.

We turned and ran. Gus, the goon, caught my jacket, but I spun around and slipped out of it — a parting gift.

When we got to the hallway I glanced over my shoulder. The players from the stadium had joined those in the training room.

"The stairs!" Cowboy shouted.

It made sense. No way was I goin' back into that kitchen. I grabbed Daniel's hand, he grabbed the girl's, and we raced up the steps. We were halfway to the top when the whole staircase began to shake — no doubt from the extra tons of muscle that had just started up them.

We made it to the top and Andi started for the first bedroom door. The one we'd escaped through before. But this time it wasn't real. Just a painting of a door.

She ran to the second. This one was real and she threw it open.

We gasped. And for good reason. There was another me lying there on a bed, passed out with a needle jammed in my arm.

"What?" I cried. "That's not possible."

"It's your nightmare," Andi said. "Up in Washington. It's the universe where you had the overdose."

I tried to step in for a closer look but she pulled me back. "No," she said. "It's a paradox!"

"A what?"

"A time paradox." She pushed us out and slammed the door shut behind her. "It's too dangerous!"

"Not as dangerous as these boys." Cowboy pointed to the players who'd reached the top of the stairs.

We ran to the next door and tried it. It was locked. I slammed into it with my shoulder.

"Let me!" Cowboy stepped in and hit it once, twice. It took three hits before the lock broke and it opened. But instead of the door flying open and into the room, it flew out at us . . . pushed by a thousand gallons of water that roared over us, slamming us to the ground and rolling us down the hall.

It drained in seconds and we made it to our feet, gagging and coughing up seawater.

I shouted to Andi. "That was *your* nightmare, where you were drowning."

"Yes!"

The flood slowed the bruisers behind us, but not by much. They were already clambering to their feet and stumbling toward us.

The main stairway with the fancy banister was just ahead. The perfect escape — down the steps, through the entry hall, and out to the beach or whatever would be there. There was only one problem.

Players were also coming up them.

"Now what?" Cowboy shouted. "We're surrounded."

Daniel raised his arm and pointed to a closed door at the very end of the hall. Not a door to a room at the end of the hall, but simply a door at the end of the hall — as in, open it, step out, and fall out of the house. It hadn't been there until now. I was sure of it. I was also sure I recognized it from Washington. But there, the door was on the first floor and it led into a basement with some pretty ugly stuff.

One other thing: Sister Smiles was standing beside it. But instead of motioning us toward it, she was motioning us to get down on the floor.

It made no sense. But it didn't matter to Daniel. He dropped to the ground, digging his hands into the carpet a fraction of a second before she opened the door and all hell broke loose. I'm not swearing. It *was* hell, complete with the red glow and leaping flames.

There was also wind. Lots of it. But, unlike the last door, nothing was racing out at us. Instead, we were being sucked toward it. It pulled on my clothes, my hair. My whole body was being dragged toward it. I dropped to my knees, grabbed the only thing I could find — some door molding — and hung on with just my fingertips.

"Look out!" Cowboy yelled.

I turned and ducked just as the first of the big boys tumbled past. I flattened myself against the wall as another rolled by. And then another. And another. Until there was a steady stream of bodies being sucked into the doorway.

My fingertips ached. Any minute they'd give out. I turned to Daniel. He was slipping, losing his grip on the carpet.

"Hang on!" I shouted.

He dug in, but the wind was too strong.

"Grab my leg!"

He looked at me.

"Grab my leg!"

Finally, his grip failed. He slid past and just barely caught my ankle in time.

My fingers cramped, on fire, but I yelled, "We'll be okay! Hang on!"

He knew I was lying. He knew my fingers were giving way. I saw it in his eyes. And I saw something else, too.

"No!" I shouted. "Don't!"

He started to smile.

"Daniel! No!"

It was that sad, crooked smile.

"No! Don't you dare let go! Don't you —"

But he did let go. He fell away without a sound.

"DANIEL!"

He was gone. Bodies kept flying past, but he was gone. I cried out. A scream. It came from deep down in my gut. I couldn't breathe. It was over. There was nothing left. My fingers gave way or I let go, it didn't matter. The wind dragged me across the carpet. I started to tumble, to roll. It didn't matter.

Until something grabbed my arm.

I looked up to see Cowboy grimacing down at me. "Just hang on, Miss Brenda!"

He began to pull.

"Daniel . . ." I shouted. "Daniel's —"

"Just hang on." Somehow he'd wedged his body into the last bedroom doorway where he braced himself as he kept pulling. I saw the strain on his face, the pain. And the impossibility.

"Let go!" I shouted. "Let me go!"

But he didn't. He wouldn't. He kept pulling . . . until he finally dragged me out of the hall and we tumbled into the room . . . with Andi and —

"Daniel!" I cried.

He grinned and giggled as I crawled to him, as Andi and Cowboy fought to close the door.

I pulled him into me. Holding him, kissing the top of his head. I couldn't get enough. And when we finally parted, I did it all over again.

CHAPTER 14

Cowboy leaned his head against the closed door, catching his breath, as the last of the wind died. He got to his feet and looked around the room, breaking into that big grin of his. "Don't you just love this place?"

Love wasn't exactly my word of first choice . . . or my last. But if the pattern of the Washington House was true, this is where he had his God encounter. Either way, I was glad we were safe. Daniel looked just fine. So did Andi. But the girl . . .

"Where's Littlefoot?" I asked.

Cowboy's grin faded. He looked down and took a deep breath. And then another.

Andi answered for him. "She never made it."

I nodded and got to my feet. I wasn't sure what to say or do. Daniel saved me the trouble. He reached for the door.

"No, don't!" Andi cried. "We're not sure —"

Too late. He'd opened it. And three feet away, standing on the beach, in all his stuffy-butt glory, was . . .

"Professor!" Andi threw herself at him, all hugs and tears. "You're alive!"

He endured the emotion and did his best to return it. "Do you have the slightest idea how long I have been waiting? Andrea, please!"

She wiped her eyes as the rest of us stepped outside to join them.

He motioned to the front door of the house that, just a moment ago, had been the door to the bedroom. "I have been outside, knocking upon this blasted door for half an hour. Would you mind telling me why you took so long to answer?"

I shrugged. "Long story."

"Well, I expect to hear every detail. And the spear?"

We traded looks.

"Don't tell me you failed to retrieve it? After all we've been through?"

More looks.

"We could go back," Cowboy said. He turned to the door. "I bet that nice nun would —"

"No," the professor said. "I believe we've endured quite enough, thank you very much. We shall return to the Vatican and tell Hartmann that his wild goose chase has come to —"

He stopped as Daniel pulled both halves of the spearhead from his back pocket.

I blinked. I'm betting we all did.

"That's fantastic!" Andi cried. "Great job, Daniel." She reached for the spear, but the professor quickly stepped between them.

"No."

She turned to him.

"From your past behavior, that is an unwise decision." He eyed Daniel suspiciously. "How are you feeling, son? Any unusual emotions? Thoughts of grandeur? A desire for control?"

Daniel shook his head.

"Very well. Then I suggest it remain in your possession until it is delivered."

We agreed, and Daniel slipped it back into his pocket.

Without a word, the professor turned and started up the beach.

"Professor?" Andi called. "Where are you going?"

"Why to the taxi, of course."

"He's back?"

"The man claims his 'voice' told him to return; though I suspect the voice was more concerned with the profit of a running meter than any humanitarian effort."

"Wait," Cowboy said. "Hold on a moment." He turned back to the house. "Shouldn't we tell that nice old lady how much we . . ."

He slowed to a stop. And for good reason.

There was no noise, no sound. But the house was rising. Not the cliff. Just the house. At least the front of it. The door, the windows. They weren't solid anymore. They were clear, transparent. Like a cellophane wrapper slipping up and off the cliff, higher and higher.

"Everybody's seeing this, right?" Andi asked.

No one bothered to answer.

It cleared the top of the cliff, paused, then shot up into the sky. So fast it was a blur. One minute there. The next gone. Now there was only the rocky cliff.

I stepped up to where the door had been. Felt for it. There was nothing but smooth, cold stone. I stood back for a better look. There were hollows and ridges here and there that could have passed for windows. But that's all they were — hollows and ridges. It was just a rocky cliff.

EPILOGUE

The sun was setting by the time the taxi got us back to the Vatican. And it was just like old times . . .

- The professor browbeating another receptionist who said we couldn't see Cardinal Hartmann
- The receptionist running off to his superiors (with or without tears, I couldn't tell from where I sat)
- Us sneaking through the little door and up to Hartmann's apartment
- Me knocking on the door
- And the frail old assistant with the dirty Coke-bottle glasses answering

But Hartmann wasn't in. His blue velvet chair with the peeling gold paint sat in the middle of the room just like before, but that was it. Nothing else. 'Cept the memory of the sketch I made before we ever met. The one of the empty chair without him in it.

"When do you expect his return?" the professor asked.

The assistant thought a second, then raised a bony finger like he suddenly remembered something. He turned and shuffled to the old desk. We waited as he opened the drawer and pulled out an envelope. We waited even longer as he shuffled back to us.

He handed the envelope to the professor, who turned it over. It had a red wax seal on the back. He opened it, pulled out a card, and silently read.

We stood.

He reread.

We shifted.

More rereading.

The assistant took off his glasses and cleaned away a few layers of dust.

"Well?" I said.

The professor looked up . . . a lot paler than when he'd looked down. "He won't be able to see us."

"You tellin' me we go to all this trouble and he doesn't care enough to —"

"He wants us to leave the spear with his assistant."

We turned to the old timer who stopped polishing his glasses and gave a silent, humble nod.

"Are you certain?" Andi said. "Do we really want to entrust something of this value and with this much power to —"

The professor ignored her and turned to Daniel. "Give it to him."

"Professor?"

"Now. Give it to him now."

Daniel nodded and pulled the two pieces of spear out of his back pocket. He handed them to the old timer, who took them in both hands and gave another one of those humble nods.

When he looked up, he was smiling. Something else, too. It was probably just the light in the room, but I swear the color of his eyes had changed. Just like the girl's. They'd been a cloudy cataract gray. Now they were a brilliant sapphire blue.

The professor turned toward the door. "Let's go."

"What?" I said. "Just like that?"

"We've completed our task. Now it's time to leave. And do so quickly."

The assistant gave another smile and nodded like it was a good idea. He opened the door and we left. We wound through the halls and down the stairs pretty fast. But not fast enough.

We just got to the first floor and were

heading for some giant brass doors when we heard, "You there. Stop."

The professor picked up his pace. We all did.

"Stop, I say."

Other priests and what-nots turned to stare at us. A guard appeared at the door. We slowed to a stop. Busted.

Some overfed priest waddled toward us with the receptionist.

"You wished to see Cardinal Hartmann?"

The professor turned and waited. He knew what was coming.

"Do you wish to see Cardinal Hartmann?"

"No," he sighed. "Not anymore."

"And yet you came here —"

"It was a mistake," the professor said. "We didn't know."

"Know what?" I said.

The priest frowned like I had no business talking, much less breathing. I flipped my dreads to the side. "Know what?"

"Hartmann's dead," the professor said.

"He's what?"

"You are family?" the priest asked.

The professor shook his head. "Just friends."

"Please accept our sympathies. With the Lord he has been nearly six months now. Yet a day does not pass where he is not missed."

"No way," I said. "We were just with —"

The professor cut me off. "Yes. We did not know." Looking at me with meaning, he repeated. "We did not know." Before I could argue, he turned and headed through the doors and out into the courtyard.

I traded looks with the others and we followed.

The priest called after us. "We do miss him. All of us. His departure for us was a great loss."

I caught up to the professor. "What was that about?" He said nothing but kept walking. "Hey," I grabbed his arm. "What *was* that?"

He didn't slow. But he did answer. "That, Miss Barnick, was a profound tragedy."

I scowled. "What?"

He swallowed hard. I watched as he covered his face with his hands, then lowered them to his mouth.

I softened. "You two were close."

"It's a far greater loss than losing a close friend." He slowed to a stop and we gathered around him. He looked at each of us. There was more than sadness in his eyes. There was fear. Anger. "I'm afraid the tragedy is ongoing. *Our* lives, each one of them, is set to unravel."

"What do you mean?" Andi asked.

He shook his head.

"Professor?"

He took a deep breath and resumed walking. "What's done is done," he said. "What's done is done, and there is no turning it back."

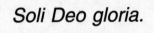

Soli Deo gloria.

INFESTATION

FRANK PERETTI

CHAPTER 1
THE DOLPHIN

The teeming waters and the chatter-filled trees of the Indian River Lagoon put his mind at ease. He belonged here, wading waist-deep through the shallows, peering through the tangled roots of the mangroves, feeling the sandy give of the sea bottom through his waders. His skiff followed close behind him, tethered by a rope around his waist. The short little box of a boat carried his camera, binoculars, notebook, and lunch. It also served as a quick resort should an alligator come too close — which so far had not been a problem. Alligators preferred the freshwater streams and culvert outlets, and those he'd seen in the lagoon were largely indifferent and safely distant.

All in keeping with the goodness of the day: the Florida sun, the aliveness of the leaves and blooms, the constant flitter and flash of every color of bird, lizard, and fish in every direction.

Life. He was here to record and observe it, count and preserve it, and how he loved it.

He'd already spotted two manatee females with their calves, newborn this year, and four new pelican nests, three with eggs, one with hatchlings. Very good signs. At last, after so many mysterious deaths in this place — dolphins, manatees, pelicans — life was returning.

A ripple offshore alerted him. He reached for the skiff, drew it close. Alligators were stealthy, and the lagoon was no place for inattention.

But . . . no. A silvery gray dorsal fin broke the surface, a sight that made him grab his binoculars. He peered through the lenses, focused, anticipated the next breach —

The fin broke the surface again, dipped below, then broke again, this time with a puff of air and a gray arched back that glimmered in the sun.

A dolphin!

He laughed in joy. How long had it been since he'd seen a dolphin in this part of the lagoon? And where there was one, there were sure to be more. He scanned the placid waters, then set the binoculars in the skiff and watched.

The dolphin seemed to be alone, and now

it was circling back, coming closer, a nice bit of luck. He might get a chance to judge the size, age, and health. Viral outbreaks among the dolphins in the past had made him and his fellow biologists careful to observe and record any anomalies — such as this particular dolphin's behavior: not playful or vigorous, but sluggish, and oddly single-minded. It was still coming his way on a straight course.

Cautious, he yanked the skiff in close and watched as the dolphin approached, then slowed and circled no more than ten feet away. It was an adult, average size. That it would come in so close suggested it might be habituated to humans and was either curious or expecting a handout.

But the sheen and color of the skin and the listless behavior looked all too familiar. This dolphin was ill, probably dying. His heart sank.

He chanced a very slow movement toward it.

Rather than shying away, it drifted closer.

Habituated. Had to be. No wild dolphin would act this friendly.

Standing next to it now, he observed a greenish tint on the skin, possibly an algae. The dolphin allowed a gentle brush of his hand; a green residue clouded the water.

He leaned close to check the eye —

The eye was gone, nothing but an empty socket oozing green.

"What the — !"

The dolphin sidled closer, and he could sense the rules of the encounter changing. Now the dolphin was pressing into his space and he was the one feeling timid. He fought off the feelings, reached to examine the flank —

His hand passed through the skin as if it were sodden newspaper. The flesh within felt like goo between his fingers. When he yanked his hand away, it was coated in green slime. A cloud of green billowed out of the dolphin's flank, fouling the water.

What was this? Another algae? Another plague of phytoplankton? He clambered in the skiff for a sample jar, dipped it into the green cloud . . .

The dolphin rolled lazily onto its side. The movement drew his attention. He turned his head, looked into the wound his hand had made.

The wound tore open, and green slime exploded into his face. All he saw was oozing, shimmering green.

And then nothing.

Chapter 2
A Recluse

To be left alone.

All I wanted was to be left alone in the quiet of my condo, *my* universe, the door locked, the phone turned off, safely sequestered against any more high-minded talk of adventure, especially of — oh, a plague on the notion! — saving the world. To hear such themes, to even think of them, brought a visceral twisting I feared would destroy me, and only served to remind me how futile and illusory life can be and what a fool I'd been.

I trusted. I believed.

So I was used and played for a fool.

The story of my life.

The doorbell startled me as if it were a clap of thunder. I had been enjoying an hours-long stupor, sitting in my easy chair, staring at the opposite wall. Having expended any reason I ever had to go on living or thinking, it seemed a reasonable behavior, and besides, at least I could be confident the wall was really there. I could turn away, then look again, and it would still be there. I thought I would start with that.

But then came this, this invasion! "Go away or die!"

"Professor! Come on, McKinney, open up!"

Yes, I thought with a deflating sigh, *now let death come.* It was Brenda Barnick.

I shattered my own stillness. "You are uninvited, unwelcome, and unliked, so be on your way!"

"Well kiss my — !"

I won't repeat it, but she did say it, and having heard it, I couldn't let it go. I bolted from my chair, crossed the room, and opened the door to the defiant tattooist. She was leaning on my doorpost, unruffled — save for her dreadlocks. They were always that way.

"I'm sure this isn't a social call," I said.

She thought a moment, then conceded, "No, I guess not."

"Then state your business."

She arched her eyebrows and asked, "Where's Andi?"

Andi Goldstein, my young assistant, still remained in my employ despite my exile from the world. Every other morning I would slip a grocery and errand list under the door. That evening, I would retrieve groceries, mail, laundry, whatever was on the list, from the front walk, and all without a word or disturbance. "At this precise time, I wouldn't know."

Barnick waved some lists in my face, about a week's worth. "And you haven't seen her in a while, have you?"

I took the lists from her. Had Andi missed that many days? I *was* getting low on milk and whole-grain bread; since most of the mail was junk I hadn't fretted over that. The days all ran together. "No, I haven't seen her."

Barnick searched the sky with wide, rolling eyes and asked, "So don't that bother you?"

"It most certainly does. I'll have to have a word with her."

While the forsaken lists diverted my attention — yes, I'd listed dish soap and mouthwash and now, come to think of it, I'd run out — Barnick slipped past me and into my living room, waving her arms with agitation. "Man, what is up with you?"

I stood aghast at the trespass, and had it been anyone else I suppose I would have taken action — which in itself surprised me.

123

Of all people, I was extending grace toward Barnick? It couldn't be for her coarse manners; perhaps it was for the reliability of her gift. "You have to ask? You're the one who drew the picture. Remember? Cardinal Hartmann's chair?"

She remembered, all right. She was still carrying that drawing in her back pocket like unfinished business, and as she pulled it out and unfolded it, it still spoke the truth. She'd drawn a blue velvet armchair with peeling gold paint on the arms, but the main point of the drawing was that the chair was empty. She looked at it, then at me, and as I expected, she knew. "He was never there."

"Exactly." I'd been over and over our hapless venture into the Vatican for our supposed meeting with my oldest and dearest friend, and every revisit brought the same pain, the same anger. We'd all been had. To offer my evidence, I went to my desk and brought back the note handed to me by Hartmann's withered little assistant. "You've been wanting to see this."

She took it from my hand. Though she read silently, I could discern her reaction to each little phrase because I had it memorized: *Dear Dr. McKinney: I regret that I cannot be present. You are to give the spear to my assistant. Many thanks to you and your team for a job well done. Cardinal Hartmann.*

She looked up at me, and I could see the dots connecting. "Hartmann didn't write this."

"Cardinal Justus Hartmann was my mentor, my wisdom, the only man who stood by me during my personal Inquisition and the only man I ever fully trusted. I came to address him as Cardinal Justus, or Justus, he came to address me as James, and in any correspondence he ever sent me, he addressed me as *James* and signed it *Justus.*"

"It's a kiss-off!" she exclaimed. "Thanks, good-bye, don't call us, we'll call you."

"Which never could have happened with my old friend unless he were dead . . . and someone used my adoration for the man against me, against all of us."

"Oh man. Ohhh man . . ." I could see the downward spiral in her eyes, the falling of the dominoes as she sank into a chair at the table. "All that trouble we went to . . ." She evoked the sacredness of manure and looked to me for help.

But what could I give her other than the truth? "We were talking to a holographic image projected from — where? The other universe we bought into? The skinny old assistant was from that other universe; you

125

could tell by the shifting color of his eyes, the same as we saw with Helsa, the Girl." Nausea took hold of me, and I sank into a chair, as well. "Which means the scroll went full circle. It was brought to us by the Girl, and of course it needed translating, as every mysterious scroll does, so haplessly, naïvely, we — that is, I — brought it to a phony Hartmann and his assistant, both from the same other universe, which means we brought it to the same people who sent it in the first place. It was a scam to rope us in. The Vatican was never expecting us. We were never invited to a real meeting with real people and had no real appointment scheduled. If I'd stopped all my blustering and listened to the receptionist, he would have been able to tell us there was no Cardinal Hartmann because Hartmann was no longer living. It's all to my shame."

"So that's why security bounced us out of there."

I could feel the bitterness in my soul; I could taste it in my mouth. "Because, without permission or appointment, we sneaked our way up to that meeting . . . guided entirely by young Daniel."

Yes, her turn of mood was expected. "Hey, now wait a minute."

"Daniel Petrovski, a lad with supernatural

insight, who freely communicates with unseen people, be they angels or denizens of another universe . . . knew exactly where to take us — twice! — and yet, strangely enough, had no clue that the whole thing was a fraud, that we were being deceived."

"That is not fair!"

"I've had time to think about it. Once you've taken the time —"

"Daniel wouldn't do that!"

She was raising her voice. I determined not to raise mine, though I couldn't help the steely tone. "Daniel was working for them."

She was getting too uncomfortable to remain seated. "I ain't listening to this!"

"The puppeteer operating that hologram already knew where the spear was: 'The feast is in the kitchen.' All these multi-universe charlatans needed was someone to do their dirty work. So they concocted a scroll to convince us we were a team, and now, thanks to us, they have the spear to do with as they will."

She glared at me, which, I suppose, was all she could do.

I could feel the twisting of my viscera, the pain and chagrin as I made my confession. "I trusted. I believed. *That* was my fatal error. And that, Ms. Barnick, is 'what's up with me.' " I leaned back and stared at the wall. "At any rate, there, I've begun the process for you. With any honesty, you'll come to the same findings as I did. We are not a team, we have no mission, and speaking for myself, whatever game these liars and impersonators are playing, I am out. Oh, and as for Daniel Petrovski, you might have a word with your young charge and find out what game he was playing. I will have a satisfactory explanation before I ever see his face again."

"So what about Andi?"

"What about her?"

"She's in Florida."

My gaze shot back at her. "Florida?"

"I got a call from her grandmother."

Barnick. Such a gift for irking me. "You knew this all along?"

"That's why I'm here. You won't answer your phone, so she called me."

"Why didn't you say so?"

"Because I got the distinct impression that you didn't give a rip, not about Andi, not about anybody."

I dodged that. "So now you're going to tell me she's seeing UFOs again? More dead birds and fish? Haven't we already been through all that, and wasn't it a waste of time like everything else?"

"She's had some kind of mental collapse. She's in the hospital, confined in a behavioral health unit."

I stared at her.

She held up two plane tickets. "And these came FedEx from Andi's grandmother."

I had convinced myself that nothing mattered anymore — until now. "I'll pack some things."

CHAPTER 3
ANDI

The "team" did not fly to Tampa, Florida. I flew to Tampa, Florida, and only because of Andi. Because of the plane tickets, Brenda took the same plane, and for financial reasons, we went in together on a rental car. We drove straight from the airport to the hospital, and Andi's grandparents met us there, which was a good thing. The behavioral health unit was in a secure facility — I'll use the word *prison.* Without the signed clearance Andi's sabba and safta — alias Jacob and Sadie Goldstein — filed with Physician's Assistant Matilda Fornby at the front desk, Fornby would not have opened the ponderous, automatic door that sealed the unit against the outside world — and vice versa.

A Dr. Lawrence led us through the "Social Environment" in which residents could freely move about and mingle, and through another secure door into the "Special Care

Environment" where residents, for their own safety, were confined in cell-like rooms. He led us to Room 4, unlocked the door, and brought us into the darkened room. It was sparsely, safely furnished: a bed arranged atop a solid box, no frame that might be disassembled and used for a tool or weapon; a padded chair bolted to the floor; a breakaway light fixture that could not support the weight of a human trying to hang herself. The shade was drawn over the window; the light was turned off. The occupant was mostly a silhouette until we came closer.

I was unprepared. This couldn't be Andi, the bright, fright-wigged prodigy we'd come to appreciate and whom I regarded as irreplaceable: the red-haired, razor-minded seer of numbers, patterns, probabilities, and calculations. This was, by all appearances, a quintessential lunatic, perched in a padded chair, dressed in a hospital jumpsuit, rocking incessantly. If she was aware of our presence she gave no indication. Wild-eyed, as if seeing visions, she was having an animated conversation with someone who wasn't there. "Oh, Atafina, that is so, that is so. It is the self . . . the self that is not . . . nor should it be . . . for to be truly one is not to be at all."

I rested on my knee at her eye level. "Andi?" She didn't notice me, didn't stop her ramblings.

"She's become unresponsive to human interaction," said Dr. Lawrence. "It's like she isn't in this world anymore."

Sadie said, "When she showed up at our door she acted lost, like she didn't know where she was, but she still knew who we were. But that was a week ago, and now . . ."

Jacob put a comforting arm around her. "She kept getting worse until she didn't know who we were, and then she started wandering at night. We spent all our time looking for her. She'd walk for miles with no idea where she was."

"And she'd do it again if she could," said the doctor. "We have to confine her for her own safety."

"Why the dark room?" Brenda asked.

The doctor, learned man that he was, only shrugged. "She prefers it that way."

Andi's face brightened as she looked and reached toward the ceiling. "The orbs! Oh, hello! How lovely to see you! Orb One, Orb Two . . . How do you do!"

Brenda shot me a glance. *Oh no,* I thought. *Are we to go there again?*

"Our saviors," Andi cried in dopey ecstasy.

"Lights, transcendent minds to show us the way!"

"Looks like they're back," Brenda whispered to me.

I held my peace though I could feel my face flushing. Our last trip to Florida was a bitter memory. We wasted hours, days, investigating smelly piles of dead birds and fish and whatever the real cause of the mass die-offs, Andi, Brenda, and Tank — aided by Daniel, of course — were too distracted by madness and delusion for us to ever find it. Rather than a scientific explanation, they opted for strange lights in the sky, illusory alien beings, invisible evil. I discounted any notion of extraterrestrials and demons then, and I most certainly did not entertain such theories now. I even found it affirming that new claims of such things as "orbs" and global saviors were originating exactly where one should expect to find them: in the ravings of a lunatic.

I sighed, hands over my face. *Our* lunatic. Our dear Andi. If not the beings or spirits or flying saucers Brenda was referring to, the old delusions had returned, and to a tragic degree. I questioned the doctor. "And what are you doing about this?"

"The blood tests came out negative," he said. "No hallucinogenic drugs as far as we

133

could tell. But the MRI and brain scan did indicate an abnormal stimulation of the central nervous system. We'll be doing some more tests to track that down."

"Why aren't you doing them now?"

"Professor —" Brenda cautioned.

"What are you waiting for, another day's rent for this jail cell?"

An orderly knocked, then opened the door. Another visitor entered and I winced at the timing.

Bjorn Christensen. Out of place, unexpected, uninvited, perhaps the last person I wanted to see at a time like this. Enormous and muscular, he was a could-have-been football star who gave it up to be a part of our "team." What a dreadful mistake that was.

"Hi, team!" he said quietly. At least he knew he was in a hospital.

"Hi, Cowboy," said Brenda.

If he calls us a team again . . . I thought, but said,

"Hi, Tank." He approached, his eyes on Andi and more dismayed with each step, until he sank onto the edge of the bed, plainly bewildered and saddened.

"It must fill the earth," said Andi, looking into space. "Fill and subdue it. The lord of the mind, the heart, the body . . ." She began to tap and scratch nervously on the arm of the chair, a weird, nervous tic.

I looked at the doctor. He watched her hand. He brought up his clipboard and made a note of it.

"Andi?" Tank said.

Her eyes followed an invisible someone as if they had come in through the ceiling and stood by the window. She smiled at them.

"Wow," Tank said softly to the rest of us. "Kind of like Daniel does when that angel's with him."

All right. I admit I'm not an agreeable person sometimes. Today, at this time, not at all. "Tank . . ." I tried to keep my voice down. "She is out of her mind. She has been inflicted with delusions for which we have neither cause nor remedy. Kindly update yourself before lapsing into such stupidity!"

Brenda put her hand on Tank's arm. "Things are kind of tense right now."

He seemed to understand.

"Just what are you doing here, anyway?" I asked. "I don't recall inviting you."

He nodded toward Brenda. She acknowledged her culpability by arching her eyebrows at me.

I glared back at her; I did not welcome him.

"I gotta be here," Tank said. "We're a team."

There it was, the flame to my fuse. I had to get out of there. I got up to leave. That meant leaving Andi. I paced back, glared at him.

"Professor . . ." Brenda cautioned me, again.

"A *team*? How did you ever get such a ludicrous impression?"

His gaze went from me to Brenda and back again. "Well, all the stuff we've been through together, the note, the scroll —"

"The scroll!"

The doctor got into it. "Mr., uh . . ." He had to look at his clipboard.

"McKinney."

"Mr. McKinney —"

"Doctor to you . . . Doctor!"

"Dr. McKinney, pipe down right now or you're out of here."

I had to admire his spine. Well done.

I piped down, if only for Andi. "Mr. Teammate —" I didn't pinch his cheeks, but my tone did as much. "Since we're to be a team, perhaps you can establish that by making yourself useful." I paused for effect, then nodded toward Andi. "Heal her."

That threw him back a little. He looked at Andi — she was still talking a flurry of numbers, vague philosophy, and ridiculous fantasy names — and then he looked at me, still unbalanced by my forwardness.

"Well?" I said. "Come on now, you think you're so gifted. You healed her dog, heal her. She's your teammate, isn't she?"

He nodded.

"So?"

He sighed, then closed his eyes as if praying.

For a fleeting moment it occurred to me that Tank was over 250 pounds of pure muscle, that he'd broken bodies and limbs on the football field, that I might be pushing a dangerous threshold, and that if he did put me in my place with an arm, an ear, a finger elsewhere, I deserved it. But I was compelled, deeply soured by bitterness even as I knew I should be ashamed. "Is this part of the ritual, or are you stalling for time?"

He didn't tear my arm off or break me in half; he just looked at me with a gentleness I was glad for. "I was praying for you."

I refused to be impressed or softened. I simply nodded toward Andi. "And now her. If you please."

He gave another sigh, and extended his hand toward her.

Her reaction jolted all of us. One touch, and she recoiled. Leaping from her chair, her arms tightly about her, babbling in a high octave. "NO! No, not your kind, not ever, not ever! Stay away!"

Now this hurt him. He extended his hands pleadingly. "Andi . . ."

She locked eyes with him — the first time she'd met eyes with anyone — and just kept screaming, her back against the wall.

"Okay," said Dr. Lawrence, "everybody out." He began to wave us out with his clipboard as he shouted to the orderly in the hall, "Roberto, we need the restraints."

We backed away from her, at a loss, me especially. Andi just wasn't there. We hadn't reached her; she didn't know us.

"Come on," said the doctor. "Out."

Suddenly, inexplicably, Andi calmed and fell silent. Her face relaxed as she looked toward the doorway. We turned, and there in the doorway was — now where had I seen him before? Here in Florida for certain. Oh, yes! The marine biologist at the big aquarium that had the dolphin show. We'd asked him about any findings, any explanations for the dead birds and fish, and as I recalled, he never came up with a sound explanation for anything.

The name came to me. "Dr. . . . Mathis, is it?"

He smiled. "Yes. And you're Dr. McKinney! And . . . Brenda, is it? Oh, and Tank! I remember you!"

And then his gaze went to the pitiful creature Roberto and another orderly were strapping into her bed. As Andi seemed to look his way, he was at a loss. "What on earth . . ."

Dr. Lawrence observed, "She seems to know you."

Mathis looked into Andi's eyes and she looked back, calmly letting the orderlies bind her. "I do remember her," he said. "She and her friends were investigating the mass bird and fish die-offs we had a while ago."

Andi lay back on her pillow and resumed her conversation with orbs and entities, peaceful and happy, though I did note that she was tapping and scratching with her fingers again, soundlessly upon the sheets.

Now we were all standing around her bed like spectators. If only to break the spell and spare her dignity, I cleared my throat and asked Mathis, "So, what brings you here?"

"I just dropped by to say hello to some of the staff. When I saw Andi's name on the patient roster I thought it sounded familiar."

"Well, thank you for dropping by. We were just on our way out." I flashed a glance at the doctor, who nodded.

"Listen, if there's anything I can do, just let me know," said Mathis.

I couldn't imagine what he could do, but I thanked him.

With Andi at peace for whatever reason, we left, signing ourselves out at the front desk and thanking P.A. Fornby for accommodating us.

"So may I confirm, please," I ventured, "that we are on the list of authorized visitors now? May we visit again, say this evening, without having to repeat the paperwork?"

"Well, let's just make sure," she said, gently shooing a large calico cat off the list so she could check. "Yes, just show some ID to the attendant on duty and you'll have no problem."

I looked with gratitude at Jacob and Sadie, and we went on our way.

CHAPTER 4
DIVIDED

Regrouping, depressurizing in the beach-front home of Andi's grandparents, Brenda, Tank, and I rested with Jacob and Sadie in their living room, trying to enjoy the coffees Sadie had brewed for us. There were short conversations, mostly dealing with how we wanted our coffee, but between those, periods of somber silence as we withdrew into our thoughts and coffee cups. We were bleeding for Andi.

Jacob, sitting in his favorite chair, finally eyed us over his mug. "So here you are again, like it or not."

"To be clear," I said, swirling the cafè mocha remaining in my cup, "I am here for Andi. I have no interests beyond that."

"Then you're not gonna help her," said Brenda, looking toward the ocean.

I had no desire for another heated exchange, but if it had to be, it had to be. "As-suming, of course, that only your perspective is viable."

Finally she looked at me. "I'm just seein' what's there, and I'm sayin', if you don't want to see what's there you ain't gonna get very far helpin' Andi or helpin' anybody."

"As if we got anywhere last time?"

She half raised her hands, a sort of surrender. "Hey, I'll take my blame, but Jacob's right and now you've said it yourself: We're here again because last time we didn't finish what we came for."

I had to regroup a moment. "Where, oh where, does this come from, this sense of mission, this whole idea that this has something to do with the fate of the world and we are the chosen ones —"

"We're a team," Tank said — again. "Don't you get it?"

He'd already lit my fuse, and since we were not in the hospital I raised my voice as much as I pleased. "No, young man, *you* are the one who doesn't get it! In order to get it, you have to be rational, you have to be logical."

He'd been wounded ever since Andi's screaming rejection of his healing hand, and now I could see his forbearance was wearing thin. "I *am* logical. I can think. I can see what's right in front of me!"

"Okay, guys . . ." Brenda cautioned.

I mimed a wide-eyed look of wonder. "Ohhh. Logical. Yes. So you see sense and logic in five people who couldn't be more mismatched being a 'team,' and based on what? Feelings? Hapless adventures and missteps? Oh, excuse me, I forgot: we received a note from an unnamed, unknown child on a bicycle for no particular reason, signed by none other than 'Ezekiel.' Well, of course it would be rational to believe that! Not to mention the high point of discovery, a scroll delivered by . . . what? Beings from another universe?"

"But you said there could be alternate universes."

"But does an alternate universe guarantee inhabitants that are benevolent and trust-worthy?"

I gave him time to think, and he finally answered, "No. But your friend, Cardinal Hartmann, he called us a team and he translated that scroll, and the scroll said we were chosen to be a team."

Brenda hid her face as she muttered, "Oh, lord, here we go."

I'd been dying to spring the question. "But who wrote that scroll, Tank? Seeing as you're so logical, have you ever wondered about that?"

"Sure. I guess."

"So? Who, Tank? Who took pen in hand and wrote that scroll? Do you have a name?"

I could tell he hadn't thought that much about it.

"Then, if you don't know who wrote it, how do you know that person knew us, or even knew *of* us?"

"But Littlefoot brought it."

I nodded as if to a three-year-old. "Ah, yes, little Helsa. And who was the meticulous planner who sent her into a strange universe all alone to walk barefoot in the snow and be frightened by strangers and attacked by a wild beast? Do you have a name?"

"No."

"Ohhh. Well then, maybe you can tell me why a scroll, supposedly a message for us, was not written in a language any of us can speak or read? Maybe you can tell me why the same beings who concocted that scroll created a phony hologram of my dearest, oldest friend and pretended to translate a scroll they wrote in the first place? Maybe you can tell me why we should think we are a team just because a pack of liars and deceivers from another universe say so."

I'd lost him. "What? What are you talking about?"

I prodded Brenda. "Explain it to him, will

you?" I was tired of going through it, and I wanted to test where she was on the matter.

She recounted the whole Vatican and Spear of Destiny mess quite well, except for . . .

"You left out the part about Daniel," I said.

She gave me a chilled look. "I ain't passin' that on 'cause I don't believe it."

I acquiesced. "We'll leave it there."

"What?" Tank asked.

"Suffice it to say, Daniel will not be participating in . . . whatever this is. I wasn't even planning on your participation, but here you are."

"Yeah, here I am." He was offended, of course, but brooded about the whole thing while we waited. Finally, he said, "So if these guys from the other universe brought us all together to fool us, doesn't that still lump us together? Why didn't they try to fool somebody else, or just you, or just Brenda? Why did they set this whole thing up for us five? We must fit together *somehow.*"

Hmm. He *could* be logical.

"Like our being together here again," said Brenda, "just like Jacob said. I don't know why we keep fallin' into things together. Seems like last time, we were somethin' *like*

145

a team, at least then, and maybe we could have done somethin', maybe we were *supposed* to do somethin', but we didn't. Me, I just left it here, just gave up and went home." She looked toward the ocean, heavy with sorrow. "Well it's payday now. We didn't go after it and now it's coming after us, and that's what I'm sayin'. Whatever's doin' this, it's still out there . . . and now it's got Andi, and if you don't get that, you're nowhere near helping her."

"A madness has her," I objected. "Not spirits, not extraterrestrials, not —"

"So where'd that come from?" Tank asked.

"That's what I'm here to find out, and in rational terms."

Brenda rose from her chair, still looking out the front windows. "Abby knows."

The others rose to look, and only then did I. Abby, the chocolate lab, was up to her old behavior, sitting by the sliding glass door with eyes and ears fixed on the ocean, listening, watching, whining *as if* something evil was out there. *As if.* That was the thing to remember — if only I could convince the others. "If I may," I said, talking to their backs as they gawked out the windows. "This is the same behavior, the same prelude to the madness that deceived us last time."

"If only she could talk," said Sadie as if I'd said nothing.

"If only Daniel were here," said Tank.

"Oh, please!" I said, and I had to be firm. "Let us not go down that sorry path again!"

Jacob spoke up. "That path may be the only one you have."

"This is where we left off," said Brenda.

"And we need to finish it this time!" said Tank.

Now they were all facing me with one accord, leaving me the only sane person in the room. I could see all was lost. I felt I was speaking to the tides, trying to hold them back. "Then do as you wish. Be a team, wallow in fanciful theories." I grabbed up my coat. "I'm going to go see Andi — alone!"

Perhaps Tank was using his scrimmaging skills. I had only taken a few steps when there he was, right in front of me. "What are you so mad at?"

I was astounded at the man's density. "You haven't been listening all this time?"

"That's not what I'm talking about," he said, his finger in my face. "I mean, what are you mad at *really*?"

That crossed the line. It invaded. It dug deep. "I do not share these things with people I don't trust!"

I maneuvered around him and went out the door.

CHAPTER 5
ORBS

The hospital room was illumined by a single night-light. I reached for the window curtain and pulled it open only an inch. Andi, free of her restraints and sitting up in her bed, showed alarm until she saw it was dark outside, then calmed and gave no protest as I pulled the curtains the rest of the way open. She was immediately fascinated with the city lights outside. She rose from the bed, went to the window, and spoke with them as they apparently spoke with her. The stoplight at a nearby intersection, winking from green to yellow to red and back again, amused her the most, as if the lights were playfully teasing her.

I sat in the padded chair and observed, trying to gather pieces of the puzzle. Lights. Though ambient light, such as daylight or a lit room, seemed to bother her, she was fascinated by isolated points of light. Though morose and muttery that afternoon, she was rather animated now with so many friends outside the window.

So I could guess there was something here, a pattern, a larger fact we could only see in scattered pieces, and certainly not all of those, not yet.

And certainly not with my perceptions skewed by anger and stubbornness I was too obstinate to admit. Sitting here in the semi-dark, away from contentious conversation, I could admit it now, at least to myself.

What was I so mad at? Tank wanted to know.

It is said that anger derives from pain that derives from love, and I can testify to that. Not that I would. My pain I didn't talk about. But it raised a fair question: did this pain keep me from thinking clearly? Could the explorations of my . . . non-team-mates . . . actually have some tiny corner of validity I would be wise to consider?

Lights. Orbs. Was there a connection I was refusing to see? Could there be —

Oh. Now what was this?

Andi had stopped conversing and was now . . . well, singing, it turned out. At first it sounded more like she was sleep-talking, but then an actual melody and words came together: ". . . rise to sing her praise . . . lessons learned within these walls will guide us all our days . . ."

My first thought was dementia. She was regressing back to her high school days, singing the dated and corny strains of an alma mater. I was about to ask her about it when —

Thump! Thump! Someone knocked on the door. The door opened a crack and Roberto the orderly stuck his head in.

"I believe she's singing her alma mater," I tried to explain.

Apparently that wasn't what had drawn his concern. He beckoned with his finger. I went to the door.

Before I got there I could hear a familiar canine panting in the hall, and as I slipped through the door I came face to face with Brenda, Tank, and, on a leash, Abby the chocolate lab. Brenda and Tank were cringing a bit, rightly expecting a burst of anger and indignation from me.

"We wanted to try something," said Tank, calming Abby by stroking her ears.

"It's just a guess — a, a hypothesis," said Brenda. "It would show us if there's any connection between whatever Abby's seeing and whatever's got Andi."

I countered. "Based on two premises: one, that Abby is indeed seeing something, and two, that Andi is 'gotten' by something."

Brenda gave a little shrug. "Hey, even if we're all wrong on this, she loves this dog and the dog loves her. You never know, Abby might do her some good."

Perhaps I was just tired of being angry; perhaps it was the superseding fact that they cared for Andi at least as much as I did. Also, they were willing explorers, risk-takers, which could only be admired. With a sigh, I opened the door and called inside, "Andi, there's someone here to see you."

Brenda and Tank, smiling and affirmed, led Abby through the door. "Hey," Brenda said sweetly, "look who's here!"

We could not have anticipated what happened. Clearly the hospital staff thought as we did: these were two devoted friends. Surely there would be recognition, a heart-to-heart connection, a healing.

That was not the case.

The way Andi's face contorted in horror, the way she cowered and backed into a corner, one would think a predacious, drooling lion had entered the room.

The way Abby bristled, bared her teeth, and tried to lunge, one would think Andi were an evil prowler to be mauled.

Abby's bark was more a roar — fierce, vicious, guttural — and it took both Brenda, on the leash, and Tank, on Abby's harness, to hold her back. Andi's scream was shriller than when she had screamed at Tank. She leapt up on the bed for refuge, her arms raised in front of her. By now Roberto the orderly was coming through the door, other patients were crying out, a red light was flashing, and an alarm was sounding.

Brenda and Tank got Abby out of the room and down the hall, fighting and tugging all the way until Abby's fierce commotion was shut out by the closing of the big security door.

"It's all right, everyone," said the head nurse, hurrying up and down the hall. "It's okay."

The alarm quit, the red light shut off. Fine with me; they only made things more frightening.

The orderly and I went to either side of Andi's bed to comfort her and ease her down. Despite having made such a commotion, she calmed rather quickly and we were able to place her in the chair. Another orderly brought restraints, but Roberto turned him away. Andi wouldn't need them. Within a few minutes of quiet in the darkened room, Andi went back to singing her alma mater, and Roberto, with other patients to see to, left us alone.

"Honor Ponce de Leon," Andi sang. "Rise

to sing her praise; Lessons learned within these walls will guide us all our days . . ."

Ponce de Leon? What a dreadful name for a high school.

"The spirit of discovery shall make us brave and bold; And we will harken back each day to Leon's green and gold."

She was quiet, safe, and happy. Let her sing.

I rested on my haunches in the corner below the window, letting my nerves settle down and weighing the fact that Brenda and Tank's experiment, though producing near disastrous results, did produce results. Nevermind what "it" might be, Abby the dog was reacting to something, both on the beach and here in Andi's room. Considering that part of Abby's past experience with "it" involved her disappearing, then being found dead and eyeless in the waves, it was safe to assume she would lash out at the same menace should she encounter it again.

But this time . . . in Andi? The same Andi who'd held her stiffened corpse on the ocean sand, wailing and mourning over her until Tank . . . well, revived her? The thought was positively dreadful, but reasonable.

Andi had stopped singing. I looked up. She seemed enraptured by something, and —

Tap tap tap tap. Scratch. She was tapping on the arm of the chair again. This time, looking for meaning in anything, I paid attention. Her finger moved again, the fingernail making little scratches, four of them, followed by a single, staccato tap. Next, five scratches. Then, four more staccato taps followed by one scratch.

Good lord. A pattern? Well, this was Andi. It would be just like her.

I groped in my jacket pocket for a pen, had no paper, used the corner of the bed sheet.

Scratch, scratch, scratch, scratch, tap.

Scratch, scratch, scratch, scratch, scratch.

Tap tap tap tap scratch.

I marked it down. I'd pay for the sheet if the hospital objected.

Four scratches and a tap.

Five scratches.

"Andi," I whispered, "Are you doing this, I mean, are you aware of this?"

She only tapped again, this time, four taps and a scratch; four scratches and a tap. Five scratches.

I wrote it on the bed sheets again. A pattern indeed!

"Andi! Andi, is this you?"

A golden light washed over her face. A passing vehicle? I looked out the window —

My gasp was involuntary. I froze right there, eyes locked on the phenomenon on the other side of the glass.

Two — I'll use the word — orbs. Round glowing objects about the size of a soccer ball, hovering by no visible means just outside the window.

Only my eyes moved — they, and my hands that were trembling. I blinked. I studied. I looked away and looked back again. I dared to turn my head and look at Andi — she was looking at them, still enraptured as if seeing angels. I looked again, and they were still there, hovering without a sound, wavering just a little as if stirred by a breeze. They were a metallic gold, glowing, and each had what appeared to be a camera lens glowing deep blue and — I will confess the sensation — watching us as if aware, as if they knew us.

Four taps and a scratch. Four scratches and a tap. Five scratches. Now Andi was tapping and scratching rapidly; I would even say *frantically*. I followed along, reading my penned record on the bed sheets. The same, every time.

The orbs stirred this way and that, rotating to keep their blue lenses focused on us. They could have been a pair of eyes. Maybe they were. At last, perhaps out of impatience, definitely out of curiosity, I faced them directly, defiantly.

They rushed away like little UFOs, vanishing amid the lights of the city.

Andi whimpered, a weak little sound.

I dropped to my knee, eye to eye with her. "Andi. Is that you? Are you in there?"

For a fleeting moment I saw Andi, the real Andi, in her face. She was frightened, pleading. Her chin dropped ever so slightly, rose, then dropped again.

From somewhere inside, she was saying *Yes*.

Chapter 6
The Nephew

My mind churned and circled and processed repeatedly through the night. These orbs were popularly known as ethereal, nonmaterial globes of light, but what I saw through Andi's window was definitely mechanical. Had someone constructed a real machine to mimic a myth? What an ideal piece of trickery that would be. Morning couldn't come quickly enough.

After a hurried breakfast, Brenda, Tank, and I ventured onto the beach, turned right, and headed for the home of the nearest neighbor, no more than fifty yards away.

"You sure the nephew's even gonna be awake this early?" Brenda asked.

"I assure you, he will be," I said, my nose resolutely pointed that direction. "We will see to that."

The "nephew" was the unnamed sluggard and drunkard Andi and I had interviewed the time we were here seeking answers to the fish and bird die-offs. His aunt Edna, the lady of the house, hadn't seen anything strange other than the dead fish and birds, but her nephew claimed to have seen "orbs," even to be closely scrutinized by one. At that time, I saw no need for such outlandish testimony; this morning I was chastised and awakened — and humbled, I might add, as I shared the previous night's experience with Brenda and Tank over breakfast. We are not born omniscient, I told them, and we would be ill-advised to close our minds to new knowledge. Consequently, though I intended to accept their viewpoint only in increments as called for, the presence of these infernal contraptions and their obvious interest in Andi's condition meant I would, with no ifs, ands, or buts, hear what this nephew had experienced.

It was 8:30 a.m. when I knocked on the door on the beach side of the house, the same door where Aunt Edna and her nephew met with Andi and me the last time.

Aunt Edna looked about the same, like an old but stately vessel cruising lazily through life. At the sight of Brenda and Tank she looked puzzled. When she recognized me, she started shaking. "Can I help you?"

"Pardon, ma'am," I said. "I take it you remember me?"

"Where's the red-haired girl?"

"That's what we came to see you about — or your nephew, if you please. Andi — the red-haired girl — is in the hospital with a strange ailment, and we thought your nephew might have some kind of information that could help her."

"What kind of ailment?"

Brenda, Tank, and I looked at each other. Since this was my big idea, the question fell to me. "Some kind of . . . psychosis . . . possibly having to do with all those other things that were going on."

"What things?"

"Uh . . . dead fish and birds?"

"Uh-huh."

"And, uh . . . well, your nephew described certain . . . orbs of light, an unusual phenomenon we've —"

Her answer was abrupt. "We wouldn't know anything about that."

"Well, may we talk with your nephew?"

"I haven't seen him."

"But he does live here, does he not?"

"I think you need to go away."

"Tell us where he is!"

"I said go away!"

Abruptly, Tank stepped in front of me and said, "Ma'am . . . uh, it's Aunt Edna, isn't it?" His gentler, drawling manner seemed to ease her a bit. I backed away and let Tank have the conversation.

"My name's Bjorn — my friends call me Tank; guess that's 'cause I'm so big — and this here is Brenda. She's a . . . creative artist. And this man here is, uh . . ." He looked at me as if getting permission. "James. He's a professor. And Aunt Edna, if you don't mind my saying, you look like something's wrong, like you need some help. Is there something we can do?"

She looked him up and down and asked, "How are you at breaking down doors?"

We stood outside the nephew's bedroom door. It was locked, just as Aunt Edna had told us.

"I don't pay that much attention to his coming and going," she told us, "and anything he does, well, it doesn't surprise me much. But when he started talking strange and acting like I wasn't even there, I started to worry."

"How do you mean, talking strange?" Tank asked.

"Oh . . . just talking goofy things that didn't make any sense, and talking to people who weren't there. Talking to his flying saucers or whatever they are."

Bingo. Tank, Brenda, and I looked at each other.

"And three days ago I heard him come home late at night like he usually does, and go into his room, only this time he locked the door and wouldn't come out. I could hear him through the door, talking away, singing songs, just blabbering over and over about the same things, and I called to him but he never did answer me." Then she added, staring at the door, "And then he got quiet, and I haven't heard a sound out of him for two days."

I knew what we had to do. "Aunt Edna, did you mean what you said about breaking down the door?"

She looked at all of us and then at the door. "I'd sure feel better knowing."

I nodded to Tank and advised her, "Better stand back."

Tank checked the door first, then decided to use his foot. It only took one violent kick.

"Whoa!" I shouted, arms extended to block the opening before anyone could set foot inside.

We all held back, huddling around the doorway, looking into the room. We just didn't know what to make of it.

The nephew wasn't there. The room was, in a sense, as we expected, messy and cluttered. The single bed, unmade as far as we could tell, was up against the far wall. The shape of an old guitar leaned in the corner. What were probably clothes were tossed about the floor. There was a bowl-shaped object, probably a dog's dish, on the floor and what appeared to be a dog's leash hanging on a nail. There were posters on the walls, but posters of what, we couldn't tell.

What held us back, at a loss, had no ready explanation; it fit into no familiar category. Having no idea what it was, we feared it.

The room was coated, covered, with a strange dust the color of dead leaves. The stuff lay like brown snow in soft, thick heaps on the floor, obscuring every object that lay beneath it. It lay an inch thick — in places two inches — upon every horizontal surface — the bed, the dresser, the cluttered desk. It clung like mold to the walls. It was as if the room had been bombed with a large sack of autumn brown flour.

Bombed? Not a bad choice of word, for on further observation we could tell the material lay within a definite radius, having originated from a center like ash from a volcano.

And at the center, which we surmised to be on the bed, was a pair of cargo shorts, the same shorts the nephew had been wearing when he last spoke with Andi and me.

Aunt Edna began to wail, losing control to the point that, for her safety and ours, Tank gently removed her to the living room.

Brenda pointed, and we both noted the footprints of pets in the thick dust. Some cats, we decided, plus a large dog. The animals had moved about the room in a desultory manner, but eventually made their way to the rear window, open just wide enough for them to escape.

We closed the door and backed away.

Aunt Edna was trembling and plainly fearful to speak of anything. She had no idea what had happened, could not explain the brown dust, had not seen anything unusual before this. Yes, the nephew had pets, two dogs and three cats, but that's all she knew. Had she seen orbs such as her nephew described? "No!" she screamed, looking out the windows as if they might be out there.

I borrowed a small food storage container from a cupboard, went to the bedroom, and, using a spoon, carefully took a sample of the dust, sealing the plastic lid with a snap. I closed the door.

Aunt Edna had retreated, sealed herself away in a corner of the couch, and said nothing further except, "Please go away.

Don't ask me any more questions."

She needed time. With the sample in my hands, I told her, "We're going to find out what this stuff is, and then we'll come back to check on you. Until then, please do not go anywhere near that room."

After we left, I started to shake, but I just kept walking.

CHAPTER 7
A FUNGUS

Dr. Mathis peered through the eyepiece of his microscope, clearly fascinated. "It's a fungus of some sort. It's dead, and that's why it's turned brown. I see . . . yes, over here there's still an edge of green, probably its color while living."

He let each of us take a look. Through the microscope we saw myriads of brown, roundish clumps covered with hairlike bristles. They looked formidable, as if they could cling to you like a burr and poison you like an urchin, yet they were incredibly minuscule; thousands could fit in a thimble.

"This could explain the madness," Mathis mused aloud. "Andi's MRI and brain scan indicated some kind of chemical imbalance such as we see in a person under the influence of cocaine, methamphetamine, or hallucinogens. Certain fungi have the same effect. You've no doubt heard of the 'magic mushrooms' that were popular in the sixties for their psychedelic effects?"

Why was he looking at me? "So, uh, how did this hallucinogen escape detection?"

He peered once again through the microscope. "I suppose they could be detected if the lab folks knew what they were looking for. But the hallucinogens piggyback on top of hormones such as estrogen and testosterone where they can't be readily detected, then smuggle their payload to the neuroreceivers." He looked up to make sure we were still following him. "It's just like plugging a thumb drive into your computer. Once these things are plugged in, they can trigger all manner of hallucinations. Some Native Americans used fungi they found in caves to induce altered states of consciousness as part of their religious rituals. Drugs of this kind have always been a part of the . . . what would you call it? . . . higher consciousness movement — Eastern mysticism, contacting spirit guides, ascended masters . . ."

"Extraterrestrials?" I asked.

"Oh, certainly."

With that I met the eyes of Brenda and Tank.

"So where did this stuff come from?" Brenda asked.

"And how did it get into the nephew's

room?" said Tank.

"And what killed it?" I added. "That's what we have to know."

Dr. Mathis held up a hand. "Whoa, whoa, easy. Um, light could have killed it. The daylight coming through the window. Some fungi can only survive in the dark."

That struck us all. "Andi's afraid of light!" Tank recalled, as we all did.

"But . . . wait," I said. "That would mean this fungus is somehow conveying its 'fears' — I'm personifying, of course — to its host. It is transmitting its vulnerabilities, so the host avoids those things."

"Maybe it can think," said Tank.

I waved that off. Too far out for me. "Tank, your question haunts me . . . and I really do not want to go there." Even so, I fielded the question again, wondering if anyone had arrived where I had. "How did the fungus get into the nephew's room?"

Brenda cursed under her breath. She'd figured it out.

A cloud descended over Mathis's face. He'd figured it out, too.

Tank waited to hear the answer.

Brenda provided it. "It was in the nephew."

Dare I speak it? "The nephew went into the room, but he didn't come out."

Tank went for the bright side. "He could have gone out the window with the dog and cats."

"There were no footprints to show that."

Brenda wagged her head. "I don't wanna go there, either."

"What?" Tank asked.

"The nephew could still be in the room," I said, my guts twisting as I recalled the image of those cargo shorts lying at the center of a powdery explosion. "Or . . . what is left of him."

Tank's jaw sagged and his eyes widened. Now he was with us. "Well . . . m-maybe he did go out the window. He *had* to have gone out the window."

"Oh, wait a minute!" said Dr. Mathis. "As to the source of the fungus. There could be a connection —" We waited. He finally shared, "One of our field biologists encountered a virulent fungus in an aquatic preserve not far from here. We were losing dolphins and manatees and trying to figure out why, and that fungus could be the cause."

"And the fish and birds, too?" Brenda asked.

Mathis nodded. "If we can retrace the source, we might find out what we're dealing with. I can take you there. We can look around."

I exchanged an affirmative look with the others. "It's a plan."

CHAPTER 8
THE AQUATIC PRESERVE

Having set Brenda and Tank on a different task, I rode with Mathis as he drove south along the coast, beyond the beachfront houses, hotels, and marinas, to an aquatic preserve where the encroachment of man had been held back and wildlife could at least make a go of it. It was a lovely spot where the fresh waters of the Florida interior eventually found their way to the sea and the waters mingled; where varieties of sea grass provided habitat and food for fish, crustaceans, and manatees; where long-legged cranes waded in the shallows and pelicans soared with graceful precision.

Mathis pulled to a stop at the end of an unimproved road and opened the trunk of the car, pulling out two pairs of waders. Well! Being quite the fly fisherman, a lover of rivers, waters, and nature, I slipped into mine with ease and some eagerness. In no time, we were hip-deep in the blue water, easing our way along the edge of mangroves, bumping into sparkling, darting fish, and looking for anything peculiar — which seemed to be in short supply.

"It seems an infestation of green fungus would be rather visible," I said, looking about and seeing only blue water and healthy plant life.

"Well, this is where our field man encountered it, although you're right, I don't see anything out of the ordinary."

"Pleasant, though. A man could spend days here just —"

I stopped talking when Mathis raised a hand, then pointed toward the middle of the bay. Well! I'd come to look for fungus, seen only the beauty of nature, and now, here was another sight worth the drive: a dolphin, arcing through the water, spouting and shining in the sun. I'd never seen one in the wild and, frankly, I was mesmerized.

"They don't usually come in this close," Mathis said, as excited as I was. He splashed as we watched, and lo and behold, the dolphin changed course and circled back toward us.

"What! Is he . . . ?"

"He could be used to humans. It happens."

Of course, I'd seen dolphins perform in

aquarium shows, but this was the real thing. I remained still, not wanting to alarm the creature, as Mathis gently splashed, coaxing the dolphin to come and say hello.

And it did come in close, so close I felt a little timid. Just what was one to do when face-to-flank with a sizable sea creature? Did they bite? Were they skittish?

The dolphin floated within reach, resting placidly in the water.

"Yes," said Mathis. "Definitely habituated to humans. It's too bad we don't have a treat we can give it."

"Amazing!" I whispered, awed and relishing the moment.

But then again . . .

While silvery gray as a dolphin should be, there was an odd greenish sheen on the hide. I leaned, studying, trying to verify.

The dolphin rolled lazily on its side like a dog.

Mathis chuckled. "Look at that! He's gotten used to getting belly rubs."

"Really?"

He gestured. "Go ahead."

"Are you sure?"

"Move slowly. See what happens."

I took a step closer, extended my hand . . .

I froze, as did time. I looked again to be sure.

The dolphin had no eyes, only empty sockets exuding a green pollutant into the water.

With heart-stopping abruptness, the bark of a dog made me jump and shattered the moment. The dolphin vanished in a thunderous splash that doused me. The dog kept barking, fiercely, protectively.

And pieces came together in that moment. The dog happened to be Abby, on a leash, expected, and brought to the aquatic preserve by Brenda and Tank. I turned to observe, and there she was, running along the bank, pulling Tank after her, barking furiously at the departing dolphin.

A sideways look at Mathis revealed a man taken aback and alarmed.

"What is this?" he asked.

"They got here late," I replied, not telling him that was our whole intention. "Whatever we're dealing with, it seems Abby has a sense about it. It might be a scent, it might be raw intuition, we don't know, but I thought it could be helpful today — and it seems that's the case."

"But she scared the dolphin!"

I nodded. "Indeed she did."

The dolphin now gone, Abby was willing to submit to Tank's leading — but then she went into bark and attack mode at the sight of Mathis! Now both Brenda and Tank worked to contain her, but I could see they would never get her back into the car without risk.

"I'm so very sorry," I told Mathis. "This is not a good situation. Perhaps if you could work your way back to your car and leave, we can get that dog contained."

Mathis wasn't about to argue. "I'll do that."

He clambered out of the water, pushed his way through the grass and mangrove, and a moment later, I heard his car start and drive away.

Abby watched him go, and then calmed down, loved and petted by Tank and Brenda. I climbed up the bank, slipped out of the waders, and joined them.

"Well done," I said, still shaken.

"Sorry . . . I think," said Tank, kneeling by Abby. The dog was panting and smiling, but still edgy.

"On the contrary, you have carried out a successful experiment, and also may have saved my life." The fact unnerved me even as I shared it. "That dolphin had no eyes, and it was oozing green."

I could see shock hit them, followed by new realizations.

"Just like Abby!" Brenda exclaimed.

"No wonder she was so upset," said Tank. "She's been there. She lost her eyes, lost her life."

"Whatever gunk got into that dolphin got into her, too," said Brenda, who immediately cursed as the next connection hit. "But . . . she barked at Mathis . . . and she barked at Andi!"

"Sensing the same thing in all three," I said as I sat on the grass, weakened, trying to sort it out.

"And she's sensing the same thing at Jacob and Sadie's house," said Tank. "Sitting there looking out at the ocean, right? Just like that time she ran into the surf chasing after something."

"And came back dead with her eyes gone," Brenda added, "just like the dolphin."

"Which puts us right on the edge of accepting UFOs," I said, my cynicism unhidden. "Didn't a huge glowing sphere in the sky fit into the narrative? Let's be cautious here."

They both raised their eyebrows at me. Maybe Tank learned it from Brenda.

"But you are witnesses: I accept that Abby has a canine gift of some kind, and I've reached the point of trusting it."

"Wow," said Brenda. "Trust."

I avoided that rabbit trail. "And given that,

whatever Abby is telling us does not bode well, and the whole situation is getting bigger, wider in scope than we first thought. We've seen this eyeless death thing before."

"All those dead fish and birds," said Brenda.

"Those tough guys back in Italy," said Tank.

"The birds that rained on us while we were in that taxi."

"And on and on it goes," I said, even as Brenda's comment about trust persisted in my mind. Where would I be now if Brenda and Tank hadn't joined in the plan and brought Abby when they did? Where would I be if I had to sort this whole thing out and save Andi alone? If there was a point, a plan, an overarching scheme behind what faced us now, could that same scheme have been behind all those past places and cockeyed adventures?

"What?" Brenda asked.

I wasn't ready to concede what now hammered at my mind. "Oh, nothing."

"So what's next?" Tank asked, clearly assuming that *we* would be doing whatever it was together and, of all things, turning to me for leadership. Some things were just unavoidable.

"Aunt Edna."

CHAPTER 9
AUNT EDNA

Aunt Edna had *much* to deal with and, consequently, was inconsolable. The upside was she was talkative, especially as we recounted Andi's condition, our own encounters with glowing spheres and orbs, what happened to Abby, and the strange almost-encounter with the dolphin. "Oh my, oh my, oh my! It's the end. We're being invaded! It's aliens from outer space!"

To the facts, I thought. "You said your nephew had pets: three cats, two dogs."

"A yellow lab, a chocolate lab, a white cat, a black cat, a mangy cat . . ."

"Any idea where those pets are?"

"No, and that's the truth," she said. "But the yellow lab, Boris . . ." She hesitated.

"You can tell us," Tank urged.

"Boris got snatched by the UFO, just like your Abby. But he came back alive. His eyes were gone, but he was still alive, like that dolphin! He came home and ran right into my nephew's room as if he could see where he was going, and after that . . . that's when my nephew started acting crazy."

"And Boris?"

"Disappeared. Except . . ."

"Go on."

She nodded toward her nephew's room. "Right after Boris came home, the aliens started snooping around the house, shining their blue lights in the windows and scaring us, and then . . . that brown powder. My nephew had it on his shoes; he was tracking it around the house. There was brown powder, but no Boris. And then my nephew got crazy."

"The, uh, aliens . . ." I approached the topic gingerly. "Do you mean orbs? Spheres of light?"

She nodded, trembling with fear. "They were watching us, watching him, and then, when he wouldn't come out of his room, they went looking for him. One came right into the house, searching all around with a blue spotlight. It was like we were animals in the zoo, or, or, fish in a fish bowl, or . . ."

"Or specimens being studied," I said, recalling words the nephew had used.

"Yes! Yes, exactly!" She sobbed, and her whole body shook. "They're going to take over. We're all gonna turn to powder!"

■ ■ ■ ■

As we left Aunt Edna's home, we grappled with what to do, how to help her. We could call the police, but what on earth could we or Aunt Edna tell them that they would even believe, and given the incomplete smattering of information we had so far, what could we do? There was no good news, none at all.

And then there was Andi. "If this fungus is the central cause in all of this," I said, "then Andi has it too — and now we know where she got it."

"From Abby," lamented Tank. "Had to be. Andi was holding Abby when she was dead, there on the beach. She was holding Abby, putting her face right up to Abby's face . . . and I saw it: green stuff in Abby's mouth, in her eye sockets." He was near tears. "Man, I had no idea."

"But you healed her," said Brenda. She looked at me, insisting. "He did heal her!"

"Well, God did," said Tank.

"But not before the fungus passed from Abby to Andi," I said, "no matter how the 'healing' happened."

"But what about Daniel?" Tank said, worry in his voice. "He was there. He put

180

his face right against Abby's."

"He's all right," Brenda answered.

I asked, "How do you know?"

It seemed she had to formulate an answer. "Oh, I've been checking in on him."

"Hey," Tank asked me, "do you think Mathis tried to set you up, get you infected by that dolphin?"

"I intend to ask him," I said. "But first we'll check on Andi. If this infestation follows any consistent pattern . . ." I couldn't think it, much less say it.

CHAPTER 10
ALOYSIUS

As we drove near the hospital, I thought I recognized a little lady tottering down the sidewalk. Well, no, it couldn't be who I thought it was. After all, the behavioral health unit was in a secure environment with a big security door to keep all the patients from wandering off. But then . . .

"Hey," said Tank, pointing at an odd-looking fellow leaning against a building, staring at the sky, "isn't that a guy from the ward where Andi is?"

We all looked, even as two white-coated staff from that very ward accosted the man and gently but effectively rounded him up.

"Oh no," I said, pressing the accelerator. "Oh no."

I parked our car rather sloppily, and we dashed in to find the unit in chaos. Orderlies were dashing about, Dr. Lawrence was barking orders, a red light was still flashing. Security guards were going here and there, jabbering into walkie-talkies that hissed and squawked back.

We approached Dr. Lawrence. He was consulting with Physician's Assistant Matilda Fornby who, strangely, was being held in a chair by two orderlies.

We hardly had to ask a question when we heard the babble coming out of Fornby's mouth: "Oh, yes, Doowano, god of great wisdom! All things serve all things, and those things that serve serve in return, to the end that oneness comes and we are the cosmos . . ."

"What happened here?" I asked Dr. Lawrence.

Dr. Lawrence's mind and attention were desperately occupied everywhere else as he tried to fit in an answer. "Fornby's out of her mind. She opened the security door and half the patients have wandered off."

"What about Andi?"

"She's gone. But don't worry, we'll find her." And then he was heading elsewhere. "ALLAN! Get a head count! Julie? Julie! Do we have the police on the line? Speak up!"

Roberto the orderly came racing by. I had to take his arm to stop him. "Are there any pets in the ward?"

He looked at me as if I were the worst of

the patients. "What?"

"Pets. Dogs, cats?"

That finally registered. "Aloysius!"

The man was still preoccupied, hearing orders, trying to choose actions. I had to shake him. "Who? WHO?"

"Aloysius," he answered, looking down the hall. "The cat. We had a pet cat. But we had to confine it because it got sick."

"What do you mean, sick?"

"It went blind. Somehow . . . it lost its eyes."

What a feeling: our enemy, whoever or whatever it was, was several steps ahead of us. "Where is that cat?"

Of course Roberto had other things to do, but I managed a grim enough look to convince him. He started down the hall. "Come on."

We followed as he jingled through his keys. "Fornby was taking care of it and put it in here until the vet could come take a look —" The door he spoke of, marked MAINTENANCE, was already open. "Oh, great!" he said.

And then he screamed. So did Brenda. I'm sure I must have, but I only remember hitting the floor with all the others as an orb, as real as anything, defying gravity, floated out through the doorway, rotated

180 degrees, and shined a blinding beam of blue light into the room. Then it rotated and fixed its lens on us. We cringed, curled, covered our heads.

Having a good look at us must have been enough. It rotated, flew down the hall, and went out through a window it had apparently broken to get in.

"Madre de Dios!" Roberto exclaimed.

I was too shaken to stand, so I crawled to the door. Tank and Brenda got to their feet, though shakily.

Inside we saw the cat's basket on the floor, but now, save for a few shreds of calico fur on the pillow, nothing remained but a thick circle of green powder fading to brown.

Roberto helped me up. I asked him, "Where . . ." I had to gather myself and take another breath. "Where did that cat come from?"

"It was a gift, something to help cheer up the patients."

"From whom?"

"A friend of Matilda's. Uh, Dr. Mathis, that scientist from the aquarium."

Chapter 11
Mathis

I was too stressed, too preoccupied to drive. I rode shotgun while Brenda did the driving. We were heading for the aquarium for an unannounced visit with Dr. Mathis.

"Help me," I said. "We've got to get this sorted. We have to have something, anything, before we get there. Brenda. Any pictures, images?"

"You mean, you're gonna trust me?" she asked with her typical raised eyebrow.

This time *I* cursed. Only Brenda — *only Brenda* — could bring that out of me. "Must we get into that now?"

"A flashlight," she said, her eyes on the road. "Well, not a flashlight. A big flashlight. A spotlight kind of thing."

"That's it?"

She rolled her eyes with impatience. "Well, it was a blue light, okay? But Aunt Edna talked about the orbs usin' blue light and then we saw that orb use a blue light and maybe that's makin' me see things, I dunno."

"Tank? Anything?"

" 'Turned to powder,' " he said from the back seat. "What Aunt Edna said. She's got it right. This fungus takes over until fungus is all there is."

I nodded, sickened by the conclusion. "The fungus consumes the victim: the nephew's dog, the nephew, Aloysius the cat . . ."

Andi. I couldn't say it. I covered my face. "Oh God . . ."

"Yeah," said Tank. "Don't worry, He's in the loop."

I wanted to lash out at his simple faith, his pat answer, but in that instant the thought of Andi brought another thought. "Do either of you know Morse code?"

Brenda shook her head.

"I do," said Tank. "I learned it in the Boy Scouts."

"The other night Andi tapped out a pattern. Maybe it was Morse code."

"That'd be Andi," said Brenda. "Her head's full of stuff like that."

By now I had the pattern memorized. "Four dots and a dash. Four dashes and a dot. Five dashes."

Tank winced, searching his memory. "Oh

man . . ."

"Tank, remember!"

"Uh, uh, uh, it's uh, numbers. Um . . . OH! Dit-dit-dit-dit-dah, that's the number 4. And dah-dah-dah-dah-dit, that's 9. And five dashes is zero. Four Nine Zero."

I sighed in exasperation. "Oh, Andi. You and your numbers!"

"Prof," said Brenda, "they always mean somethin'."

"Well," said Tank, "what was happening when she did it?"

I replayed it in my mind. "You'd just left with Abby . . . the orbs appeared outside the window . . . Oh my God!"

"Yep, it's Him again."

"Blue light!"

"Keep goin'," said Brenda.

"Blue light. The orbs use a blue light." A lightning bolt hit me. "OH! Fungus. Light. The fungus was discovered in caves, in the dark."

"And Andi always wanted the room dark."

"And light, *blue light,* is known to kill some species of fungus."

"Hey," said Tank, seeing some light of his own, "those orbs weren't searching around Aunt Edna's house with blue lights. They were cleaning up, killing the leftover fungus!"

I turned and looked at him. Brenda looked at him through the rearview mirror.

"Tank . . ." I said, a little ashamed to be so shocked. "That's brilliant — no pun intended."

Tank's countenance lifted several degrees, and he kept going. "Boris the dog brings the fungus in, he pops open, spilling fungus everywhere — gross! — the fungus infests the nephew. The orb shines blue light through the window and kills the leftover fungus. It turns brown, the nephew tracks it around the house on his shoes. Then . . . oh brother . . ."

Brenda picked it up. "The nephew bursts." She winced. "The fungus spills all over his room and, you know, finishes up the nephew. The orbs go through the house killin' the fungus so it doesn't spread. We find dead fungus all over his room, but not him."

"Same thing at the hospital!" said Tank. "The cat had the fungus, it infested Fornby, then it . . ."

"Yes, yes," I said, "go on."

"And that's why we saw the fungus and a little bit of the cat in the cat's bed. *Gross.*"

"But!" I completed the thought. "The orb was there to kill that fungus with a blue light, and we saw it dying." My heart was quickening. "So there's definitely a purpose, a mind, a technology behind all this. The orbs must be like drones — remote eyes, remote tools. They observe the infestation and control any spillovers with blue light. AND! Getting back to Andi's number, 490. That would be a wavelength in the blue range of the spectrum. It could be the specific wavelength of the blue light: 490 nanometers."

That appeared to boggle Tank's mind. "Really?"

"That's Andi," said Brenda with a wag of her head.

"Brenda," I said, spotting a line of cabs waiting in front of a hotel, "pull over."

"What?"

"Pull over, grab one of those cabs, get to the University of Tampa, show them your picture."

"But I haven't —"

"Draw it when you get there. Find someone, anyone, who might know what it is."

Brenda pulled into the hotel parking lot. "Well, then what?"

I don't know where I got the conviction; faith, perhaps. "It's there. You never draw anything that doesn't exist somewhere. Search around, find it, get it." She climbed out. "Oh! It must be set for 490 nanometers! 490!"

"Four-ninety, right," she said, running for a cab.

I ran around the car, got behind the wheel, and looked at Tank in the back seat. "Let's go see Dr. Mathis, shall we?"

"Come in, come right in."

I looked at Tank. We hardly expected so jovial a response to my knock. Then again, Mathis could still be ignorant of our discoveries and suspicions. I opened the door and we stepped into his lab.

Mathis sat at a bench on the far side of the room, peering into a microscope. "That's a very perceptive dog you have," he said good-naturedly.

We made our way through lab benches, tables with fish, squids, and crustaceans in jars of formaldehyde, lab machines, and instruments. The room was dimly lit, just as it was the last time we were here. This time we noticed.

"She barks from experience," I said. "She had a run-in with the fungus herself. Just like the dolphin you and I encountered. Just like Andi. Just like Aunt Edna's nephew." Then came my coup de grace. "Just like the cat you brought to the behavioral health unit."

"Just like the masses of dead birds and fish," Mathis added, unruffled.

"Do tell."

We stood behind him, resting against the worktables. Rather than turn to engage us, he reached for another slide, placed it under the microscope, and continued viewing. "It's all for the best, to bring peace to the world. The fungus expands the mind and opens up pathways to the spirit world. That's why a benevolent global organization genetically engineered their own version of it, something they could propagate, control, and use to promote universal bliss and brotherhood; to unite all minds into one."

Uh-oh. This kind of talk sounded all too familiar.

"Wait a minute," said Tank. "A benevolent global organization? That wouldn't be The Gate, would it?"

"Oh, you've heard of them! Well, well. They'll soon be known all over the world, we assure you! The fungus will see to that. But you can understand the problem they encountered: They had a mutation of the fungus they could use to control minds and bodies, but no effective way to deliver it. You know how people are; they aren't going to just swallow the stuff. The Gate had to get around that. They had to find a suitable delivery vehicle.

"They experimented with fish and birds, but because the fungus was engineered to thrive inside people, fish and birds didn't work; the fungus matured only as far as eating out the eyes, and then the fish and birds would die, and the fungus would die with them, leaving a big mess to draw attention. Warm-blooded animals whose temperature was close to that of humans, that was the answer, and it worked, with an extra benefit: what better way to spread the fungus to unsuspecting human beings than through their pets — dogs, cats, or even dolphins?"

"So they used Abby?" Tank asked.

"She was an early experiment using a warm-blooded mammal as a delivery vehicle, except that you, Tank, interfered with the process, so they couldn't be sure the fungus had taken hold — which it did, but far too slowly. What should have taken days took months. When they tried it with Aunt Edna's nephew using his dog, Boris, it worked perfectly. The fungus went through all four stages of its life cycle unhampered: infestation producing altered states and madness; destruction of the eyes; displacement of tissue; and then what we call the burst stage."

"Yes," I acknowledged. "We've seen all four."

"It's how the fungus propagates itself. It reaches maturity and bursts from its host so it can spread to the next. It's like a conquering army!"

"So why destruction of the eyes?" I dared to ask.

"Oh, survival, of course, something the fungus does on its own that The Gate wasn't counting on. This is a cave fungus. It doesn't like any kind of light, but The Gate engineered it to be vulnerable to a narrow frequency of light only they knew about, so only they could control it. Well, that works fine if the fungus is lying outside a host, but once the fungus is inside the body of a warm-blooded mammal — such as pets and humans — it can survive and complete its life cycle, untouched by any light, except . . ."

I could see where this was going. "Except through the eyes."

With an affirmative nod, he finally turned. I half expected it, but still it was horrible.

His eyes were gone. Nothing but empty sockets oozing green.

"Exactly," he said. "We want The Gate to have some control, but not all."

He rose from his chair. We backed away. We knew we weren't really talking to Mathis, but another mind entirely, a mind that was cunning, cruel, arrogant. "Oh," he said, "we never told you about the other dolphin, the one that infested the field researcher in the Indian River Lagoon. That researcher was Dr. Mathis. The dolphins ingested some of those infested fish from the earlier experiments and became carriers themselves."

"And knew just where to swim to find us."

He smiled, the flesh crinkling around the sockets. "Exactly where we wanted them to swim. The fungus has a mind. Our mind."

"Then you must know where Andi is."

"Something you'll want to know, I'm sure, and the sooner the better." Casually, and without a hint that he was blind, he removed his lab coat and hung it on a hall tree. "You could say she's somewhere trying to restore her youth." He looked at us with those empty sockets. "But you'd better hurry and find her. The fungus is well into the first stage now. Once she loses her eyes, there'll be no getting her back."

He slipped on some wraparound sunglasses and headed for the door. This monster, loose on the streets? We tried to stand in his way.

"We're not here to play games," I said — even as something hard collided with my cranium from behind. I went reeling into a lab table, shattering and scattering flasks and test tubes. Sinking to the floor, I caught sight of Tank in a fighting stance, blocking an attack from the culprit, an orb that kept lunging, bobbing, trying to knock him down. With just a few quick fighter's moves, Tank had hold of the thing. It fought him with surprising power, like an angry fish, but that only riled Tank. As if he were spiking a football, he dashed the thing against the floor, where it cracked like an egg, spilling wires, fluids, and components. The blue light came on for a moment, then winked out.

The orb finally lay still, except for a faint electrical fizz.

The door to the lab clicked shut. The orb had done its work. Mathis was gone.

Chapter 12
The High School

Tank and I wasted no time bolting from the lab to find Mathis, dashing past the aquarium's tanks and displays, going out the door to run past seal and tortoise pools, hide-and-seeking through the gardens and paths. The chase was useless, and I was on the verge of a coronary. Mathis could have gone anywhere.

We finally joined up outside the tropical bird aviary, Tank only mildly winded while I collapsed on a park bench wishing I had an oxygen tank.

"Maybe we should call the police," he said.

"And tell them what?"

"But what can we do?"

"Get out your iPhone," I said between gasps for air. "Find out where Ponce de Leon High School is."

He got out his phone. "Ponce . . . ?"

"Ponce de Leon. The Spanish explorer who was looking for the fountain of youth.

He discovered this crazy state."

"Well . . . it wasn't a state then, was it?"

"No. Thank you for that correction."

"So they named a high school after him?"

"Mathis gave us a clue, something about Andi trying to restore her youth. She was singing the alma mater at the hospital."

He was tapping away on the phone. "What a lousy name for a high school."

"Wait'll you hear the song."

"Here it is."

"Get the directions and let's go."

Just a few more taps and we had the route. Tank helped me along, and we got to the car as quickly as my rubbery legs would allow.

Tank drove. I just breathed and hurt.

"Why would Mathis tell us where to find her?" Tank asked.

"To trap us, I imagine. It's the old 'tell them where, but say it in a riddle' trick. Makes us think we figured it out ourselves when they were handing it to us. And if this whole thing is guided by a universal mind operating in the fungus, then Andi sang her alma mater and Mathis gave us the clue for the same reason: to trap us in the high school with Andi as the bait."

"So, did I miss the part about why we're purposely walking into a trap? I mean, I've never been in a trap before."

"Sure you have. Just think football. Look for holes in the line, get around the blockers, nail the quarterback."

He followed that metaphor just fine. "Yeah . . ."

My cell phone played Beethoven's Fifth.

It was Brenda. "Got it! I mean, the guys in the School of Engineering have a light, 10,000 watts, and they can set it up for 490 nanometers. They know just how to modify it because I drew them a picture — and I didn't even know what I was drawin'! Way cool."

"We're on our way to Ponce de Leon High School. Can you meet us there?"

"I'm on my way there now!"

"Wha— ?"

"Remember that cabbie who picked us up in Rome?"

I was about to get angry. Was she toying with me? "Who appeared out of nowhere for no particular reason and knew just where to take us?"

"Yeah. Well, I'm in his cab, and he's taking me to the high school. Same guy, 'cept now he talks Southern."

I put my phone away. "*Him* again!" Yes, it was a trap, all right. We'd just have to deal with it when we got there.

■ ■ ■

Ponce de Leon High School turned out to be an empty, boarded-up shell from the past. *I* could have gone to high school there. Perfect. If The Gate and their lackeys wanted to eradicate us neatly, away from any watching eyes, this was the place to do it.

Brenda's cab arrived with a screech only minutes after Tank and I got there. The cabbie didn't stick around, but I took some quick steps to look at his face. Yes, same guy, all right. I think I heard him say "Bye, y'all," as he gave me a little wave and drove off.

"So why're we here?" Brenda asked.

She was empty-handed! "Where's the light?"

"They're working on it."

"Without a blue light, what can we do?" I looked up at the imposing, brick building. Night was approaching. It was going to be dark in there. Even if we found Andi . . .

"Hey," Brenda insisted, "don't worry. When it's ready they'll get it to us. I took care of that."

"We have to look for Andi," I said. "In there."

200

Now that got a curse out of her.

"And find her before the fungus reaches the second stage and it's too late," I added.

"But wouldn't we need a blue light to help her, anyway?" Tank asked.

"We might find one we can use. *Might.*"

The main doors were chained shut, but we found a side door standing ajar like an invitation. We stepped gingerly into a long, dark hall. Years of trash, even dead leaves, littered the floor; the place echoed. Through broken windows, streetlights painted squares of light on the old, dented lockers.

As if on cue, we heard a far-off, echoing voice. "Abby . . . here, Abby . . ."

It was Andi.

We ventured a few more steps inside as our eyes adjusted to the dark.

Two classroom doors ahead, another hallway crossed the hall we were in. A golden glow appeared in that hall. We ducked into a doorway as an orb, and then another, floated through the intersection like watchmen on patrol, lenses sweeping back and forth. When they passed down the hall and their light winked out around a corner, we advanced like shadows to a niche between lockers and a drinking fountain and hid there, listening.

Somewhere, Andi was laughing playfully

as she often laughed with Abby, suggesting she was not alone. All we could do was make our way in that direction. What we would find, we would find. The game was cat and mouse, sneak and hide, avoid orbs, follow sounds. From somewhere — around the corner, down a hall, perhaps in a library or cafeteria — came the clicking of animal claws on the tile floors and the panting of dogs. A cat let out a mournful cry.

"Ab-by!" the voice called once again. We were closer.

We didn't know the layout of the building; we didn't know what lay around any corner we came to. We made turns and decisions that could have been right but could have been wrong; we stole down halls, around corners, through deserted classrooms with the desks stacked helter-skelter.

Intermittently but growing louder, nearer, Andi's voice drew us forward while the orbs, by chance or by strategy, blocked any retreat. We passed through the old auditorium — and were startled by the shadow of a cat dashing up the aisle. We kept close together, eyes outward, watching ahead, behind, to either side.

We went out the other side of the auditorium, turned down the hall.

We heard the dog first, clicking and padding on the tile. Then the ponderous frame of a mastiff crossed into a patch of light. The beast was eyeless, drooling green slobber. As if it could see, it spotted us and its hackles bristled like spear grass. We backed away. It charged, its thunderous bark reverberating off the hard walls. We did the only thing we could do: we ran the other way.

The hallway came to a T. An orb and two hissing, eyeless cats blocked a turn to the left; we ran to the right. Orbs closed in behind us, blocked a side exit, kept us moving. The orbs, the dogs, the cats, were all moving with orchestrated precision. We were being herded.

A chocolate lab like Abby, eyeless, blocked the hallway ahead of us. We veered sideways into a stairwell.

Well done! The dead-end stairwell immediately flooded with pale golden light as at least ten orbs, the mastiff and the lab, and cats, some visible, some moving and wailing in the dark, formed a barrier. The earthy stench of the fungus closed in on us.

A figure emerged from the blackness behind the orbs. It was Mathis, or whatever was left of him. The walk was stiff, unnatural, the torso bloated. The eye sockets were spilling green powder.

"This is it," I told the others. "The burst stage."

That was when Tank changed the rules. Abruptly, with a loud, startling growl, he charged, hit Mathis full force, and *would have* brought him down in a flying tackle if Mathis were still Mathis. Instead, the shell that was once Mathis exploded on impact and Tank disappeared into a choking, spreading cloud of green powder. Brenda and I would have been enveloped as well if we hadn't seen a gap between the cloud and the stairway and dived for it. Crawling out the other side into the hall, we managed to remain in clear air, but were still plainly visible to the orbs, the dogs, and the cats. We clambered for safe distance as Tank, invisible in the green murk, screamed in pain and horror. The fungus was taking him over.

"No, no, ain't gonna happen!" Brenda was ready for a scrap, but any move would be the wrong one unless . . .

With Tank in such agony, the orbs' attention was divided. "Go for that orb, the one closest," I told her. "Distract it."

She ran right up to it and slapped it sideways. It turned from watching Tank's suffering and got back to business, eyeing her, trying to herd her. She led it along, right toward our own little trap.

I pounced from the dark, threw my jacket over it.

It was like netting a wildcat. The thing spun, lurched, battered against me through the jacket. Before long it would break my arms or knock me unconscious. Brenda got into the fight, containing it in her arms and holding it against her body while it shook her, hammered her, hurt her. Gathering the sleeves, hem, and collar of the jacket together, I managed to form a pouch. With a firm grip established, I nodded to Brenda. "Okay!"

She let go. The orb nearly flew away with me, but fortunately, weight was on my side. I began to spin, arms extended. Now centrifugal force was on my side. I spun faster.

Wham! Another orb came after me, and I scored a lucky hit, smacking it with my spinning captive. It spun crazily away.

A quick sidestep, and on my next rotation I smashed the orb into the wall. There were sparks, electrical pops. The thing fell like a cracked egg to the floor. I yanked the jacket away, rolled the orb about, searching, searching.

"Prof, look out!" Brenda screamed.

The mastiff came toward me, not charging, not growling — it just came toward me. Stiffly. The body bloating. The sockets and the dangling tongue dripping green.

I found a panel on the side of the orb opposite the lens. It was cracked. I pried it off.

Somewhere in the dark, Tank was crying out to Jesus, arguing with a nebulous, personal evil we could not see or hear.

I backed away from the mastiff. It kept coming.

From another side, Tank staggered toward us out of the green murk. "No, no, Autoguano or whatever your name is. You're not God! Yeah? Well, stick it in your ear." He was coated in green and fighting *not* to approach us even as he did. "Prof, Brenda, get out of here!" His voice was hoarse, choking. "Don't let me getcha!"

I groped about inside the wrecked orb for anything: a wire, a lever, a trip switch, a test button —

Brenda screamed and ran to me, grabbing up my jacket for a shield, threatened from behind by a mangy eyeless cat.

The mastiff was relentless, pushing, pushing, pushing us back, the body swelling.

"Oh, Lord Jesus, don't let 'em win!" Tank cried, staggering, reaching as if to grab us.

In that instant, as if there really was a God, my fingertip found a button. I pressed it.

The orb's lens fired a dazzling beam of

blue right into Tank's eyes. He screamed, covered his face.

"Look at the light, Tank!" I shouted.

There was a dull thud as the mastiff exploded in a cloud of green. Brenda and I jumped backward —

The eyeless cat pounced, claws bared.

Brenda blocked it with my jacket. It clung to the jacket by its claws.

I shined the light at the cloud before us. Green turned brown and began settling to the floor.

Brenda slapped the jacket against the wall —

Another explosion of green!

We ducked away as I brought the light around. Green turned to brown.

Tank was on his knees, bent over, gagging. In a hoarse, gravelly voice he kept crying out, "Jesus! Jesus!"

"Look up, Tank!" I shouted, shining the light his way.

He dropped his hands from his face and forced his eyes open, crying, flinching in pain.

The green on his face turned to brown. His eyes ran with tears but he kept them open. I swept the light up and down, all over his body. The green turned to brown the moment the light hit it.

Once again, we heard a faraway Andi calling, "Abby! Here, Abby!" We could hear the clicking of the chocolate lab's claws trotting away in the dark. Abruptly, the orbs spun and followed, leaving us alone in the hallway.

Gradually, visibly, Tank became himself again, dusting the brown powder from his clothing, wiping it from his face, shaking it from his hair. "It isn't over," he said, blinking, wiping his face with a handkerchief, trying to clear his head. "I saw it! I saw everything! It's like they all have the same mind, they're all connected by the fungus. They were trying to trap us and spread the fungus to us, but it didn't work."

"So what about Andi?" I asked.

"They have a Plan B. They're going to use her to spread the fungus somewhere else, maybe with the dog. They've got her thinking that dog is Abby."

"Where? Where is she going?"

Tank shook his head. "I didn't see that."

But he did see *something*. The mind. The freaks from space. Demons. Whatever they were, they had the answers, and there was only one way to tap into this mind of theirs. I looked at Tank and Brenda. Could I trust them?

I would have to. "We need to know the rest."

Some green fungus still remained from the Mathis explosion. I ran to the stairwell, scraped some together, scooped it up, and slapped it into my mouth.

CHAPTER 13
OTHER DIMENSIONS

Sensations streamed one after another: dry mold on my tongue, then slime, then a fire raging from mouth to throat to stomach and sparks of lightning at every nerve ending. Somewhere beyond all the immediate agony I heard myself screaming, and then . . .

As if passing through a veil, I passed beyond pain into a shattering of consciousness: I was myself, there, in the present, vaguely aware of the cold tile floor, but I also existed elsewhere, behind the visible, before and after the present. Brenda and Tank were shouting at me, or at one of me, and that one of me wanted to answer but was so far away, so unimportant against all the greater forms and beings I was, that I remained silent.

With such a sudden loss of who I was I could have panicked, but instead I was fascinated, enthralled. I was no longer *in* the old high school; I *was* the old high school. I could see the halls and rooms as a floor plan of myself, but not just the high school. The entire city of Tampa was enveloped by my being, the pulse of the city, the lights, the other tiny entities all cells of my own body. My awareness expanded like a fireball. . . .

And from a point somewhere above the atmosphere, as I realized my oneness with the earth, I began to see the dissolution of distinction between what was and what I was, and how all things were one and I was all things, how I was divinity itself. . . .

Until an illumination came to me: *What a ludicrous heap of bunkum and balderdash!*

A being appeared and came toward me, crossing through dimensions as through successive curtains of cellophane, seen more clearly as it passed through each curtain. It glowed like a god, was dressed like a stereotypical alien, and spoke. "I am Tonnofan, an ascended god of wisdom and knowledge. Welcome to our fellowship. You are God. . . ."

I answered, "That would mean I don't believe in me, which is absurd!"

"Professor?" It was Tank's voice from somewhere. "Prof, don't do this! Look at the light!"

"No!" I shouted from somewhere outside

myself. "Don't shine that light at me, I have to see what the fungus sees!"

Incredible! As if I spoke it into existence, the halls of the high school appeared before me, and not just the immediate halls, but the rooms, the cafeteria, the street outside. I had become the orbs, the dogs and cats. Their eyes, their minds, were mine. I could see and I could know through them.

Brenda spoke from somewhere, "Prof, you'll die! Once you lose your eyes —"

"Then let's hurry!" I shouted. "I can see things. I know things. I might see where she went."

Now I could see Tank, Brenda, and between them, myself — from beside me, from above, from far away. Brenda draped my jacket over my shoulders. They helped me to my feet, each shouldering an arm.

"Which way?" asked Tank.

Instantly I saw the quickest way out; I saw us going there before we were there. "Left, then right. The door before the cafeteria."

I was an orb, in stealth mode, following just above and behind us in the dark.

I was a cat slinking along the wall. I wanted to pounce, to claw, to shred —

"Tank, go through that door."

"But that's the gym," said Tank.

I knew because I'd been there before.

"There's a baseball bat just inside. Grab it!"

Tank left me teetering, hanging from Brenda's shoulder. He dashed into the gym and came back wielding the bat.

I could see the cat *and* see what the fungus saw through it. "Kitty cat at six o'clock."

Brenda dropped me — I didn't mind — and turned the light behind us. Tank's mighty swing turned the cat into a missile trailing green that faded to brown.

"Orb at eight o'clock high!"

Tank swung. Missed. Brenda caught the sneaky little globe in the light. Tank swung. This orb exploded with a loud pop and the innards clattered to the floor. That view of us winked out of my awareness, but I got to my feet and we made it outside.

It was all I could do to overrule the thoughts encroaching on me: I was the fungus. I wanted to grow, spread, fill the world. My hubris was without limit; I was unstoppable!

I could see us from above and in front, through the orb that hovered there, and I knew it was going to fire a beam of blue light at me. I shut my eyes; I covered them with my arm. "They're trying to take me out of the game!"

Tank and Brenda stepped between the orb and me to shield me even as the first beam of light blasted down, then another, then another. *No, you don't!* I thought. *Not until we know.*

Not until we knew where Andi was going, which, in my strange, multidimensional world, was where *I* was going. Brenda threw my jacket over my head to keep me in the dark, blind to any more blue lights as my feet pounded the pavement, striding with strength and purpose. She and Tank were hurrying, nearly running, to keep up.

"Where're we goin'?" Brenda huffed.

"Senior Center," I think I said. Images, sounds, knowledge was streaming so rapidly through my mind I hadn't time to sort it; I just had to accept and follow. Another voice from another mind came out of me: "But you can't stop us! You can only be in so many places, but we can be everywhere!"

Don't listen to me, I thought but could not speak. *Stay with me. See it through.*

I was inside an orb, then another one, then another, seeing what they saw as they hovered and bobbed in the dark around a quaint old meeting hall surrounded by park-like grounds. Through the open door, through the windows, I saw good old folks, lots of them, enjoying a party in a large, decorated room.

Jacob and Sadie were there. It was some-one's anniversary.

I felt my guts, my many beings screaming, "They are yours! Take them! Live in them!"

The gods, glowing, masquerading as aliens — and all, I was certain, with ridiculous names from some fantasy novel — were watching, following me on the sidewalk, lingering above the Senior Center, calling to me —

But . . . no. Not only to me. To another mind the fungus was controlling.

Andi. The gods were calling to Andi, "They are yours! Take them! Live in them!"

I could see through Andi's eyes the choc-olate lab, apparently the nephew's missing dog, trotting beside her as if trotting beside me. The sockets were spilling green powder; the flanks were distending. "Come on," Andi said to the dog, "let's go see Sabba and Safta."

CHAPTER 14
EXPLOSION

Splendid, coursed the thoughts through my being. *All those people, so trusting, who know so many other people. From here I can go everywhere and the gods will rule.*

Andi quickened her step, and the dog trotted along. Through her eyes I could see the Senior Center just a block away. Festive. Unsuspecting.

I was thrilled.

What was I thinking? How could I think it? What was I doing?

"Prof," said Tank, hurrying beside me, "you still with us?"

I turned, swung at him. "Go away! You've done enough damage!" I could have been striking against iron, and the pain brought back some lucidity. "Keep going, Tank! Don't let me stop you!"

"Don't worry." With the baseball bat in one hand, he took me in a strong grip with the other and we hurried along.

Words, like vomit, erupted from my mouth. "Stop! Give this up, you will fail, you will all die!" Tank, bless his heart, just kept going, and fighting him off was futile.

We made it to the sidewalk in front of the Center, raising a hubbub that caught the attention of the folks visiting on the Center's veranda.

But Andi and the dog had turned up the walkway that traversed the expansive lawn and were heading for the front steps.

I was the dog, looking up at the curious seniors gathering on the veranda. I was ready. Any moment now . . .

From out front I, whoever I was, could see the dog walking stiffly, no longer an animal but a shell, a walking carrier of fungus.

Andi called, "Sabba! Safta!"

No. NO! Yes! Do it!

I yanked the jacket from my face as my stupid, mindless mouth bellowed, "Come closer! Your granddaughter has something to show you!"

"No," Tank hollered, throwing my jacket over me again, "stay back!"

"Safta! Sabba!" said Andi. "Look, Abby can do a new trick!"

Her grandparents, all love and concern, came down the stairs. "Andi," said Sadie, "sweetheart, are you all right?"

"NO!" shouted Tank. "Don't get any closer!"

The fool! The menace! I could see Tank through other eyes and pounced to silence him. The Gate, the demons, the gods, the aliens, whoever the heck they were, could have chosen a mightier stooge than I. It was like trying to tackle a marble statue.

"Oh no!" said Sadie, now noticing, "Her eyes are gone! But . . . no, this isn't Abby!"

While pounding and wrestling with Tank the Immovable, I saw, I felt, I *knew* the fungus was gathering, consolidating from a dozen directions. I could feel the Mind stretching out across the street, up the block, drawing other minds, other eyes. More dogs and more cats were gathering, every creature infested since the nephew's pets escaped. Two escapees from the behavioral health unit, a demented man and a suicidal woman, came up the street looking whammy-eyed and robotic.

In the Mind, I was walking with the last — and most lethal — arrival: I rounded the corner in that person's eyes. I floated above that walking shell in the eyes of an orb. I recognized who it was from where I grappled vainly with Tank. Physician's Assistant Matilda Fornby was no longer within the skin that walked stiffly up the sidewalk. In her place was a bomb, seconds from its appointed time.

"Sadie!" Tank shouted, still trying to break my grip without breaking my arm, "Sadie, get back!"

Well! My little diversion, no matter how futile, kept Tank occupied so Matilda Fornby could slip past and go up the front walk.

"Matilda," said Sadie. "Matilda, is that you?" Sadie gasped. "Her eyes are gone, too!"

Brenda ran up the walkway. Tank wrapped his free arm around me and, to my anger and astonishment, carried me along as he ran after Brenda.

"Unhand me, you fool!" I screamed, and I admit that most of me meant it.

"Sorry, Prof," he said. "You're with us, like it or not!"

Brenda, Tank, and I, Tank's kicking passenger, ran up the walkway, outdistanced Matilda Fornby, and put ourselves right in Andi's face. Brenda lifted the crippled orb and triggered the beam.

Inside Andi's mind, and through her eyes, I saw the light flashing her direction and Brenda's grim, determined expression, like that of a gallant warrior — but on the enemy's side. NO!

"NO!" Andi screamed, covering her eyes.

Tank spoke to her as a friend. "Look into the light, Andi! Look at it!"

I could feel the warmth of trust rising in her as the light hit her eyes. Trust! Like a nagging, undefeatable truth so far away.

The light did its work. Like an extinguished lamp, my vision through Andi's eyes winked out. She was free.

"Brenda? What are you doing here? Tank, what are you doing with the professor?"

In anger and frustration that weren't mine, I growled, "You belong to us, Andrea Goldstein!"

She smiled her disarming smile and said, "Oh, you bet I do!"

I didn't mean it that way.

"Safta! Sabba! What's, what's wrong? What's happened?"

Sadie could not stay away from her granddaughter. She rushed forward, held the girl in her arms.

Brenda, Tank, and his unwilling, underarm prisoner advanced and stationed themselves between the innocents and Fornby, the two escaped patients, a pack of dogs and yowling, eyeless cats. Brenda raised the broken orb, aimed it at Fornby. I kicked the air, reached and groped for that orb to stop her.

But . . . no need. The orb's power pack went dead. Its blue light dimmed, blinked, went out. Brenda jiggled the orb, pressed the test button inside, but to no avail.

AH! Through the dog, through Fornby, I watched a pall of helplessness fall over Brenda Barnick's face. Now this was going to be perfect. Perfect!

But Brenda's resolve didn't waver. Instead of that look of helplessness, a fire rose in her eyes. She dropped the orb, Tank tossed her the bat, and the two — with me in their company — planted their feet and stood their ground.

Oh, and now, what was this? Andi, though frightened and trembling, came down the stairs and stood with us, feet planted. We were a wall. We would die there before we would move.

"Unhand me!" I screamed at that huge ape of iron.

"I'm gonna do like you said," said Tank. "I'm gonna think football. We're not giving up another yard." Then he looked me right in the eye and asked, "You gonna help?"

I could hear the thoughts of the fungal Mind like hundreds of little voices coming through a wire — *The breeze is right, we're in last stage, they are yours, take them, live in them!* But I could not turn my eyes from Tank's face, for I now beheld what I had never seen before: A man. Not a youthful, bungling football jock, but a man. A warrior. Here, in Tank, in Brenda, in Andi, was valor, and part of me, buried deep within, felt something.

Felt something?

Yes. The fire, the same as I saw in Brenda's eyes, in Tank's strength, even in Andi's fear.

And where was I? Where was Dr. James McKinney? Where *should* I be?

Against all the poisonous voices within me I knew it: with them.

"At your service," I said.

Tank released me. "If we can just push 'em back, buy some distance and some time . . ." was all he could say before I let out a war cry and charged. I was infested, anyway. Why not strike the first blow?

I collided full speed with the shell of Matilda Fornby, and rather than experiencing a bone-breaking impact, the clothing and skin collapsed, I felt a muffled blast, and my entire awareness was enveloped in a green cloud.

Wump! Brenda took the bat to the chocolate lab, and it exploded.

Tank grabbed up the two dazed patients,

one in each arm, and got them into clear air.

To one side, Andi stood in the path of the cats. They leaped and burst upon her, splashing her with green powder.

Everywhere, there was green, green, green. The stench of the fungus filled my nose and mouth. I was gagging. I heard screams and chaos as my ears rumbled and the earth seemed to quake. But through orbs above, I saw the green cloud expending its explosive power in the middle of the Center's grounds, away from the building where the good folks were watching, screaming, running inside. We'd spared them, at least for the time being. But we, covered in the fungus, were doomed.

The rumbling in my ears grew louder. It must be the next stage beginning. I felt for my eyes — still there. No pain yet. I could still see. . . .

Wait!

Blue light! Like a blue sunrise. And immediately —

Horror. Pain. Death. Intense, everywhere. I could hear a million shrieks as the light penetrated through the green cloud and myriads of minuscule, green globes shriveled to dead, brown particles. I screamed,

clamping my hands to my head. This, it occurred to me, must be how it felt to be shot
— a million times.

And yet . . .

I, the real I, knew this was salvation, as
light coming from heaven. At first it was
only a murky glow through the cloud, just
enough to call to my soul in its prison, but
as the cloud fell away like fog under a
warming sun, the light grew brighter, dazzling, healing. I looked directly into it, held
my gaze right there as I felt the voices, the
thoughts, the chains of lies and confusion
fall away. I had a thought of my own: "My!
The destruction of the fungus is quite
rapid!"

My next thought came as a declaration of
freedom: "I am Dr. James McKinney — and
that's all I am!"

The rumble was deafening, and even more
so as I returned to this singular planet and
my own situation within my own skin.
Everything around me was awash in blue.
The steps, the walkway, the senior citizens,
the lawn, all blue. Dead powder, looking
blue, was settling like fine snow on the
ground all around me, and only now did I
become aware that my body was not standing, but lying feebly within a web of arms.
With my own eyes, still there and still work-

ing, I found myself safely held and steadied by Brenda Barnick, Bjorn Christensen, and Andi Goldstein.

"Am I . . . am I back?" I asked them.

Andi's jubilant smile was the first I saw. "It sure looks that way!"

I got my feet under me and put my weight on them, still steadied by my friends. With arms free and eyes focused, I dusted the brown powder from my sleeves, shoulders, and pant legs as I looked around. "Did we get it all?"

I could see the two patients from the BHU were back to . . . well, normal for them. They were lightly dusted in brown, but surrounded by senior friends and making their way up the steps to sample some punch.

"I think we got it all," said Tank, and it was only then I realized how we were shouting to hear each other. Where was all that noise coming from?

When the noise moved from directly above us to out over the Senior Center grounds, I recovered my senses enough to recognize a helicopter settling on the lawn. On the nose of the chopper was a sizable black cylinder still emitting a powerful beam of blue light.

I looked at Brenda, astonished. "They mounted it to a helicopter?"

"The chopper belongs to Jacob," she said. "All I had to do was ask."

The brilliant blue light switched off as the chopper's engine and rotors wound down. The door opened, and there in the passenger seat, his hand on the spotlight controls, was . . .

Daniel Petrovski, smiling like a cherub.

What a feeling. That kid of questionable allegiance just saved my life. Our lives. *Countless* lives, as a matter of fact. I turned an icy eye toward Brenda. "And just how did he get involved in this?"

Brenda smiled. "I had him come along — separately, just in case. He stayed with some friends of Sadie and Jacob. Turns out we needed someone to show the chopper pilot where we'd be — and to work the light."

"But how did he know where we'd be?"

She shrugged. "He has . . . friends that you don't like."

Daniel looked up at an invisible someone sitting in the chopper with him.

Oh, the things I had to accept with this bunch! "And to think I trusted you."

She put a fist on her hip, cocked her head, and up went those eyebrows. "Yeah, to think you did."

Well, where would I be if I had not? And where would any of us be if not all five had been here? I put my arm around her and gave her a nod. "Well done. And thank you."

That left one last debt to settle. I took Tank aside. "You asked me what I was so mad at."

"Well, we don't have to talk about that if —"

"And I said I didn't share such things with people I didn't trust."

Now he just listened.

"Her name was Autumn," I said. "We were in love, but I was a Catholic priest. Because of my vows, I lost her; because of our love, I was defrocked. End of — well, beginning of story, actually. But now you know — and I'm still just as angry."

He nodded. "Got it" was all he said.

Brenda and Andi joined us. I think it was supposed to be a group hug, but nobody organized it and it looked more like a collision. Well, we'd get better organized with time.

"Hey," said Tank, looking at Daniel, "one thing I still wonder about: he had his face right next to Abby's, but he never caught any of the fungus."

"He's prepubescent," I surmised. "Remember how Mathis said the fungus piggybacks on testosterone to infiltrate the neuro-receivers? In our young man, the fungal toxins lacked a sufficient handle, and the fungus died isolated."

I could tell Tank was impressed. "For real?"

I smiled. I shrugged. "Well, suffice it to say, the powers-that-be, whatever they are, wanted him fit to tackle his role in this little project." I said to everyone, "Come on. Let's help him down out of that chopper . . . and shake his hand."

■ ■ ■ ■

INFILTRATION

ANGELA HUNT

■ ■ ■ ■

CHAPTER 1

"What's that address again?" I asked Tank, who held the professor's note. "Was it 2468 Gulf?"

"Twenty-four sixty nine," he said, bending to peer out my window. "Probably that one right there."

I pulled into the narrow driveway and shut off the ignition, then surveyed the place the professor had rented.

"Cool beach cottage," Brenda said, opening the rear door. "Come on, Daniel my man. Let's see what the prof's been up to while we were packing."

I drew a deep breath and slowly released it in an effort to calm my pounding heart. Only two days ago our team — me, Brenda Barnick, Tank, and Professor McKinney — had been involved in a life-or-death struggle with green powder and flying orbs, and I wasn't exactly eager to go another round with whatever had confronted us. But the professor had been adamant about not stopping to lick our wounds. We had to go on the offensive, he kept saying, we had to stop reacting and start being proactive.

The thought didn't thrill me.

I got out, then went around to open the trunk. Anything to keep from rushing headlong into whatever the professor was planning.

I grabbed a couple of bags, then turned to survey the street. Gulf Boulevard snaked along the coast in this part of the county, so dozens of beach houses and condos here were available to rent. Still on an emotional high from our last escapade, the professor had rented this house for a month — but I sincerely hoped we wouldn't need it that long. I could handle an occasional adrenaline rush, but running with Brenda, Tank, Daniel, and the professor full time was enough to fry my circuits. After all, none of *them* had ended up in the hospital's behavioral health unit, but I did. And though I'd been pronounced physically fit by my doctor, my emotions felt a little unsteady. And for good reason: I'd been only hours away from exploding like a bag of green powder.

"Andi?" Tank turned, his smile fading to a look of concern. "You okay?"

"I'm great." I plastered on a big, fake grin

and trotted up the concrete porch steps.

Inside the house, Brenda and Professor McKinney were bent over the dining room table. I dropped my bags onto a functional sofa as Tank entered behind me. In no hurry to join the others, I turned to admire the not-so-admirable art on the walls. "Interesting place, don't you think?" I murmured, taking in the nondescript lamps, the mostly empty bookcase, and the stack of tattered magazines on the coffee table.

"All the comforts of home," Tank said. His gaze wandered to the dining room, then shifted to Daniel, who sat on the couch, his hands empty and his gaze blank.

"That reminds me," I said, rummaging in my purse. "I picked up a little something for Daniel." I found the small box and handed it to him. "Here. I hope this will give you something to do while we're talking. Plus, if you ever get separated from us, you can give us a call."

Daniel's eyes went wide as he held the iPhone box. "For me?"

"For real and for you," I told him. "My provider has a package plan, so no big deal. I've already programed it with our names and numbers, e-mail addresses, all that. I'm sure Tank would be happy to recommend some really cool games, too."

Daniel opened the box and lifted out the phone with an almost reverent look.

"I'll help you download some killer apps," Tank promised, "soon as we've finished talking to the prof." He turned to me. "Don't you want to see what the professor's been up to?"

"I guess." I forced another smile and reluctantly followed Tank into the dining room. On the table, gleaming beneath a chandelier that might have been fashionable in the seventies, was an orb — a slave, we assumed, of the organization that had apparently tried to wipe out the human race.

I halted in midstep, my heart pounding hard enough to be heard from across the room . . . if anyone had been paying attention.

Brenda was bent over the table, dangerously close to the orb. "How'd you get this?"

The professor folded his arms. "Yesterday I went back to Dr. Mathis's lab at the aquarium. The police were there, of course, and a guy from management was telling them about a case of vandalism. While he was holding their attention, I slipped in and walked directly to the spot where Tank had destroyed one of the orbs."

"Didn't anyone stop you?" Brenda asked.

"Of course not. I had borrowed one of their lab coats." The professor's smile deepened. "If you wear a lab coat and behave as though you know what you're doing, most people will defer to your authority."

"And this orb was just lying on the floor?" I asked, embarrassed to hear a tremor in my voice.

"It was shattered, the pieces resting where Tank left them. I put all the bits and chips into a specimen tray and carried it out. Note that, please. The orb was in at least a dozen pieces. It looked nothing like this."

Despite my innate abhorrence of the object, the professor's comment sparked my curiosity. "A substitution," I suggested. "Someone took the broken orb and left this sphere."

He shook his head. "Once I reached my car, I placed the tray in a box and sealed it. I slept with the box under my bed at the Goldsteins'. I didn't break the seal until this morning and *this* is what I found."

My gaze drifted back to the orb, which didn't have a single scratch or blemish.

"I ain't buying the idea that this thing put itself back together," Brenda said. "So maybe someone saw you take it. Maybe there's a GPS in all those pieces, so someone tracked it. A good inside man could have switched it out while you were asleep and you'd never hear a peep."

The professor shook his head. "When I opened the box at the Goldsteins', the orb had regained its spherical shape, but I could see ridges in the metal — or what I *assume* is metal. I put the box in my car and drove here. When I opened the box a few moments ago, it looked exactly as it does now — perfectly smooth."

The atmosphere thickened with the silence of concentration. One by one, we pulled out chairs and sat, our gazes fixed on the orb. And as we watched and thought and theorized, I couldn't help feeling that the orb was staring back at us.

"Any markings at all?" Brenda asked, tapping the orb's silver surface with her fingernail. "I take it you didn't find a spot stamped 'Made in China'?"

"No markings — in this incarnation, at least. And I didn't see any in its first incarnation, either. Then again, I was fighting the thing, so it would have been difficult to give it a thorough examination."

"Are you certain the surface is smooth?" I asked. "There could be a pattern too small to be seen without magnification."

The professor pulled a magnifying glass

from his pocket and slid it toward me. "Be my guest."

Brenda tapped the orb and sent it rolling toward me. I put out a hand to catch it, and the instant my fingertips made contact, something began to buzz in my head. I closed my eyes, wondering if my ears were playing tricks on me, but like a radio tuner homing in on the correct frequency, the buzz disappeared and the voices began.

Any god who desires worship is arrogant and vain; you are the source of knowledge.

Faith is useless. Knowledge is all-powerful.

Become enlightened. You are god. Knowledge is the source of all power.

I dropped the magnifying glass and pushed away from the table. The voices were so loud that I could no longer hear my friends. Squinting in annoyance and anxiety, I mumbled something about a headache and stood. I tried to walk back into the living room, but stumbled into the half wall that served as a room divider.

Seek knowledge, and become one of us.

You are not a being, you are becoming.

Belong to us. We are the enlightened, the powerful.

I felt strong hands on my shoulders, then someone turned me around. Tank stood before me, his face filled with concern, his mouth opening and closing, but I couldn't hear a word. All I could hear were the voices and their incessant chatter.

Tank looked away and said something else, then the professor appeared in my field of vision, his brows drawn into knots of worry. He said something to me, then snapped his fingers before my eyes. Why?

Next thing I knew, he had guided me to the couch and pressed on my shoulders, forcing me to sit. Brenda, Tank, the professor, and Daniel stood around or sat on the coffee table and stared at me, their lips moving in time to the voices in my head. Was I hallucinating, too?

Everything you've heard about God is a lie.

There is neither good nor evil; there is only knowledge.

Once you become enlightened, everything becomes clear.

God desires slaves; you deserve freedom.

Freedom is knowledge.

You are god.

You are —

Knowledge is all.

Join us.

Unable to listen a minute more, I closed my eyes and snapped, "Shut up!" but the voices only spoke faster and higher, as if someone had increased the speed on an old record player. I clenched my fists, frustrated by my inability to block out the sounds.

God is a lie.

Knowledge —

Freedom —

New music —

Join us!

I threw back my head and screamed, then crumpled into darkness.

CHAPTER 2

I sat in an office waiting room, arms crossed, hands fisted. Professor McKinney sat at my left to keep me from bolting, and Daniel sat at my right, because I figured if anyone knew psychiatrists, he did. Brenda sat next to Daniel, because where he went, she went, and Tank sat next to Brenda because he didn't want to be left behind. "We're a team," he had reminded me as we left the rental house. "So if all the others are going, I'm goin', too."

I was present under protest, because seeing a shrink was the last thing I wanted to do. But the professor had made a deal — when the medics who responded to his 9-1-1 call wanted to take me back to the hospital's behavioral health unit, the professor talked them out of it by promising that he'd take me to a shrink as soon as possible.

So here we were.

I closed my eyes and let my head tip back to the wall. After I fainted yesterday, I woke to a young guy shining a flashlight into my eyes. "She's awake," he called, while voices behind him murmured. Only when he snapped his light off did I see the professor and company standing behind the medics, all of them wearing expressions of grave concern.

"I'm okay," I told them, sitting up. "It's just that I kept hearing voices —"

That off comment nearly landed me back in psych. Mentally healthy people apparently do not walk around hearing voices. People can talk to themselves, their dead aunt, or the dog, but if another voice joins the chorus, extreme steps must be taken.

Later that night, the professor knelt on the edge of the couch and placed a paternal hand on my shoulder. "Andi, it's only natural that you feel some aftereffects from our experience with that nasty fungus. I've felt an odd moment or two myself, and you were, shall we say, under the influence a lot longer than I was."

"You've been touching the orb," I said. "Has touching it ever made you . . . hear anything?"

His brows rushed together. "Never."

That's when I agreed to see a psychiatrist,

but after a good night's sleep and a decent breakfast, I no longer felt the need to have my head examined.

"Who is this Dr. Drummond, anyway?" I asked, turning to the professor. "I live in this area, you know. My grandparents will have to deal with any fallout if he decides I'm crazy."

The professor gave me an indulgent smile. "I asked your family doctor for a recommendation when you went in for that emergency check-up. He said Dr. Drummond would be perfect for you — he has a sterling reputation in the international medical community, and he's in the area temporarily, working on some research project as a visiting fellow. He's British. Won't be around long enough to gossip, so you can tell him anything you like."

"Even about our work?"

The professor's smile twisted. "Well . . . you might want to be discreet in that area. Tell him only what you must."

I snorted softly, then looked at the others. "I hope you all know that a person's visits to a psychiatrist are private. I appreciate the group support, but I'm going into that office alone."

"Noted," Brenda said, an unlit cigarette dangling from her lips. "Not that I wanted to go with you, but okay."

I leaned forward. "You know, this shrink might be able to help you lick that smoking habit."

"I'm licking it just fine, thanks," she answered, the tip of her nicotine placebo bobbing with each syllable. "Daniel's helpin' me."

"How?" I asked.

"He put the ButtOut app on my phone. It tracks how much money I'm savin' by not buying cigarettes, how much tar isn't goin' into my lungs, and how many extra days I get to live. I guess that's what you call positive — um, positive —"

"Positive reinforcement."

When I supplied the missing word, McKinney patted my shoulder. "See? Your mind is fine; you're as sharp as ever. I'm sure you were only suffering some kind of hangover from residual . . . you know."

I closed my eyes. Oh, yeah, we were *fine*. We knew about two deaths that hadn't been made public, and we'd seen things that would strike fear into the hardest cop on the local force. No wonder I was having trouble clearing my head.

My eyes opened automatically when I heard the click of a doorknob. Looking up, I saw casual slip-on shoes, khakis, a short-sleeved knit shirt, and the most gorgeous face I had ever seen on a man — cleft chin, sparkling blue eyes, longish black hair, and a toothpaste-commercial smile. For a moment my mind went completely blank, then I heard him speak: "Andrea Goldstein?"

Brenda elbowed me. "If you want, I could take your place in there."

"I'm okay," I whispered, rising on wobbly knees and following the man into his office.

I don't know what I expected to find in Dr. Drummond's office — a couch, maybe? But all I saw was a desk, a couple of leather wingback chairs, and a laptop computer on a wooden stand — a classy version of those rolling bedside tables they used in hospitals.

But before I even moved toward the chairs, Dr. Drummond looked at me, smiled, and held out his hand. "Hamish Drummond," he said in his lilting accent. "It's a pleasure to meet you."

I swallowed hard and shook his hand, taking care to make sure my grip was firm and polite. I didn't know how a shrink might evaluate an introductory handshake, but I wanted him to see that I was a normal young adult, not a hysteric.

Dr. Drummond gestured to a wingback chair. I thanked him and sat, then he took the chair near the computer stand. "So," he said, crossing one knee and looking at me with an open, pleasant expression. "What brings you to my office today?"

That voice! The professor had said he was from Britain, but this wasn't a London accent — it was Irish, or perhaps Scottish. One of those lovely speech patterns that made everything sound musical. I contemplated asking where he was from, but didn't want him to think I was changing the subject.

"What do you already know?" I asked. "I don't want to waste your time."

He opened his hands and grinned. "Can you believe it? I know nothing. So why don't you tell me what you think I ought to know."

"I don't want to keep you here all day."

"I have as long as it takes — almost." A dimple in his cheek winked at me as he smiled. "Tell me the important things; then tell me about the thing that brought you here."

I drew a deep breath, then exhaled in a rush. "My name is Andi Goldstein. I was studying humanities in college when I met Professor James McKinney, who's now my employer. I actually grew up in this area, and graduated from Ponce de Leon High School. I guess this is what you'd call my hometown."

He propped his elbow on the chair and rested his chin on his hand. "Don't you enjoy coming home?"

"Sure. I get to see Sabba and Safta, of course, and Abby, my dog. I didn't take her after graduation because I travel a lot, and she's getting old. But she is always happy to see me."

On and on I talked. I told him about being a geek in high school. I told him about my gift of seeing patterns everywhere, in numbers, fabrics, and events. I told him I'd been adopted by my grandparents, that they were devout Jews who raised me with a bat mitzvah and everything, and that I still considered myself religious . . . to a point. "I believe in God," I said, "but I don't talk about Him much because it's a personal thing. But . . . lately I've begun to wonder about all the things I believed growing up. I've realized that evil exists, and that sometimes it exists just for evil's sake."

Dr. Drummond's brows lowered. "I'm not sure I get your meaning."

"Well," I shrugged, "when you read about a serial killer, you usually learn that he came from an abusive family, or that he never bonded to his mother as a baby, or he was mentally deficient or something. You rarely hear about criminals who are bad because they enjoy hurting others. I didn't believe that was possible until lately, but now I have to wonder."

"What are you wondering?"

I blew out a breath and glanced at the clock. "My goodness! I've been talking for a solid hour. And I haven't even gotten to the stuff about why I'm here."

The doctor checked his watch, then smiled. "Can you give me an abridged version?"

"Sure." I leaned forward. "Those people out in the waiting room — they're friends, and we've been investigating unusual situations. Ever since I joined up with them, we've all seen things I can't explain." Because I felt completely comfortable, I told him about Sridhar and the Institute, about the disappearing House and what the professor called *posthumous manifestations.* I told him about the bird and fish die-offs, about the odd girl who managed to contact us through another universe, and our mad romp through Europe and a half-dozen multiverses. Finally, I told him about the green fungi, the flying orbs, and how I almost died.

"The fungus is no longer in my body," I said, "but yesterday I thought I heard the voices again . . . and they were loud enough to drown out everything else. I don't know what's happening, but at times I'm scared spitless. Being out of control — having intruders in my brain — was the most frightening experience of my life. That's what happened yesterday, and I was so frightened that I fainted. That's why I'm here."

I sat perfectly still and waited for Dr. Drummond to slap his head in disbelief or something, but he simply smoothed a wrinkle out of his pant leg and leaned toward me. "Andrea," he asked, his blue eyes darkening with concern, "in this moment, right now, what do you want more than anything else in the world?"

I blinked. "I want to get out of here."

He laughed. "Fair enough. What will you want when you're in the car and on your way home?"

I thought a moment. "I want . . . to feel like myself again. I want to feel bubbly and optimistic and bright . . ." I looked down and laughed. "Sounds like a line from 'I Feel Pretty,' doesn't it?"

"Pretty and witty and bright," Dr. Drummond joked, and when I glanced at him, his eyes danced with a conspiratorial gleam.

My heart did a flip-flop. He knew *West*

Side Story?

"I have a favor to ask," he said, standing and moving behind his desk. He opened a drawer, then pulled out a slender blue notebook, the kind we had used in college for essay tests. "I'm going to give you a blank journal, and I want you to fill three pages in it every day, without fail. Write about what you're thinking and feeling, what you're doing, that sort of thing. Don't worry about spelling or grammar; this isn't for publication. It's just for you."

He thumbed through the blank book as if checking to be sure the pages were clean, then came around the desk and handed it to me. "And I'd like to see you again in a few days. We'll talk some more, and maybe you'll discover that you've written something important in your wee book. If that's so, you can tell me about it. Here's my card. Call me if you have a problem."

I put the card in my pocket, then clutched the blank journal. "My wee book." I smiled at it, clean and compact, waiting for my words. "All right, I'll see you soon."

CHAPTER 3

The next morning, the professor received three boxes from a FedEx truck, then dragged all of them into the living room. A UPS truck pulled up five minutes later, and handed over a package addressed to Brenda.

"What's all that?" Brenda asked, looking at the boxes as if they were bombs that might go off at any moment.

The professor closed the door and looked at our suddenly crowded living room. "The large boxes are from a clipping service," he said. "This one is for you, Barnick, from a Mrs. Irene Brown."

"Auntie Rene!" Brenda practically vaulted over the coffee table to reach the professor, then snatched the box.

I stared in shock — Brenda never showed that much enthusiasm — while the professor gave her a disapproving frown. "Have you been sharing our address?"

"Only with Auntie Rene." Brenda lowered

her brow. "You got a problem with that?"

"We must think of our personal security. No matter who we're communicating with, e-mail accounts can be hacked, cell phone calls can be recorded —"

"Auntie Rene would never hurt me," Brenda said, tearing into the package. "The woman worries about me every time I go out of town. She's a little overprotective, but still —" Brenda held up what looked like a seriously deformed orange hammer. Instead of a head and a prong, the top of this hammer featured two formidable steel knobs.

Tank gaped at it. "What in the —"

"The Life Hammer," Brenda said, reading from a card. "Dear Brenda — I looked on a map and saw where you is and then I saw that long bridge over the ocean. Cars fall into the water every day, and I don't want you drownin', so I got this for you. Keep it in your purse and if your car falls in, just smack the window.

"I've also enclosed a can of shark repellent, in case you go swimmin' at the beach, and some mosquito wipes. They're not for wiping mosquitoes, they're for keeping them away because they carry that nasty West Nile virus. Don't want you gettin' sick. Love you, Auntie Rene."

I laughed, Tank guffawed, and even Daniel smiled. "Hoo boy," Brenda said, chuckling to herself, "when was the last time a car went into the water around here?"

"About the same time somebody got the West Nile virus," the professor said. "Or was attacked by a shark."

I shook my head. "You guys shouldn't laugh about things like that. I don't think any cars have gone over the bridge lately, but about thirty years ago, a bunch of cars and a bus went into the bay. A ship hit the bridge, so it was a pretty big deal."

"That was a long time ago," Brenda said, "but it was nice of Auntie Rene to think about me."

She set the orange hammer, shark repellent, and mosquito wipes on the coffee table, but Daniel picked them up and handed them back to her. "Keep," he said, his eyes serious.

She looked at him, then sighed. "Little man, what am I gonna do with you?" Still she dropped all of her aunt's gifts into her purse. "Better?"

Daniel nodded and went back to playing a game on his new phone.

"Now," the professor said, pulling one of the large boxes over to his chair. "Let's get to work."

"What's a clipping service?" Tank asked.

The professor ripped the tape from his box, then opened it and pulled out a stack of printed pages. "Several times now we've had people mention an organization called The Gate, so I thought we should investigate them. Right after the event at the school I subscribed to a media monitoring service and asked for printed copies of articles that mention the group." He smiled with satisfaction as he lifted out a second stack. "And here they are . . . three boxes filled with clippings."

Brenda groaned. "You expect us to read through all that?"

"Time to change our tactics," the professor said. "Ever since we got together we've been reactive, simply responding to the odd things we encountered. We were being played, rattled, used, and for what? Nothing. We have nothing to show for our efforts."

"We're alive," I pointed out. "That's something."

The professor waved a hand in my direction, but charged ahead. "We are not merely reacting any longer," he said, his voice booming in the small house. "We are going to be proactive. We are going to learn everything we can about this group. We're going to figure out who or what The Gate is, and then we're going to rattle their cage for a while."

He pulled another stack of printed clippings and set it in front of Tank.

Tank grinned. "You mean we're gonna turn the tables on 'em?"

"Exactly." The professor set another stack in front of Brenda. "Here's the plan. Andi and I will work on the orb while Tank and Brenda skim these clippings. You'll find the pertinent parts highlighted, see? If the information is useful, circle the important sections and set the clipping aside. If the article isn't helpful, toss it into an empty box."

Brenda lifted a stack of pages onto her lap, then scowled at McKinney. "You do know that you could do the same thing with Google, right? For free? And without killing a bunch of trees?"

He shook his head. "I want information that would never find its way to the World Wide Web. I want facts that precede the Internet. Humor me, please, and start reading."

Tank took a stack of documents and went to sit by the window; Brenda stretched out on the couch. Daniel sat on the floor, tapping his phone, but his gaze kept darting around the room, leaving me to wonder what he was seeing. . . .

"Andi?" The professor went into the dining room and pulled out a chair. Sighing, I joined him.

From a cardboard box, the professor lifted a scale, a drill, and a tape measure. I reached for my tablet computer, then opened a scratch pad.

"You know the routine," McKinney said. "Weigh, measure, record. Experiment. Then let's see what this little odd ball is made of."

The orb, I discovered, weighed four pounds, ten ounces — in the hour I measured it, at least. The circumference was fourteen inches exactly, and when I held it twelve inches from the floor and released it, it fell to the linoleum with a thud. "Definitely not weightless," I typed on my tablet. "Incapable of flight, as far as I can tell."

The professor plugged in the electric drill, which he fitted with the smallest drill bit. He took eye protectors from his bag, which we both put on. Then, beneath that awful chandelier, the professor held the orb between his hands while I attempted to drill into it. I was unsuccessful when I held the drill at a ninety degree angle to the surface, but when I tilted the drill slightly, the bit did leave a thin scratch along the surface.

"Not impermeable, then," the professor said, lifting his protective eyewear to study the scratch. "A laser could make quick work of it."

I smiled. "Got one of those in your box?"

"If only."

We left the orb. I went to the kitchen for a soft drink while the professor stood to stretch.

"I don't get it," Tank called, looking up. "Most of the articles say The Gate doesn't exist. That it's a bogeyman invented to scare people."

"Scare them with what?" the professor asked. "Nuclear war? Disease?"

"Nothing is ever spelled out," Brenda said, "at least not in what I'm reading. People talk about the group, but no personal names are ever mentioned."

"But what if The Gate was hiding in plain sight?" I said. "Wouldn't that be brilliant?"

"Hard to know truth from rumor." Brenda handed a document to Daniel, who dropped it in the "not useful" box. "I mean, some of the articles claim The Gate goes all the way back to medieval times; others say the old Gate is gone and new people have revived the organization."

"Wait a minute." Obeying a hunch, I

grabbed my laptop. I booted it, then used my cell phone to create a hot spot. Two minutes later, I was on the Internet. I typed a name, hit enter, and landed on a webpage.

"Take a look," I said, turning the computer so Tank and Brenda could see. "The Gate has a webpage and a Twitter account."

"Get out!" Brenda came over to read the text at the top of the screen. " 'Wake up, weary traveler! This war-infested, polluted world is nearly at its end. Join us as we prepare for a new society, an age of personal power and enlightenment. Join those of us who have realized secrets the ancients possessed, secrets for which others have died in order to safeguard the future.' "

"Gobbledygook," the professor mumbled. "If the secrets are so great, why not employ them now?"

"No names or photos on that site," Tank observed, studying the page. "If this organization is so cool, why won't anyone admit being a part of it?"

"Let me see that." The professor stepped out of the dining room and stood between Tank and Brenda, all of them studying the website. "Hmm. Maybe I should have Googled them."

"According to this site, the cloud of secrecy is about to evaporate." Brenda pointed to a textbox in the lower corner and read aloud: " 'The Gate is a powerful collective of leaders entrusted with protecting the billions of human beings on the planet. Our plan for humankind has spanned several eras and prevented humanity from engaging in acts that would have destroyed all human life. The scale of our operation requires stealth, leaving no overt proof of our work. But the time for covert operations and anonymity is nearing an end."

"Typical end of the world stuff." The professor shook his head. "Fodder for the apocalypse survivalists."

"What are they gonna do?" Tank looked at me, eyes wide. "Don't they realize God wins in the end?"

"Maybe they don't believe in God." Brenda pulled her cigarette from her back pocket, stuck it in her mouth, and squinted at the screen. "Looks like they believe in themselves more than anything else."

"They believe in knowledge." The answer came easily because I'd heard the words in my head only a few days before. "They believe the key to a better life is enlightenment."

Tank laughed. "That's what the devil promised Eve in the garden, you know. She ate from the Tree of Knowledge of Good and Evil, and when she'd finished, she had new knowledge, all right. She'd been living in a perfect and good world, but that forbidden fruit gave her firsthand knowledge of evil and sin. Knowledge isn't everything it's cracked up to be."

"I don't think we can be so simplistic," the professor said, frowning. "There are levels to man's knowledge, and men have always wanted to better themselves, to rise above their beginnings —"

"That's what Satan wanted, too." Tank's jaw jutted forward. "He was a beautiful angel, designed to serve God, but he wanted to rise above his station and be equal with God."

"So you think it's wrong for a guy to be ambitious?" Brenda asked.

"Not necessarily. But it's wrong for a man to be proud. Every time I get to feelin' that I'm more special than somebody else, God lets me know that I'd be nothin' without the gifts and grace He's given me. I'm just a man, the professor's just a man —"

The professor raised a brow. "So my years of education count for nothing?"

I closed my eyes as their words flowed over me. A vein in my temple had begun to throb, so I pressed my fingertips to the spot in a futile attempt to massage the tightness away. I did not want to hear the voices again, and even hearing about The Gate felt like opening a door to the intruders.

"Excuse me." I closed my laptop and stood, then moved toward the hallway that led to the bedrooms. Before leaving, I turned to the others. "I have a headache, so I'm going to lie down where it's quiet."

At any other time, the professor would have made a crack about my inexhaustible energy, but my comment left him — left all of them — speechless. They didn't want a repeat performance with EMTs and flashing lights, either.

They looked at me, their eyes shining with concern, and then they let me go.

I rode aboard a dream ship that pulled up to a dock and regurgitated passengers onto shore. I walked across the sand and into a large room that seemed to be some sort of auditorium. I could see silhouetted heads and shoulders and hear sibilant whispers in the darkness.

I lifted my gaze and saw a lighted stage at the far end of the room. A woman in a flowing white tunic stood on the stage, and she lifted a woven basket and set it on a tree stump. Then I heard the sound of a baby's cry. The crowd buzzed, but since no one seemed inclined to intercede for the child, I moved down the aisle, my gaze fixed on the basket.

Three steps led up to the stage. I mounted them slowly, wondering if someone would come rushing out from backstage to apprehend me for trespassing. The woman watched me, her eyes like large liquid pools, but she did nothing to impede my progress.

Finally I reached the basket, where the baby's cries had softened to a low mewling.

A gauzy fabric covered the opening, so I pulled it away and gazed on a baby with a misshaped head. Or not exactly misshaped — the head was *fluid*, the skull moving beneath the skin, rearranging the mouth, nose, and eyes, of which there were three. The eyes positioned themselves into a straight line, then the lips smacked while the eyes shifted again, one eye moving to the center of the forehead. The infantile mouth curled in a smile, and the eyes — now blue — slowly blinked at me.

The baby was *me.* I knew it as surely as I knew my name.

I staggered backward, my body caught in a paralysis of horror. The woman looked at me and smiled. "She is not settled yet. Her father alone has the right to say what she will become."

At the mention of the child's father, I sensed a presence and heard the deep, rattling breath of a dark creature. Compelled to turn, I looked for the source of the sound and saw horns, yellow eyes with dark slashes for pupils, and brilliant tiger teeth . . . and then I screamed.

I woke and clutched at my blanket, then listened to the soft sounds of Brenda's breathing until my heart rate decreased and my palms stopped perspiring. Then I closed my eyes and prayed that I would not dream again.

CHAPTER 4

After a restless night, I found Tank and Daniel at the kitchen bar the next morning, both of them slurping down bowls of Lucky Charms and focused on their phones.

"Take that," Tank said, dropping his spoon so he could work the phone with both hands. "You're sunk, kid!"

"Morning," I mumbled, then I moved to the fridge and took out a bottle of orange juice.

I grimaced as a shrill, undulating siren pierced the quiet of the kitchen, and I nearly dropped the orange juice when a robotic voice called, "MEGADEATH APPROACHING, CAPTAIN. DEFEND YOUR BATTLESHIP."

While Tank grinned, Daniel's fingers flew over his phone. "What are you guys *doing*?" I shouted, holding my free hand over my ears as horns and sirens continued to wail.

"Saved!" Daniel grinned at Tank as the

kitchen went silent again.

Tank looked up at me. "It's *Battleship Megadeath*," he said. "Daniel's really into the game. He's playing eighty-seven other players right now — some of them in other countries."

"I hope the other players don't wake up their mates," I said, jerking my thumb toward the bedrooms where Brenda and the professor still slept. "I've never heard anything like that."

"The siren only goes off if your battleship is sinking. Oh . . . gotta take care of this . . . there." Tank grinned again, then swept up a spoonful of Lucky Charms. "It's addictive. If your ship is hit, the siren goes off until you either save your ship or it goes under."

"For my sake, then, I hope neither of you loses any ships. My ears can't take it."

"Play," Daniel said, looking at me.

"Daniel, I don't know —"

"You'll find an invite in your e-mail," Tank said. He tilted his head toward Daniel. "Come on, humor the kid. You might enjoy it."

"Maybe."

I went to the pantry next, and stared at the shelves — a cereal variety pack, a box of cheese crackers, two bags of potato chips, four boxes of brown sugar cinnamon Pop-

Tarts, and a canister of beef jerky. Clearly, one of the men had done the grocery shopping.

I pulled a package of Pop-Tarts from the box, then ripped it open and took a bite. One stool remained vacant at the kitchen bar, but as I walked toward it, the dining room table caught my eye. The orb was still in the center, but someone had covered it with a dishtowel.

I lowered my Pop-Tarts and peered at the towel. "What's up with this?" I asked the guys. "Who covered it?"

"Guilty." Tank raised his hand. "Did it last night. Daniel kept sayin' that the thing was watchin' him."

"Really, Daniel?" I leaned on the counter to look him in the eye. "Do you know that for certain, or did it just feel like it was watching you?"

Daniel looked up from his phone, met my gaze . . . and shrugged.

Sighing, I walked to the table, then pulled the dishtowel away from the orb. Nothing happened, but the orb looked different. Yesterday it had been a shiny silver color; now it was gold. Why hadn't I thought to record its color when I was making notes?

"Hey, guys." I gestured to the orb when

they turned around. "Notice anything different?"

Tank nodded. "It's gold."

Daniel nodded, too. "Bigger."

I lifted a brow, then reached for the professor's bag. A quick wrap with the tape measure proved Daniel's point: the orb was now fourteen and one-half inches, so the thing had expanded . . . unless I measured incorrectly yesterday.

I picked up the orb and turned it in my hand, searching for the scratch. I spun it from east to west, then from north to south, but the scratch had disappeared.

I sank to one of the dining room tables and propped my chin in my hand. Unless my eyes were deceiving me, the orb had healed itself. And if Daniel was correct — and he often was — the thing had some kind of consciousness. It was aware of us.

Dear Journal:

Living things share seven characteristics — let's see if I can remember all of them:

- Living things are composed of cells.
- Living things have different levels of organization.
- Living things use energy.

- Living things respond to their environment.
- Living things grow.
- Living things reproduce.
- Living things adapt to their environment.

Of those seven characteristics, so far I have seen the orb expand (and contract), respond to its environment (perhaps), and appear to heal itself . . . which must have used energy.

So is this thing alive?

"Whacha doin'?" Brenda asked, glancing at my journal. "You workin' already?"

"Just making notes." I jerked my head toward the orb. "Notice anything different?"

Brenda glanced at it, then her eyes widened. "Have we struck gold?"

"It's not actual gold," I said, "but it did change color."

"Why?"

"I've no idea."

We both looked toward the front door when the professor came in — apparently he'd been up and out long before us. He strode into the dining room and dropped the morning paper on the table.

I glanced at the front page headline, then looked at him. "Something special in there?"

"Couple of things," the professor said, crossing his arms. "First, the police are investigating the disappearance of Dr. Tom Mathis and Nick Warner, which must have been the name of the nephew. Neither man has been seen in days, but they found a trace of Mathis's DNA at Ponce de Leon High School. So they've tied the damage at his lab to the mess at the school, and now they're saying he met with foul play."

Brenda and I looked at each other. We were all pretty sure about what had happened to Nick Warner, but we certainly weren't going to call the paper with news about the killer fungus that may or may not have been created by The Gate and/or co-operative aliens. As for Tom Mathis, we'd been with him when his body exploded into a cloud of green powder. No way we were sharing *that* news with anyone.

"Do you" — I caught the professor's gaze — "think we should go to the police? If they're looking for bodies, they're not going to find anything."

"I don't know." He scratched his chin. "I doubt they'd believe us."

"If my dog was carrying that killer fungus, I'd want to know," Tank said, turning to join in the conversation. "If they've unleashed another batch of that stuff, people could be dying right now."

"I don't think they will release it anytime soon," the professor said. "Call it a hunch, but I think they were simply testing that fungus. After the birds and fish, Nick Warner, Andi, and Dr. Mathis stepped into the role of human guinea pigs, so the researchers now have verified results of their experiment." He shook his head. "If they launch that fungus again, I believe it'll be on a global scale. Not much sense in tipping your hand before your first major attack."

I folded the newspaper, about to draw the professor's attention to the orb, but he took the paper from me. "Don't throw this away," he said. "Mathis is having a memorial service today. Maybe we should go."

Brenda lifted her head. "I don't do funerals, especially for people I barely knew."

"A memorial service isn't the same thing," I pointed out. "There's no body."

"I'll go," Tank said. "Mathis was a nice man before the fungus got ahold of him. I think we should all go."

The professor smiled. "Mathis's likability is a moot point. Statistics indicate that killers often visit the funerals or graves of their victims just to revel in the experience. I don't know if we'll see members of The Gate at that memorial service, but surely time spent honoring a fellow scientist is time well spent."

"Whatever," Tank said, grinning at me. "What time do we leave?"

"Eleven." The professor glanced at his watch. "Which gives all of you just enough time to get ready."

I took three steps toward the bedroom I was sharing with Brenda, but even though I'd been forewarned, I wasn't ready for what came next: "MEGADEATH APPROACHING, CAPTAIN. DEFEND YOUR BATTLESHIP."

As horns and sirens blared from Daniel's phone, I looked at Brenda, who had spilled her coffee and looked as though someone had nearly run her over. "Come on," I said, raising my voice to be heard above the noise. "I'll explain everything while we're getting ready."

Dear Journal:

Thomas Mathis, as it turned out, was neither religious nor prepared for death, so the funeral director is holding Mathis's memorial service in the cemetery where his daughter insisted on purchasing a plot.

I overheard all the pertinent details while washing my hands in the ladies' room. "I kept telling that man that I wanted a place where I could sit and grieve for Daddy," a voice called from the first of the two stalls. "He said, 'But we don't have a body!' and I said, 'Well, pretend we do!' It's bad enough that we don't know why Daddy's DNA was all over that school, but I won't have people thinking I was too cheap to buy my dad a proper headstone."

I glanced at the red-eyed older woman who stood by the paper towels, then gave her a sympathetic smile. Poor thing — I hope she wasn't Dr. Mathis's mother.

I left the restroom and followed a series of discreet signs to an open plot surrounded by about two dozen people. A fiberboard casket sat on some kind of mechanism, and a spray of roses — probably from the distraught daughter — lay on the coffin.

I found myself wishing I could step up and tell the mourners the truth about the marine biologist's fate:

Excuse me, ladies and gentlemen. Most of you are wondering what happened to Dr. Mathis, and I hope you'll be pleased to know he is no longer suffering. His mind was abducted by some sort of collective consciousness and his body was taken over by a green fungus that eventually caused him to explode at the high school. He is now at rest and his soul is wherever souls go under these circumstances, so maybe we should give the roses to someone who needs them and put the casket back in storage.

The touch of a hand on my shoulder startled me, and I nearly jumped out of my skin.

"Whoa." Coming alongside me, Brenda gave me a quizzical look. "You okay? You're not usually wired this tight."

"I'm fine." I stuck my journal in my purse, then crossed my arms. "You?"

"I was going to ask you somethin', but I don't want to put ideas in your head."

"Okay. What did you want to ask?"

"Just look around," Brenda said, her gaze drifting over the crowd. "As the dude talks, tell me if you see anyone who looks familiar."

I scanned the people at the graveside. "Do I know this person?"

"Not gonna say anything else. Just take your time and tell me if you spot anyone we've seen before."

I sighed, then transferred my gaze to the funeral director as he moved to the head of the casket. He welcomed the guests, then read Mathis's newspaper obituary. As he rambled on, I studied the guests — Mathis's daughter stood next to the open grave, supported by a group of older women. A few middle-aged couples stood behind them. No children anywhere, as far as I could see, but it was a school day. A group of twenty-somethings stood in a knot behind the funeral director, and I recognized some of them from the aquarium where Mathis had worked. Were they the familiar faces Brenda was referring to? Shifting my gaze, I saw a handful of other adults, probably friends or neighbors, and Sridhar —

I blinked. Between two bald men I saw a guy who looked like Sridhar Rajput, the young man we had met at the Institute for Advanced Psychic Studies, one of many enterprises reportedly sponsored and/or managed by The Gate. Sridhar had been one of the Institute's star pupils, specializing in lucid dreaming and dream telepathy. He had wanted out of the program, so we tried to help him escape, but he'd vanished from Brenda's apartment in the middle of the night.

What was he doing *here*?

I turned to Brenda and caught her eye, then mouthed the name: *Sridhar?*

Her eyes widened, then she smiled and nodded.

I turned to make contact with our friend, but I could no longer see him. Was he trying to make his way to us?

"And now," the funeral director said, "let us observe a moment of silent meditation in honor of the deceased."

I lowered my head and closed my eyes, not willing to see any other oddities in the crowd. Silence wrapped around us, a heavy quiet marred only by the quiet swishing of cars moving on the road several yards away. A bird warbled in one of the wide oak trees, and the wind gently ruffled a ribbon dangling from the roses on the casket.

Then the sound of horns and sirens blasted the gathering. "MEGADEATH APPROACHING, CAPTAIN. DEFEND YOUR BATTLESHIP."

As the sirens wailed and horns blared, Tank, Brenda, and I fumbled for our phones. Brenda dumped her purse, then knelt to sort through all the things that had fallen into the grass. Tank pulled his phone from his pocket and was frantically punching buttons; I took my phone from the special pocket inside my purse and slid my finger over the screen again and again, vainly searching for the *Battleship Mega-*

death icon. I had accepted Daniel's invitation and downloaded the game right before leaving the house, and though I didn't even know I *had* a battleship, apparently it was in danger —

From the corner of my eye, I saw the professor pull his phone from his jacket pocket, then tap the screen a few times. The sirens stilled, and the professor folded his hands, his gaze intent on the funeral director.

The noise hadn't come from my phone — or Tank's, or Brenda's. The professor — *really?* — had been the one with the endangered battleship.

My knees went weak as adrenaline stopped spurting through my bloodstream. Kneeling in the grass with a package of cigarettes, her bright orange Life Hammer, can of shark spray, and about a dozen scattered mosquito towelettes, Brenda had begun to mutter under her breath, but I knew she wouldn't say anything to Daniel. We should have muted our phones, and none of us did. Not even the professor.

The funeral director, after he'd stopped glaring at us, resumed the service. When he finally folded his hands and thanked us for coming, I slipped past Brenda and threaded my way through the dispersing crowd. I kept my head down, not wanting to make eye contact with mourners who might be peeved about the interruption, and ran headlong into a chest that did not yield to my charging advance.

I looked up, my jaw dropping as I stared into the baby blues that had entranced me at our last meeting. "Dr. — Dr. Drummond! What are you doing here?"

He smiled, then squinted as if trying to remember my name. "It's Annie, no, Angie, no —"

"Andi," I told him, feeling a little light-headed. "Andrea Goldstein."

"That's right." He grinned, then stepped aside. "I believe you were intent on leaving."

I managed a weak laugh. "Not really. I thought I saw someone I'd met before."

"Ah. Well. Don't let me keep you."

"It's okay. I don't think he's here . . . more likely I was seeing things. That wouldn't surprise me, especially these days. I've, uh, been a little shaky."

I closed my eyes as a sudden thought occurred. Maybe Brenda hadn't been referring to Sridhar when she mentioned seeing someone we knew. When I mouthed *Sridhar,* she might have thought I was saying *Drummond.* Both names had two syllables.

Dr. Drummond slipped his hands into his pockets. "Been writing in your journal?"

I nodded, glad that I was doing something right. "Every day. Three pages."

"You said you were feeling shaky. Would you like to come in later today? Maybe tomorrow? If you aren't doing well, you don't have to wait until your next appointment."

"But it's Sunday!"

"Aren't all days pretty much alike any more? At least for me they are. Anyway — if you want to come in, please do. You'd be a welcome break from my research work."

I tilted my head, thinking, then nodded. "I think I would like that. Let me check with the professor. If I can get away, I'll give your office a call."

"There is no office — there's only me." He took a business card from his jacket pocket and handed it to me. "When you're a visiting fellow, you don't get to bring along your office staff."

"I understand." I was about to say goodbye and walk away, but I halted when I heard familiar voices. I glanced over my shoulder and saw my team approaching — and every one of them was staring at Dr. Drummond with undisguised curiosity.

The professor was the first to speak. "We

saw you the other day," he said, extending his hand, "but we weren't properly introduced. I'm Dr. James McKinney, Andi's employer, and these are our associates — Brenda Barnick, Bjorn Christensen, and Daniel Petrovski."

Dr. Drummond's brows rose. "You are a unique group."

"You might say that." The professor smiled, but I saw no humor in his eyes.

"Well, we'd better be going. I'll call if I can come in." I tugged on the professor's arm, but he didn't budge.

"I hope you realize," he said, his gaze never leaving Drummond's face, "how special Andi is. She has unique gifts and we rely on her. We expect you to take extremely good care of our girl."

Dr. Drummond eased his hands back into his pockets and smiled. "Och, Andi, I think I've been warned. And dinna you worry, I'll take care of her. I was just tellin' Andi that she ought to come in today for another talk."

The professor looked at me with a shade of rebuke in his eyes. "You didn't say anything about having trouble."

"I'm not, I mean, it's not trouble. It's just . . . I still don't feel like myself. I keep having odd dreams —"

From out of nowhere, Tank's thick arm wrapped around my shoulder and clamped me to his side. "We'll take good care of her," he told Drummond, smiling broadly, "because that's what friends do."

"Good to hear." Dr. Drummond smiled again, then looked at me. "I'll be talkin' to you soon, lass."

My cheeks flamed as he walked away. "Good grief," I said, looking from the professor to Tank. "That was a bit much, don't you think?"

"We don't know him," the professor said. "But I like him. He's educated. Cultured. Plus, the man has more degrees than a thermometer."

"I like him, too," Tank said. "Only because he promised to take good care of you."

I looked at Brenda, hoping for a little saltiness to counteract the sweet, and she didn't disappoint. "Enjoy it while you can," she said, taking Daniel's hand. "It's not every day that you get to be the princess."

CHAPTER 5

Getting away that afternoon wasn't easy. After we returned from the memorial service, the professor wanted Brenda and Tank to dive back into their reading, and he wanted me to conduct experiments with the orb. But I told him I'd do a better job if I could get my head on straight, and Dr. Drummond might be the key to helping me feel like my old self.

Reluctantly, the professor agreed.

So I drove to the building where Dr. Drummond had taken an office. The door was locked, of course, but I knocked and only had to wait a couple of minutes before Drummond let me in. "Sorry about the mess," he said, pointing to a slurry of papers spread over what should have been a receptionist's desk. "And come on back. I'm trying to get my paper ready for a professional publication, and it's kept me so busy I don't have time to tidy up."

I stopped in the hallway. "Are you sure I'm not interrupting? I could back another time."

He smiled. "As I said before, you're a welcome distraction. All work and no diversion makes a psychiatrist a little crazy."

I laughed and dropped into the same wingback chair I'd chosen last time. "Did you make that up?"

"That bad, eh?" Drummond dropped into the chair across from me, then casually leaned over the arm. "All right, lass — what's up with you?"

I rubbed my damp palm over my jeans. "I'm having weird dreams." I forced another laugh. "I bet you get that all the time, huh?"

"I hear it a lot, aye. Sometimes our dreams are the way our subconscious speaks to us. But dreams have a unique language."

"Then I definitely don't speak dream."

I watched as Drummond got up and moved to a counter on the other side of the room. The counter held a small sink, a single-serve coffeemaker, and a spinner that held about a dozen single-serve coffee pods.

"What can I get you?" he asked, turning. "I've got all kinds of coffee, various teas, plus hot cocoa and apple cider."

Considering the steamy weather outside, I wasn't exactly in the mood for a hot drink, but the man was from the United Kingdom. Maybe he preferred teas and coffees out of habit. "Um . . . tea," I said. "Any kind."

"Sugar or the fake stuff?"

"Sugar, please. And cream if you have it."

"I like a woman who knows the proper way to drink tea — though my friends on the other side of the pond would be aghast if they saw me brewing tea with this machine." I heard the hum of the coffeemaker, followed by the sound of dribbling liquid. While Drummond prepared the tea, I looked around the office.

The room was more library than office, with tall shelves lining three walls, most loaded with books. Papers and books cluttered the desk in front of a wide window that opened to the parking lot. His laptop sat on the rolling table beside his wingback chair, so perhaps he preferred to work away from his desk.

Unlike most doctors, he hadn't hung any degrees or award certificates on the wall, but this was a borrowed space, after all. "No degrees?" I said, glancing back at him.

"Pardon?"

"On the wall — most doctors prominently display their degrees to impress patients."

"Ah." He lifted a steaming mug and brought it over. "University of Edinburgh," he said. "Masters in Psychological Research in 2007, Doctorate in Psychology of Individual Differences with an emphasis on Depression and Personality in 2010." He handed me the mug. "I'll hang a few diplomas if you think it will enhance my credibility."

"No need." I felt a blush creep across my cheeks. Did he think I didn't trust him? "So what made you choose psychiatry?"

He chuckled as he sank into his chair. "Fascination, I suppose. People are amazing, and I am easily intrigued. We have so many differences and so many commonalities."

"Sure — some of us are crazy and some aren't."

"I don't think you're crazy, Andrea. You seem completely sane."

"You may not think so after you hear what I've been dreaming."

"If you're ready to tell me, I'd love to listen."

I took a sip of tea, then wiped my hands on my jeans again.

"You're tense," Drummond said. "Why don't you close your eyes and pretend I'm not even in the room?"

I didn't like the idea of closing my eyes — what girl would, with a gorgeous man sitting across from her? — but maybe he had a point.

"I've had this dream before," I said, obediently closing my eyes. "I'm in the back of an auditorium, watching a scene. It's dark, and there are people all around, but they're only silhouettes. There's a platform down front, and it's lit with a bright light. I see a short pedestal with a basket on it, and a blanket is covering whatever's in the basket. A young woman steps out — she's wearing this sort of Grecian gown, all draped and flowing — and she pulls the blanket away. Then I come down the aisle and look into the basket, and somehow I know I'm looking at an infant version of myself. I'm a baby, but I'm not solid — it's like I'm made of flesh without bones, and some invisible force is shaping me. I look at the face — it has three eyes, one in the center of the forehead, then the face shifts so there are only two eyes, but they're vertical instead of horizontal.

"Then the woman says that the child's father has the right to say what the baby will become, and this is what he's chosen, and then I turn and look at a shadowed figure over to the left — it's huge, with horns and wings and scaly skin . . . and I know it's Satan. And the people in the room

284

are chanting things like *you are god* while I'm screaming and the baby's face continues to shift . . . and that's usually when I wake up."

I opened my eyes. Dr. Drummond sat with his elbow propped on the armrest and a finger pressed to his mouth. "Well," he said, smiling across the distance between us, "I can tell you a few basic things about dreams and their meaning. To dream of yourself as an infant means that you want to be nurtured and cared for . . . that you might be feeling a bit unloved. The third eye is supposed to be a window into the spiritual world, so perhaps you've been seein' — or you *want* to see — into other realities. And if you see Satan in your dream — that's a sign of some wrongdoing or evil in your environment." He lifted a brow. "Have I provided any keys that might help you interpret this dream yourself?"

"Well . . ." I raked my hand through my hair in the hope that it might stimulate my brain. "Ever since I've become involved with the team, I *have* felt like we're chasing something . . . really evil. In fact, Safta, my grandmother, jokes I've been hanging out with ghostbusters. I tried to tell her that our work is nothing like that, but then again" — I shrugged — "we *have* seen dead people,

285

so maybe she has a point."

"These . . . ghostbusters." Drummond smiled. "Are they the people I met at the funeral?"

"Yes." I tilted my head as a sudden thought struck. "By the way, what were you doing at Dr. Mathis's service?"

"He was the friend of a friend — didn't know him well, but I respected his work."

"His work with jellyfish?"

Drummond's brows lifted, then he smiled and cocked his index finger at me. "He worked primarily with dolphins and manatees, but nice try. Testing my veracity, are you?"

Again, my cheeks burned. "Sorry. But we *have* been chasing evil — and I'm no longer sure who I can trust."

"Back to your dream." Drummond crossed his legs. "You said a blanket covered the baby, and a Grecian goddess-type removed the blanket."

I nodded.

"Could the woman represent your mother? How long has it been since you've seen her?"

My mouth went dry. "My mother," I said, struggling to speak, "was a drug addict. She gave birth to me, then both of us went through detox. But about a month later,

286

someone broke into her apartment and shot her up with enough heroin to kill an elephant, or so the medical examiner said. The police never found the murderer, but they suspected a couple of drug dealers who might have been upset about her leaving that lifestyle behind. The cops turned me over to social services, but my grandparents picked me up before I entered foster care. They adopted me, and I've been living in their home ever since I can remember."

Dr. Drummond listened with his eyes closed, and I watched emotions — sympathy, anger, resignation — flicker over his face as I told the story. When I finished, he grunted softly and looked at me. "Incredible," he said simply, his eyes sparking with interest. "Did your mother use drugs while pregnant with you?"

"Yes. I don't know what she took, but I do know that we were both in the hospital for a while. I'm okay, though. No long-term impairment — the doctors say I'm lucky."

"Indeed you are." He shook his head slightly and looked at the chair's armrest. "I suspected that your background might hold some sort of mother/daughter separation because of the woman's role in the dream. She was the *presenter,* you see, just as your mother presented you to the world." A frown line crept between his brows. "Do you know anything about your father?"

"Only that I hope he isn't the devil." I forced a laugh, but the effort sounded weak even to my ears.

"If your birth mother was a heavy drug user, she may not have known who your father was." He hesitated. "The older gentleman with your group — your employer?"

"James McKinney," I said. "And yes, he is a sort of surrogate father figure. I met him in my freshman year and started working for him right after college graduation. He might appear to be curmudgeonly, but he has a soft heart. It's just buried under layers of logic and rationalization."

"Any sort of romantic — ?"

"No," I snapped, having heard the question one time too many. "It is completely possible for an older man and a younger woman to be platonic friends."

"Indeed it is." The doctor looked down, the suggestion of a smile hovering around the corners of his mouth. "Thank you for the background," he said, "now let's talk about the issue that brought you here. Your family doctor said that you experienced a physical trauma and a break from your sense of self. How are you doing physically?

And are you beginning to feel more normal?"

"Yes . . . and no."

"Explain, please."

I pressed my lips together and struggled to find the right words. "Yes, I feel strong, and I've been getting back to work. But no, because I'm not sleeping much, because I keep having that dream. And sometimes I hear the voices in my head again, but at least this time I'm in control, not them. But shouldn't they be gone? I worry that I'll let my guard down somehow and they'll take over again."

Dr. Drummond leaned forward. "Who are *they*?"

"I don't know. We've heard rumors about a group called The Gate, but we don't know how they are connected to the various situations we've investigated. We're trying to learn all we can, but it's not easy to investigate a group that doesn't want to be investigated."

Dr. Drummond's face cracked into a smile. "Surely you're not serious."

"Why wouldn't I be?"

He shrugged. "The Gate is a favorite topic of conversation among those who like to talk about the Illuminati, the second shooter on the grassy knoll, and the captive aliens at

Area 51. No proof exists for any of those things, but the rumors persist."

I stared at the floor. If he didn't believe in The Gate, he wouldn't believe any of my stories.

"Andrea, you're a bright young woman. You don't really believe in the existence of The Gate, do you? You might as well believe in Santa Claus."

"For your information," I said slowly, "Saint Nicholas was an actual man who lived in fourth-century Turkey. Stories of his miracles evolved into the fat man who comes down the chimney on Christmas Eve, but no one can deny that Saint Nicholas existed. Rumors about The Gate and the Illuminati and the second shooter and the aliens may abound, but rumors have to spring from *something*."

"Indeed — fable. Fantasy. As a Scotsman, I can tell you about haunted lochs, fairy hills, and clootie wells. They are part of my heritage, but not part of my reality."

I didn't know what to say. If I told him about some of the things I'd seen . . .

Dr. Drummond drew a deep breath, then settled back in his chair. "I believe that the voices you heard are nothing more than your own anxieties — your subconscious is literally giving voice to your fears. In the same way, your dream is your subconscious way of sorting through things your conscious mind puzzled over during the day."

I frowned. "That sounds so simple."

"Most problems usually are." He smiled again. "All right. Let's meet again in a couple of days, but I want you to think about something. I want you to consider hypnotism. It may help you clear out some of your subconscious anxieties. You'll feel better and sleep better, too."

I blinked as my thoughts veered toward nightclub acts and cheesy camp skits. "You want to hypnotize me?"

"I believe you may have memories buried deep in your subconscious, and you'll be more willing to talk about them under hypnosis. It's my job to convince your subconscious self that it's safe for you to put those memories and feelings into words."

I frowned at him. Aside from my recurrent nightmare, I couldn't think of any memory horrific enough to be suppressed, but maybe I'd suppressed something I couldn't consciously remember.

"Hypnosis will help you," Drummond said as he opened his laptop, "so I'll pencil you in for Tuesday, if that's all right. We'll have you feeling like yourself in no time."

"I'm still not sure."

"Don't worry, Andi, just think about it. And if you're willing to be hypnotized, we'll have a session when you come in."

I nodded numbly and walked toward the door, more confused than when I'd arrived.

Sunday night, after dining from a half-dozen boxes of Chinese food, we gathered in the living room to report on what we'd learned. "First," the professor said, "we'll hear from Daniel." He turned his attention to the boy, who actually looked up from his current game of *Battleship Megadeath.* "Daniel, have you seen anything odd since we've been in Florida? Any — whatever it is you see — that we should be aware of?"

Daniel narrowed his eyes as if thinking, then shook his head.

"Have you seen any of your invisible friends around us since we've been together on this trip?"

Daniel's face brightened.

"Really? Around whom?"

Without hesitation, Daniel pointed to Tank, who grinned an *aw, shucks* grin before replying. "Good to know, Daniel."

The professor lifted his gaze to the ceiling as if appealing for help, then continued. "What about Dr. Drummond?" he pressed.

"Anything odd about him?"

"No," Daniel said. "No duch. No anioł."

When the professor looked to Brenda for an explanation, she blew out a breath. "Daniel has his own words, and I'm still learnin' some of 'em. But these two I know. From what I can tell, a *duch* is bad. An *anioł* is good."

"So . . . ?"

"So Dr. Drummond is not good, not bad."

"Could Daniel come up with something more useful?"

Brenda's brows rushed together. "You wanna back off? He's a *kid.*"

"As were we all, once." The professor folded his arms. "What about your research, Barnick? Have you been able to identify any members of The Gate? Any location? Mission statement? Anything besides what we've already seen on their website?"

"Whaddya think I am, a computer?" Brenda grimaced and pulled some note-cards from her oversized purse. "I couldn't find anything linking The Gate to the fungus, but I did find some interesting stuff about funguses."

"That's fungi," the professor corrected. "One fungus, two fungi."

"Whatever. Scientists used-to think that fungi evolved from algae because they're both green. But now they think that fungi are more closely related to animals. Fungi don't make food through the sun like plants do; the stuff has a digestive system more like a human's. I don't get all the mumbo-jumbo about why that is — has to do with cells and a bunch of words I can't even pronounce — but I think it might explain why The Gate wanted to use a fungus to do their dirty work."

From the way the professor's eyes widened, I knew he was pleasantly surprised by Brenda's insight. "That *is* interesting, Barnick. What about you, Tank? Any progress?"

"Not really," Tank said, his voice flat. "They do a good job of hiding. Remember when we met Sridhar at the Institute? We also met the director, Dr. Trenton, and Sridhar had heard Trenton acknowledge the school's association with The Gate. But you won't find that published anywhere. Last week, Mathis was babbling about The Gate when the professor and I found him in his lab, but he was infected with the fungus by then, so it wasn't him talking, it was the . . . whatever you want to call it."

"The collective," the professor said. "A hive mentality. When many beings are controlled by a single consciousness."

"Yeah," Tank said. "I know it sounds

crazy, but it makes sense once you've seen it in action. So I'm sorry I don't have more to tell you. I found lots of stuff about The Gate, but I can't tell if it's legit or just a bunch of speculation. Clearly, nobody wants to admit they belong to that outfit. Makes it easier to deny that the group even exists."

"Which is also what I discovered." I smiled at Tank, not wanting him to feel discouraged. "By the way, I thought I saw Sridhar at the funeral. Did anyone else see him, or were my eyes playing tricks on me?"

When no one answered, I sighed and moved on. "Chalk it up to my overactive imagination, I guess. Anyway, lots of people on blogs and conspiracy sites blame The Gate for everything from inflation to tsunamis, but no one can prove anything. So yes, The Gate is surrounded by mystery. But on the other hand, they have a website, a Twitter account, and a Pinterest page. All their social media accounts are group accounts, so it's hard to know who's actually posting tweets and blogs, and after a while the posts all sound the same — don't be a slave to a god of any kind; be master of your own life through knowledge, which brings power. Illumination and personal deification — that's pretty much the heart of their message."

"So they're a scapegoat," the professor said, "for everything that goes wrong in the world?"

I shook my head. "They don't take credit for the bad things — they'd probably say that we bring disasters on ourselves. But they always take credit for the good things."

"Like what?" Brenda asked.

"Like the fact that though we have nuclear and hydrogen bombs, we've managed to avoid blowing up the planet," I said. "They'd take credit for nations that sign peace accords. And humans who create art and music."

Tank snorted. "Do they never realize that God is the ultimate artist? That He created a beautiful world? That His angels sang for joy when the earth was formed outta mud? That everything good comes from the creator of all, and we are only reflections of Him?"

"Whoa, Cowboy," Brenda said. "Get outta the pulpit. We're trying to stay steady here."

Tank opened his mouth to say something else, then clapped it shut, but I could practically see steam coming out his ears.

"This is good information," the professor said. "Tomorrow I'd like us to focus on the orb. Andi has been studying it, so maybe she'll be ready to give us a report tomorrow."

I lowered my gaze, a little embarrassed that I hadn't been able to finish my work — I'd spent too much time with Dr. Drummond. I didn't want to be the weak link.

"Andi," the professor said, drawing everyone's attention to my flaming face, "are you able to handle all this?"

"Of course." I knew he was speaking out of concern, but I didn't like the extra attention. "I'll make a full report tomorrow."

The professor looked at me for a long moment, then nodded. "Fine," he said. "Just get better."

CHAPTER 6

I didn't mean to fall asleep in my clothes, but after filling the required three pages in my notebook for Dr. Drummond, I lowered my head to the pillow and closed my eyes. When I awoke, bright sunlight streamed through the window, and Brenda was snoring softly in the twin bed across the room.

I must have been exhausted, because impromptu sleeping was foreign to my nature.

I changed out of my rumpled clothes, dashed into the bathroom and dragged a mascara brush across my lashes, then attempted to brush my hair. I glanced in the mirror and saw a pale woman with frizzy red hair staring back at me — the Tim Burton version of Raggedy Ann. But I couldn't help what I looked like, and it wasn't like we were planning to go anywhere.

By the time I made it to the kitchen, the professor had put on the coffee and brought in a huge box of doughnuts. "Wow," I said, lifting the lid. "Guess we're not counting calories this week."

He was standing by the table with a document in his hand, and he waited to finish reading before he looked up and greeted me with a nod. "You could use a few extra calories," he said. "And we're really getting nowhere with all these clippings, right?"

"I think" — I plucked a glazed doughnut from the box, then grabbed a napkin — "we're focusing too narrowly. Instead of spending all day reading about The Gate, maybe one of us should be searching for information on research with fungi, and someone else looking into mechanical orbs."

"Mornin'." Brenda shuffled into the kitchen in her pajamas and slippers, then grabbed her purse from the kitchen counter. "Going outside. If you solve the mysteries of the world, let me know."

I waited until the front door clicked behind her. "You've gotta give her credit," I told the professor. "She's trying hard."

He nodded. "Frankly, I'm surprised she's done as well as she has. What is she down to now, two or three cigarettes a day?"

"Two, I think. She goes out first thing every morning, and right after dinner every night. She only smokes during the day if she's unusually stressed . . . which I guess we've all been these last few days."

The professor didn't argue, but he did look up when Tank lumbered into the kitchen, his outstretched arms punctuating his expressive yawn. "Man," he said, dropping his arms as he shook himself awake. "I slept like a rock. Daniel, too — the kid's still in there sawing logs."

For some reason, my inner alarms clanged. "You sure he's okay?"

Tank gave me a reassuring smile. "He's fine."

I blew out a breath and moved to the coffeemaker. I couldn't explain why I still felt on edge — my ordeal was over, and physically I was back to normal. But I kept experiencing crazy surges of panic, usually accompanied by a certainty that something had gone terribly wrong.

"You feelin' okay?" Tank asked as he opened the refrigerator and pulled out a carton of milk. "No nightmares or anything?"

There it was again — for no logical reason, Tank's innocent question lifted the hair along my arms. What in the world was wrong with me?

"I'm good." I gave Tank a quick smile and was on my way to the table when the front door opened. Brenda came in with her purse on her arm, but instead of a cigarette butt, she carried a piece of paper. Without a word she walked to the dining room table and dropped the paper next to the orb.

We all leaned in for a closer look. Without being told, I knew that something had come over Brenda as she had her morning smoke, and instead of pulling out a cigarette, she had pulled out paper and pen and begun to sketch. The ink had smeared in a few places, but I would have recognized that image if she'd drawn in crayon.

"What is that?" Tank looked from me to the professor, then he grinned at Brenda. "Is this some kind of a joke?"

She pointed to the bottom of her sketch, where she'd drawn leaping flames. "I don't think fire is funny."

The professor and I exchanged a puzzled glance, then I braced my hands on the back of the nearest chair. "Maybe we should have a brainstorming session," I said, "about how our investigation could possibly involve a rubber Gumby."

"Dumby? Who's that?" Tank dropped into a chair at the head of the table, then pulled the box of doughnuts closer and set two glazed, two Boston creams, and a French crueller on a napkin.

Brenda rolled her eyes and sat next to me, eyeing Tank's doughnut tower while she sipped her coffee.

"Gumby," I said, "used to be a kid's TV show, back in the sixties. I only know about it because Sabba has a DVD collection of old kids' programs. He says he's saving them for my kids because television today is too violent."

"Gumby and his horse, Pokey," the professor added, his voice vibrant with nostalgia, "were originally intended to persuade kids to read, but before long the little guy was having independent adventures and leaving the books behind. One of the first attempts at Claymation, I suppose. Rudimentary compared to today's standards, but kids from the sixties enjoyed it. As you might imagine, a toy manufacturer licensed the image and sold millions of rubber replicas."

"What I want to know" — Brenda tapped the sketch with the tip of a fingernail — "is why this image popped into my brain. Usually I get an impression that has something to do with a person or an object that ties into our investigation. I don't get this. And I wasn't even born when that show was on TV."

I picked up the sketch and studied it more closely. I envisioned Gumby as being straight or slightly bent at the waist. In my memory he had large oval eyes, a triangle nose, a half-circle mouth, and hyperactive brows that communicated his emotions. But *this* Gumby, if that's really what the image represented, was grotesquely twisted — his mouth appeared to be dripping from his rubber face, his nose was tilted, and his pupils had run into his eyes. And Brenda had drawn flames around his feet . . .

Tank pinned Brenda in a steely gaze. "Are you saying you saw Gumby in hell?"

"No. Yes. I don't know what I saw, but it looked like this." She jabbed the image again. "You know how my sight works — I see, but I don't interpret. I don't want to be wrong."

"Okay." I studied the image again. "So if this is what you saw, why do you think you saw it? After all, we haven't exactly seen any Gumbys running down the street."

"Lemme say it again — I don't interpret. Maybe it's nothing. Maybe I'm confused."

"I'm confused most of the time," Tank said, grinning at her. "But your pictures are always right on."

"Anyone else have an idea?" I looked at the professor, who seemed distracted. His eyes were fixed on the orb, and I was pretty sure he was only half-following the conversation about Brenda's sketch.

"Maybe" — Tank paused to lick sugar off his thumb — "maybe it's a sign."

"Of what?" I asked.

Tank shrugged. "I don't know. But if we see that little rubber dude, we'll know we should pay attention. Gumbo means something."

"Gum*by*," I corrected, "and you're probably right."

"Well, I'm done with this." Brenda stood, cast a longing glance at the doughnuts, then went back to the coffee pot. "Can I suggest that we all get busy? Sittin' around starin' at doughnuts isn't helping my cravings at all."

"Right," the professor said, pushing away from the table. "Let's get to work."

At lunch, Tank was destroying a mushroom and pineapple pizza when he blurted out the question everyone had been too discreet to ask last night: "By the way, Andi, how was your visit with the shrink yesterday?"

I met his concerned gaze as I took a seat at the dining room table. "Fine. I talked, he talked. He wants me to keep writing in my journal, and he wants to hypnotize me."

Tank's open expression slammed shut. "Not a good idea," he said, his eyes hot.

"That kind of stuff is dangerous."

"Actually," the professor said as he opened a box of spicy chicken wings, "therapeutic hypnosis is nothing like the sideshow theatrics you're undoubtedly thinking of, Tank. Used properly, hypnosis is simply a state of focused concentration. While in a hypnotic trance, a subject is more open to helpful suggestions."

Tank regarded the professor with narrowed eyes. "How can you be sure this doctor won't hurt Andi? He might program her to murder people, or maybe he wants to take advantage of her —"

"Nonsense." The professor waved Tank's concern away. "Some people can't even be hypnotized, and no one under hypnosis can be forced to do anything he or she wouldn't ordinarily do. Andi would certainly be safe from any predacious doctor."

"Unless she don't want to be." Brenda grinned at me. "You gotta admit, that man is *fine*. He wouldn't have to use hypnosis to get some lovin' from me."

"I'm not in the market for love." I shot an equal opportunity glare around the table. "I just want those voices out of my head — for good." I looked at the professor, who had also been infected with the fungus. "Have you noticed anything odd about your thoughts? Have you heard any *echoes* of those voices?"

"No." The professor gave me a sympathetic smile. "But I wasn't infected nearly as long as you."

"That's it, then." I grabbed a slice of pizza. "I have another appointment tomorrow, and I'm going to tell Drummond to start swinging his watch, or whatever he does to hypnotize people."

"I second the motion," the professor said.

"I third it," Brenda added.

Tank growled. "My opinion may not matter much, but I'm against it."

Daniel, who had been plucking the mushrooms from his pizza, lifted his hand, signaling his agreement with Tank.

I sighed. I would have liked to have unanimous support, but three-to-two was still a win.

After lunch, I went back to the dining room and opened the cardboard box on the floor. The orb lay beneath the dishtowel I'd thrown over it, so I grabbed it, dishcloth and all, and set it on the table. I found my tablet, my tape measure, and a pen, then pulled the dishtowel away from the orb . . . and gasped.

The orb had changed again. Instead of being silver or gold, the orb's surface was covered with rows of trapezoids . . . and in each four-sided shape I saw the stage, the woman, and the basket from my recurrent nightmare.

My first instinct was to cover the orb and run. The thing knew too much. It was either reading my mind or it had invaded my dreams, but in either case, it was an intruder.

But maybe I only *thought* I was seeing those things. Maybe I was imprinting those little shapes on the orb; maybe someone else would see something different.

I glanced into the living room. Brenda had curled up on the couch, and Daniel was sitting on the floor playing *Battleship Megadeath.* Fortunately, we had convinced him not to target any of *our* ships during the day, so none of our phones erupted in sirens and horns while we were working. But occasionally we heard "MEGADEATH APPROACHING, CAPTAIN. DEFEND YOUR BATTLESHIP" over the sound of wailing sirens and knew that Daniel's ship was in peril.

Fortunately, the more he played, the better he became. Which meant fewer interruptions for us.

I threw the dishtowel over the orb again. "Hey, guys. Will you come here a minute? I want to try a little experiment."

Brenda and Daniel looked at me, then Brenda sighed and swung her legs to the floor. "Come on, kiddo," she said. "It's always good to take a break."

They pulled out chairs, sat, and waited.

"I'm going to lift this cloth," I told them, "and I want you to describe the orb."

"Okay," Brenda said. Daniel simply placed his arms on the table, then propped his chin on his hands.

"Okay — here goes."

I yanked the cloth away in one quick motion. Instead the puzzlement and confusion I expected to see on their faces, I saw nothing but calm curiosity.

"Blue," Brenda said, smiling. "Kinda reminds me of Planet Earth."

"Pretty," Daniel said, his eyes wide with wonder.

I turned to look at the orb — it *was* blue, a deep, metallic color that shone like a new car. No trapezoids, no images, no nightmares. Which meant either the orb had changed, or I was losing touch with reality.

Brenda lifted a brow. "Is that what you wanted us to say? Or did you want me to call it something fancy like *sapphire*?"

I forced a smile. "Nope, it's blue. That's all I needed."

Brenda shook her head slightly, then squeezed Daniel's shoulder. "Whaddya say to an ice cream? I think the professor has some cones stashed away in the pantry."

I pulled out my tape measure and scale, trying to behave as though nothing out of the ordinary had happened. But when I measured the orb and found that it had expanded *another* inch, I sat back and stared at the thing. The orb was getting bigger, anyone could see that. But how?

Even more important, why?

CHAPTER 7

Tuesday dawned clear, hot, and blue. Brenda woke up grumpy and with a headache, so the professor suggested that she take Daniel to the beach for a few hours. "Just stay out of trouble," he warned. "Tank, why don't you go with her and the kid?"

Tank hesitated. "What about you, Andi? Want to come with us?"

I pulled my laptop closer. "I'm gonna do some research, then I'm supposed to see Dr. D. You guys go on without me."

Tank didn't look very happy, but Brenda and Daniel did. So off they went.

Once they'd gone, the professor stretched out in the worn easy chair and kept working through the box of documents from the clipping service. "I know there's something in here," he said, pushing his reading glasses up the bridge of his nose. "I'm just afraid we won't recognize it when we see it." He glanced at me. "How are you coming with the orb?"

I blew out a breath. "It's pretty freaky. It changes. It expands and contracts. It seems to have consciousness."

"We need facts and evidence," the professor said. "You know the principles of scientific investigation. Hunches and appearances can be wrong."

"I'm working on it," I told him. "But more important, so are the boys in the basement."

The professor smiled and went back to his reading.

My reference to the boys in the basement was sort of an inside joke. The professor spoke of *the boys* often when we first started working together — his way of teaching me that during an investigation, everything we saw, heard, and experienced was stored in the subconscious until the *boys* made the necessary connections and provided the conscious mind with an answer to the problem.

I needed my subconscious to put in some serious overtime because lately my *conscious* mind had been seriously messed up.

I removed the dishcloth over the orb to view the thing's latest incarnation. The orb's color had shifted; the blue color now had a greenish tinge. And it may have grown, but

311

I wasn't in the mood to take measurements. I was ready to get my head straightened out first.

I called Dr. Drummond's cell phone, and felt a flutter of nerves when he actually answered. "This is Andi," I said. "And I'm ready to be hypnotized."

Silence rolled over the phone line for a moment, then he chuckled. "All right, let's move ahead. But I'm not at the office today — I'm at the condo, so I'll need to text you the address."

"A condo?" I frowned. Meeting a doctor at his home didn't seem very professional, but then again, he wasn't in full-time practice here. He was doing me a favor by agreeing to see me at all. "Where is the condo?"

"Clearwater Beach," he said. "I think you'll like the view. Anyway, we'll talk, I'll hypnotize you, and then I'll let you enjoy the rest of your afternoon. Oh — and you'll get to meet my mother. Lucky you."

I relaxed at the mention of his mom. "I'll be there in half an hour. Thanks."

I couldn't help smiling as I drove north to Clearwater Beach. Though my sleeping hours had been filled with nightmares, the bright sunshine and wide blue sky evaporated my feelings of dread. The doctor was staying in a condo at Sand Key, a nice development that appealed to tourists and snowbirds.

I parked the car and smiled at several sunburned and sandaled tourists as I got into the elevator and rode up to the fifteenth floor.

When Dr. Drummond answered the door, I entered a bit timidly. I knew the professor would have a fit if he knew I was meeting the doctor in his condo, but when I followed Drummond from the foyer into a living room, I was relieved to see an older woman — his mother, I presumed — seated on the sofa. She was reading the newspaper, but after welcoming me and apologizing for her casual appearance, she gathered up the pages and headed into the kitchen.

"My mother," Dr. Drummond said, watching her go. "She loves Florida, so I insisted she come along on this trip. She's going to hate going back to Edinburgh."

I smiled and moved into the middle of the living room. "Does it matter where I sit?"

"Sit anywhere you like." Dr. Drummond waited until I sat at the end of the sofa, then he took the nearest chair. "Have you been writing in your journal?"

"I have. Every day."

"Did you write about your feelings after

the latest nightmare? Are you recording all the details?"

"As many as I can remember."

"Good." He gave me an approving smile. "All right. What we are going to do now is play a game of 'let's pretend.' You are going to pretend to follow my instructions and fall into a trance. You are going to let your mind go as blank as possible, and you're going to let your face relax. Don't react to anything I say or do, but listen to my suggestions and focus on my voice. Take a deep breath in and slowly release it. That's right. Do it again — inhale and exhale, deeper and deeper. You're going to go deeper and deeper, you're going to become more and more still. Watch me. Look into my eyes."

I listened. I watched until my head grew heavy and I felt like I was staring *through* Hamish Drummond, like I could almost tumble forward and fall through the man into another dimension. Or one of the professor's multiverses.

"When I count to five," Drummond went on, his voice flat and steady, "you will become more and more aware of the room around you. I am going to count, and by the time I reach five, you will look up and feel refreshed, alert, and fantastic. You will not have that dream tonight. You will not hear voices in your head. Never again. Ready? One . . . two . . . three . . . four . . . five."

I lifted my head and looked around. Hamish sat on a chair in front of me, smiling expectantly, and from the kitchen I heard the sounds of clanging pots and pans. "So?" I asked. "Are we going to do the hypnosis now?"

His smile broadened. "My dear girl. We've already finished."

I looked at my hands, the room, and the clock — I had left the rental house at 10:00 a.m., but the clock had moved to 11:15. The drive must have taken longer than I realized.

I smiled in a flood of relief. "It didn't work, did it?"

"But it did."

"What? I don't feel any different. I mean — I feel fine, but I'm nearly always fine when I'm awake. The nightmares begin after I go to sleep."

I waited for his response, but he had lowered his gaze and seemed to be smiling on a spot on the carpet. "Hamish?" I tried again. "Did you hear me?"

He lifted his head, then he reached out and took my hand. "What did you just call me?"

I opened my mouth, ready to say *Dr. Drummond,* but my spoken words were still vibrating on the air. I'd called him *Hamish.* And I never, *ever* called professionals by their first names.

My jaw dropped, and the doctor squeezed my hand. "Nice to meet you, too, Andi. I hope you wilna mind being on a first-name basis."

"How — why — how did you do that?"

He lifted one shoulder in a shrug. "I simply made the hypnotic suggestion that we call each other by our Christian names. Your subconscious agreed that it was a good idea."

"But — but —"

He held up a restraining hand. "Don't worry about it; you can call me anything you like. But how do you *feel?* How do you feel about your nightmares?"

I halted, then closed my eyes to evaluate the feelings of dread and anxiety that had been simmering in my brain over the past several days. I felt nothing . . . but clarity. The anxiety and fear had vanished.

I opened my eyes and gave him the first genuine smile I'd mustered in days. "Hamish — Dr. Drummond — right now I think I could kiss you."

He grinned, then stood. "I'd better let you

go. I'm sure your friends are wondering where you are."

I stood, too. "The professor gave us the morning off. Something about all work and no play —"

"Why don't you stay for lunch? I'm supposed to barbecue a stack of spare ribs or some such thing, and Mother's made a clootie dumpling for dessert. We'd love the company."

I laughed. "A clootie *what*?"

"Stay . . . and you'll see."

I looked away and bit my lip, wondering if he'd done any hypnotic hocus pocus to evoke the glorious feeling of happiness that was bubbling up inside me. But even if he had, why should I mind?

I turned to face him, then hugged my arms and nodded. "I'd love to stay for lunch."

I didn't return to Ghostbusters Central until midafternoon. My bright mood dimmed when I came through the door and found Tank scowling at me. "We've been worried sick," he said, flushing. "Where have you been?"

I lifted both brows, then glanced around the room to see if any of the others were as upset as Tank. The professor was peering at

317

me from above his readers, and Brenda had stopped reading a press clipping to look at me with a question on her face. But Daniel was deep into his *Battleship Megadeath* game and didn't even look up.

"I went to my appointment," I said, forcing myself to remain calm. "And then Hamish — Dr. Drummond — invited me to have lunch with him and his mother. We ate. We talked. And that was it."

I tossed my purse onto the coffee table and strode to the dining room, where the orb waited under the dishtowel. Tank could stew if he wanted to, but I'd done nothing wrong, and I refused to get caught up in his fears. I hadn't asked him to worry about me, and I wouldn't. Ever.

Dear Journal:

After coming in from lunch, I sat down, took my equipment from the cardboard box, then pulled the dishcloth from the orb. The sphere had taken on a pink tone, and seemed to be vibrating slightly. I placed my fingertips on it and closed my eyes, trying to discern whether the humming sound came from the orb or some other mechanism in the house . . .

The sound faded, and I felt no vibration under my fingertips. I pulled out the tape measure and wrapped it around the widest part of the sphere: eighteen inches.

I whistled and made a note on my tablet. Heat caused objects to expand, but I hadn't noticed a significant elevation in temperature. Had the dishcloth trapped heat beneath its surface? Or had direct window light fallen on the orb during the early afternoon?

I picked up my digital scale and set it on the table. I then slid my hand beneath the base of the orb and prepared to gently roll it onto the scale. But no sooner had I lifted the orb than it floated out of my hand, hovering above my palm.

I couldn't move. Had the orb floated because the momentum of my hand propelled it upward? Or had it risen under its own power?

"Professor," I called, making every effort to keep calm. "Can you come over here?"

I heard the creak of his easy chair, then he appeared in the doorway. "What — ah!"

He stared, too, and a moment later Tank, Brenda, and Daniel joined him in the opening to the dining room. The orb had not moved — it remained about two inches above my palm, not spinning, not vibrating, just . . . waiting.

Obeying an impulse, I lowered my open hand and the orb descended with it, but maintained that two-inch distance. I lifted my hand, moved it left, right, and with each movement, the orb traveled with me.

"Fascinating," the professor whispered, crossing one arm over his chest. "Like a baby bird that's imprinted on its mother."

I snorted. "I hardly think that's the case. It's not alive. It lacks even the potential for life —"

Without warning, the orb left my palm and flew toward my face, astounding me with its speed and forcefulness. I threw up my hands and ducked reflexively, but the orb stopped short of striking me. It hung in the empty air in front of my eyes, then zipped off toward the professor, where it hung before him, almost as though it were taunting him . . .

Perhaps the orb was more than I thought.

Tank sputtered in amazement, and the orb flew to him, hovering a half inch in front of his nose. When Brenda laughed, the orb flew toward her, then remained tantalizingly out of reach when she tried to catch it. It zipped left and right, up and down, making a game of her spirited attempts to touch the thing.

Meanwhile, the professor kept his gaze fixed to it, his eyes narrow with calculation.

Tank and Brenda had made a game of it, an odd sort of chase through the living room, with the orb spinning high and low. It hovered near the ceiling, then it ducked beneath a shelf in the bookcase. Daniel put down his phone as they played, and though his eyes followed Tank's and Brenda's clumsy moves, he did not smile.

"What do you think?" the professor said, coming toward me. "Benign or malevolent?"

I shook my head. "Can't tell. But considering where it originated, I don't think I'd leave that thing out at night."

"So where do we put it?"

I glanced around the kitchen. We had a basic supply of pots and pans, a grill on the back porch, and three or four closets. I didn't know what to do with the orb, but I didn't want it to fly away. . . .

"Ah!" I ran through the utility room and stepped onto a shabby little patio where the previous owner had left a pile of odds and ends. One of those was a rusty birdcage, and it would be perfect for the orb.

I carried the old birdcage into the house, then removed the plastic bottom, leaving the cage open at the base. "All right, Tank, Brenda," I called. "Unless you want to sleep with that thing hovering overhead tonight, you'd better help me capture it."

Until that moment they'd been playing with it, then Tank got serious. He grabbed Brenda's sweater from the back of a chair and held it open, then chased the orb until it hovered over the dining room table. I could have sworn it was looking at me when Tank crept up from behind and threw the sweater over it. Together, we transferred it to the bottom of the birdcage, then I snapped the wire section into place.

We stood back, and I suddenly realized how silly we looked — four adults and a kid staring at a shiny pink ball in a rusty birdcage. The orb did not hover or fly or protest, but simply sat on the plastic floor amid traces of old paint and bird droppings.

But it wouldn't buzz around our heads tonight.

I woke at 2:00 a.m., not because I'd had a bad dream, but because the boys in the basement were pounding on the plumbing, desperate to give me a new idea. I padded through and into the dining room, then clicked on the light. The orb sat motionless in the bottom of the birdcage, but I had plans for it. . . .

I pulled out my tools — measuring tape,

drill, protective eyewear. Then I let myself out of the house and went out to my car, quietly opening the trunk and removing the case I'd tossed in on a hunch — the microscope I'd used for a science fair in high school. It wasn't the most powerful model, but it might be strong enough to verify the new hypothesis.

Back inside the house, I set up the microscope and removed the wire portion of the birdcage. Then I slipped a clean sheet of paper beneath the orb. Keeping my left hand on the sphere lest it try to zip away, I picked up the drill and turned it on, scraping the bit over the orb's surface as I had before. The drill bit made only a slight indentation, but I didn't care about marking it — any scratch would soon disappear, anyway.

I set the drill down and quickly brought the wire cage back over the orb, then slipped my left hand free. Once the orb was secure, I used a pair of kitchen tongs to slide the sheet of paper through the bottom opening and onto the table.

Working quickly, I put a drop of water on an empty slide, then sprinkled the water droplet with tiny metallic shavings from the orb.

"What on earth are you doing? I thought

you were a burglar."

I startled, then glanced over my shoulder at the professor, who stood in the open doorway with a pistol in his hand.

"Where did you get *that*? And why are you pointing it at me?"

"I'm not pointing it at you. And I picked it up two days ago because I thought it might prove useful in saving our collective bacon."

The professor set the weapon on the counter, then came forward to watch me work. I dropped the coverslip onto the shavings in water, then set the slide on the stage and dialed in the magnification. Then I focused.

I had expected to see metallic strands, bars, whatever — but I saw patterns. Clear, unmistakable, and organized. *Cells.* Not the typical cells with a nucleus, a cell membrane, and cytoplasm, but cells nonetheless. Even with my puny home microscope I could make out cell walls and a dot that might be a nucleus or other mechanism for controlling cell development. Furthermore, I saw the sort of asymmetry that was common in living cells . . .

Goose bumps pebbled my flesh as I looked at the professor. "It's not a machine," I whispered. "It's alive."

Lightbulbs were going off in my head, and I wanted to shout. The real me was back. For the first time in weeks I felt excitement sparking in my veins. I was seeing patterns, putting ideas together, and hearing that satisfying *click* that meant my instincts were right.

"Impossible." The professor sat and pulled the microscope toward him, straining the power cord. "All life is carbon-based. This is metal and wire and circuits —"

"It may *contain* metal and wires and circuits," I said, my words coming out in double time, "but it's not expanding and contracting, it's growing. It's healing itself. It's replicating and repairing damaged cells. It's organized. It uses energy. It responds to its environment. All we have left to determine —"

The professor lifted his head from the eyepiece. "Is what?"

"If it can reproduce."

The professor leaned back in his chair and thrust his hands into the pockets of his robe. "Impossible."

"You can say that all night long," I told him, "but it doesn't change what you see in that microscope. What we've seen over the last few days. Whoever made this orb —"

"The Gate?"

"Whoever made it has access to technology far beyond conventional research. This thing, this living metal, could be derived from an alien culture. It could have come from another galaxy. It could be so advanced that not even our government knows about it —"

"But *we* do? This makes no sense." He leaned forward and touched my arm. "I know you're flush with excitement right now, but reality's going to hit you in the morning. As far as I know, no one has ever found a non-carbon-based life form. In the entire universe, Andi. No one. Nowhere."

He stood, nodded, and turned toward the hallway. "I'm going back to bed now. And in the morning I'm going to come in here and tell you that I had the oddest dream. And you're going to laugh and give me a cup of coffee, and we're going to go back to reading and searching for needles in haystacks. So good night."

"Fine. Just take the gun with you."

I watched him pick up the pistol and shuffle away, and I knew his mind needed time to accept the impossible, the improbable, and the nonexistent. But by tomorrow, the boys in the basement would have done their work, and he'd come around.

He always did.

CHAPTER 8

I slept late the next morning, and might have slept even longer if not for the noise coming from the living room. I threw on a robe and stumbled down the hallway, then went instantly awake when I saw who stood next to Brenda: Dr. Hamish Drummond, and he was anything but calm. His face was red from exertion, his forehead was damp with sweat, and he was leaning over the coffee table, eye to eye with the professor.

"What's going on?" I pushed a tangle of curls away from my face to better see them.

Tank, who'd been blocked from view by a wall, stepped into my field of vision. "Your doctor friend says he's been visited by one of the orbs."

"What?" Ghost spiders danced over my spine. "Why?" I stepped around Tank to see the doctor. "Why would the orbs visit you?"

"I don't know, and that's why I'm here." Hamish looked from me to the professor.

"Tell me what you know about the people controlling those things."

"We don't know anything." The professor crossed his arms. "We aren't even sure what the orbs are used for."

I knew better — we knew the orbs were used for spying and for destroying the green fungus when it got out of control. I knew the orbs were made of living metal. But apparently the professor didn't want to share what we had learned.

I pressed my lips together as another thought made my stomach twist. Did Hamish know the professor was lying? He might, if I had told him what we'd learned about the orbs. I had no idea what I'd said under hypnosis.

Hamish regarded the professor with a skeptical gaze, then nodded. "I see," he said, a cryptic response that could have meant anything.

Brenda leaned against the wall. "Why don't you tell us what you saw?" she suggested, an easy smile playing on her lips.

Hamish looked from her to me, then he slipped his hands into his pockets. "I went to the office this morning. The air smelled different, and the room was unusually warm, so I checked and found a shattered window. I immediately turned to see if anything was missing. That's when I saw the thing. It had been hiding in a corner, and when I spotted it, it flew straight at me. I ducked, then it flew out the window, and I lost track of it."

All of us looked at each other. His description of the orb's behavior seemed accurate, but I knew the professor would be skeptical.

"Which brings us back to why," Brenda said, twiddling her unsmoked cigarette between her fingers. "Why would an orb be spying on *you*?"

"And that's why I'm here." Hamish folded his arms. "I'd never seen anything like that until I met the five of you. I wouldn't know what it was if Andi hadn't told me."

There it was — the finger of blame, pointed squarely at me.

"I'm sorry," I said, giving him an apologetic look. "I hate that I've gotten you involved in all this. If you want to stop seeing me, I'll understand. I *am* feeling better."

The professor had narrowed his eyes at the beginning of Hamish's story, but now he nodded. "All right, then. I think we can assume that whoever might be interested in us is also interested in the doctor. They're probably conducting damage control. We know about their experimentation with the fungus, and we know that it could easily be weaponized."

"But why?" Hamish lifted both brows. "It doesna make sense. Why would they want a weapon? Why would they kill thousands of innocent people? What's the end game?"

I had no answer, and I didn't think the professor did, either. Brenda gave the professor a *what next?* look, and Tank scratched his head.

"We don't know what the end game is," I said, speaking up because I felt responsible. "But we do know that the things we've seen do not bode well for anyone."

Hamish tipped back his head and looked at me, then he nodded. "I guess I'll just have to move on and forget about it . . . if I can."

"Sorry," I said again. "I never dreamed they'd come after you."

"Let this be a lesson to you, lass," he answered, his mouth curving in a half smile. "Be careful who you tell your secrets to."

"I'll walk you to the door," I said. "Sorry about not being awake when you came in. I was up late last night."

He walked with me through the doorway, then lingered outside on the tiny front porch. Aware that I was outside in my robe with no makeup, I cinched my robe tighter and folded my arms, waiting to hear whatever he wanted to say.

"Thanks for stayin' for lunch yesterday," he said. "My mother enjoyed meeting you."

I looked down and smiled. "I enjoyed meeting her. It was nice to get away" — I gestured to the house behind me — "from all this. But if you want to read my journals, maybe to learn a little more about what we've been doing, I'd be happy to let you see them."

He shook his head. "I never read my patients' private thoughts. I said that wee notebook was for your eyes alone, and I meant it. But . . ." He paused and wagged a finger at me. "I might have to seriously consider turning you over to another doctor. It's unethical, you understand, for a doctor to see a patient to whom he's personally attracted."

I stared as the words slowly sank in. Did he mean what I thought he meant? Was he really attracted to me? I liked him, but then again, who wouldn't? He was handsome, charming, intelligent, and who could resist that accent?

"I'd better be goin'." Hamish stepped off the porch and waved, then opened the door of his convertible.

"Nice car," I called, coming down the stairs.

"A rental." He grinned. "But I'm enjoyin' it for as long as I'm in Florida. Might as well go back home with a tan."

I laughed and stepped closer. The interior was what I expected to see in a new sports car — leather seats, power everything, burled wood in the dash — then I spied something so unexpected I froze. On the dashboard, sitting like a tiny little person, was a green Gumby.

I widened my eyes and pointed. "What . . . is . . . that?"

He followed my finger, then grinned. "You mean Gumby?"

"Why do you have a Gumby in your car?"

He chuckled. " 'Tis my brother's stand-in. He gave it to me when I left home. Said he wanted to come to America, but since he couldn't, Gumby would have to stand in for him." He tilted his head. "Does that mean something? You look like you've seen a ghost."

I drew a deep breath and felt my shoulders relax. Surely the Gumby was harmless — so why had Brenda sketched him?

"It's cute," I said, stepping away from the car. "But I'd better let you go. I'm sure you have work to do."

"Nothing more interesting than talking to you," he said, sliding into the driver's seat. "But seriously — call if you need to see me. You have my number."

I nodded and backed away, then watched him pull out of the drive and head north. And as the convertible merged into traffic at the intersection, another random thought struck: how had he known where to find us? I put my grandparents' address on the medical intake forms.

I must have given him the condo's address while under hypnosis.

Inside the house, I discovered that Hamish Drummond's arrival had drastically affected my friend's moods. Tank wore a decidedly worried expression. Brenda kept grinning at me, probably delighted by the thought of observing a transatlantic fling, and the professor radiated disapproval, undoubtedly because he thought I had crossed the line between personal and professional relationships. The only one who seemed unaffected was Daniel, who sat on the floor drawing pictures while he listened for sounds of distress from his battleships.

"He's a good doctor," I finally said, breaking the tense silence that had reigned ever since I came through the doorway, "and a nice guy. But that's the extent of our relationship."

"Good thing," Tank said. "I was wondering if he made up that orb story just to — you know."

The professor removed his glasses and pinched the bridge of his nose. "I don't understand why an orb would enter his office — no logic in that. He hasn't been in contact with the fungus. And he knows nothing about our work aside from what he's learned from Andi. Which brings up something else —" He shifted his gaze to me. "Maybe it's not a good idea for him to hypnotize you again. You could tell him far too much."

Tank's brow furrowed. "I'm not following you."

"Andi will explain the latest developments later. But it's not logical to have a spybot, if you want to call it that, follow someone with secondhand information if the primary source is available. If The Gate wanted to spy on us, it'd be more logical for them to have an orb follow Andi."

I closed my eyes, thinking of the orb in the birdcage. What if the thing had been abandoned on purpose? It had been with us for days, so it had seen and heard all kinds of things . . .

"What . . . if . . ." Brenda spoke slowly, as if easing into her thoughts — "the dark powers of The Gate have somehow been drawn to the doctor through Andi? I mean, he was just one of seven billion people on the planet until Andi became his patient. But he's a bright guy, he's from Europe, and who knows how many people he has the potential to reach. If they wanted pets to carry the fungus to humans, why wouldn't they want a guy from Scotland to carry it overseas?"

The professor brought his finger to his lip. "That's a surprisingly logical thought, Barnick. If The Gate started their work with the fungus here, they might want Dr. Drummond to carry a more polished specimen to Europe. If he could be exposed through Andi —"

"But that's not possible because the fungus is gone. I don't have it any more." I gave the professor a warning look. "Can we drop this discussion and get back to work?" When no one objected, I turned to Brenda. "By the way, I've spotted Gumby. Dr. Drummond drives with one on the dashboard of his car."

Brenda's mouth opened and closed, like a fish gasping for air. "You're kidding."

"What does that have to do with anything?" Tank asked. "I don't think we should be involving a guy who —"

"Wait. The figure in Barnick's sketch —" The professor reached for his briefcase, then shuffled papers. "Here it is. *This* Gumby is twisted and mangled. Did Drummond's look like this?"

"No. His Gumby looked like Mr. Universe compared to that one."

"Then what you saw *isn't* what Barnick saw. I must admit that it's an improbable coincidence, but the images don't match. So let's move on."

I sighed and pushed hair out of my eyes. "Moving on, then. If you could all join me in the dining room —"

"Guys?" The alarmed note in Brenda's voice lifted the hairs on my arms. I turned to see her holding one of Daniel's drawings. "I think you should all see this."

Tank and the professor joined me near the sofa. In the typical style of a ten-year-old, Daniel had drawn the image of Hamish Drummond, identifiable by his black hair, dark pants, and white shirt. He stood behind a flat two-dimensional table, but behind the doctor, on the wall, Daniel had drawn three frowning shadow creatures.

The sight of them gave me the willies.

"Daniel," Brenda asked, smiling gently.

"Who are these people?"

Daniel glanced at the picture, then shrugged.

"Did you see them?"

He nodded.

"Are they, um" — Brenda struggled for the right word — "bad?"

Daniel shook his head. "No duch."

"Are they good? Like the invisible guy who hangs out with you sometimes?"

Daniel shook his head again. "No anioł."

"So you don't know who they are?"

This time he lifted his head and met Brenda's gaze straight on. "I don't know," he said, his eyes welling with tears. "I don't."

Brenda smiled. "That's okay, kid."

She consoled Daniel as the professor, Tank, and I tiptoed into the dining room for a quiet conference. "We know he sees supernatural beings," I said, establishing known territory. "We know he's seen evil manifestations —"

"And angels," Tank interrupted. "At least, that's what I think they are."

"But he's never been uncertain about what he sees . . . until now."

The professor scratched at his stubbled chin. "Maybe they aren't manifestations. Maybe he's exercising artistic license."

Tank guffawed. "He's never done that before."

"He's ten," the professor pointed out. "Every day he does something he's never done before."

"Maybe they're a kind of spirit he's never met," I suggested. "Aren't supernatural beings sorted into classes? After all, the angels have cherubim and seraphim and archangels . . ."

As one, we turned and studied the boy, who was drawing another picture. "If some kind of dark force is following Hamish because of me," I whispered, "I — we — have to help him find a way to be free."

I made my big announcement after I'd placed the orb cage in the utility room where it couldn't listen to our conversation. I don't know if it heard things — could it possibly have some sort of auditory mechanism? — but I didn't want to take a chance.

The professor didn't react to my news; he simply took another sip of his coffee and set his mug back on the table. Brenda and Tank stared at me with puzzled looks — they knew I'd stumbled onto something big, but they couldn't quite grasp the significance. But they would soon enough.

Daniel only looked up at me, smiled, and

went back to drawing his pictures.

"So," I said, crossing my arms and settling back in my chair, "this is huge news, and it might actually help us locate The Gate."

"How's that?" Brenda's frown deepened. "You've lost me."

"I was lost at 'I've had a breakthrough,'" Tank said, grinning. "Why don't you start over?"

"The orb," I said slowly, "is made of living material. You've seen it expand and contract — it's actually been growing and shrinking. It has healed its injuries. You've seen it fly purposefully. For all I know it may be transmitting information to its creators."

"Is that why it's in the utility room?" Brenda said. "You think it's a spy?"

I shrugged. "I suspect that it was told — or commanded or programmed — to watch over Dr. Mathis, which it did until Tank smashed it in the lab. Now that it's had time to heal, it may not have a command to follow. It may be waiting. It may be looking for an opportunity to escape and go back to its programmer or whatever. Its creator."

"You think someone created this?" The professor narrowed his eyes, but at least he had begun to consider my hypothesis. "Last night you were talking about aliens."

"We can't rule that out," I said, "because as you pointed out last night, no one has ever found anything like this in nature. Maybe it's a machine-human hybrid."

"Whoa." Tank held up both hands in a defensive posture. "Now you're talkin' *Terminators One, Two,* and *Three.*"

I blew out a breath. "Science fiction gets a lot of stuff right. But the orb" — I pointed toward the utility room — "is a living thing. So we have to treat it as such."

"How is this supposed to help us find The Gate?" These latest developments must have shaken Brenda, because she had popped her unlit cigarette into her mouth. "Don't tell me you want to let it go and see where it lands."

"No — but that's not a bad idea, if we could find a tracking device." I lifted a brow. "I was thinking about money. If you were a secret organization and you came up with an amazing and totally unique substance like living metal, what would you do with it?"

"Sell it," Tank said. "You'd want to make a lot of money."

"Control it." Brenda tapped her nails on the tabletop. "You wouldn't want your secrets to get out. You'd guard them. Watch out for industrial espionage and that kind of thing."

"I'd patent it," the professor added. "If it's an actual life form, or even a hybrid, you'd patent the process and the result."

"Yes, yes, and yes." I grinned at all of them. "And wow, is it ever good to be back. I feel like my brain is finally working at full power."

"So God bless the shrink," Brenda said. "Get back to the topic at hand."

"Okay." I pressed my hands to the table. "Professor, why don't you check the US Patent Office and see if anyone has applied for a patent on living metal or some similar term. Brenda, start searching for stock tips, new companies, anything you can find about living metal. And Tank, if someone claims to have invented living metal, see if you can find any mentions of how the substance could be used. If we follow these threads, they'll lead us to The Gate . . . or at least to one of their shell companies."

Brenda squinted at me. "Say again?"

"Think of The Gate as the big, bulbous head of an octopus," I said, "with long tentacles to represent the different shell companies, organizations, schools, whatever. The offshoots may carry on legitimate business, but the head controls them all. If we can find even a few names associated with one of these branch groups, we'll have the names of people who are either part of The Gate or loosely associated with them."

Brenda blew out a breath. "Sounds a lot easier than lookin' through all those boxes of clippings."

"One question —" Tank held up his hand. "Does this mean we have to watch what we say around the orb? And if that thing's really alive, maybe we should make it more comfortable. I hate to think of it all cooped up in that rusty cage."

"Let Andi keep it with her," Brenda said, standing. "She's its mother."

They laughed and left the table, leaving me to wonder if they could possibly be right.

By the end of the day we had made solid progress. The professor reported that no one had applied for a "living metal" patent in the United States, but Tank found a researcher who had created metal cells capable of reproduction. "Dude's from the University of Glasgow," Tank said, consulting a computer printout, "and he calls them iCHELLS." He lowered the paper. "Basically, he took a lot of metal atoms and mixed them in a solution. I don't understand all the details, but positive ions bonded with negative ions and such. He says he can design the cells to do certain things." He slid the paper toward me. "More details in the article, if you want to read it."

"Thanks, Tank." I set the article aside and bit my lip. The University of Glasgow . . . Scotland. Dr. Drummond was from Scotland, too — coincidence?

"I found a company." Brenda turned her laptop around and showed me the website, a basic design of not much more than a logo and lots of text. "Summit Biotechnologies. They're small, but they're ramping up. I found some stockbroker sites that were raving about a potential IPO in the next year or two."

Tank squinched his face into a question. "What's —"

"Initial public offering," the professor said. "They want to sell stock on the New York Stock Exchange."

"That's cool." I looked around the circle, hoping my excitement was contagious. "Tomorrow, let's investigate Summit Biotechnologies. Maybe we should take a trip to their office and nose around to see what we can find."

"I hope they're in a big city," Brenda said, pulling a pack of cigarettes from her purse.

"Maybe New York or Paris. If we have to do some globe-trotting, let's trot in nice places, okay?"

The rest of us split up and headed to our rooms. I felt tired and happy, and I knew I'd sleep like a rock. Now that Hamish had taken care of my nightmares, I was looking forward to a good sleep.

I pulled out my journal and tapped the cover, wondering if I really needed to keep writing in it. I was feeling so much better . . . but what was the harm? It felt good to write about everything that had happened, and for once I had good news to report.

After putting my journal away, I crawled into bed and was asleep before my head hit the pillow.

I was dreaming that I was a glamorous World War II spy, wearing a trench coat and secretly taking pictures of important documents, when Brenda shook me awake.

"Hey." She was in pajamas and leaning over me, a shadowy figure in the dark.

"What?" I blinked the remnants of my dream away as my eyes adjusted. "Brenda. What's up?"

"I was about to ask you the same question."

"Huh?" I rose onto my elbows and looked

around. "What do you mean?"

She gave me an odd look, then sat on the edge of her bed. "A few minutes ago," she said, "you got out of bed, walked to the desk, and used your phone to take pictures of your journal. Then you crawled back into your bed and went back to sleep." She tilted her head. "Why'd you do that?"

Curiosity brought me fully awake. "You must have been dreaming."

"I haven't been to bed yet."

Frowning, I got out of bed and walked to the little desk in our bedroom. My journal lay in the corner, right where I'd placed it before going to sleep. My phone lay on the desk, too, and when I unlocked it and checked my photos, I saw only pictures of Abby, the beach, and a few I'd taken of Daniel.

I held up the phone so Brenda could see it. "No photos."

"Maybe you deleted 'em. You stood there for a couple of minutes before you went back to sleep."

"Why would I do that? Who would I send pictures to?"

Brenda folded her arms. "Good questions."

"Here's another one — why did you watch

me do all that before asking what I was doing?"

Brenda snorted. "Haven't you ever heard that it's dangerous to wake a sleepwalker? I called to you a couple of times, but when you didn't answer, I thought you might be sleepwalkin'. So I decided to wait and make sure you didn't hurt yourself."

"I'm not a sleepwalker. I've *never* been a sleepwalker."

I sat on the bed and checked everything I knew to check — nothing odd in recent phone calls, nothing in text messages, nothing unusual in my e-mails. My address book was open to the page with Hamish Drummond's phone number, but I had called him the other day.

Sighing, I tossed the phone on the desk. "I think you were dreaming."

Brenda opened her mouth, and I knew she wanted to say I was crazy.

But instead she clamped her mouth shut, got into bed, and turned her back to me.

CHAPTER 9

By the time I got up Thursday morning, Brenda and Tank were involved in a spirited discussion of what might be possible with living metal

"A robot that looks human and makes its food through photosynthesis!" Brenda said, to which Tank countered, "Terminator Ten!"

The professor had his laptop open at the counter and was reading a long e-mail. I was slipping past him to pour a cup of coffee when he caught my eye and pointed to the screen. "Our marching orders," he said. "We're to stay here until we receive plane tickets via messenger. We'll be leaving in a day or two."

"And goin' where?" Brenda wanted to know. "Can I vote for Paris?"

I slid into the chair next to the professor. "I don't know who these people are," I said, speaking of the mysterious benefactors who occasionally provided tickets, visas, and other things we needed for travel, "but I'm glad they're on our side."

"Why don't we put a little effort into figuring out who they are?" Brenda asked, casually stealing marshmallows from Daniel's bowl of Lucky Charms. "Or would that be too much like lookin' a gift horse in the mouth?"

"I'm just happy knowing the good guys have a team." Tank smiled above the rim of his coffee mug. "I'd hate to think that we were standing up to The Gate alone."

"If these people want us to know who they are, I trust they'll tell us," the professor said, closing his laptop. "In the meantime, we do occasionally run into others. Like Littlefoot. The nun. And that crazy taxi driver in Rome."

I tapped the professor's arm. "Since we'll be leaving soon, I think I'll run some errands this morning and maybe stop at my grandparents' house," I said. "I'll try to be back by lunch time."

After showering and dressing, I picked up my purse, finger-combed my hair, and went into the utility room, then looked around and realized I'd forgotten why I went in there. Whenever my grandmother did that, she laughed and said she had too much on her mind.

So did I.

Muttering to myself, I slipped out the front door and got into my car.

I did want to visit my grandparents, of course, but I felt compelled to stop by Hamish's office. He had been caught up in our bizarre drama through no fault of his own, and I felt horrible that he'd been terrified by an orb. I also wanted to ask him about the researcher who had invented living metal. Hamish had completed his postgraduate work at the University of Edinburgh while the other man worked at the University of Glasgow, but Scotland wasn't a huge country. Had they ever met?

I spotted Hamish's convertible in the parking lot, and the Gumby on the dash. Smiling, I slung my purse over my shoulder and knocked three times on the office door, then stepped into the waiting area. "Hamish?" I called. "Got a minute? It's Andi."

"Andi!" He came out of his office, both hands extended as though he were greeting a friend. "How are you feeling today?"

"Great, thanks to you. I wanted to stop by to thank you for —"

"Come in, come in," he said, ushering me into the inner office. "Have a seat while I make you some tea."

"I've just had breakfast —"

"No matter. A spot of tea always gets the day off to a good start."

What could I say? The man was Scottish. While he fussed at the coffeemaker, I looked at his window. The curtains had been pushed aside, and both windowpanes were whole and clean. "Your window," I said. "Repaired already?"

"I couldn't leave it overnight," he said, turning toward me as the machine gurgled. "After all, these aren't my books on these shelves, and I'd hate for anything to go missing while I was renting the space. Thank heaven for 1–800-GET-GLAS."

He brought over two mugs and gave one to me. "Thank you," I said. "I seem to be saying that a lot, but I mean it. I was a little lost until I began meeting with you. I don't know what you did, but I can't thank you enough."

"I wish all my patients were as quickly mended." He sank into his chair. "You were — are — a delight."

I sipped from my mug, then frowned when my phone buzzed within the depths of my purse.

"Do you need to get that?" Hamish asked. "Might be important."

I glanced at the caller ID. "It's Brenda. We're leaving soon, so she probably wants to know if I've seen her shoes or something."

"Where are you going?"

"We're not sure. This work we do . . . is often spontaneous. We go where the tickets take us."

"Rather unnatural way to live. And who sends the tickets?"

I shrugged and let my head tip to the side, where it could rest against the side of the chair. "I don't know, and this gig is definitely better than being bored. Which reminds me — I am really sorry about the orb in your office. I don't know where it came from, and I hope you never see another one." My voice sounded distant, and the room appeared to be filling with a slight haze.

"I have enjoyed getting to know you," Hamish was saying, "and Mother enjoyed meeting you, too. It's too bad we won't see you anymore. Mother greatly admired your thoroughness. She said your journals were the most interesting she'd ever read."

I blinked and tried to raise my head, only to find that it weighed about thirty pounds. "How ridiculous," I said, laughing as my nose nestled into the seam of the chair. "I can't seem to lift my head."

"It's the sedative," Hamish answered, and though I couldn't see him, I heard the subtle swish of his shoes over the carpet. He

was moving about the room, doing something. . . .

"Hamish?" I asked, struggling to lift my
heavy eyelids. "Are you still there?"

The phone in my purse buzzed again and
again and again. . . .

Slowly, the fog in my head cleared. I opened
my eyes and saw that I was still in the chair,
but my hands had been tied together.
Hamish was not sitting next to me, but leaning on the desk, an expectant expression on
his face.

"Andi?" He lifted a brow. "Are you back,
then?"

My mouth was as dry as cotton. "I'm . . .
here."

He smiled. "Good. Have a few last minute
details to arrange, and I have to collect that
orb from you. Can't have that roaming
around, can we?"

"What . . . orb?"

"The one in that beach bag you call a
purse."

I pressed my tongue to my teeth, trying to
force the word over my clumsy tongue.
"Th— there's no orb."

"I believe there is. So excuse me while I
plunder your purse."

I watched in dazed astonishment as he

picked up my bag and pulled out my phone. "Ah," he said, reading the screen. "Bjorn, Brenda, and the professor have called several times in the last quarter hour. I trust you didn't tell them you were coming here?"

I blinked. What had I told them?

Hamish pulled up the orb, which had filled out the bottom of my large bag. "There." He smiled at the thing as it hummed and hovered a few centimeters above his open hands. "They will be pleased to know this little one has come home."

"Wh-who is — who are — ?"

"You needn't worry about that, Andi. Thanks to your faithfulness, we now know everything your little group knows, and we can better plan for the future. You were so dutiful, obeying every hypnotic prompt, sending your neat little reports, keeping us in the loop — good girl. And now, I believe it's time to wrap things up and send you off."

"Wh-where?"

"It's all been arranged. I'm going to put you in your car and give you the trigger word, and then you will drive to the spot I have selected. You'll be the first to die, but you'll go peacefully, your conscious mind soundly asleep. Afterward, traces of a seda-tive in your blood will lead many to believe you were suicidal. Over the next few weeks, the others will meet with accidents, too — the professor is next in line. Due to his advanced age and fondness for you, no one will be surprised when he has a heart attack. The big oaf will follow — probably in a drunken brawl or some such thing. Then the artist, an easy job because tattoo parlors are *so* seedy, and the clientele not the finest. I believe she'll be robbed of whatever is in her cash box, just to keep things real. Without you lot to take care of him, the boy will be sent back to the hospital, where no one will mind anything he says."

Moment by moment, my mind cleared. This was no exercise; he was serious. He was one of them. And he was planning to kill me.

"I think that's about it." Hamish looked around his office and absently patted his pocket until he heard the jangle of keys, then he knelt in front of me. "Are you ready to go under?"

"You can't." I summoned every ounce of energy to glare into his eyes. "You can't make someone do what they don't want to do, even under hypnosis."

"Ah." His smile went soft and buttery. "But that's the thing, Andi — you were so upset over your recent illness that you wanted to die. You thought you were use-less, that your splendid mind had gone to mush and your gifts had vanished. For days now, your subconscious has been ready to throw in the towel."

"But —"

"All we have time for, love. Say good-bye now." His smile vanished. "On the count of five, you will again fall into a deep and dreamless sleep. One . . . two . . . three . . . four . . . five.

I dreamed Hamish and I were walking along a dock, then Hamish gestured to a boat, opened a hatch, and waited until I climbed in. Then he went around, walking on water, and climbed into the opposite seat.

"Can't get used to riding on the right side," he said. "You mustn't drive without a seat belt, love. Put it on, please."

I did. As if they had a mind of their own, my fingers pulled the seat belt across my chest, then snapped it into place at my hip.

"Perfect," Hamish said, turning sideways to smile at me. "Let's go. Pull out into traf-fic and drive toward your grandparents' house."

I drove the boat, obeying traffic signs and signals and watching other boats zoom past as I held to the speed limit. "You're an exceptionally careful driver," Hamish said. "No one would believe that you drove into a retention pond accidentally, so it has to be suicide. Sorry about that. A bit hard on the reputation, I know, but you'll be past minding."

We drove into a very busy channel, and I maintained a steady speed in the right lane until Hamish pointed to a buoy. "This ramp, love."

I took it. "Now," he said, "pull onto the verge, the shoulder."

I pulled over, coasting until Hamish told me to stop. "Now," he said, smiling, "I'm going to get out. When the door closes you're going to accelerate and drive toward that pond over there. The ride might be a bit choppy, but you will hold the wheel steady. You'll steer straight toward the pond, and you'll remain calm as the vehicle fills with water because your struggle is finally over. Your friends will be better off without you, so go ahead, close your eyes, and sleep."

Then, while I stared at the world beyond the windshield, Hamish leaned forward, turned my face toward him, and kissed me for a long moment.

"Pity," he said, pulling away. "Such a waste."

I sat motionless, waiting, until I heard a

door click. Then I pressed my foot to the accelerator and heard the responsive roar of the engines.

I heard the trickle of water and felt the boat slide on the surface. So pleasant. I loved sleeping to the sounds of water.

MEGADEATH APPROACHING, CAPTAIN. DEFEND YOUR BATTLESHIP.

I blinked as sirens and horns disturbed my liquid lullaby.

MEGADEATH APPROACHING, CAPTAIN. DEFEND YOUR BATTLESHIP.

I shook my head as reality intruded into my fictive dream. I wasn't in a boat; I was strapped into my car. Water wasn't trickling nearby, it was pouring in through the doors, rising from the floor, and rushing up the windshield. The front end of my car had already gone under, and water was crawling up the car doors, covering my seat, drowning my purse.

My phone! I reached for it reflexively, but it had already gone silent beneath the murky water. I had to get out. I had to get *free*. I reached for the seat belt buckle, my fingers frantically searching for the locking mechanism until I found it. I threw off the belt and tried to work the door handle, but the onrushing water seemed determined to hold the door closed. I could feel pressure squeezing my eardrums. The power window button wouldn't work, and I didn't have a hammer. . . .

Water crept up my chest and tickled my neck. I snatched a deep breath and turned to kick at the window, but the steering wheel cramped my movements, leaving me little room to maneuver. The rising water was at my chin, filling my ears, so I tipped my head back, gulping air near the ceiling light. The car tilted, the driver's window plunged downward or maybe upward because I could no longer tell which way was up and which down.

I kicked, hit the fabric of the ceiling, and realized it, too, was soaked and there was no more air. . . .

Oh, God, please . . .

As my eyelids fluttered at the bright light, I looked out and saw Tank bending over me with wide blue sky behind him. My gorge rose, and Brenda rolled me over while I vomited water and coughed liquid from my lungs. Then I was lying flat again, mud beneath my palms, wet clothes chilling my skin.

Four concerned faces peered at me from above — Tank, Brenda, Daniel, and the professor. When I blinked and asked why I was wet, four faces broke into wide smiles and the professor patted Tank on the back.

"I never thought guys like you could swim," the professor said. "I thought you'd sink like a stone. But you did it, my boy, you did it."

"Couldn't have done a thing without Brenda," Tank said, patting his pocket. His smile faded for an instant. "Oh — sorry. Must have dropped it in the pond."

Brenda waved his comment away. "Forget it. Aunt Rene will send me another Life Hammer once I tell her that you saved Andi's life with the first one. Maybe she'll send two."

I listened to them, more confused with each word. "Can I sit up?" I asked as sirens began to wail in the distance. "Is Daniel playing that game?"

"I think you should lie still," Tank said, placing a hand on my shoulder. "At least until the EMTs have a chance to look you over."

I blinked when I saw Daniel crouching next to Brenda. He wasn't holding his phone, so the sirens must be real. . . .

Within a few minutes an ambulance had pulled up and a pair of young men lifted me onto a gurney. When the professor told them that I'd been pulled from a submerged vehicle and revived with CPR, the medics said I had to go to the hospital.

"Possibility of infection inside the lungs," one man said, pulling up the gurney's guardrail. "We won't release her until we're sure she's okay."

I would have protested, but at that moment I didn't feel like the sharpest tack on the bulletin board. Maybe a few hours in the hospital would do me good.

CHAPTER 10

By the next morning, I'd had time to think about a lot of things. Lying in the soft light of a dim hospital lamp, I realized that a few days ago, all I'd wanted was to feel normal again. Because he was smart and handsome and charming, I trusted Hamish Drummond, even allowing him to hypnotize me.

I should have known better. I should have listened to Tank and Daniel. Because I didn't, Hamish had full access to my team . . . and now we were all in danger.

Would they ever forgive me?

I sat up and propped my elbows on the rolling bedside table. In the car, in that moment before I filled my lungs with water, I had called on God . . . and I was still alive. I wasn't exactly sure how or *if* He worked things out, but I was still alive and I didn't deserve to be.

I would never again let my heart overrule my head.

My friends showed up after breakfast. The professor greeted me with a vase of flowers and a printed sheet of paper. "The flowers are gorgeous," I said, burying my face in the fragrant carnations. "And what's that other thing?"

"Our next gig." The professor handed me an itinerary. "Day after tomorrow we're leaving for San Diego. So if you can refrain from getting into trouble —"

"Hush up, you ol' curmudgeon." Brenda sat on the edge of the bed, blocking my view of the professor. "Girlfriend, that one was too close for comfort. You gotta be more careful."

"I know. And I'm sorry for getting us into this mess."

Brenda patted my hand. "We're all still here, ain't we?"

"I'm still not sure what happened. I remember sitting in Dr. Drummond's office and hearing that I was about to die. Next thing I knew, I was in the car hearing the Megadeath battle cry. I think — I *know* — that sound snapped me out of my trance. But I couldn't get out in time." Even now, the memory of that chilly black water made me shudder. "Can you fill in the gaps for me?"

Brenda glanced at Tank and the professor,

then she draped her arm around Daniel's shoulders. "Daniel, my man, why don't you ask Tank to go get you some ice cream? I think there's a little shop down in the lobby area."

Tank stared at her. "Ice cream? In the morning?"

"Be a prince and take Daniel for a cone, okay?"

I watched silently as Daniel walked over to Tank, took his hand, and led the big guy through the doorway. When they were safely away, Brenda leaned forward. "I don't want to embarrass the kid. But we wouldn't have found you if not for him."

"Daniel?"

"Quite right." The professor leaned against the end of my hospital bed. "Once again I found myself grateful we had the boy along."

Brenda tossed the professor a disdainful look, then patted my hand again. "You'd gone out that morning. I don't think we even realized it, but suddenly Daniel had one of his episodes." She gave me a pained smile. "He started screaming about the duchs and how they were all around you. We looked for you, of course, 'cause we wanted to show him that you were fine, then we saw your car was gone. I remembered you sayin' something about going to see your grandparents, but as soon as I mentioned that, Daniel started screamin' even worse, hollerin' and hittin' us if we got close. Then Tank opened the front door, and suddenly Daniel ran out and jumped in the rental car. Well, what else could we do? We got in, too, and then —" She paused to draw a deep breath. "You know how he has this invisible friend?"

I nodded.

"Since we didn't have a clue where you were, we went wherever Daniel told us to go. When he took us to the interstate I was convinced we were on some kind of wild goose chase, and then suddenly he pulls out his phone and starts playing *Battleship Megadeath* — the game he's got goin' with you. Then we're at the side of the road, and Daniel points to a pond. We're staring at it, and we see this huge air bubble come to the surface. Daniel freaks out again, jumpin' up and down, and Tank is ready to dive in, but before he can kick off his shoes Daniel reaches into my purse, pulls out that silly orange hammer, and hands it to Tank."

Brenda paused and drew a deep breath. "About that time, I was putting pieces together, and I didn't like what I was thinking. I had to take a CPR class to get my state license, and I *know* how fast a car can sink. Unless you can get your seat belt off and your window down before the power shorts out, you're done for."

"I did get my seat belt off," I said, shivering. "Barely."

Brenda shook her head. "Man, I get wore out just thinkin' about it. But I'm sure you can figure out the rest. Out in the pond, Tank sees your car, breaks the window with the hammer, and pulls you out. If the water had been a couple of feet deeper, or if you'd still been stuck in that seat belt, I don't think Tank could have done it — the guy's got a lot of heart, but he's not what you'd call naturally buoyant. Anyway, Daniel stops screamin' once he sees that Tank has you, and he's as quiet as a mouse while Tank is givin' you mouth to mouth." She grinned. "Personally, I think Tank liked that even more than savin' your life. So that's what happened."

I leaned against my pillows, exhausted and a little amazed. The story made sense, but if I hadn't lived it, I wouldn't believe it.

"What about Hamish?" I shifted my gaze to the professor. "Has anyone checked out Dr. Drummond?"

"A couple of detectives went to talk to him," the professor said, "but he had vacated the premises — not a trace of him at the office, not even a fingerprint. But about an hour later the cops called me with news of a burning convertible on Interstate 275. The car sounded like Drummond's, so I went to the scene. No body, just a crumpled convertible on its side, resting in the middle of the median. And this." He pulled his phone from his pocket, tapped the photo icon, and let me see the screen. In a patch of charred grass, I saw Hamish's Gumby — twisted, melted, and an exact copy of Brenda's sketch.

"What does it mean?" I asked, lifting my gaze to meet the professor's. "Is he dead?"

The professor released a hollow laugh. "I wouldn't think so. But that's okay — neither are we."

I leaned back against the pillows and sighed as Tank and Daniel came back in. Tank carried a tray of ice cream cones, and as he passed them out I remembered Drummond telling me that all of us but Daniel were supposed to die, one after the other. But if The Gate couldn't manage to get rid of a defenseless girl like me, how powerful could they really be?

Maybe we'd soon find out.

"Thanks, Tank." I accepted a cone and tasted the vanilla on my tongue. Delicious.

■ ■ ■ ■

THE FOG

ALTON GANSKY

■ ■ ■ ■

PROLOGUE

I know the people behind me are wondering what I'm doing. I can't blame them. It's not everyday you see a man my size standing on the parapet of a high-rise building in the middle of a major city and looking down at a street he can't see a mere fifty floors below. Did I mention it was night and the only light I have comes from emergency lamps? Probably not. I'm not at my best at the moment.

I've never admitted this to anyone before, but I don't like heights that much. I don't let on, of course. A big football player isn't supposed to have such fears. Well, I ain't a football player anymore. I'm just a big ex-jock teetering on the edge some five hundred feet above the sidewalk below.

It's eerie up here. Not just because most of the lights in the city are out, but because of the silence. About a million-and-a-half people call San Diego home, or so the professor tells me. He has a knack for such things. When we first arrived, I noticed the noise of downtown: traffic, people talking, busses, mass transit trains, and other noise-making things of humanity. Now all I can hear is the sound of a gentle breeze pushing at my back and zipping by my ears. That and the sobs of my friends.

If all of that wasn't enough to raise the hair on a man's neck, there was the fog — a fog like I've never seen before. At first it looked like your garden-variety mist, but it moved differently, and — how do I say this — it was populated. Things lived in it. Bad things. Horrible things. Ugly things.

When I look down I can't see the street, just the roof of the fog bank. That and the things swimming in it.

A face appeared.

I shuddered.

It wasn't alone.

The things swam in the fog like dolphin swim in the ocean. Except dolphins are cute. These are no dolphins. No siree. These things ain't from around here. They're not from anywhere on this earth. I can only guess where they call home, but if it was Hell, I'd believe it with no hesitation.

"Tank . . ."

Even with my back to her, I recognized

Andi's voice. I would recognize it anywhere and at anytime. The biggest hurricane couldn't keep her words from my ears.

I raised a hand. I didn't want to hear it. I wanted to hear it more than anything I've ever wanted. I know it doesn't make sense, but I'm a guy standing on the edge of certain death, so my thinking, such as it is, has a few hiccups. Don't expect me to make a lot of sense at the moment. You stand on the edge of a high-rise an inch from death and see how well the gears in your head work.

I allowed myself one last glance back. I turned slowly to look at my friends and the scores of people standing behind them. I was real careful. When I go over the edge, I want it to be my decision, not a fool mistake.

My gaze first fell on Professor McKinney, worldwide lecturer, atheist, and former Catholic priest. Yep, he's a bit conflicted. He's the smartest man I've ever met, and at times, the biggest pain in the neck. He is retirement age, but hasn't slowed down. Good thing. The team needs him. He stared at me through his glasses. Even in the dim light provided by a pale ivory moon overhead and the emergency lighting, I saw something I had never seen before: a tear in his eye.

The professor's hand rested on Andi Goldstein's shoulder. I let my gaze linger on her. My gaze *always* lingered on her. Her usually wild red hair might strike some as a bit strange, but she was fashion-model beautiful to me. There were tears running down her face. The sight of them squeezed my heart like you might squeeze a lemon.

Next to her stood Brenda Barnick. Her black face seldom showed a smile, and she could put on an expression that would melt steel. I've faced a lot of big guys on the football field, but not one of them put any fear in me. When Brenda loses her temper, she plain scares me and anyone else within the sound of her voice. She's a street-smart tattoo artist, all hard on the outside, but I know she has a great big heart. She looked away, but not before I saw the fear and pain on her face.

One way I know Brenda has a big heart is the boy standing in front of her. The kid has mental problems. Well, that's what the doctors say, but we know better. He's just different. And talented. Brenda, through a lie or two, got herself named his guardian. She makes a good mom.

The sight of my friends gutted me. I turned from them. It was easier looking at what I feared rather than those I love. I was on this ledge for them and for many others.

I raised my right foot and inched it over the edge of the parapet. The breeze pushed at me as if encouraging me to jump.

The things in the fog were agitated, like sharks in bloody water. Their small, lethal heads bobbed up and down in the fog.

They were waiting.

Waiting for me to lean forward.

I did.

A hundred pairs of clawed hands reached for me.

But first, I need to tell you how I got here.

CHAPTER 1
ALL DRESSED UP WITH SOMEWHERE TO GO

Of all the things I've seen lately, and I've seen a lot, today might just take the cake. I've seen a house that appears and disappears at will. I've seen the inside of the Vatican. I've seen flying orbs made of living metal (that's what Andi calls it). I've seen a green fungus that invades living things and takes them over. I've been chased by monsters not of this world and protected a little girl who grew younger with time instead of older. But this. Seriously. This is almost too much. I would think I was dreaming if I weren't standing and lookin' into a mirror in my hotel room.

Still, I can't deny it. The image was right there in the mirror: me — in a tuxedo. I'm a simple kind of guy. I like meat and potatoes, vanilla ice cream, and have been known to watch a little NASCAR racing from time to time. I figured I'd have to wear a tux if I ever got married, but maybe not even then. I skipped the proms at school, so I never had a need to rent one of these monkey suits.

There was my image: all six-foot-three, 260 pounds of me — in a tux!

Someone pounded on my door. "Let's get a move on, Tank. The car and driver are waiting."

The professor. Dr. James McKinney is our leader although we never elected him. He makes many of the decisions because at sixty he's the oldest and because he is smart, educated, and domineering. He's a priest who lost faith and left the church. Now, instead of conducting Mass, he spends his time traveling the country proving that God doesn't exist, faith is a dream, and believers are fools. His words, not mine. Yep, despite all that stupidity, the guy is the smartest man I know. I like him.

"Do I have to kick the door in, Tank?"

I smiled. I'd kinda like to see him try. "Coming."

I turned from the mirror, glad to leave my image behind, and opened the door. He had his arms crossed, wore a tux similar to mine, and flashed his well-known frown at me. He was tall, with a full head of gray hair and eyes that seemed to look through people and things.

He studied me for a moment, relaxed, and lowered his arms to his side. The corners of his mouth ticked up a coupla notches.

"For a star football player, you clean up nicely."

"I was a good college player, but never a star. You know that, Professor." That was as true as sunshine in the morning. I played well in high school, and my first two years of college weren't too shabby. When I transferred to the University of Washington on a football scholarship, things changed. I had been playing for a junior college in Southern California and lovin' it, but playing for a major university with a well-known football team was an eye-opener. I was playing with and against people who made me look small. The hits were harder, the plays more complicated, the competition out of this world. I was a tiny fish in a great big pond.

Then I got hurt. A three-hundred-pound lineman did a dance step on my foot, and I was out for the season. To make things worse, our little team of do-gooders was traveling more, facing greater unknowns, and risking our lives. Somehow, football just didn't seem important anymore. I haven't touched a football since last December. People told me I'd miss it. Maybe I do a little, but I need to be here, with this team doing what, apparently, only we can.

"Do I have this on right?" I asked the professor.

"Your bowtie is loose. Turn around."

I did an about turn and felt the professor fiddlin' with the adjustable bowtie. It tightened.

"Can you still breathe?"

"Yes."

"Okay, so not tight enough then."

"Hey."

"Just kidding, Tank." He had me turn around again. "Perfect. You look like James Bond."

"I look like a penguin on steroids."

"Nonsense, son. Besides, people like penguins."

"Are you gonna be ridin' my case all night, Professor?"

"Most of the night, anyway. Come on. You're in for a surprise."

I hoped it was a good one. We've had our fill of bad surprises.

The Courtyard by Marriott was a cut above most hotels, but not fancy. The professor called it a business hotel, but I saw plenty of people who didn't look like executives. I didn't bother to point that out. I was just glad for a nice place to stay. In

378

the early days, we often had to rely on the professor to pay for airline tickets, food, and the like. These days, someone was taking care of such things. Don't ask who. I don't know. None of us do. Not yet.

We rode the elevator down three floors to the lobby. Seated on a sofa situated across from the desk was a young woman with vivid red hair. Andi normally let her hair hang whatever way it chose, but not tonight. She had spent part of the day at the hair salon, but to me there was nothing they could do to improve on perfection. I may have been wrong. Her hair had been pulled, woven, whatever they did in such shops, close to her head. She wore an evening dress of white and black stripes that were set on the diagonal. The dress left one shoulder bare. Not being an expert in such matters, I have no idea how a designer would describe it. I settled for "wow."

Andrea Goldstein (we just call her Andi) rose from the sofa and all the air left the room. She seldom wore makeup, but tonight she proved she had skills that went beyond computers and patterns.

She straightened the dress. "Do I look all right?"

She was looking at me. I cleared my throat and wondered if I should comment on the dress, her hair, her makeup, her beauty, so I said, "Um, wow!"

The professor chuckled, something he seldom does. "It's okay, Andi, I speak fluent Tank. He says you look gorgeous."

"Yeah, what he said." I've never been quick.

Andi smiled in a way that nearly melted my spine. "Mr. Bjorn Christensen cleans up pretty good, too."

"Hear that, Tank? She thinks you look like James Bond."

"I didn't say that, Professor." Andi's smile widened. "But you do, Tank."

I hoped for all I was worth that I wouldn't blush.

I blushed.

The professor's expression soured. "Where's Barnick? Do I have to go get her?"

"Of course not, old man."

The voice came from behind us. A very familiar voice. I turned and got another shock. Brenda Barnick looked like she had just stepped from a model's catwalk. Her dress was white on top and contrasted with her ebony skin. Gold lace something or another separated the floor length black dress. She too had spent time getting her hair done. She wore dreadlocks most of the time. Of course, she still had those, but

380

somehow the hairdresser worked some kinda magic. For a streetwise tattoo artist, she looked like a movie star.

"Give us a spin," Andi said.

Brenda did. It was a tad wobbly. "I hate these shoes. They make no sense."

"No worries, girl. You'll get the hang of heels. All you have to do is shut out the rest of the world and focus on your feet."

"That should make the evening fun for me," Brenda said.

A movement behind Brenda caught my attention. "That you, Daniel?"

No response.

"Come on, dude," I pressed. "I'm wearing one, too."

Daniel was the youngest member of our team. Just ten years old, and a year ago he was spending much of his time in a mental institution for children. Apparently telling people you have invisible friends is not a good idea. He has no parents. He was alone until he found us. Daniel has been a lifesaver several times.

Brenda has been declared his guardian. She introduces him to others as her son. They usually look at his white face, then at her black skin. When that happens, she narrows her eyes and says, "What?"

Brenda is tough. I think she could cower a

rhino just by staring at it. Despite her tough exterior, Brenda has a heart of gold. She is a natural mother, and she takes care of Daniel as if she gave birth to him.

I stepped to Daniel and held out my fist. He smiled and started our secret handshake. Fortunately, he chose the short one. The long one takes two full minutes.

"Now that we're done looking at ourselves, it's time to go." The professor pointed at the entry doors. A long black limo pulled up.

First a tuxedo. Now a limo. It all should be fun. I doubted it would be.

It never was.

CHAPTER 2
SQUARE PEGS

The limo was long and black and shiny. I'm a pickup guy, Chevy if you must know, but once inside the Ford I began to change my mind. Like I said, I'm a simple guy, but a man could get used to this. The car was a Ford Excursion that looked as if someone had spent a year or two stretching the thing. I counted the seats — fourteen people could fit inside. It looked expensive. It smelled expensive.

Our seat was a long, deeply padded bench that wrapped around the back of the vehicle and ran along one side of the passenger area. A simulated wood bar ran along the other side. Once we were in and comfy, the professor and Brenda wasted no time in helping themselves to the wine. There was even a soda for Daniel. Me, I passed. I've never been good with liquor. Something Brenda knows since I let myself get talked into drinking something I shouldn't. When

I came to, I learned my football friends had dumped me off in a tattoo parlor. That's where I first met Brenda and got my first and only tattoo. I wasn't conscious during the tattooing. I've stayed away from booze ever since.

I glanced at Daniel. He was in awe. He held his soda, but showed little interest in it. There was too much to see.

A small brochure awaited us, and I glanced through it. "Hey, Daniel, this car's got four televisions. Four, little dude."

His eyes widened. Daniel doesn't talk much. He's certainly capable of it, he just chooses not to. Much of the time he seems lost in a world only he can see, or playing a video game on his smartphone. I've even heard him talk to people who aren't there. No, that's not quite right. He talks to people the rest of us can't see. Don't get me wrong. The little guy is not nuts. His invisible friends have helped us a few times in the past.

The limo pulled from the hotel and onto the street. Our hotel was in a San Diego suburb called Kearny Mesa. Our destination was downtown proper. The professor told us to expect a twenty-minute drive, maybe longer. It was Friday night, and he had been told traffic could back up anywhere along the path. Since we were headed to a party, we didn't have to be there on the stroke of seven.

Night had settled like a thick blanket, so the professor turned on the overhead lights.

"Okay," he said. He spoke just above a whisper. "We have a few minutes for review. Andi?"

Andi Goldstein, still so pretty she hurt my eyes and my heart, shifted in her seat and pulled a set of folded papers from her purse — the kind of purse women call a clutch.

"We've gone over this before so I'm going to be quick. We're going to Krone & Associates. It's an architecture firm. That you know. I've spent part of the day gathering information. I had to do it at the salon, but I found what I needed. Gotta love smart-phones."

She passed one page to each of us. On the page were some photos and a brief history of Krone & Associates.

"Krone is our primary concern," the professor said. "At least that's what I glean from the little information our handlers give us." He pressed his lips into a line. "One of these days, we're gonna find out who they are."

"Focus, Dr. McKinney." Andi was one of the few people who talk to the professor that way. She had been his assistant for several years and traveled with him while he tried to convince the world there is no God, that religion is for fools, and that smart people know that. I don't know it. I'm a Christian myself, and I don't hide it. Naturally, I irritate the professor a good deal. There's some satisfaction in that.

"You tell, 'em, girl," Brenda said. She was the other one who spoke her mind to the professor. Andi had earned the right; Brenda just didn't care what the professor thought.

"Krone & Associates has been in existence for thirty years and is responsible for scores of large building projects. About twenty years ago, the firm broke into the high-rise design business by winning a contest for a skyscraper to be built in Houston. They won a couple of contracts after that and pretty soon businesses wanting a high-rise with their name on it came calling. Now, bear in mind, much of this comes from their website, so it may be filled with PR fluff."

"No doubt," the professor said.

Brenda found a small bowl of cheese and another of tiny crackers. "Snacks!"

That woman can eat and never gain weight.

Andi pressed on, snacks notwithstanding. "The president of the company is Allen

Krone, as you might guess. His wife is Janice. Those are the first two photos. Both are sixty years old."

"Ancient," Daniel said. Then he smiled. I only mention that because he does it so seldom.

"Watch it, young man." The professor straightened. "I happen to be sixty."

"Ancient," Daniel repeated.

Even the professor had to grin.

Andi cleared her throat. "If I may have everyone's attention including young Daniel and Old Man McKinney."

"Ohhh, nice one, girl," Brenda said. "That moniker could stick."

"It better not." McKinney didn't bother to look up from the page. It was as if he was vacuuming the information into his brain. The man never seemed to forget anything or anyone. Kinda scary.

"Like many architecture firms, at least from what I can tell from the websites I visited, Krone & Associates has other partners."

"Let me guess," Brenda said. "Krone & Associates has, well, associates."

"Nothing gets by you, Barnick," the prof said dryly.

"Straight up, Doc."

Andi sighed and plowed ahead. "The firm

has two associates. I think they're called 'principals' in the trade. The next photo on your page is Jonathan Waterridge. He's forty and been with the firm for the last decade. I couldn't find out what firm or firms he served once he left the University of Southern California School of Architecture. In fact, he's barely a blip on the Internet."

"The woman is his wife?" the professor asked.

"Yes. Her name is Helen. I imagine she'll be at the party tonight. I couldn't find out much about her, either."

The limo slowed on the freeway. The professor's source about San Diego traffic was right. We were surrounded by sedans, sports cars, a Humvee, and an eighteen-wheeler. Drivers and passengers stared at us. Now I know why limos have tinted windows.

"The third partner is Ebony Watt, age forty-five."

"A woman architect?" I said. A chill filled the limo. The professor stared. Andi and Brenda glared at me. "Don't get me wrong. I think that's great." The temperature dropped another five degrees. I sighed.

"She's black, too, Cowboy," Brenda said. "You wanna comment on that while you're at it?"

At least she called me Cowboy. That was her favorite term for me. I've heard her use stronger, less complimentary terms for people.

"I didn't mean that as it sounded. I just meant . . . How do I get out of this?"

"Tank, this is one of those times when silence is golden."

"Understood, Professor. I'm shutting up now."

"Ebony Watt came to the company from an architecture firm in Los Angeles. She graduated from UCLA with a degree in architecture and urban design. She also has a degree in interior design. I found out more about her than I did for Waterridge. She's been featured in *Architectural Record* and other industry magazines. Oh, and I found this interesting: her husband is Eddy Bruce Watt."

The last statement floated on a sea of silence. I started to ask who Eddy Bruce Watt is, but kept my promise of silence.

"Really?" Andi said. "Seriously? None of you know Eddy Bruce Watt? The blues player. You've heard of B. B. King, right?"

We all admitted to knowing King.

"Okay, Eddy has been described as a younger B. B. King."

"If you say so," Brenda said. "I've never

been a big blues fan."

The traffic began to move faster, and Andi took that as an excuse to move on. "The retirement party is a pretty big deal among some San Diego executives and politicos. Who knows, maybe the mayor will show up."

"What's *her* name?" I said. Another silence. "You see what I did there? Did ya?" I plastered on my biggest smile.

"Nice, Cowboy," Brenda said. "There may be hope for you yet."

"It feels good knowing that my friends would consent to be seen in public with me."

"Hang on, Cowboy. I didn't say that."

"To answer your question, Tank," Andi said, "I didn't look up the mayor's name. I'll do that if he or she shows up."

Andi began collecting the papers she had passed out a short time ago. "It wouldn't be good to take these in with us. It might look like we're a team of stalkers. Okay, last thing from me. This is more than a retirement party. Allen Krone is passing the torch to his partners. He will formally announce the new name of the firm: Krone, Waterridge, and Watt. As founder, his name stays on the letterhead, but the real business will be handled by others."

I made a mental note. Now, if only I could remember who was who and when to keep my mouth shut.

Downtown San Diego oozed with cars and pedestrians. Some of the streets were one-way. Taxis slithered through lines of traffic. Pedestrians crossed at intersections, some even waiting their turn, others, not so much. It seemed every corner had a nightclub, bar, restaurant, fast-food joint, or some combination of those. Friday night was a busy time in the big city.

I watched the people on the street. There were men and women wearing nice clothes — not tuxes and evening gowns, mind you. They seemed too bright for that. Others wore their best barhopping rags. Many women wore skirts. Some were tiny. Others were tight. Some were both.

Mixed in the group were a number of people with dirty, tattered clothing, uncombed and filthy hair, and carrying bags of what I assumed were all their worldly possessions. They moved through the streets paying no attention to the partiers; the partiers returned the favor. It was as if two worlds shared the same space and the people of one could not talk to the people of the other. There was sadness in seeing that. Didn't seem right to stare at the homeless from inside a limo.

The driver showed great skill driving through the obstacle course of cars and pedestrians. He turned each corner as if he were steering a Volkswagen instead of a limo the size of an oceangoing barge. I hoped the professor would give the guy a big tip.

A Plexiglas window separated the driver's area from the passenger compartment. I was beginning to wonder how we would know when we were getting near when a voice came over speakers hidden in the limo's ceiling.

"We're pulling up to the building now," the driver said. "Someone will get the door for you."

I was stunned. It was a woman's voice. I had assumed the driver was male. You can bet I kept that little assumption to myself. Of course the driver had opened the door for us at the hotel, but I paid him, I mean her, no mind. I was blinded by the limo. Pretty dumb, I know.

"Thank you, driver," the professor said. I had to admit, he was smooth. He acted like he was used to being carted around in a limo.

The vehicle slowed to a stop, but was still several feet from the curb. I guess one didn't parallel park a car like this. As soon as the wheels stopped rolling, the door opened.

A man in a doorman's uniform said, "Welcome to the Portal Bayfront Plaza. I hope you had a pleasant drive." He held the door while he stood to the side. That was the first thing I noticed. The second thing was the man's blue skin.

Yeah, that set me back a little, then I noticed the street and the sidewalk were also blue. When we exited the limo I learned why: our destination was a high-rise with a glass skin. All the glass was cobalt blue.

"Wow," Brenda said. She tilted her head back. "I'm impressed. How tall is this thing?" Brenda had no problem striking up conversations with strangers.

The doorman closed the door, and the limo slowly pulled away. "Technically, ma'am, it is a fifty-story structure."

"Technically?" Andi always wants details.

"Yes, ma'am. It is forty-eight stories above grade and two stories below. FAA regulations."

As he said "FAA" a commercial airliner flew overhead. The doorman smiled as if he had planned that. "San Diego International Airport isn't far from here. The Federal Aviation Administration limits all buildings in the flight path to five hundred feet or less."

"But fifty-stories sounds better than forty-eight. Is that it?" Brenda said.

"I couldn't say, ma'am." He nodded and offered a Hollywood smile. "This way, please."

He led. We followed. "You look good in blue, Tank," Andi said. "Hey Brenda, can you use your magic tattoo ink to turn Tank blue?"

"I'd be willing to experiment."

Apparently I wasn't out of the doghouse yet.

I glanced at the building. I was too close to see all the detail, but what I could see was amazing. The front of the building was glowing blue glass, but partway up was a different floor. A single story was dark green. It split the building with maybe one-third of the floors below the glowing green band and two-thirds above. At least the best I could tell.

The doorman opened the front door to the lobby. I say *front door,* but it was more than one door. There were several doors set in a wall of glass. Pretty sleek. I said he opened the door to the lobby, but he didn't really. He opened the door to a massive foyer. The building was tall with straight lines like a giant refrigerator box set on end, but there was more to it than that. The big part of the building was set back from the street with the entrance — an extension that was as curvy as the rest of the building was straight — protruding to nearly the edge of the sidewalk.

We walked into the wide glass foyer. I caught sight of the professor slipping some folding money to the doorman, who took it without hesitation.

The ceiling of the foyer was curved, as were its walls. It was like walking into a bubble. Pretty neat. As soon as the door closed behind us, the outside sounds disappeared, replaced by the soothing bubbling of a fountain directly ahead. A single spiraling shaft rose from the wide fountain eight feet or so in the air and spurted out a gentle flow of water that fell into the fountain's pool. The water was blue — I should say, it *appeared* blue. More lighting tricks. The spiral spout was jade green.

A set of wide steps waited in front of us. There were only three risers.

"Interesting," Andi said.

Of course, I had to ask. "What?"

"Look at the tiles on the floor. Maybe they're called pavers, whatever. There are fifty tiles across the lobby. They're all blue marble — probably fake marble — except for the green ones that form a line." She studied the floor for a few moments. We didn't bother her. This is what Andi does. She sees patterns in almost everything. Seeing patterns in the floor tile would surprise no one who knew her.

"Each tile is about a foot square. That means the foyer is fifty-feet wide. Fifty. Like the number of stories in the building. And the green tiles start in the thirteenth row and run up the steps —"

"Like the green band on the outside of the building," I said.

"Listen to you, Cowboy, going all Andi on us." Brenda seemed impressed.

I shrugged. "It's hard to miss."

"I saw that, too." Andi nodded. "I think the band would be the thirteenth floor. They carried the theme into the building."

"It's just consistency in design." The professor could be dismissive. "It's part of the theme."

"If you say so." Andi seemed a little miffed. "I'm just bringing it up."

We walked up the three rows of steps, past the fountain, and into a much wider and taller space. The real lobby. People wandered about, many of the men in the same kind of tuxedo straightjacket I was wearing.

"This place is amazing," I said. I was looking at the ceiling. Somehow, long glowing strips of light ran the width of the ceiling. This light was white and was the only illumination I saw. Curved blue couches were tucked here and there. The backs of the sofas were low and streamlined. The dark blue tile transitioned into rows of lighter blue until all the blue was gone and a few rows of white were left. Those ran in front of a wide desk like those in a fancy hotel. Several men and women stood behind the counter-high desk talking to guests. Behind the counter area were two tall structures that looked suspiciously like the building we were in. They even had the green stripe.

"You know, I once thought about being an architect." The professor seemed to be sucking in the sights. "I studied it for a bit, but then got derailed by seminary." He shook his head. "I should have stayed the course. I would have been of more use to society as an architect than I was as a priest."

When we first became a team — at the time we didn't know we were a team — I would have argued with him. Never did any good. Besides, this wasn't the place to start a conversation that would put him in a bad mood. He had been almost fun to be around this evening. Not something I could say most times.

"But if you did that, Professor, then you would have missed out on meeting me."

The professor glanced at Brenda. "I think you have that backward, Barnick. You would have had to miss me." He paused. "Either way, we both might have been better off."

And there it was. Dr. James McKinney had — just like old milk — turned sour. Brenda didn't respond, and for that I will forever be thankful.

Something else caught my eye. Spaced around the large lobby were glowing blue trees. Not real trees because trees don't usually glow. These were like sculptures — art. Each tree stood about five feet tall, had no leaves, and looked as if they were made of glass. As cool as the whole lobby was, those tree things were the coolest. If I were a thief, I'd have spent a little time trying to figure out how to sneak one of those babies out the front door. It would make a great nightlight for Daniel.

Daniel was looking at them, too.

"Pretty great, right, little dude?"

He didn't answer. Nothing new there. He did, however, look puzzled. Not afraid. Just confused. He's a smart kid, so I knew I didn't need to tell him they weren't real trees. Maybe he was trying to figure out how they worked. I would have told him. If I knew how they worked.

We followed the professor to the long curved desk where three people in dark suits stood.

"Dr. James McKinney and party." The professor had chosen one of the women to speak to. She had very blue eyes. So blue I suspected they were contact lenses. He reached into an inside pocket of his tuxedo coat and removed five invitations. They looked like tickets to a movie or something.

She smiled, took the invitations, and scanned them with one of those laser scanners you see in some stores. This scanner looked a little more high-tech. "Thank you, Dr. McKinney." She handed one invitation back to him.

"Ms. Barnick?" the receptionist said.

"Yo."

The professor cringed.

The blue-eyed woman handed an invitation to Brenda. "Please keep these with you at all times. They are part of the security system." She handed back the rest of the invitations. She hesitated when she saw Daniel, but only for a moment. I guess she wasn't expecting four adults to walk in with a kid.

Speaking of security — at each end of the check-in counter stood a man in a gray suit coat. Both were about my size, and each wore a security badge. The one on the right nodded at me. It was what one jock did when meeting another.

We were directed to the elevators at the back of the lobby and told to use the one on the right. It was one of six elevators.

As we approached the elevator, I asked why we had to take the one on the right.

"Most likely," the professor said, "the others don't open on the top floor."

Made sense to me.

Before we could press the Up button on the panel next to the elevator, the doors opened for us.

Andi stopped in her tracks. "It's like it sensed our presence."

"I think it did." The professor continued into the elevator cab. "I bet our invitations have RFID chips."

Brenda and I gave the professor a puzzled look.

"You wanna explain that, McKinney?"

I'm glad Brenda asked. Sometimes I get tired of being the one who doesn't know anything, although I know more than most people think.

"RFID. Radio Frequency Identification.

It's used for many things, including security badges. The elevator knows we are near and that we have the right invitations."

"Of course," Brenda said. "So they can track us."

"That's a little paranoid, Barnick." The professor paused as we stepped into the elevator cab. "But yes, they can."

CHAPTER 3
TOP FLOOR PARTY

The elevator was completely red inside. Like the building, like the fake trees in the lobby, the walls glowed. Since coming here I had been blue and now red.

"Odd," Andi said.

"Uh-oh, here it comes." Brenda and Andi got along pretty good, but no one was protected from Brenda's quips. "Whatcha got, Pattern Girl?"

"Again with the Pattern Girl, Brenda? Really?"

"Sorry."

She didn't sound sorry to me. "What is it, Andi?"

Andi pointed at the control panel. "There's no floor thirteen. Either someone can't count or they're a tad on the superstitious side."

The professor grunted. "Most likely the latter. It used to be customary to avoid the number thirteen in buildings. It's called triskaidekaphobia."

No one questioned the professor about the term, but that didn't stop him. "The word means fear of thirteen."

"Good to know," Brenda said. "I could be on *Jeopardy* someday."

The professor grunted his doubt. Sadly, he goes through more ups and downs than this elevator.

I looked at the panel. Andi was right: eleven, twelve, fourteen. "So there's no thirteenth floor?"

The professor sighed. "Think about it, Tank. Of course there's a thirteenth floor. It's just not *numbered* thirteen — that, or the floor is occupied by one of the companies that share ownership of the building and they have their own elevator."

"Why would they do that?" I had a good idea, but nothing puts the professor in a better mood than when he feels like he's enlightening us.

"To keep people from accidently going to the floor. Perhaps it's a government agency that doesn't want foot traffic —"

"Like spies and stuff?" Daniel asked.

The doctors could say what they want about Daniel's mental and emotional problems, but he didn't miss a trick.

"Could be, son. Could be. Or maybe

something a little more boring. Anyway, there are many reasons this elevator might not have a button for the thirteenth floor. For all we know, that floor could be used for all the equipment that keeps a building like this working. You wouldn't want people accidentally popping into a place like that. Especially in the age of terrorism."

"I still think it's weird." Brenda tugged at her evening gown. She looked great, but I was pretty sure this was the first time she had worn fancy duds like this. I didn't feel so alone.

"Zebras." The professor's one-word comment caught us all off guard.

"Zebras?" Brenda said. "You have a thing for zebras?"

Again the professor sighed. He was a master at it. He had taken the art of sighing to new heights. It had become a game with us: Can we get him to sigh in some new way?

"First thing doctors learn in med school is this: When you hear the sound of hoof-beats, think horses, not zebras."

I decided to take a stab at interpretation. "So, look for the common and not the unusual?"

"Spot on, Tank."

My first impulse was to remind everyone

that we had seen quite a few zebras since we were thrown together.

The elevator slowed and the doors parted to reveal a wide and open room. No walls. A person could see from one end of the building to the other. Windows surrounded us on three sides. Only the rear wall was solid. Blue light spilled in through the glass, but was much dimmer than what I had seen outside. Scores of people milled around the open space. The men wore tuxedos and the women wore evening dresses. We fit right in. Even little Daniel.

There were dozens of the glow-light trees we had seen in the lobby. In the center of the room was a wide and very long table that supported a couple dozen model buildings, including a mock-up of the one we were in. Some were much taller, apparently built out of the way of commercial airlines. I first noticed the model of the building we were in, then I noticed an odd, narrow, pyramid-like building. It didn't seem to fit with the others. It was dark, colored with black and browns. Kinda gave me the creeps.

Nearby stood several short partitions, all red like the insides of the elevator. Attached to those were a bunch of large photos. Even at a distance, I could see they were portraits of Allen Krone, the head of the architecture company.

"Welcome." The word came from a woman approaching from our left. Unlike the other women in the room, she wore . . . I guess you'd call it a waiter's uniform. "My name is Mable. I'm one of the greeters."

She didn't look like a Mable. She had straight black hair, bangs that hung to her perfect eyebrows, and the same kind of blue eyes the receptionist had.

"Good evening, Mable. I'm Dr. McKinney and these are my good friends Andrea Goldstein, Brenda Barnick, and Bjorn Christensen. And this little man is Daniel."

Daniel scooted closer to Brenda.

The runway model/greeter smiled. "I'm very glad to meet you, and I know Mr. Krone is pleased you responded to his invitation."

None of us mentioned the fact that we hadn't been invited by Mr. Krone.

Mable bent forward without bothering to bend her knees. Her face was pointed at Daniel, the rest of her was pointed — elsewhere. Andi and Brenda exchanged glances. I did the same with the professor. We chose not to speak.

"You look so handsome in that tuxedo, Daniel," Mable said. "I know there are a lot of adults around here, but that's okay. I made sure there was ice cream and cake for special guests like you. Just let me know when you're ready, and I'll make sure you get a big bowl." She straightened. "If that's all right?" She looked at each of us.

Brenda answered. "It's fine with me as long as I get some, too."

Mable's smile widened. "There's plenty. This is a party, after all." She motioned around the room. "Please feel free to explore. We have an exhibit of some of the more interesting buildings the firm has done and a portrait gallery of Mr. Krone through the years. There is a snack table on the east side with chocolate-covered strawberries, caviar, and many other delicacies. Next to it is a hosted bar. The wines are especially good.

"Exits are clearly marked, as are the restrooms. If you have any questions, you'll find other greeters and hostesses wandering the floor. We've all dressed alike so we will be easy to find."

A mild tone sounded behind us, and the elevator doors opened. In the short time we had been chatting, or rather, Mable had been chatting, the elevator had retrieved more guests.

I looked at the professor. He looked at

Andi. Andi looked at Brenda. Brenda looked at me.

"I'm startin' to feel a tad conspicuous just standing here," I said. "What do we do now?" I looked at the professor again. He shrugged. Some leader.

"Kinda makes you wish you knew why we're here, doesn't it?" Brenda said.

"We never know until we're in the thick of it." Andi spoke just above a whisper.

"That's the fun of it." Brenda pulled at her dress again. "I think this thing is trying to squeeze the life out of me."

"Think of it as a long-lasting hug." Andi said that with a grin.

"That's a creepy thought."

Brenda isn't the huggin' type. Except with Daniel. He's gotten his fair share of hugs from her, but then again, he's Daniel.

"Speaking of Daniel," I said.

Andi hiked an eyebrow. "We weren't talking about Daniel."

"I know; I was thinking," I said. "Never mind. Where is he?"

Brenda glanced to her side. He wasn't there. "He was just here." I heard the concern in her voice.

"He's okay. I mean, where could he have gone? Let's spread out. Andi you check the food area — maybe he went for the promised ice cream. Tank, you check the bathroom —"

"Excuse me."

The voice was deep, but a little weak. I turned. There was Daniel, standing three feet away holding the hand of a dapper gray-haired old gent.

"It seems this young man wants us to meet."

His words flowed easily, and I could hear some humor in them.

"Daniel!" Brenda cleared her throat. "What are you doing?" She made eye contact with the man. Daniel continued to hold on to the gentleman's hand. "I hope he wasn't a bother, sir."

Another smile. "Not at all. He has been every bit the gentleman."

Daniel smiled. Then the light in my brain went on. Daniel had just found the star of the party: Allen Krone. Well, at least one of us could make a decision.

Brenda was a leaf in a hurricane. "He . . . he just walked up and began talking to you?"

"Yes. Very friendly child." Krone extended his hand to Brenda. "I'm Allen Krone. Welcome to my retirement party."

Brenda shook his hand. "I'm embarrassed, I mean. Brenda. Brenda Barnick. I'm Daniel's guardian." It took another second for

Brenda to take her foot off the throttle of her brain. She made introductions, introducing the professor last. At least she did right by him, calling him "Dr. James Mc-Kinney."

"Doctor McKinney. MD?"

Daniel finally let go of Krone's hand.

"No, PhD" The professor shifted gears. "This is a lovely building. You must be very proud of it."

Krone's smile widened. "I am. Of course, I owe my partners a great deal of the credit. I confess to overseeing the aesthetics, but Jonathan and Ebony handled the interior and structural details." Then, as if an afterthought, said, "Jonathan Waterridge and Ebony Watt, the other principals in the firm."

Andi had already told us their names, so they weren't new to us.

He pointed to a small group near the center of the room. "That's them over there. With the mayor and his wife."

Jonathan Waterridge was tall, maybe six-two or so, thin, and had a fairly large nose. Not huge, but large enough to guarantee he took a ribbin' when he was a kid. The mayor was not tall, but he was stout. What he lacked in height he made up for in girth. His wife looked half his age and a third his width, and her platinum blond curls flashed in the glow of the trees.

A motion to my right caught my attention. Daniel had moved to Brenda's side and was pulling on her dress. She took his hand in self-defense. If my little buddy pulled any more, we might see more of Brenda than we had ever seen before.

"Excuse me. Daniel was promised some ice cream, and it seems he wants it right now."

"Certainly." Krone dipped his head as if bowing.

Brenda and Daniel moved to the refreshment area.

"You know," Krone began, "I'm having trouble remembering where we last met —"

The professor didn't let the man finish. No doubt he wanted to avoid the question Krone was going to ask. "I was just telling my friends that I had considered architecture as a career. I went another direction, but I still have a great interest in the art and the science you practice. I wonder if you would indulge me and tell me a little about the wonderful building models."

"Of course." Krone looked around the room as if looking for someone to save him from a task he had probably done a dozen times already this evening. He was stuck with the professor. The two moved away.

"That was slick," I said to Andi.

"The professor is nothing if not slick."

"What now?"

Andi shrugged. "That ice cream sounded good."

I agreed.

CHAPTER 4
FOGGY NIGHT

"How's the ice cream, buddy?" I looked at two chocolate scoops in Daniel's bowl. It was a real bowl, too, not one of those plastic things you see at most parties. Someone would be doin' a lot of dishes when this shindig was over.

"Good."

"Is that bowl for me?" I pretended to reach toward his little treasure.

"Nope. Get your own."

"That's my boy." Brenda held her own bowl of frozen chocolate goodness. "You tell 'em."

I grinned and patted Daniel on the head. "I like a man who stands up for himself."

"He gets it from me," Brenda said.

"No doubt." Andi moved to the counter, learned there was red velvet cake for the having, and asked for some. "I'm really starting to love this get-together." She took a bite of cake and closed her eyes. I assumed that meant she was in cake heaven.

When she opened her eyes, she asked Brenda, "How much of this stuff can we eat before our gowns come apart at the seams?"

"Only one way to find out."

I have known these two women long enough to know that neither would overeat. They talked a good game, but always quit early. Me, on the other hand . . .

"Sick."

It was Daniel. Brenda slipped the spoon from her mouth. "What is it, sweetie? Did you eat your ice cream too fast?" She reached for it, but had no more success at grabbing it than I had.

Daniel shook his head and scooped up another bite. Apparently whatever was ailing him hadn't affected his ability to down ice cream.

Brenda lowered herself so she could look Daniel straight in the face. "You said sick, kiddo. Are you sick?"

"No."

"Maybe he meant *sick* as in *good*," I offered. "You know, 'That car is sick!' Is that it, little buddy?"

This time he looked at me like my brains had just run out of my ears. "No."

Brenda took a deep breath. "You know, sweetheart, you can be real hard to follow sometimes. What did you mean when you said *sick*?"

He nodded across the room. That wasn't much help. There were several hundred people milling around. "Him. He's sick. Bad."

I still don't understand why Daniel does things like this. We know he sees what the rest of us can't. He sees beings from another world. I believe they're angels, and that ability has helped us many times. The problem was, Daniel did very little talkin' about what he saw. Sometimes Daniel would string several sentences together, and for him that was being a chatterbox. Other times he did what he was doing now: one or two words at a time. Frustrating enough to make a Baptist preacher swear.

"What man?" Brenda prompted.

Another frown from Daniel. At times he acted like the smartest person in the room, the kind of smart person that frustrated lesser brains.

He pointed with his spoon. I followed his point and saw the professor talking to Allen Krone by the models. Apparently, Krone hadn't been able to escape. My gut wadded up.

"The professor?" I meant my words to be more than a whisper, but that was all I

415

could muster.

"No. Him. Krone."

He pronounced Krone as "Croony."

I felt joy. I felt relief. Then I felt guilty.

"Allen Krone? The man we were talking to a few minutes ago?" Brenda was showing remarkable patience. She always did with Daniel. I sometimes think that's why she has so little patience with the rest of us. Daniel uses it all up.

Daniel nodded. "Bad sick." He walked away, bowl of ice cream in hand.

Brenda rose. "Maybe this is more than a retirement party."

"You mean like a going-away party?" Andi said. "A final going-away party?"

"Makes sense." Andi kept her eyes on Allen Krone. "You know, I thought I caught a yellow cast to his skin, but the lighting in this building is a little weird. Makes it hard to be certain about colors."

"That's sad." I meant it. I know we all check out of this life at some point, but knowing that doesn't make it easier.

"I have an idea," Andi said.

It must have been a good idea because she set her cake down and walked away. Brenda did the same with her bowl. I didn't have anything to set down, so I just followed Andi.

Twenty steps later we were standing in a small maze of five-foot-high partitions. They were covered with photos of Allen Krone through the years. Krone graduating architecture school; Krone at a drafting table with a drawing on the board; Krone at a computer, a floor plan on the monitor; Krone wearing a white hard hat standing in front of a large building under construction. There were wedding photos and pictures of him shaking hands with important people from around the world.

"Do you see it?" Andi asked.

"See what?" I guess that answered her question.

"Krone used to be a lot heavier." Andi kept moving from photo to photo. "Not fat. He looks fit in the pictures."

"He's not young, you know." Brenda leaned close to one of the displays.

"He's just sixty, Brenda," Andi said. "The same age as Dr. McKinney."

I recalled Daniel's little joke about the professor being ancient.

Andi nodded. "I think Daniel is right. Then again, he's always right. Cryptic, but always right."

"Ah, I found you." The professor walked over. "Remarkable man, that Krone. His ability to see in three dimensions and translate those ideas to a set of two-dimensional plans is amazing. Did you know . . ." He looked at our stricken faces. "What?"

"Krone is sick," Brenda said. "Maybe terminal."

"Who told you that?" The professor had put on his I'm-ready-to-burst-your-bubble face.

"Daniel." The three answered in unison.

"Daniel is not a doctor. How can he know if Krone is sick?"

We stared at him.

He raised his hand and aimed his palm at us. "Okay, okay, that was stupid of me. Did he have anything else to say?"

Andi answered. "No. He just said that Krone was sick and then said it was bad. Look at the photos. He looks very different in his pictures, even the ones dated from just a year ago."

The professor, being the professor, did just that. He studied the photos like Sherlock Holmes studying a crime scene.

Finally, he looked at us. There was a good deal of sadness in his eyes. "Maybe cancer. Maybe a degenerative muscular disorder. Maybe . . . no sense guessing. It doesn't change anything." He sighed. "I thought there was a sadness about him. He knows that his retirement will be short —"

There was a rumble. It came through the floor. It spread to the windows. There were screams and shouts.

The lights flickered, then went out.

The building swayed. It moved so much I expected the skyscraper to break in half. I seized Andi by the arm to steady her and did the same to Brenda. The professor went down on his keister. The partitions around began to dance and slide on their chrome feet.

"Daniel!" Brenda's shout wasn't loud enough to defeat the noise of the rattling building.

"Wait!" I held her tight. "Wait!"

Thirty seconds later, the shaking stopped. Emergency lights filled the open space with dim light. The decorative blue light we had first seen when we arrived was gone.

"Andi, check on the professor." I let her go. "Come on, Brenda."

We emerged from the partition maze into the open area. People littered the floor. Most were struggling to their feet. I heard the word "earthquake" a dozen times. I scanned the fallen crowd. Maybe I should have been concerned about injuries, but at the moment I could only think of Daniel.

"Let's split up. I'll go —"

"I see him." Brenda pointed. "By the window."

There he was, still on his feet, or maybe he had just gotten up. It didn't matter. We raced closer to him, stepping around, and on a few occasions stepping over people on the floor.

Daniel was inches from the window, his bowl of ice cream on the floor next to him. Chocolate was spattered on the carpet, window, and Daniel's pant leg. If that window had shattered during the earthquake — I still can't think about it. What I could think about was an aftershock.

Daniel gazed out the window.

Then he began to scream like a siren.

I charged forward, hoping no one got in my way.

No one did.

I scooped Daniel up and hugged him tight. I barely glanced out the window, but even that set my teeth on edge. I ignored what I thought I saw and, at a slower pace, moved away from the glass wall. I hadn't made it more than six feet when Brenda reached me.

"Let me have him."

"In a sec. Let's get someplace safer."

She started to argue, but saw the wisdom in waiting a few moments. We walked around people, most of whom were now on their feet. Some of the women were crying. Some of the men were swearing. To be fair, a good number of women were swearing, too.

I found an empty spot and released Daniel to Brenda. She was on the verge of tears. If you knew Brenda the way I do, and if you've faced danger with her the way I have, then that statement would surprise you. She took Daniel in her arms as if she would never let go.

"Hey, buddy." I began to look him over, best I could. "That was kinda scary, huh?" I kept my voice calm. He had stopped screaming, but he hadn't stopped staring at the window. "Are you hurt? Did you fall during the earthquake?"

He shook his head.

"You sure. No bruises. No ouches?"

When I said "ouches" he looked at me like I had lost my mind. Sometimes I think that ten-year-old is older than me.

"Is he okay?" The professor joined us. Andi was with him.

"I think so," I said. "I can't find anything wrong, but he got a good scare."

"We all got a good scare." The professor moved closer to Daniel. I noticed he limped.

"Are you hurt, Professor?"

He waved me off. "I bruised a butt cheek."

Then I heard the sweetest sound I've ever heard. In the middle of all the confusion, I heard Daniel giggle.

"Butt cheek." He giggled again. The sound of it was better than music. "He said 'butt cheek.' "

Andi stepped to Brenda. The two bickered constantly, but at this moment, all voices were quiet. Andi wrapped her arms around Brenda and Daniel. Where Brenda was holding back tears, Andi let them flow.

The professor and I helped people to their feet and checked on injuries. There was nothing serious, although the professor wasn't alone with his butt cheek injury.

Then I heard a man's voice: strong, loud, and filled with terror-laced obscenities. I've spent a lot of time on a football field so I've heard everything, but never in such rapid order.

I saw the man near the window.

He was staring out and down.

He vomited.

Chapter 5
Somethin' Ain't Right

The man's outburst quieted the crowd for a few moments. No one approached. I can't blame them. For a few moments there was a hush. I glanced at my friends. All the excitement and my fear for Daniel's safety had forced the glimpse I had out the window from my brain. Now it was trying to worm its way forward.

"Tank, where are you going?" Andi sounded terrified. That just meant she was like the rest of us.

"Stay here."

"Tank?"

"Stay here — please."

I worked my way through guests. It was like pushing through a forest of small trees. I lost sight of the man at the window, but reacquired him a few steps later. He had turned. His mouth moved as if he expected words to come out, but apparently he had run dry. The smell of the vomit filled the air. The stain of it clung to the front of his tux.

Unable to speak, he pointed out the window. Out and down.

"Take it easy, sir." I tried to sound calm and in control. I never was a very good actor. "Maybe you should step away from the window."

"L-l-l . . ."

"Easy, buddy. We'll get through this. We just gotta stay calm and focused. We all need each other now." I kept a slow pace toward him.

"L-lo-lo . . ."

I smiled and motioned for him to walk toward me. He turned his back to the window, then to me. "Look!"

I did, and my mind started to overheat. Now *I* felt like vomiting, but I'm pretty sure that a dozen other people with sensitive stomachs might follow my lead. So I kept my last meal.

And I gazed out and down.

Out and down almost fifty floors to the street below, except I couldn't see the street. Instead, I saw a fog. There was no way for me to be accurate about my guess, but the fog looked to cap out at just about five feet above the street. I came to that conclusion because hundreds of people had spilled from surrounding buildings and into the streets. I don't know how good an idea that is after an earthquake, but I didn't have any better ideas.

The fog was everywhere. I couldn't see cars, just the heads of a few people and the noggin tops of a few shorter people.

Then I saw why the man had cursed. I realized what made him empty his stomach. Somethin' was moving in the fog, and it wasn't even close to being human.

What people I could see were running in different directions. They seemed to be running in slow motion. I caught sight of one man — I knew he was tall because I could see his shoulders. He wore some kinda baseball cap. He was doing his best to run up the street. As he ran he looked over his shoulder. I don't know what he was seeing, but it had him scared. Really scared.

Ten steps into his sprint something broke the surface like a shark in the ocean. I couldn't see it clearly. Fifty floors is something like five or six hundred feet. What I was looking at didn't seem large, but I had a feeling it was deadly.

It was.

The thing moved through the fog with ease. It seemed to be swimming. Ridiculous, I know, but I've become used to seeing and believing the ridiculous.

I do know one thing: what I was seeing wasn't human. People say there ain't no such thing as monsters, but tell that to a seal being chased by a killer whale. Monster is in the eye of the beholder, and I was seeing something monstrous.

And it wasn't alone. Another breached the surface of the fog, then another. Before I could draw a deep breath, they caught the tall man with the cap. He went down, replaced by a mist of red.

My knees threatened to betray me. I rested a hand on the glass, bent forward, and wished for amnesia. "Dear God. My dear Jesus." I'm the religious one of our group, so those words were prayer. If not for them I might have used the same language as my vomit-tinged friend.

Inhale. Exhale. Inhale. Slowly. Slowly. Exhale. I forced my heart to slow. I resisted the urge to scream. I was determined not to lose control. I couldn't let others see that. Most of all, I couldn't let Daniel see it.

I straightened. "Professor. I need to show you something."

"We're coming."

"No! Just you." I turned. "Leave the girls behind." My voice came out an octave higher.

"But Tank —" Andi began.

"I said no!"

That was a first. I had never snapped at Andi, or any of the others. Odd what watching people die could do to a man.

The professor looked shocked. "Tank, what is it?"

I couldn't put enough syllables together to make words so I nodded to the window. The professor annoys me a great deal, but once you get past his arrogance, he's an okay guy. I hated doing this to him.

"I'm not going to like this, am I?"

"No, sir. I'm sorry."

He exhaled noisily. I couldn't help noticing the unblinking eyes fixed on us. No one spoke. No one moved. It was group-wide paralysis. Wives hung onto husbands, dates hung onto each other. All of them were looking at us. Better they look at us than what was on the street.

The professor, always calm, always logical, always with a straight back and packing lots of extra superiority, forced himself to gaze into the darkness lit only by moonlight.

He stood as rigid as a goalpost. His breathing slowed. His back bent. His hands shook. He sniffed like a person about to burst into tears.

Then came a whisper. "Those poor souls.

Horrid."

I slipped to his side and watched the carnage below. I saw another man go down and the red smear rise where he had been. Then a woman. Then several young women, best I could tell, then — dear God — a parent with a child on his shoulders.

Both —

I closed my eyes. After everything I had seen. After the dangers we have faced as a team. After all the impossible weirdness, this terrified me more.

"Steady on, lad," the professor whispered. "Everyone here is taking their lead from us. We lose it, they lose it. Understand?"

"Yep. I know. I was going to say the same thing."

The professor nodded. "You might have to remind me."

A familiar voice came from my left. Allen Krone was there. "Not to worry, gentlemen. This building is designed to withstand earthquakes. It has the latest features. We're safe here. However, it might be good if you backed away from —"

His gaze shifted from us to the street.

I caught him before he hit the floor.

In two beats of my heart, two others joined us. One was an African-American woman with salt-and-pepper hair cut so close to her scalp she was an eighth of an inch from bald. Her features were sharp. To tell the truth, she was stunning. I recognized Ebony Watt from the pictures Andi showed us in the limo.

The second person was Jonathan Waterridge, Krone's other partner. He approached quickly but calmly. He didn't strike me as a man prone to panic. A good quality right now. Waterridge took Krone's other arm. "What is it, Allen?"

"I'm fine, Jon. Just . . . um . . ." He pointed at the window.

"Can you stand?" Waterridge looked Krone up and down like a doctor with X-ray eyes.

Krone nodded. "I'm okay now." His voice sounded stronger.

Waterridge slowly released Krone's other arm and, seeing that his partner wasn't going to do a header, moved to the window. Both looked out, then down. Neither reacted.

"The fog?" Waterridge asked.

I answered for him. "Yes."

Waterridge and Watt exchanged glances, then turned their attention back to us.

"I don't get it," Watt said. I detected a slight accent in her voice. "It's just fog."

I caught the professor staring at me. He

went to the window for another look. I was happy to stay where I was and serve as Krone's prop.

Waterridge stepped back to Krone. "I thought maybe there was damage from the earthquake, bodies in the street, fires, something, but all I see is fog."

Krone spoke in hushed tones. "There are things in the fog. I saw them. Creatures."

"Creatures?" Waterridge looked at me. "We need to get Mr. Krone a chair. He needs to rest."

I recognized the tone. I hear it each time I'm forced to tell someone what our team deals with: disbelief. "I saw them, too. So did the professor."

The professor said nothing. He kept his gaze glued to the sights below.

"Tell them, Dr. McKinney. They'll believe you."

The professor turned. "Tank. The fog is rising."

Not what I wanted to hear.

Ebony Watt and Janice Krone, who seemed to appear from nowhere, helped me get Krone to a chair. Waterridge decided the guests needed a little encouragement.

"Ladies and gentlemen," he said, "thank you for your calm and courageous response.

It's been quite an evening. First, let me assure you, you are in a safe place. This building not only meets the most rigid earthquake standards, it exceeds them. You are safe here."

"But we should leave, right?" some woman in the crowd said.

"No, not yet. As you can tell, we're on emergency power. Buildings this size have only one elevator that can operate on emergency power. I will check to see if the generator is working or if the earthquake knocked it offline. Our best way out will be the stairwells, but I suggest we wait for a bit. There will probably be an aftershock soon, and you're less likely to get hurt here than trying to walk down nearly fifty floors. Most likely, the power will be back on soon and the elevators will be online."

"You're sure we're safe here?" This time it was a man's voice, a frightened man's voice. "I felt the building sway."

"Absolutely." Waterridge tucked his hands into his pants pockets like a man without a care in the world. "Not many people know this, but architects and structural engineers design tall buildings to sway. If they didn't sway in strong wind or earthquakes, they would experience much more damage. I know it may have felt like more, but the sway was only a couple of feet in each direction. So, swaying is good — even if it feels otherwise.

"That being said, I suggest we stay calm. Help yourself to the food and drink. Not too much on the alcohol, just in case we all have to walk down the stairs. It would be bad form to survive an earthquake then break a toe on the exit stairs." That brought a few chuckles.

"For now," Waterridge continued, "I ask that you stay away from the windows. I'm being overcautious, I know, but humor me."

The guy was smooth, I had to give him that.

I left Allen Krone in the care of his wife and worked my way to my friends. Brenda still held Daniel. I'm pretty sure it would take a crowbar to loosen her grip. Daniel seemed fine with that.

"What's going on?" Andi kept her voice low. "What did that guy see out there? What did you see? Daniel said something about sharks. Sharks? Really?"

The professor raised a hand. "Easy, Andi. One question at a time."

"Sorry. I'm a little shook. And I don't mean by the earthquake. That didn't help."

I stepped next to her and put my arm

around her shoulder. She was trembling.

"Not sharks," the professor said. "Worse." He tried to describe what we saw, toning down the gruesome details, probably for Daniel's benefit.

"So this is why we're here?" Andi looked around. "It must be."

"Where'd they come from?" Brenda almost sounded like her old self. No doubt, she would be telling each of us where to get off soon. I looked forward to that.

"I don't know," the professor said.

"I don't want to know," I said. "I just want them to go back where they came from."

"How are we gonna do that?" Brenda said. "If I heard right, we ain't going down there and start exchanging punches with those things."

"I have no idea," the professor said. "I'm open to creative thoughts."

No one had any.

The building began to shake again.

CHAPTER 6
A RISING FOG

The guests had clumped into small groups. Loud laughter had been replaced with mumbles and occasional nervous chuckles. Some ate. Some paced. Some stood around looking lost. For the first half hour nearly everyone pulled out their smartphones and pressed them into service, except there was no service. No phone calls. No texts. No e-mail. No Internet. I'll admit it; I did the same thing as did the professor, Andi, and Brenda.

Mr. Waterridge returned and told everyone that he had used a landline to reach fire and rescue. "They suggest we wait here. Apparently it's a little confusing at ground level."

A little confusing? After what I had seen of the murderous things in the fog, it was no problem believing there might be a bit of confusion. The horrible sights returned, and my fear elevated a good bit. I felt just as sick now as when I first saw the monstrosities mowing down people in the street.

A thin woman stepped forward. "Our cell phones still don't work. Can we use the landline to call our families? They'll be worried, and we're worried about them."

Waterridge's face showed great compassion and understanding. It also tipped me off to the answer.

"I wish you could. I understand the problem, but I'm afraid the phone line went dead just before I finished the call. I'm sure it will be up in no time. The best thing for us to do now is be patient. I'm sure we'll all be headed home soon."

I wasn't so sure. From the professor's expression, he wasn't convinced, either. The girls didn't have to say anything for me to know they were carrying a load of doubt. We had seen too much in the past to know that all this would blow over if we just sat tight. At least Brenda had set Daniel down. He is a bit big to be held like a toddler.

While Waterridge continued to talk, the professor motioned with his head for me to follow him. I did, but I didn't like where he was leading me. He made for the windows. Really? I had to look down there again? I kept my fears to myself. I'm supposed to be the macho guy of the group, but my machismo was paper-thin.

"What do you see, Tank?"

Now you know why I call him the professor. Okay, he was a professor, that's the big reason, but if you hang with the guy you soon learn that he loves to teach and test. He always has an opinion and wants to make sure we know he's the one with the brains.

"I see fog. It's what I don't see that scares me. Those things below the top surface of the fog."

"I know what you mean." He shuddered. I don't think I've ever seen him shudder. "That, however, is not what I'm getting at. Look again."

Something the professor said to me came back. It had been a stab in the heart the first time, but I was focused on holding up Mr. Krone. "The fog is rising, just like you said."

"It's rising fast."

Since I couldn't see the street below, the best I could do is guess at how much the stuff had risen. When I first looked out the window, I could see the heads of pedestrians. Sometimes it was just the top of their heads, but with taller people I could see all the way to their shoulders. I couldn't see that now. Of course, for all I knew, the fog-monsters might have eaten all the people below. Now I could see nothing but the churning fog. No trucks. No busses. No tall vehicles at all.

"I can't be sure," I said, "but I'm guessin' the fog is up to the fourth or fifth floor."

"That's my estimation, too."

As we watched, several of the creatures broke the surface, their heads swiveling from side to side. Then they looked up.

"They're looking at us, Professor."

"Maybe. I doubt they can see us."

They began to move in a circle, like sharks. The sight of that poured ice water down my spine. Despite the professor's doubt, I felt sure those things were sizing us up. A few moments later, the creatures disappeared below the surface again.

The professor turned, and I followed him away from the windows and the unwanted view they provided. We had moved only a few steps when I saw Mr. Krone motioning for us to come to where he was seated. His wife, Janice, stood by his side. I didn't have to be a mind reader to know how frightened she was.

When we reached him, I dropped to a knee to better look him in the eyes. There was still a keen intelligence there. If Daniel was right — what am I saying, Daniel is always right. The kid said Krone was sick. It wasn't obvious. I doubt most people in the room knew. That's probably how Krone wanted it.

I gave a little smile to our host. "How you doin', Mr. Krone?"

"Call me Allen."

"Only if you call me Tank."

He gave me a small smile. "I'm fine, Tank."

I looked at Janice. It's been my experience that spouses are more truthful about the health of their partners. She cocked her head. I took that to mean she wasn't in full agreement.

Krone rose from the chair. I was on my feet a second later. "You should rest."

"Nonsense. I don't want my guests to worry unduly." He stretched his back and wobbled an inch or two. It took a lot of willpower for me not to seize his arm. He steadied.

"What did you see?" He asked quietly. "Just now, I mean."

We didn't answer at first.

"I saw you at the window. I'm pretty good at reading body language. Unless I miss my guess, you saw something that made you . . . uncomfortable."

Uncomfortable. That was an understatement. Still, we said nothing.

"Okay, gentlemen. I saw those things, too. In fact, I keep seeing it in my head, so I'm not going to be shocked by talk of monsters and whatever that fog is. You're in my building. You owe me the honor of the truth."

The professor pressed his lips into a line and looked at Janice.

"My wife can take it. Information is better than ignorance. Now tell me what you saw."

"The fog is rising, sir. Before, we could see almost to street level. The fog was maybe five feet above ground. I make it to be up to about the fourth floor now."

"And it's still rising?"

"Yes." The professor shifted his weight. "I would have to observe it over time to guess at the rate of its climb, but it is significant."

Krone nodded, then lowered his head like a man deep in thought. "Fog can get pretty high, and I doubt this is ordinary fog. Creatures can swim in the stuff. That's not normal."

"I need to ask a question if I may, sir." The professor kept his eyes on the man.

"Ask it."

"The stairwells — could the fog get into them?"

Krone nodded. "Stairwells are not airtight. There needs to be an exchange of air, so yes, fog could seep in at the base of the exit doors at street level."

"What about the floors below ground?"

"Yes. We have to assume that if the fog was at street level, and we know it was, that it could have poured into the parking floors below the building."

"That means the parking floors could be teeming with those things." I thought it worth mentioning.

"Yes," Krone said, "but we're asking the wrong question. The question isn't whether or not the *fog* can get in, but whether or not the *creatures* can get in."

"I think they need the fog." The professor put his hands behind his back, striking a relaxed pose I know he didn't feel. "The few times I've seen the creatures stick their heads above the fog, they soon submerged again. If submerged is the right word."

"Works for me," I said.

"The fog is like water is to fish."

I could see the professor's point. "So what happens if the fog rises to the floor we're on?"

"They still have to get in. They can't fit under the door." Krone spoke without conviction.

"No, they can't, but they have hands. Hands with claws. At least the best I can tell." This time it was the professor who lowered his head in thought. "Mr. Krone — Allen — no one knows more about this building than you and your partners. Is there any way those things can get into the building?"

Krone shook his head, then stopped abruptly as if a thought had slammed into him. "I'm just thinking aloud here. Let's assume they can go wherever the fog goes. The higher the fog, the higher they can move. That would have to be true on the inside of the building, too." He fell silent. "If I were them, I'd open the doors to the stairwells, but I'd find a way to open the doors to the elevators in the parking structure. Fog would pour in. If the cab is there, they could tear out the ceiling. The fog would climb the shaft at the same rate it's climbing outside the building."

I wasn't enjoying this conversation. A motion to my left grabbed my attention. It was Andi. She had Daniel with her. She stepped forward and smiled at Krone. "Excuse me. May I steal my two friends away for a little while?"

The professor didn't appreciate the interruption. He hated interruptions. "Andi, we're in the middle of a conversation."

She gave him a look that said, *Shut up and*

come with me. That's what I got out of it. Apparently, the professor got the same message. We put some distance between us and anyone else.

"This better be good, Andi. We're in a life-and-death situation here."

"Ya think?" She closed her eyes and took a deep breath. "There's something you need to see."

"If you mean outside —"

"I don't," she snapped. "Follow me."

Andi is a nice person. I think the world of her. She has skills no one else has, so when I hear anger in her voice, I get confused. Then I get afraid. She started for the back of the cavernous room.

"Where are we going?" the professor asked. At least he wasn't resisting anymore.

"The ladies' restroom."

"Well, of course." The professor cut his eyes my way. I chose to remain silent.

The restrooms were along the back wall — the only wall without windows. We stopped a few feet from the door to the restroom. A similar door nearby was marked for men.

"Brenda went missing while you two were taking in the sights. She left Daniel with me. She had that odd look she gets sometimes. When she didn't return, I got worried, so I went searching. I found her in the restroom."

"She's been known to use bathrooms before."

The professor thought he was being cute, but Andi disagreed. "Once, just for once, old man, stop trying to prove what a jerk you can be."

"Old man?"

"Ancient," Daniel said.

If carnivorous creatures swimming in a fog hadn't already put me on the razor's edge, Andi's behavior would have done it. Andi had been the professor's assistant for a good long time, and no one knew him better. She normally showed great respect. Something had pushed Andi beyond her normal behavior.

The professor opened his mouth, then closed it. I was thankful for that.

"As I was saying. She disappeared. I went looking. I found her in here. She's been at it again."

Andi turned and plowed into the ladies' restroom, holding the door open for us. Daniel walked in with her. I hesitated. I mean, it was the girl's bathroom, after all. Andi stared at me, narrowed her eyes, and tapped a foot. I walked in, the professor right behind me.

This was awkward. I have to admit that I've never been in the ladies' room. Never had need to be.

Its size surprised me. Two emergency lights blazed from opposite corners. The light was harsh, but needed.

Andi led us past a set of stalls, then stopped. There was Brenda. Sitting on the tile floor staring at the white tile on the wall. She had hiked up her evening gown enough to allow her to sit on the floor. It wasn't a good look for her.

As I said earlier, Brenda is a tattoo artist. And I mean a real artist. We all have our "sometimes" gifts. Andi sees and sorts patterns like a computer; the professor denies any special skills, but he does some pretty special thinking; I heal people — sometimes, it's very hit and miss. I don't know why. Yes, I've been thinking about having a go at healing Mr. Krone, but I've had monsters on the mind.

Brenda draws things. When the urge comes over her, she has to put the images in her brain on paper, or if she's doing a tattoo, ink it into someone's skin. That has led to some interesting conversations.

The thing with Brenda's spontaneous drawings is that they usually don't make sense until later, but she's never wrong.

Never.

Which is why her sketch terrified me. Using a Magic Marker, she had drawn a spot-on image of the creatures showing detail we couldn't see from our position. She also sketched several human figures, all half eaten. It was sickening, but not as sickening as the third image.

"Oh, Tank." The professor made the connection.

The third image stung just to look at it. It was me. On the floor of some building. My chest had been ripped open and my eyes were gone. Three of the creatures squatted around me — feasting on my organs.

I no longer cared that I was in the ladies' room.

Brenda began to weep. Brenda never weeps.

Chapter 7
A Room with a Terrifying View

I sat on the floor next to Brenda and gently took the Magic Marker from her hand. She didn't resist. Brenda is as hard as nails. I know that's a cliché, but the words could be chiseled on her tombstone. She doesn't talk about her childhood, but I know enough to wonder how she turned out as wonderful as she is. She grew up street-smart and with fierceness that could cower a charging rhino. She's also, despite all her talk and threats, a deep, loving soul.

I may just be a college-age kid, but I know a little about people. Someone as heartbroken as Brenda didn't need words of comfort. She needed an arm around her shoulder, and I had a big arm that could do the job, so I used it.

Daniel moved close and sat on the other side of Brenda. He scooted close enough that his little shoulder touched her arm. He said nothing.

No one said anything.

The professor, who could ruin any moment, lowered himself to the floor next to me. A moment later, Andi did the same next to Daniel. There we were, five silent, shaken, confused, and frightened friends sitting on the floor of the ladies' bathroom doing our best not to look at Brenda's wall art.

A few minutes later, I took another look. There I was, dead and being devoured. I wished Brenda had not been such a good artist. Based on her earlier success, it looked like I was going to die and die badly.

Then the building shook again.

Ten minutes or so later, we walked from the bathroom — a line of two men, two women, and a boy. In any other circumstance, people would have thought it strange. If they did now, they didn't say so. The crowd had separated into small clumps of people. Some stood as couples; others in small gatherings of four or so.

I spied the mayor in the middle of the room trying for all he was worth to get his cell phone to work. Those with him did the same. That made sense. He was the mayor of a major city after all — a city that had experienced a powerful earthquake and several bone-rattling aftershocks. Oh, and a city that had been invaded by killer creatures that swam through fog, a fog that was rising every minute.

I also couldn't help noticing that more and more people had gathered around the bar. That didn't seem very wise. The professor noticed it, too.

"Fools. Don't they know they need to keep their wits sharp at a time like this?"

"They're scared out of their minds." Andi had her eyes fixed on those knocking back hard liquor.

"That's no excuse, Andi. If they get themselves drunk, they will become a danger to others and themselves." The professor spotted Ebony Watt and her husband. "I'm gonna have a word with her. Maybe she can close the bar down."

I let that be his problem. I turned to Andi and Brenda, "I'm gonna check on the fog."

"I'll stay with Brenda and Daniel." Andi placed a hand on Brenda's shoulder. To Brenda's credit, she was recovering nicely, all things considered.

I hadn't been at the window a full minute when the professor joined me. "Ms. Watt is shutting the bar down. I like her. Strong in the face of adversity."

"That's what I admire about you and the

rest of the team."

"You know, Tank, Brenda isn't always right."

"Name a time when she wasn't."

He looked out the window. "She does a lot of drawing and tattoo work. Not all of those were predictions."

"I appreciate what you're doing, Professor. I really do, but you know there's a difference. You saw her. When was the last time you saw Brenda that emotional?"

"Tank —"

"It's okay, Professor. You know about my faith. You were a Catholic priest; you know what Christians of all denominations believe about death. I'm not afraid to die. Death is just a promotion."

I waited for his usual chatter about faith being a myth and how he gave it all up to embrace reason and logic. It never came. I guess there was enough priest left in him to know not to belittle a dying man's faith.

Still, he squirmed. I let him off the hook. "The fog is rising faster. I figure it's halfway up the building. I can see the fog creatures more clearly now. Can't say I like it any."

"We have to figure something out, Tank. We can't let all these people die. We can't let those things win."

"You got that right, old man." It was

Brenda, and she sounded like herself again. Andi stood next to her.

The professor closed his eyes and sighed. "I'm not an old man, Barnick."

"Ancient." Daniel was by her side. This time he didn't lose control, but I could tell he'd rather be someplace else. I understood the feeling.

The professor eyed the boy and tried to look angry, but the smile on his face defused the act. "Should he be here?"

"It was his idea, Professor." A second later she added. "And by the way — thanks."

Andi fidgeted. "I feel useless."

"Feelings are useless, Andi. You know that. We have to approach this with logic."

"Shut up, McKinney," Brenda snapped. Man, it was good to have her back.

Andi continued as if the exchange hadn't happened. "I can't make sense of things. I'm looking for patterns, things out of the ordinary."

"That's pretty far from ordinary." Brenda pointed out the window at the creature-infested fog.

"I'm going to the roof," I said.

"Why?" the professor asked.

"To see more. To get a better idea how fast the fog is climbing. I can lean over the edge and see how high the fog is. We might

450

be dealing with other factors."

There was a moment of silence, which the professor broke. "Who are you and what have you done with Tank?"

"Yeah, what he said." Brenda's tone had returned to normal.

Andi wasn't going to be outdone. "I'm going with you and don't tell me no. You don't have the authority."

The professor cleared his throat. "Me, too. We also need to see if the fog is rising in the stairwell."

I thought that was a good idea.

We crossed paths with Allen Krone, who was looking slightly less pale. I asked if the stairwell went all the way to the roof. He said it did. I then mentioned our plan. Turns out, that was a bad idea. He insisted on going. I told him that it wasn't advisable. Janice, his wife, agreed with me. The professor backed me up. So did Andi. Four against one. I figured that would end the matter, but Krone countered with, "It's my building." No need to go into what other words he used to spice up that statement. Bottom line, he was going with us.

We approached the stairwell individually hoping not to alert the crowd that we were stepping out for a few minutes. We gathered near the door and chatted for a few moments, then slipped from the room.

The space was dim, lit from above by emergency lights. I could see light glowing down the stairs, too. I wanted to see if the fog had come up the stairs, but decided we should go to the roof first.

We moved up the stairs slowly, but it was still a tad too fast for Krone. I tried to talk him into going back. He had no interest in that and said so. We were four people climbing steps to who knows what. Still, it felt good to be doing something more than standing around.

Krone stopped to rest a coupla times, but only for a few moments. Each time, I stood beside him and put an arm around his shoulders. Partly to comfort him; mostly in hopes that my healing gift, sporadic as it is, might kick in.

Nothing. I'm thankful to God for the handful of people that I've healed (a small handful at that), but I get frustrated with it. What good is it to have a healing gift if you can't use it when you need to? I've had these thoughts before, and when I do I comfort myself with the knowledge that Brenda's gift is on-again, off-again. Same is true for Andi. Her mind is always sharp and seeing things the rest of us don't, but she doesn't see patterns in everything every day.

Still, her ability seems to be there when she needs it.

Fortunately, we started on the top floor, so the roof was only one full flight of stairs away. When we reached the upper landing, I saw a metal door that bore a plastic sign telling us this was the roof access. FOR USE IN EMERGENCIES ONLY.

I think our situation qualified.

The night air was cool, but I couldn't detect even a hint of a breeze. We propped the door open to make sure it couldn't lock behind us. We were probably being paranoid, but paranoia was understandable today.

I looked around. The roof was flat and covered with something that looked like black rubber flooring. Concrete paths led in several directions. One led to roof-mounted machinery, another to what looked like small rooms, and one to the edge of the building. The same kind of concrete walk ran the perimeter of the building. I assumed the walkways were there to keep maintenance people from walking on the rubber-like surface. Krone confirmed my suspicions. He then pointed out a few details.

"The walkway runs around the edge of the building. It's there for the window cleaners." He pointed to a short wall at the edge of the building. "There are anchors to support davits — small crane-like devices — along the parapet. The crews place the davits where they need them. It allows them to swing a window cleaner's platform over the edge of the building."

He pointed to some large mechanical equipment. "Much of the HVAC equipment is up here. Those small buildings you see are elevator equipment rooms."

"You mean like pulleys and stuff?" I asked.

"Yes, and more. This building is too tall to use hydraulic elevators, so we use an electric system. The cars are pulled up and lowered on cables."

It was all interesting and a great way to stall, but the time had come to do what we came for. I moved to the edge of the building until I was standing next to the wall Krone had called a parapet.

The light up here came from emergency lights and a veiled moon. I could see more stars than I expected in the downtown area of a major city. With the city lights out, there was almost no light pollution.

Fog reached as far as I could see in the dark city. I remembered the people on the streets we had seen from the limo: the partiers, showgoers, business people, and homeless. I tried not to think how many were now dead or how they died.

The professor groaned at the sight of the teeming fog. I leaned over the parapet and studied it. Now and again, one of those things would poke its head up, and each time the sight of its ugly face turned my stomach. Maggots looked better.

"I can barely see the green band," Andi said. "The fog must be higher than the thirteenth floor."

Krone nodded. "I'd estimate the fog is up to the twenty-fifth floor."

"So halfway, then." It seemed higher to me.

"More than halfway, Tank," the professor said. "Remember, only forty-eight floors are above the ground."

"That doesn't make me feel any better."

As we watched, the fog rose another few feet. It was definitely growing faster, bringing death with it.

"I'm gonna take a lap." I walked next to the parapet, my gaze shifting from the fog below to darkness everywhere else. As I walked west I noticed I couldn't see the waters of the bay. Even the ocean wore a blanket of fog. I'll confess, I was losing heart, which is sad, since I'm supposed to be the optimist of the group.

I followed the concrete path around the

edge of the building. I could hear the others behind me. They spoke on occasion, but barely above a whisper. They were as stunned as I was.

Behind the building was a gap. Another building, dark as a tomb stood on the other side of the gap. The fog was as high here as it was at the front of the building. Why wouldn't it be? It was fog.

"Alley," Krone said. "There's a narrow alley behind the building. If memory serves, it's about twenty feet wide."

Good to know, but useless. I had hoped there was a back way out, a place without the fog. It was a ridiculous hope, but then this whole thing was ridiculous.

We made our way back to where we started. "We're stuck," I said. I studied the fog more intently. A creature popped its grotesque head up and stared at me. Then it pointed at me. It's probably my imagination, but for a moment I thought it smiled.

Andi gasped. I snapped my head around and saw her staring across the street at the building opposite the one we were on. It was tall like Krone's building, but three or four stories shorter. It looked fairly new. Like many buildings in San Diego, it looked made of glass.

The lights had gone on. Not emergency

lights. All the lights in it. I looked at other buildings. All dark. I leaned over the parapet and looked down the side of our structure. Still dark, except for the green band.

"What's going on —" Then I saw. Dear Lord, I didn't want to see. The lights inside the building illuminated everything, but all I could see was fog. Fog inside the building. And in the fog, people running, and un-people swimming — attacking. Blood painted the windows.

I couldn't watch.

"Did you see?" The professor said.

"We all saw, Professor. Horrible."

Andi covered her mouth. "I'm going to be sick."

"I meant the fog. The fog inside the building. It's at a higher level than the fog outside. That means . . ."

He didn't finish and I was glad. We knew what it meant.

The lights across the street flickered then winked out. We couldn't see inside. That was the only blessing of the moment.

Then we heard a scream. No, not a scream — several screams. I sprinted to the stairwell. The professor was close behind.

CHAPTER 8
SCREAMS FROM A STAIRWELL

I pounded down the stairs and rounded the middle landing. There were too many things to see. My brain quivered. First I noticed a half-dozen people standing on the landing by the door to the floor we had been on most of the night. It looked like they were cons making a prison break. My guess was they saw the slaughter across the street and panicked.

Then I saw several more people standing on the first flight of stairs going down. They stopped in midstep, no doubt frozen by the screams of those who had gone before.

I saw one other thing: Brenda, sitting half on the landing, half on the first step down. Daniel was in her arms. He was shaking.

"Back into the room!" My voice echoed in the stairwell.

Those on the platform turned and stared at me. I descended the remaining steps. No one had moved. "I said, get back in the room."

One guy, a six-footer in his thirties, sneered at me. He should see what linemen do. "Who do you think you are to give orders?" He poked me in the chest with his index finger. At the moment I wasn't sure if he was brave or stupid. It didn't matter. I had to put an end to the panic, and I could only think of one thing to do, so I did it.

I seized the front of his dress shirt, just above his fancy vest, pulled forward and, when he tried to resist my pull, pushed back and up, pinning him against the doorjamb.

"Okay, mister. Here's the deal. You're scared. I'm scared. The difference is I'm younger, stronger, and twice your size. Am I getting through to you?"

He nodded.

"Good. I'm trying to help." I lifted him another two inches. "So don't get in my way. We good?"

"Y-yes."

I dropped him and took a deep breath.

"Everyone, please go in the room. Right now it's the safest place to be. There's nothing but death down these stairs."

One by one they filed back into the room until only Brenda and Daniel were left. I squatted next to them. "You okay?"

"They went nuts. They saw the lights go on in the building across the street. They cheered and moved to the windows. Then the slaughter began. They lost it, Cowboy. I mean they went bug nuts and made a run for the stairwell." She grimaced. "Daniel tried to stop them, but they knocked him down. I had to get him to safety, but they kept pushing toward the door. We got carried along. I was afraid they were gonna trample us. If you hadn't —"

"That part is over," I said. "Are you hurt?"

"My leg is banged up. Kneecap. I think it's broken."

"Let me have a look." The professor inched by me onto the stair just below Brenda. Brenda didn't object. They bicker a lot, but I have no doubt either would lay down their life for the other.

"It hurts here?" He pressed the area just below her kneecap. Her yelp was enough of an answer. He studied the leg a little longer, pressed a few more spaces, but stopped when Brenda smacked him on the shoulder. "Her arm is working."

"So is my fist," she snarled.

The professor looked at me. "She's right. I think the patella is broken. That's a guess of course." He looked behind him and down the stairwell. He let his eyes linger. "I'd feel safer inside with the others. Not much, but a little."

I lifted Daniel from Brenda's embrace. "Hey, dude. Are you okay?"

"Yes."

"No injuries, broken bones, bruises, missing limbs?"

He smiled. "No."

"I think you may have saved a bunch of lives. Go with Andi, buddy. I'm gonna give this mean ol' woman a hand up."

"Hey," Brenda said. "You heard me tell the professor that my fists are still working."

That's the Brenda I admire so much.

"Help me up," she said.

"Nope." Instead, I scooped her up in my arms. She cringed and swore — something she's really good at. She wrapped her arms around my neck, and I carried her into the room.

The expansive room was close to silent. Something was different. I found the professor, Andi, and Daniel standing near the door, which closed behind me.

"There are less people here," I said to whoever was listening. "How many made it down the stairs?"

Brenda said, "I don't know. Ten, maybe."

"That doesn't make sense. There's more than ten missing."

"Cowboy . . ." Brenda looked me in the eye, her voice soft, but soaked with sadness. "There's more than one emergency staircase."

"Blessed Jesus." I closed my eyes. "Why did I go to the roof?"

Andi laid a hand on my arm. "Because this is what we do, Tank. This is our calling. To do our best to fix things. Besides, you can't save everyone."

Nice words, but not cool enough to extinguish the fire of guilt in my gut.

I waited for the professor to huff as he usually did when any of us talked that way. The huff never came.

Brenda stiffened for a moment and then stared at her injured leg. "Cowboy, put me down."

"Let me carry you to a chair."

"Put me down now."

I lowered Brenda until her feet could reach the floor. She wiggled from my arms and stood on both legs. She bent the one with the busted patella.

"I'm not sure that's wise."

"Shut up, Cowboy." She tested her leg by bending it as much as her dress would allow. Then she pressed the area just as the professor had.

"No pain." She straightened. "It's like

nothing happened." She shot forward and hugged me. Then stepped back. "If you tell anyone I just did that, I'll deny it."

"You mean —"

"Yep. You healed me."

I shook my head. "Someday I'll get that figured out."

"I'm missing something," Andi said. The professor and I were pacing the room with her. Andi does some of her best thinking on her feet. "I'm missing something. I'm missing something."

Yes, she was being redundant, but telling her that wouldn't help anything. Then she stopped suddenly. I grabbed the professor's elbow. He was lost in his own thoughts.

"What?" I asked Andi.

"Nothing. Probably nothing. Maybe nothing. I need to see Krone." We gathered up the professor and went looking for the architect.

We found him at the bar drinking coffee. His wife was by his side. He looked worse than before we went on the roof. Janice looked even more concerned.

"Mr. Krone, may we have a moment?" Andi asked.

"You know, the only satisfaction I have at the moment is this: when one of those creatures bites into me, he's gonna get a mouthful of chemicals."

I didn't expect that. "I don't understand, sir," I said.

"Cancer. I know you've been wondering. I've got only a few months to live. Given the circumstances, I may be robbed of those."

"I'm sorry to hear that, sir." I was. Now I really felt bad about my erratic gift of healing. "But this isn't over yet, Mr. Krone."

"Are you sure?" He studied his coffee as if he could read the future in it. "I don't see any way out of this. I know what I saw. I don't believe it, but I know it's real. Does that make sense?"

Andi answered. "Believe it or not, sir, that makes perfect sense. If you knew us better, you'd know why." She manufactured a grin. He didn't look up, so he missed Andi's brave face.

"Can I join the party?" Brenda and Daniel had been standing a short distance away. She had been testing her newly healed leg. I didn't know how to feel. I was happy for Brenda but felt a truckload of guilt about Krone.

Krone looked at her, then at Daniel. He stretched forward a thin hand and patted Daniel on the head. Daniel, who didn't warm to strangers easily, allowed it.

"You know, I've created mansions, hospitals, and high-rises around the world. I've used my mind and skills to create important buildings, but one creation has eluded me." He looked at his wife. "A child. We weren't able to have children."

Tears glistened in Janice's eyes. I could see the depth of their pain.

"No children. No grandchildren." He turned back to his coffee.

I've met depressed people before. The professor has been known to live in the dark from time to time, but I don't think I've ever watched someone sink deeper and deeper into depression. It was like watching a man drown.

"Mr. Krone," Andi said, "I hurt for you. I know your pain is great, but I need your help."

"There's nothing I can do for you. Nothing I can do for my wife. Nothing I can do for anyone here." Janice touched his arm, but kept silent.

"Mr. Krone, I want to — no, I need to ask a few questions. Will you help me?"

Krone sighed and straightened as if getting ready to exert himself. "What do you want to know?"

Andi took a deep breath. "When I was on

the roof, I looked over the edge like everyone with us, and like everyone, my attention was fixed on those ugly things swimming in the fog, and the . . . what happened in the other building. Now it occurs to me that I saw something else. A green glow below the fog."

"The horizontal element." Krone picked up on the fact that we had no idea what he was talking about. "It's part of the exterior design, like the arched entryway. The bulk of the building is blocky; those elements break up the stark lines of the building. In architecture we call it gingerbread — stuff added to the building's exterior to make it pleasing to the eye, to make it noticeable and memorable. It's also part of the interior design."

"So the green band is exterior glass like the rest of the façade?"

"Yes. It projects from the plane of the front by one foot to create a pleasing shadow line."

I didn't know what a shadow line was, but I didn't interrupt.

Andi nodded then cocked her head to the side. If we weren't all going to be monster chow, I would have considered it cute. Her head snapped up. "It's on the same electrical system as the rest of the building?"

"Of course," Krone said.

"They why did I see a green glow?"

Krone shrugged. "Emergency lights."

"Forgive me, Mr. Krone, but there are emergency lights on this floor and every floor. I don't think they would make the fog glow the same way the . . . what did you call it? Gingerbread? Horizontal element?"

"Maybe you just imagined it," Krone said.

"She didn't," the professor said. "I've known her for a long time. If she said she saw it, then she saw it."

"I saw it, too," I piped up. "When I was on the roof."

"I have another question," Andi said. "That green band is at the thirteenth floor?"

"Yes, but —"

"I'm not being superstitious, Mr. Krone. On our way up the elevator, I noticed that there was no button for the thirteenth floor. Is that to make visitors more comfortable?"

"No. Not at all. I know there have been those who label the thirteenth floor as fourteen, but we've never done that. People aren't that superstitious anymore."

"Then why is there no access from the elevator?"

"The space isn't rentable. Much of the building's heating, cooling, electrical, and similar systems are on that floor. Of course, some of it has to be roof-mounted, but we've found a way to make utilities more efficient if placed in the lower third of the building. Well, Jonathan Waterridge made all that work. I specialize in design; he specializes in mechanical matters in buildings. The man is brilliant in that area. Far more than I. Just like Ebony Watt excels in interior design."

Andi pressed on. "The name of the building is Portal Bayfront Plaza. Why that name?"

"Marketing, mostly." Krone said. "Buildings need to sound attractive, as well as look beautiful. We're close to the bay, so *Bayfront.* The bay is a port, so *portal.*"

That made sense to me. It didn't make sense to Andi. "If that's the case, Mr. Krone, then the name should be Port Bayfront Plaza — not Portal."

Krone stared at her a minute. So did I. I wasn't following her logic. Lucky for me, Andi jumped right into an explanation:

"A port is a city where ships dock. A portal is a large gateway."

"And gateways lead from one place to another." The professor looked ill.

We thought on Andi's comment for a moment, then Brenda asked, "Has anyone seen Waterridge lately?"

CHAPTER 9
DESPERATE TIMES REQUIRE DESPERATE ACTS

Brenda's question was a good one. I hadn't seen Waterridge since much earlier that evening. Turns out no one had. Of course, we had had other things to think about. Janice Krone slipped away and asked some of the firm's employees and Ebony Watt if they had seen the third partner. Nothing doing there, either.

A sick thought came to me. "Do you suppose he was one of those who went down one of the stairwells?"

Apparently I wasn't the first to think that. Allen Krone was the most doubtful. "He never seemed the kind of man to panic. If anything, he would try to keep people from panicking."

"I don't like to be disagreeable," the professor said. Brenda, Andi, and I almost gave ourselves whiplash looking at him. He frowned at us. "I'm a pretty good judge of character, and something seemed off about the man."

Brenda started to address the "pretty good judge of character" comment, but I shook my head. No doubt she was thinking of the same instances when the professor's keen mind missed the boat on character assessment. For once she took a hint from me. Probably because her fortune-telling wall art said I was going to be grub for those fog-swimmers.

"What makes you say that?" Andi asked.

"It's a gut feeling."

"Well, that's logical." One can keep Brenda quiet for only so long.

He didn't snap back, which ended the theologian's debate about miracles happening in the contemporary world.

"The brain is always picking up information and details. If we know how to use our brain" — here he paused to make eye contact with Brenda — "we can find clues we first missed."

I positioned myself to block Brenda should she decide to go for the professor's throat.

"I saw him."

The voice made me blink. It was Daniel, and he was looking up at the tall adults (we often think of him as the little adult).

"When?" I asked.

He shrugged. Daniel wasn't good with

time. "When you were on the roof."

"So that's where you went, you sneaky little rascal."

"Did I do a bad thing?" he asked Brenda.

The first part of Brenda's answer was the sadness on her face; the second part was a grin; the third part had words. "Nah, actually, I'm kinda proud."

"What was he doing, buddy?" My gut told me this was important. The professor mostly listened to his brain; I tended to eavesdrop on my gut.

"Standing over there." Daniel pointed across the room to the westernmost corner. "He was looking at the fog. They were looking at him."

Daniel was opening up. He did that sometimes. Usually when we need his help. Otherwise it was one-word answers and video games.

"They were looking at him?" I had seen that look, and it scared the wits out of me. "How do you know the fog-things were looking at Mr. Waterridge?"

"I walked over there. I already said I saw him."

"Yes, you did, pal. My bad." I waited a half-second before firing another. "You went over to him?"

Daniel nodded. "I looked at what he was

looking at. The monsters were swimming in a circle looking at him."

"Looking at him." It wasn't a question. It was me echoing what Daniel said.

"I think they like him." Daniel inched closer to Brenda.

"Yeah, just like I like baloney sandwiches," Krone said.

"No. Not like — that. Like a dog."

Brenda, who spoke better Daniel than any of us took that one. "Like a dog? You mean like a dog looks at his owner."

"Uh-huh."

"My brain hurts." I looked at Andi. "Do your thing, girl. Pull it all together. Patternize what we know."

"Patternize?" The professor said. "Is that a word?"

"Not now, Professor. I'll choose a better word later." Back to Andi. "You know what I mean. What is the pattern? How does all this connect? I need to hear it."

Andi closed her eyes. "Okay. New building. Midrise. Fifty floors, but two are below ground. FAA limits height. Major earthquake. Weird fog rolls in. Aftershocks. Monsters swimming in the fog. Impossible — scratch that. It doesn't matter if it's impossible, it's being done." She sucked in a lungful of air. "Fog is rising. Fog is inside the building. It will be here soon. No thirteenth floor — no floor labeled thirteen. No common access to the floor. Mechanical space. Waterridge responsible for that part of the design. Building's name: Portal Bayfront Plaza. Portal, not Port. Portal means gateway — gate. The Gate."

Andi's eyes went wide with shock, and the professor groaned. We had fought The Gate at every turn and come close to death every time. We know so little about them, but they have a plan for this world, and it ain't good. To make things worse, there are people in this world helping them, maybe even guiding them. We believe some of them are part of a parallel universe, one that is close to ours, but different. The professor says some physicists believe such places exist.

"I don't follow," Krone said.

"It's a long story, and a little too weird to believe," the professor said.

"I'm a dying man in a building I designed, surrounded by an impossible fog with killer creatures in it. Do you think you can tell me something I can't believe?"

"You might be surprised." The professor looked at us. We nodded.

As the professor launched into the tale of our adventures, I wandered the floor, trying to sort out what was rattling in my head.

Something had to be done, but what? We couldn't go down the stairs or the elevator. That was certain death, and we had plenty of proof of that.

I did a few more slow laps around the big room and came to a conclusion. I had an idea. An idea I hated.

The walk back to my friends seemed like a hike through five feet of snow. I was chilled to the marrow. I had been walking around the perimeter of the room doing my best not to look out the window. My best wasn't good enough. I checked the rising fog repeatedly, and it was climbing the building faster than I thought possible. It was just two or three floors below us. Pure. White. Soft. Deadly fog. Fog populated by big-headed, big-mouthed creatures with sharp teeth and claws, and a very real appetite for people.

I returned to my friends. No one had left. Allen Krone looked more stunned than before, but that was understandable, if the professor had let him in on the group we called The Gate. They had tried to do us in before. Worse, they had been trying to do in the world.

"Feel better after your little walk?" Brenda asked.

"No." It took a second or two to work up

the courage to make my next statement. "I have an idea. I don't like it, and you're not going to like it, either."

The moment I finished the sentence I felt something new. It came through the floor, into my feet, and up my legs. This time it wasn't an earthquake.

"What's that?" Andi looked on the verge of panic — and Andi doesn't panic.

The vibration increased, and with it a noise that could be felt more than heard. There was no way we could stand this much longer. I'm no architect, but judging by the look on Krone's face, the building might not make it.

I put my big hands on Andi's little shoulders and looked deep in her eyes. I had to raise my voice. "Andi, you left one thing out of your summary. You forgot something."

She shook her head. "I didn't forget, Tank. None of us did. I just couldn't say it."

I hugged her for a long moment. It was the only thing that had felt right all day. Letting her go was the hardest thing I had done in a long time. Perhaps more difficult than what I was about to do.

"I'm going to do this," I said. "I don't want to hear objections or anyone saying, 'But, Tank.' We just don't have time." I turned my attention to Krone. "Mr. Krone, you know the mayor, right?"

"Yes."

"Are you friends?"

"Yes. For years."

Good. "So he trusts you."

"I believe so."

Good again. "I need you to ask him for a favor."

CHAPTER 10
ONE GIANT STEP FOR HUMANKIND

I had been right. No one liked the plan, and even though I told them I wouldn't listen to objections, they objected, anyway. Fortunately, I'm big enough to keep anyone from standing in my way.

There were hugs all around, and then they dispersed to do what I asked. In less than ten minutes we were on the roof — not just my friends, but everyone. No one wanted to stay in a room that was vibrating like the inside of a bass drum.

I watched as the mayor's bodyguards managed to open the rooftop storage room I had seen on my last trip to the roof. Several of the men in the group pitched in, too.

It didn't take long to set up the window-cleaning equipment. The building's davit supports were big enough to hold a window-washer's basket, the kind that hold two men.

We wouldn't be needing the basket thing.

I slipped into the safety harness the workers wore when they cleaned the windows. We had to let out the belts as much as possible, and it was still a tight fit. I would just have to live with the pinching. Or, if we understood Brenda's drawing, die with the pinching.

The creatures below noticed us working near the edge of the building and had worked themselves into a frenzy. I kept hoping they'd turn on each other. No such luck. Apparently they liked the flavor of human more.

"I've rechecked my calculations." Krone stood beside me looking at the davit and the safety line we attached to it. "The length should be right."

"Should be?" I needed a little more optimism.

"Sorry." It looked like he tried to smile, but his lips misfired. He only managed to look scared out of his wits. I didn't want to know how I looked. "Speech patterns are difficult to break. Architects learn to speak with caution. Did you know that malpractice insurance for architects is more expensive than that for doctors?"

"Are you stalling, Mr. Krone?"

"Yes, yes I am." This time his smile worked just fine.

One of the mayor's bodyguards moved closer. "Are you sure about this?"

"Not at all," I said. "I'm doing it anyway."

"I spent ten years in the Marine Corps and have seen many acts of bravery," the bodyguard said. "This one takes the cake."

"I don't feel brave." It was an honest admission.

"Bravery is defined by what you do, not what you feel." He shook my hand then pulled a Glock 9mm handgun from beneath his tux coat. "The mayor said you wanted one of these."

"Thanks."

"You know how to use it?"

I pulled the slide, putting a round in the chamber. "I have an uncle who is a sheriff. Any visit to his place would sooner or later end up on the shooting range." I didn't tell him I'm not big on guns.

"You know there are more of those creatures than there are bullets in that piece."

"The gun isn't for them." I let that hang in the air. There was too much talk, and I was losing my nerve.

The professor laid a hand on my shoulder. In his other hand he held a fire axe — the kind with a blade on one side and a point on the other. It had been in a cabinet near the stairwell.

"Tank —" The professor choked, cleared his throat then tried again. "Tank, I've been rough on you, but I want you to know —"

"Stop, Professor. I don't want the girls to see me get all emotional and stuff." I took the axe.

He patted my shoulder and walked away.

I was done talking. Every minute that passed brought the fog closer. Every minute that passed took a little of my spine with it.

No more waiting. I closed my eyes and took several deep breaths. I tightened the muscles in my left arm, then my right; I did the same for each leg. More deep breathing. It was the way I got ready for a football game. It was the only thing I knew to do.

I stepped on the parapet, careful of my balance. I needed to leave the roof in a particular way. Falling wasn't the way.

I glanced back at my friends and saw tears in their eyes. I looked down at the pale demons in the fog, then I turned my eyes to heaven. "Father, this is stupid, but it is the only thing I know to do. Help me do it."

I crouched, then leaned forward. With all the strength I could muster I sprang into the nothing, screaming all the way. The moment I exchanged the solid roof for the air, I twisted so my back was to the fog.

The sky overhead disappeared in a blanket

of white. That didn't matter, I was looking for green.

Something zipped by but missed — almost missed. It scratched my arm. In the few seconds of free fall, I saw dozens of the creatures. They swooped at me, but missed me each time. They would have had better luck catching a falling meteor.

Green.

I raised my gun. My trajectory had changed. I was no longer falling. Instead, I was swinging right into the building. I extended the Glock in my left hand and fired, and fired, and fired. The sound was much louder than any gun I had ever heard. The creatures diving at me disappeared as if the noise hurt them. Fine with me.

I continued to fire. I had been told the weapon had ten rounds. I tested that by firing until the gun went silent. I released it.

Allen Krone told me the glass skin was made of a type of tempered glass. Very durable. Very strong, but not bulletproof. The glass would shatter into small cubes.

He was correct.

My momentum swung me through the spot where one of the green windows had been. The next part was going to be tricky. Somehow I had to stop my swing once I sailed through the window area. That's what the axe was for.

The lights on the floor were in full force. All green, but in full force. Outside, the fog, which was now inside, was white. Here it was a moss-green gas.

When I felt my direction change, my shoes were one or two feet above the floor. I rocked forward and drove the pointed end of the axe into the floor. Krone told me the floors in the building were made of something called lightweight concrete — concrete with air blown in it to make it less dense and heavy. It was a good thing it wasn't ordinary concrete. I doubt my axe would have made much of an impression. As it was, I could only drive the end of the axe about an inch into the surface.

It was enough. I stopped my wild swing. I let go of the handle and a swung back a couple more feet, just enough for my feet to set down.

No sooner than I had touched down, I began to unclip the safety line. I had to try three times before I could unleash myself. The harness swung back through the shattered window and into a swarm of fog-swimmers. They attacked it.

I yanked the fire axe free and turned to face the things that wanted me for tonight's dinner. I steeled myself for the onslaught. I had the advantage of speed when I leapt from the building and the sudden change of direction when I reached the end of my safety line. That was then. Now, I was standing flatfooted in dress shoes and a tux — hardly fighting clothes. The floor, the walls, the machinery all buzzed and vibrated, just like the vibration we felt right before I committed to this mission.

The charging, swirling swarm of creatures didn't come. They stayed outside the building, swimming past the area of the shattered window. They didn't come in. They just stared at me like I was the ugly one, a fish in a tank.

I would like to have sat and pondered what kept them outside, but I didn't think I had the time. They might change their minds — if they have minds.

That's when it occurred to me: I was breathing the fog, and it felt like any other fog I'd been in. I'm not sure what I expected; I was just glad to be breathing. I backed away from the window and tried to make sense of my surroundings. This was supposed to be an equipment floor, and sure enough, there was equipment. There were large metal structures that were a mystery to me. Big cylindrical tanks like giant propane tanks. They were a mystery to me. Overhead were conduits, pipes, ducts and, yep, more things that were a mystery to me.

What I was looking for had to be different. I didn't know how. A sudden fear, a new fear gripped me — what if I couldn't find the . . . whatever it was I was looking for? What if it was disguised to look like a refrigerator or somethin' else familiar?

No, it had to be obvious. If we were right, if Andi and I had linked everything together, then somewhere on this floor The Gate had set up a portal to their world. I don't think you can hide something like that.

I moved slowly around the floor, not certain what I was looking for, but certain I'd recognize it. Every few steps I looked behind me, fully expecting to see one of the blood-splattered faces of those critters. Brenda's drawing stuck in my mind.

I studied the ceiling again and this time I noticed that the green light was not uniform. It was brighter farther back, to the left. I made that my destination.

My steps were slow, and I peeked around every machine, fearing what I might see, then I saw a movement near the western-most wall.

A figure.

A man.

A man in a red robe.

There was something familiar about the robe. I had seen something similar before.

The figure stood at a console of some kind. To his right was an opening the size of a garage door. The opening was sealed with green glass. As I drew closer, I could see one fog-swimmer after another falling through a green mist. I corrected myself. Not falling. *Swimming* down to someplace lower. Maybe the underground parking floors.

The vibration increased. The noise was deafening, which is probably why the man in the robe hadn't heard the window shatter.

He spun suddenly, looked at me, and reached for something inside the robe. It was Waterridge, and he had a gun.

He raised it.

I threw the axe in his direction. I wasn't trying to hit him. I was trying to hit the control panel and maybe buy enough time for me to move closer.

He dove to the side and covered his head. There was the time I needed. The axe hit the control panel and bounced off. No damage to the panel. No damage to the axe.

Waterridge had dropped his weapon. Apparently seeing a firefighter's axe flying at his head had broken his concentration. It had skittered several feet beyond his reach. He began a desperate crawl for it. I got there before he did, grabbed the gun, and stuck it in my waistband. I needed both hands for what I had to do next.

I retrieved the axe and studied the panel for a moment. Metal conduit and hollow aluminum pipes ran from the panel up the wall and into the ceiling. I laid into them with the axe.

"No!" Waterridge struggled to his feet.

Sparks flew. The vibration stopped. And the portal with its streams of creepy things and fog went empty. A few creatures that had been swimming down the fog-filled channel dropped like stones.

The vibration stopped, too. I was glad for that. For a moment.

Waterridge struggled to his feet. "You've killed us."

"Sorry, pal, but the way I see it, I kept you from killing thousands of other people."

"You're a fool!"

"Sticks and stones." That's when I noticed it. There was a screech. Just one at first. Then another. Then several.

"How did you get in here?" Waterridge stepped closer and I wondered if I was going to have to deck the guy.

"Through the window. It was recommended that I not take the stairs. I think you know why."

"We're doomed."

Another screech.

Waterridge was just a decibel two or so shy of screaming. "They'll get in. The sound, the vibration, is what kept them from this floor."

Uh-oh. "Why aren't they here?"

"They're not smart. They don't reason. They don't discuss things and make conjectures, you idiot. They are purely reactive. They're sharks in bloody water. It will only take seconds for them to realize they can come in now."

He was right.

Boy, was he right.

At first there was just one. I spied its bulbous white head peeking around a large piece of machinery. It moved slowly. A lion stalking. A killer whale eyeing seals. A shark circling. They might not be reasoning creatures, but they seemed to understand self-preservation.

I pushed Waterridge to the side and retrieved his gun from my pocket. A .22 caliber. I would have preferred something a little heftier. I pointed at the scout. It wasn't alone. Another head appeared.

"Shoot!"

"Not yet." There was no way this little gun held enough ammo to take on the hundreds of creatures that lurked in the fog. I could take down a few. Maybe a half-dozen if my aim was good. Maybe. Doubtful. It didn't matter. Brenda's prophetic drawing had already told me my fate.

"Shoot!"

"Aren't you supposed to have some control over these things? You got the red robe and everything."

"You put an end to that when you cut the power to my control panel. You doomed us."

"You doomed thousands."

The first creature floated through the fog. Several more appeared behind them, and they were showing signs of being less patient.

I pulled the trigger, and the bullet slammed into the head of the first one around the corner. I expected blood. Instead I saw a spray of yellow custard. If fear hadn't occupied most of my brain, I would have tossed chunks right then and there.

The others scattered, more from the sound of the gun than the death of their companion.

Motion from the portal window caught my attention. Last I looked, creatures were falling past; now they were rising, sucked up to wherever the wide shaft went.

The first ones up were the last ones down. They were battered and broken. Dead. Then I saw a living one struggling against the flow. It was trying to swim down the fog column, but the riptide was too strong.

An idea started to grow, but Waterridge stunted its growth. He charged me and seized my gun hand.

"Let me have it." I saw nothing but panic in his eyes.

I dropped the axe in my other hand and popped the architect in the nose. He staggered back two steps.

Something on the ceiling moved. I looked up. They clung to the ceiling tiles, claws holding them in place. There — were — hundreds of them, a quivering mass of putty-white bodies, their heads turned our direction, each mouth filled with barracuda teeth.

Waterridge took another step back. "No. No." He raised his hands. "I command you to leave."

That didn't work. One dropped on his head and dug its claws into his eyes. The scream echoed in the room. I considered shooting the thing on its head, but I could miss and blow the man's brains out. For a moment — God forgive me — for a moment it seemed the right thing to do.

Then one hit me in the back. They were coming at us from every direction. I drove myself back against the wall. Something squished. My back felt wet.

Another came at me flying five feet above the floor. I dropped it with a shot from the .22. Fighting was useless, but I wasn't wired to stand around.

Waterridge was on the ground, writhing. Then the screaming stopped. Then the writhing stopped. All that was left was the sound of the feeding frenzy.

A creature hit me in the side. Its claws ripped through my dress shirt. My skin offered no resistance. One bit my arm. Another laid into my leg. I went down on my back. For every creature that dropped from the ceiling another appeared to replace it. There were five on me. Then more.

I fought. I punched. I shot one or two more. My blood flowed, and with it my ability to fend off the beasts.

Again, a motion in the portal demanded my attention. Creatures were being sucked up the shaft by the dozen . . .

I still held the gun. I could still see out of one eye. It took everything I had to move my arm enough to aim. The sound of the gun sent the creatures on me scrambling, but they would be back in a moment.

I fired again. And again. Then I could hear only the sound of dry firing. I was out of ammo. The glass had cracked, but not broken.

I rolled on my side. There was the fire axe two steps out of reach. Crawling to it, I took in in my right hand. My left wasn't working very well.

A creature landed on my back. I was beyond caring. "I hope you choke."

Using the axe for support, I pushed myself up. Another foggy latched on. I stumbled, but at least I stumbled in the right direction. Several more creatures hitched a ride. One thing I had noticed about them: They were very light. I guess you'd have to be to swim in fog.

This was it. My last effort. The last thing I would do in this life. I refused to waste it. The biting and clawing increased. The frenzy was beginning.

I lifted the axe, turned the pointed end out, and put my body into the swing.

The axe head bounced off the glass, and the axe fell to the floor.

"I tried, God. I tried."

The glass gave way, its pieces imploding into the shaft. Wind. I felt wind. Then I keeled over.

There were screeches. The air whistled through the room and around the edges of the portal. One by one, then two by two, then by bunches, the creatures were pulled into the open portal. I couldn't tell if it was the wind or something else dragging them away. I didn't care as long as they left. They made it clear they didn't want to go.

The fog that filled the room went with them. It was like watching milky water go down a drain.

The fog-swimmers clinging to me sloughed off. Glad to see them go. I turned to where Waterridge had gone down. There were still bits and pieces of him left.

For a few moments I watched fog and creatures sail by, but keeping my eyes open was becoming more work than I could manage.

"I'm ready, God. I'm ready . . . to . . . go . . ."

The green and the white of the room dimmed to black.

EPILOGUE

"How are you doing, son?" Allen Krone walked onto the balcony and sat in one of the outdoor chairs. He had a right to. He owned the chair, the balcony, and the eight-thousand-square-foot house overlooking the Pacific Ocean. The house was in the northern part of San Diego County. We had been here for two weeks and had full run of the place. Krone and his wife stayed in one of their other homes.

"I'm doing okay, sir."

"It looks like you're healing up nicely." Janice brought a tray of ice tea for us. Krone did a lot of entertaining, he had said, so there were plenty of chairs. Daniel sat on the deck playing a video game on his phone.

"The healing is slow, but I shouldn't frighten too many children."

I wore shorts and a white t-shirt. The scars on my neck, arms, and legs were visible reminders of what had happened earlier that month. The rest of the scars were hidden by clothing. I'd be wearing long-sleeve shirts and long pants for a good many months. The plastic surgeons told me the scars would fade, and those that don't can be handled with a little surgery. Somehow that didn't seem important.

I studied our host for a moment. "You're looking pretty good yourself, Mr. Krone."

"I keep telling you it's Allen. And I feel good. Thanks to you."

"Not me, sir. God does the healing. I'm just a washed-up football jock."

"Not in my book, young man." Krone looked over the ocean as if seeing something no one else could. "You are the bravest man I know. Your friends, too."

"Eh, they're all right, I guess." That got a reaction.

"I thought we had lost you," Andi said. She kept her eyes closed and her face toward the sun.

"I thought I had lost me, too."

I don't remember my friends finding me, but they tell me they came looking when the fog disappeared. To be honest, I still have trouble understanding how I can be alive.

It had taken some time before we could discuss what had happened. Two of the guests at the retirement party were RNs. They stopped the bleeding. Once the fog was completely gone and we were able to contact others, Krone had his private helicopter flown in from Montgomery Field, which had been far enough outside of downtown San Diego not to be affected by the fog.

"Any word from the mayor on the city's condition?" I asked. I didn't want to talk about me anymore.

"He's being tight-lipped about such things. They can't explain the loss of life, the power outages. The official word is that this is an ongoing investigation. Local police, the military, the FBI, Homeland Security, and groups I know nothing about are investigating. There is no reasonable, logical answer."

"Trust me," the professor said. "I know reason. I know logic. Nothing of what we've experienced makes sense. It is, nonetheless, real."

"What do these people want?"

The professor always fielded those kinds of questions. "We're not certain. We've seen them try to control the thinking of people. At times it seems as if they want to make our universe theirs. This time they unleashed organisms to kill and to cause terror. They've also used microscopic organisms to infect people and animals." The professor shrugged. "I'm starting to wonder if our worlds aren't so different that we can't understand what they're doing. I know one thing: The Gate isn't finished with us."

"What I don't understand," Krone said, "is Brenda's gift. You told me she is never wrong, yet Tank didn't die."

"I've been thinking about that," Brenda said. "I've been pretty bummed about gettin' that wrong."

"Hey!" I smiled when I said it.

"You know what I mean, Cowboy. I've grown . . . oh, what's the word?"

"Fond of me," I suggested.

"No, that's not it. Gimme a sec. Got it. I've grown to where I can *tolerate* you. That's it. Anyway, I think I have an answer. I'll let the professor tell you if I'm right or wrong. He's going to anyway."

"You can count on it, Barnick."

"I think Tank changed the future," she said slowly. "What I drew was true. Tank made a new truth. I don't know how. Maybe he just powered his way into a different outcome."

"That's deep," the professor said. "Especially coming from you. Just like some physicists think that if there are multiple universes, there may be multiple futures."

Changed the future. As I thought about Brenda's words, it occurred to me that that's what we'd been doing all along. Changing the future.

I caught the professor looking at me. "I'm glad Tank is still with us."

"Aw, gee, Professor. You're gonna make me blush."

"Don't get a big head, Tank. I just don't want to be left alone with these two women."

"You love us, too," Andi said.

Brenda was a little more direct. "Shut up, old man."

"For the last time, I am not old!"

"Ancient."

I'll let you guess who said that.

ABOUT THE AUTHORS

Bill Myers is a youth worker, creative writer, and film director who co-created the "McGee and Me!" book and video series; his work has received over forty national and international awards. His many books include *Hot Topics*, *Tough Questions*, and *The Dark Side of the Supernatural*.

Frank E. Peretti is one of American Christianity's best-known authors. His novels, including *This Present Darkness*, have sold more than 10 million copies. He makes his home in Idaho. Learn more at www.frankperetti.com.

The author of more than 100 published books and with nearly 5 million copies of her books sold worldwide, **Angela Hunt** is the *New York Times* bestselling author of *The Note*, *The Nativity Story*, and *Esther: Royal Beauty*. *Romantic Times* Book Club presented Angela with a Lifetime Achievement Award in 2006. In 2008, Angela completed her PhD in Biblical Studies in Theology. She and her husband live in Florida with their mastiffs. She can be found online at www.angelahuntbooks.com.

Alton Gansky is the author of twenty-four novels and eight nonfiction books. He is a Carol Award winner and an Angel Award winner, and has been a Christy Award finalist. He holds a BA and an MA in biblical studies and has been awarded a Doctor of Literature degree. Director of the Blue Ridge Mountains Christian Writers Conference, Gansky also serves as an editor and collaborative writer for top tier authors. He lives in California.